Hope Road

Campanile Books
244 5th Ave., Suite N-242, New York, NY 10001
United State of America
www.CampanileBooks.com
The name Campanile Books® and its mark are the property and trademark of Campanile Books, Inc. All Rights Reserved, 2015.

Printed in the United States of America.

Publisher's Cataloging-in-Publication
Singe, Thomas.
Hope road / Thomas Singe.
p. cm.
ISBN-13: 978-0-9852393-4-3
1. Fiction.   2. Bible—Allegorical interpretations.

HOPE ROAD

THOMAS SINGE

CAMPANILE BOOKS

1.

PERHAPS I never really knew my son. Now that I am growing towards the outer edge of middle age, I feel more and more that it is hard to know anyone at all, to really know them. And so I wonder about my son.

In the technical sense, he was never mine. I adopted him when he was only a year or two old—he had been so neglected early on that they were never quite sure how old he was. I know less than he does about his "real parents." When my son was angry at me, especially in puberty, that phrase came all too readily to his lips—"my real parents wouldn't do this," "my real parents would let me stay up late"—and other such epithets. He meant to wound me, of course, but he could have no idea how deep such wounds go. I have since forgiven him for that, forgiven him for being a child and petulant with rage. So should we all be forgiven.

But I do not know if he forgives me. There was always that gulf between us, always that distance, borne of his origin and the lack of blood between us.

It is hard to explain; what happened, I mean. All these chaotic events, and portentous happenings. Of course, in middle school everything seems to mean much more than it really does. This is my memory of that age—events jumbled and indistinct, shot through with vacuous longings and powerful changes, all of it tending to exhaust and to thrill one at the same time, all of it filled with portents of the future. I would like to think that it is my son's experience as well, that all he went through was simply a lesson, portending one way to live and demonstrating the finality of death at the end. The lessons of life, as I see them.

Actually this is, through the filter of years, what I learned in middle school. I have no true knowledge of what he learned.

Jake was a small boy and hard to know. He kept to himself a great deal, always off in a distant corner.

Once out of the many hundred times, I remember driving to pick him up after school. This time that I remember was only a few weeks before he started walking to school permanently and the distance between us widened even further.

I pulled into the parking lot and looked around at the children playing. My gaze went past a bent figure sitting small and alone on a bench, and I thought to myself *What a strange, dark child,* and glanced elsewhere across the playground. I looked at the boys playing basketball, and four-square, and a variety of other games. Only slowly did I look back at the periphery of the games. Only when my gaze was drawn back to that child, sitting alone, with a drawn face at the edge, did I realize that it was Jake.

Of course, when I realized it was he, my entire perception was transformed. I recognized his backpack and his jacket. I saw his face not as drawn and long, but as interesting and perceptive, watching the game. And his posture was not bent and awkward, out of sync with his fellows, but recumbent, waiting to spring into action. Perhaps he was tired from the game, I thought, perhaps he has already scored his many baskets for the afternoon, and is taking a break on the sidelines. He did look happy to see me. I smiled at him, waving from the car as he stood and came toward me.

Yet the experience of seeing him like that, of seeing that small dark isolated child disturbed me. Oh, it wasn't a great shock—in one's heart of hearts, I suppose one always knows the truth. Your heart plumbs through the darkness of the world underneath, even while your mind convinces itself that it is looking into clear daylight. The only disturbing thing about it was the thought that I had was that this was how others might see Jake. There wasn't anything I could do to fight the fact that others would see him as I first saw him, as someone alone, aimless and unhappy—one of those odd and ill-suited children, so inexpressibly uncertain and shy that even the popular press mocks them as socially inept, the ones with tape on their glasses, the ones who fumble the ball or trip over their own shoes, or on the other hand—and what is worse—one of those dark and malcontent children who nurse a bed of rage inside themselves, as they watch the endless basketball games from which they've been excluded, who nurture an inner violence seen in every cruel word and phrase so casually tossed their way by the insensitive crowd, until their rage finally bursts the thin membrane of civility that society has given them. And these are the children who kill their fellows, who make the plans and find the guns, the round pegs in the square holes, the dark ones at the sidelines. Forgive me, but this is what I thought of my own child on that day.

I had thought similar things before, wondering—as every parent wonders—how others saw my child, willing myself, urging myself to step back from my parental function, to push outside to a more objective position so that I could see my child as others might see him. Yet I had always resisted this urge because I feared the insight I might have, I feared I would not be proud of him, that the distance between us would rush in like a floodwater, pushing us even further apart. I wanted as long as possible to be close to him, yet the deeper he retreated into himself, the more difficult that became.

So it is possible this is what made me feel that Jake's initial friendship with that man could not hurt him worse. It was the first un-childish friendship he'd ever had, and the knowledge I carried inside myself of Jake's disconnection made me rejoice at the possibility of any connection, no matter how slight, how uncertain or disruptive. I was also pleased, I'll admit, to know that even at the surly age of 12, Jake could carry on a pleasant conversation with a fellow son of man, an adult no less.

He carried himself a little higher that day, when he arrived home. A small light shone in his eyes. Something nearly unnoticeable, except that I am his parent. I did not broach the topic at first, as I prepared a small snack for him to wolf down after school. I sat with him, drinking my tea, watching him eat, knowing that any sign of excessive interest on my part would kill the possibility of communication. When he was satiated, he sat back, and even more clearly than before, that light was in his eyes, a gentle smile—one I felt I hadn't seen in five years or more—was on his lips. He bent over to get his books out of his backpack and then I asked. I spoke casually, straining to keep curiosity out of my voice, saying the same rote phrase I've schooled myself to say.

"So, anything happen at school today, old man?"

"Nah," Jake mumbled. His head was near the floor now. He fumbled in the depths of his pack.

"Oh, okay." I stood and began to wash Jake's plate. But then I couldn't resist. As I stood at the sink and faced the window, I probed. "So, nothing happen in class? Nothing made you feel good, man?"

"Nah," said Jake again. And then he added, like a death-knell: "And quit saying 'man,' Dad, it sounds stupid."

"Right." But I continued on, impetuously. "How was lunch?"

"Oh, it was okay," said Jake. "Nothing much—hot dogs, I think."

I frowned. The fact that junk such as hot dogs weren't on the menu at Rockhorn was one of the reasons I had sent Jake to a private school.

"Hot dogs?" I asked.

"Or sausages—I don't know, Italian sausages and potatoes. Why do you bug me with all these questions, Dad, huh?"

"Because I want to know," I said brightly. "I care about you."

Jake waved his hand in a desultory manner. "Yeah, yeah." Then he looked up from his backpack. "You know what did happen though?"

Then the phone rang. As I was expecting a business call, I felt obligated to take it. Just for a moment before I launched into conversation, I turned back to Jake. His face was expectant with the hope that I would hear him. It was an expression I longed for, his face full of light and meaning, waiting for my ears.

Impatient with myself—never with Jake, but impatient none the less, and no doubt visibly frustrated with my inability to ignore my work while at home—I said to him, in a short tone of voice: "Well, what happened? I want to hear about it, but I have this—I have to take this. Tell me what happened." and I tapped the receiver that I'd covered with one hand.

Jake's face fell. In retrospect, when one remembers these moments, it is astonishing how apt the metaphor really is. It happens so quickly.

The expression that was so illuminating, that gave windows, voice, and vision to the bright soul is suddenly covered, as with a heavy curtain falling solid to the ground, covering it in the heavy folds of the old weariness, the old aimless ennui and disgust.

Although the yearning was still in his voice, he said only "Ah, nothing much, man. It's just that I met this guy on the way home, and he was good—he was okay. He was okay to talk to, y'know?"

Then the demand of the phone call in my hand became overwhelming, and for the next hour I was on the phone. Jake told me, later when they had grown closer, that this was not just "a guy" of his own age and station in life—it was an older man, a stranger, who fell into conversation with him. It was only later that he told me the details, and perhaps not even then did he tell me all of what he had experienced.

As I piece the past events together, I believe that on that day Jake was simply walking as he usually does, in the way I've seen him walk, a little purposeless and a shadow on his brow, but nevertheless directed generally towards home. He is kicking a stone or doing something similar, when perhaps the man broached the silence. I say 'perhaps' because I do not know for certain that it was not Jake, in fact, who was first attracted to the man, attracted by his appearance and demeanor, who worked up the courage to strike up a conversation. But for the moment, I will assume it was the man, as the older one, the one less self-conscious and uncertain. He was never uncertain. That much, at least, is true.

The man, whose nickname I was later to know as "Ben" or as "Carp" and whose proper name was as Spanish as his swarthy looks—Bendito Delacruz– was walking in the same direction as Jake. At the beginning of the conversation, Bendito pointed out their shared path in an amusing fashion. They were crossing a small bridge over Albe Creek, and the man happened to mention that he had once fallen in the creek—or that he had been thrown in the creek, I've never been quite sure which. Or perhaps the man was walking a different direction and nearly ran into Jake, perhaps nearly knocked him into the creek as well, and this was how the subject came up. For all I know, Jake was in fact knocked into the creek, and the man hauled him out, and Jake has concealed this from me. It would be like Jake to conceal this, not wanting me to worry over him getting soaked in creek water. I do know that Jake was reading a book and that he lost the book in the Creek, which leads me to believe that one or both of them fell in the Creek that day. I've never been entirely clear about a number of these details. All I know for sure is that Jake ended up going in the same direction as the man who called himself simply "Ben." Jake seemed to find this man engaging or amusing. At the very l east, he seemed to be a change from the usual rat-race of Jake's harried life.

Of course, one might wonder whether or not I was concerned on hearing these details later—my only son engaged in long and laughing conversation with a man entirely strange to us, from a different culture and perhaps a complete itinerant.

And if, in fact, my conversation with Jake had actually taken place on that day when his face was filled with light, on the day he first met Bendito, I would have been quite concerned. Most probably, I would have prohibited Jake from further conversation with strange men, and may even have continued to drive him back and forth from school for a few weeks, just to be certain.

As with most parents today, I often feel that once my child has left the safe environs of school or home that they have entered a type of wilderness of fear. My thoughts too often turn to unsavory topics when I think of my child alone with strangers—I think of sexual abuse, of innocence lost, of abduction, of children kidnapped, tortured, starving, neglected, sexually exploited. It's easy to blame popular culture and the press for this. After all, the media are where the images in my head come from. I can't avoid the knee-jerk fear of strangers talking to my child, or what is worse, touching my child—all because I've seen too many children kidnapped in too many movies, read about too many children fighting off rapists, or being rescued from abusers, in too many schlocky best-selling novels. It is perhaps too easy to blame the media for such exploitation of a primal fear, because that protective instinct is at the core of our beings, it is primal.

Yet like many parents, I worry about how far we've gone with this, I worry about my child—about all children—losing all trust, losing the sense that the world can be a good place, that the people you connect with randomly are willing your good, and that you can work together with them to improve the world. People are fundamentally good, and in need of no redemption. That is, at least, what I would hope.

On that particular day, in this particular circumstance, faced with Jake's exposure to possible danger and disruption, I most probably would have forbidden further conversation. I would have taken steps.

But I didn't, because I did not hear about it until it was much too late. I received the details of this random conversation only later, after Ben was part of Jake's daily litany of the events in his life, after we knew already that Ben worked at the same school that Jake went to, and after we had heard story after story about the man. Only then did I gradually discover that the way Jake and Ben—and by extension, every other child Bendito Delacruz became known to at Rockhorn—had first encountered each other was through this first conversation in the wilderness between school and home, between traveling strangers on the same road.

2.

OUTSIDE OF my knowledge, Jake continued to walk with Mr. Delacruz after school nearly every day. They would meet near the creek, cross the bridge, and walk further into town together, chatting amiably.

It occurs to me now to wonder what a hard-bitten man around thirty years of age—a man living hand-to-mouth as a day laborer—would have to say to a young and privileged boy. After a long day of manual labor for Delacruz and book study for Jake, what would they have to discuss, what common point of reference would they have?

In so many ways, though, it seems to me that this man—Ben Delacruz—was like a child. He wondered at everything still, and he found pleasure in nearly everything. He had a child's passions for understanding, a child's love of learning, and a child's sense of morality, naïve and compassionate even in the most extreme circumstances. In some important way, he had never grown up; this perhaps I should have marked at the beginning, for it affected the end of it all.

What is more interesting, and what sets my mind at ease when I think of Jake and Ben walking together, what helps me understand how their conversations continued, day after day, is that Ben could seemingly find a common frame of reference with any fellow human being. Ben could seemingly find a common frame of reference with any fellow human being. Months later, when I at last actually met the man, I was astonished to discover that after the initial handshake and greetings, I continued to want to talk with him. This made him engaging, even striking in his level of engagement. Despite his lack of formal education or of the outward accoutrements of success and distinction, Ben somehow had the instinct to ask the right questions, probe in the right areas, and find the points where you and he could connect.

Thus, when he met me some months after Jake's initial encounter, it was Ben's evident interest in tax collections management that drew me in. He seemed to care more about me than he cared about his own agenda in a conversation. He was, in this regard, the most un-selfish, un-self-focused individual I've met.

Despite the fact that on that particular day, he was wearing a set of clothes that didn't seem to have ever been changed, he seemed to know a good bit about the business of accounting for taxes. Perhaps he was once a small business owner or a low-level federal employee—I never thought to ask. In any case, we discussed aspects of my accounting business at some length, and Ben had some remarkable insights into the state of mind of many of my corporate clients and in fact, some insight into my approach to the work of tax-shelters and trust fund management. I left our initial meeting impressed with Jake's choice of friends and at peace with the fact that Ben was part of his life.

Yet this was a long time away for us—I would not meet Ben until well into the spring, relatively close to what I did not realize then would be the end, the end of Jake's friendship with him, and the end of it all for Ben Delacruz.

The next actual shift in the slowing growing relationship between Bendito and Jake took place on a rainy day in October.

Jake was in the school library at lunchtime. Lunch had just finished, and everyone else had left the library except for a few clerks filing books. Jake dawdled over his book for a few more minutes and then stood to go. It was then that he noticed a man he thought he recognized sitting in the roped off section of the west wing.

The shelves and ceiling in this wing of the library had suffered water damage some years ago, and a new endowed grant had just made possible the renovation of the library. They were starting with the west wing; the stacks there were covered in plastic, and the walls and ceiling were beginning to be ripped apart. Of course, young boys like Jake were fascinated by the prospect of a library that was also a large construction site, and they did their best to get in the way.

The repair work was a long time coming, but it was absolutely necessary. Pigeons and doves had begun to roost in the damaged eaves and had already begun to make their way into the library proper. When the carpenters took off the under-eaves, the interior lathe and plaster was already liberally spattered with droppings and half-built feathered nests, demonstrating the permeability of the roof in this section.

The man was sitting on a small step-ladder, surrounded by pieces of new lumber, pigeon droppings and torn antique shelves. He was reading while he ate a simple lunch, something from the cafeteria—I believe it was fish and chips that day.

Jake went past him warily once or twice, unsure if it was his friend from the road after school. Finally, when the man did not so much as glance up from his book so that Jake could catch a look at his face, my son worked up his courage and pointedly asked him: "Who are you?"

Bendito—for it was he—looked up at this point, straight at him and said, oddly enough: "Who do you think I am?"

Jake looked at him and said: "You're Bendito, aren't you?"

"Yeah," said Bendito.

He grinned, and then they both laughed.

It was one of those odd moments, when a person you see repeatedly in a certain context is lifted from that context, changed into another context, perhaps simply seen out of uniform—in another suit of clothes—and you doubt your own eyes. There is a moment of disjunction, of trans-figuration between the two contexts. I've had the same experience myself when a former window-washer came in wearing a suit, as a new client. He was lifted from the great heights to the floor, and he looked different. It was only when he went to the window to check the most recent job that I recognized him. Like Bendito and Jake we laughed about it as well.

Jake began again, asking Bendito what he was doing in the library, out of his context of the after-school walk. It turned out that Bendito had been working for many weeks as a laborer on the new greenhouse section on the north end of the school grounds—the newly built Mary E. MacArthur Horticultural Center, to be precise. He had been responsible for moving a tremendous quantity of earth out of the way, digging foundations for a large grape trellis outside one of the greenhouses, and in fact, pouring the foundations and beginning the work of the trellis construction. The school had a dispute with the lead carpenter around that time, who left the project.

Thus, in one of those happy accidents, Bendito ended up in charge of the entire project—he was responsible for making the grapes grow. He actually built the remaining large sections of the trellis himself, finished and weatherproofed the trellis and added some elegant bits of carpentry magic to the overall project. I believe, in the end, he was also the one responsible for planting the large grape vines that the school had purchased from a nursery and twining their branches carefully around the trellis. The following year, when I first saw that section of the grounds—at a summer wedding of two teachers—I was impressed. On the day of the wedding, the leaves of his grapes were a luxuriant green backdrop to the bride and groom; the vines filled that area of the grounds with lush leaves and rich hanging fruit. He was a master grape-grower. Perhaps Bendito should have taken up the vintnering life; it would have made all of our lives less complicated.

When the greenhouse project was completed, the crew left the school. The job was done. In an exception to the rule though, Bendito did not leave. There were other odd jobs that needed to be done around the school. The maintenance and grounds supervisor, Bill Girus, had noticed Bendito's evident handiwork on the grape arbor. He requisitioned Bendito's carpentry skills to work on the sagging shelves and water-damaged ceiling of the west end of the library. He probably failed to mention that part of the task would be cleaning up extensive amounts of bird guano, but Bendito didn't seem to mind.

On that day, after Jake and he discussed how Bendito had come to land in the library, working as a member of the school's semi-permanent maintenance and carpentry staff—after Jake's curiosity was satisfied on that particular topic—the reason for Bendito's employment made itself evident.

Out of some concealed opening in the eaves, a pigeon emerged into the midst of the library and flew over them both. Startlingly white against the exposed oak rafters, the bird swung in one slow circle after another over them. Slowly, it came closer to the book stacks and the floor, looking—it appeared—for a likely place to roost. Jake ran from one side of the stacks to the other, trying to see where it was, and frankly, trying to see if he could catch it. At the end of one row, Jake almost collided with the bird, and it swooped up out of his reach, feathers blasting in every direction, an exploding ball of snow. The bird was agitated by this point, and flew haphazardly down the narrow aisles of books, ricocheting back and forth, shedding guano and feathers in its frenzy.

Then Bendito intervened. He made some small sounds—Jake later described them as whispering, whickering sounds—and the bird calmed immediately. It did not come to rest immediately, but seemed to home in on Bendito from across the room. He continued talking to the bird, and Jake stood in awed silence as the pigeon slowed perceptibly in its frantic flight, and then gently dropped its wings and came to rest on Bendito's upheld fingers.

Bendito put his other hand over the bird's head, calming it further, and then walked to the crumpled corner of the west wing. He reached out and tore a piece of lathe and plaster from the water-damaged wall, making a gap into the rainy day outside. Then he opened his hands and released the bird to the outdoors. Soon, it was gone in the distance, a white speck in the rain.

Bendito wiped his wet and guano-streaked hands off on his jeans. "Well, that's that, son," he said. "Bless the beasts and birds, huh?"

Jake looked at him with astonishment and new respect. Bendito was not only a friend, he was now a deity to my son: a man who with impunity could rip down walls with his bare hands and furthermore, could tame wild creatures, bidding them to come down to his fingers. Bendito's place in Jake's pantheon of childhood gods was now established.

From my perspective, when I heard this story, I simply reminded the excitable Jake that a life without solid professional training could be one of near-chaos, filled with constantly changing odd jobs. I imagine Bendito had held all manner of employment over the years, yet whispering to wild pigeons had to be among the oddest of them all. On top of his grape-growing and carpentry skills, Bendito had perhaps worked in a veterinarian facility. Nothing amazing about Bendito's abilities, I told Jake.

Soon after, the bell for the end of lunch rang, and Jake went back to his classes, while Bendito evidently continued to work on the keeping the pigeons out of the library. I presume one of his first acts was to replace the crumbling lathe and plaster in the corner with some fresh drywall.

3.

DURING THE next few weeks, Jake was largely occupied with the set of friends he'd recently begun to acquire. It wasn't that he was avoiding Bendito, or avoiding me—it's just that he had finally begun to establish a social group of boys of his own age and station, and he often stayed late after school. He told me that he wanted to spend time with his friends in study hall—yet in retrospect, I suspect that Jake was actually staying after because he was in detention for some offense that he chose to keep from me. It was tax season and I was away from the house for many hours in the evening, so Jake was left to his own devices, and his own new friends.

To be frank, it wasn't the group of friends I'd hoped that Jake would begin to meet at this age. Among them was not a single future Young Republican or Young Democrat, not a single future National Merit Scholar, not a single star athlete or promising young artist. By and large, the group of boys that Jake found himself drawn to focused their energies on antics of an asocial nature—ranging from graffiti and breaking windows in the construction site of the library to homemade tattoos and self-inflicted body piercings without anesthesia. The least of their offenses included cadging cigarettes and alcohol from upper classmen and brawling over their booty, yet these were the ones that most often landed them in trouble.

At the beginning, I thought of the group as simply an alternative social milieu. I supposed their activities were as equally diverse as social activity that was more publicly accepted—from my perspective, they seemed to derive as much pleasure and satisfaction from being chased by the police or from an evening spent smoking marijuana as the pleasure that their counterparts on the lacrosse team or the debating club derived from their more artificial and less risky contests.

It seemed to me at the time that Jake needed an environment in which he was accepted for who he was—darkness and all—and he had found it in a group of like-minded kids with similar views on life. I told myself that Jake's friends were a valid social group, despite their gothic attire and their periodic outbursts of anti-social behavior. This was how I explained it to myself, but I doubted that the explanation would have convinced any of my colleagues or my therapist. I am not sure that I even convinced myself.

The truth became increasingly obvious as the weeks went on. Over the next month or more, I began to find out more about Jake's new companions and rapidly came to see that these children were a group of "friends" only in the most accidental sense. Hints as to character and friendship came through in brusque and occasionally profane phone calls, off-handed introductions when I went to pick Jake up after study hall (or unstated detention), and even a few randomly strange encounters with some of his compatriots on weekends. Reluctantly, I came to know the loudmouth coward named Symon; the two out-of-control Ritalin addicts, Jimmy and Jon, both seemingly full of hyperactive, nearly comic rage; frightened Tom, who was the butt of jokes; the junior-league thief Lev (I had to talk Jake out of going shop-lifting with Lev one day); and of course the lower-caste, working class boys like José and Andy who drifted aimlessly, having no models at home as their fathers and older brothers were in Alaska fishing throughout the year, which was the only way such families could have afforded Rockhorn at all—not that the school did these malcontent and lonely souls much good.

Slowly it came clear to me that none of the members of this disparate crowd were really connected to each other—not in the way I'd expect, at least. Instead, all of them seemed to have sunk to the bottom of the social barrel, where they found each other like Brownian particles drifting together, no connection but that of being in the same place at the same time, of being trapped in the same untenable, derelict situation. They didn't look to each other as a way out of the situation, or even for the obvious support or commiseration. Instead, they all just seemed headed in the same meaningless direction, adrift in the same adolescent current that constantly left them marooned together in the back rows of a classroom, mired in the depths of anonymity and maladjustment.

Unfortunately, about the time that I began to see the reality of Jake's new set of "friends," it was too late. By the time tax season ended and I could once more re-engage with my son, Jake had firmly enmeshed himself with this group, and it would have been difficult to separate him. The reality was that Jake had selected the dregs of the lower echelon of Rockhorn's social classes to identify with; he was now firmly associated with the disaffected. I won't say that this did not pain me—it pained me to the quick.

Yet the perception of Jake as part of this odd social milieu did not bother me as much as the possibility that Jake would be drawn into destructive situations. The first such situation occurred late in tax season, when the accounting was most heavy, and when my attention could least be distracted.

One early evening, long after the school had shut down for the night, I was called at work by Catherine Foss, Rockhorn's school librarian. Of course, the reason she called me there was that I was not at home. It seems that Jake wasn't at home either; apparently, the maid was asleep, for when Miss Foss had called my home, she'd only gotten the answering machine.

Jake had been caught breaking into the library through one of the broken windows. Some other boys were with him when this happened, but they managed to make good their escape. He was the only one caught, and I was the only parent to get the call. She said it wasn't just a childish prank; perhaps, she said, he meant to burn the library down. The pocketful of candles, the lighter fluid, and matches he was carrying didn't bode well.

I took the call from Catherine Foss very seriously. Besides the simple fact that she was a hardworking employee at Rockhorn, and responsible for my son's welfare in an abstract sense, she was also soon going to become the only endowed staff member at the school—the only one who had more job security than the Dean, the Headmaster or myself. In fact, it made me angry that Jake hadn't shown enough foresight to cross swords with some other member of the faculty— someone not nearly as powerful or influential.

In fact, Miss Foss' father was Norman Alan Foss. Now retired, Norman Foss had been a protégé of legendary CEO Jack Welch at GE and had gone on to manage several very successful companies himself. Foss had reaped a king's ransom in the dizzying spiral of the stock market, and was worth many billions. In fact, he had been instrumental in persuading a very prominent local family to donate to the Library.

It wasn't entirely due to her father though—she had picked the right former student to endear herself to. Ten years after graduating, successful entrepreneur Jackson Argurion had approached Rockhorn about setting up an incredibly generous Grant: the full amount, once fully endowed would be in the range of $30 million. However, the J.M. Argurion trust was carefully locked to two uses: to renovate and expand the library facility and collections, and to create the first "Chair" at Rockhorn—the position of Librarian, which would henceforth be an endowed position with full lifetime tenure. The first, and primary, beneficiary would be Catherine Foss. If we were lucky, the rest of the school might also profit—from the crumbs off her table.

This summer, the initial grant from the trust had finally been released from the Argurion estate, and Catherine Foss had risen to her new power with grace and aplomb. Immediately, she began releasing funds from the trust to renovate the water damage and to plan a new $4 million expansion, which would break ground the following spring. After the New Year, the rest of the Grant would be released, and there was already much discussion about whether or not the funds would be designated in advance, or would be released to the discretion of the faculty to use as they saw fit. There was already one constraint on the fund that was giving everyone headaches. The Argurion Trust terms stipulated that only the Librarian had the power or authority to hold and disseminate funds. Thus, practically overnight, Catherine Foss had become one of the most politically powerful people at Rockhorn.

When she called, Catherine Foss explained the circumstances of Jake's nighttime antics to me. She did not seem surprised or shocked—as I would have been—by the fact that students were breaking into the library after hours. She said instead that the construction project in a working facility was like a magnet, drawing in every nascent delinquent. She told me that her first instinct was to prosecute for trespassing, but that she would be willing to show mercy, given the fact that Jake had never done something like this before, and presumably, because of my position as the school Treasurer. I was fortunate that Catherine Foss had a deep and abiding affinity for the powerful and the wealthy, and I was both (in the right circumstances and when the stock market had a good day).

There were some conditions on her mercy. I would have to immediately retrieve my son, and be present as she explained the potential consequences for late night burglary and arson. In the future, she said, I must also keep careful tabs on his whereabouts in the evenings.

Grateful for her favor, I drove to Rockhorn. It must have been nearly midnight. By the time I reached the school, I was fuming, and I spent the time at the Library with Jake and Catherine Foss in an angry fugue state. He was, of course, defiant, which didn't help matters. The fog of rage overwhelmed me; I couldn't understand the way Jake's behavior was disintegrating before my eyes. I barely heard Catherine Foss describe the possible consequences, and I barely heard her talk about how Jake had been caught. I was too frustrated at being entrapped by my own child.

I am not sure how far other parents' patience stretches, but in the years to come I personally did not want to experience the phone call from jail after ever-more-dangerous late night escapades, the hushed payments for damages to property or to the parents of other children, the earnest meetings with other parties' lawyers, the concerned calls from Rockhorn's Dean or Mental Health Counselor, the frantic ambulance revivals after drug overdoses, the blood in the bathtub from suicide attempts and eventually, the embarrassing arraignments in a psychologist's office or juvenile court. I've seen those all on television, and I never thought I would be in these distasteful situations. Yet in a few short weeks, this seemed already to be the direction we were headed. I already had Jake in therapy, but despite the cost, it didn't seem to be helping. In a word, I was concerned.

However, between the beginning of tax season—when I was last in evidence around the house—and the end of tax season—when I returned to the fold—Jake had also acquired the adult skills of privacy, evasion, indirection and obfuscation. In the Library that night, I realized that he was suddenly of an age when it was impossible to intervene; any attempts on my behalf to change his social group would have simply made his disaffection worse. Jake seemed to have grown up overnight. He was, if anything, more distant and dark than before, and his new companions didn't seem to have helped him come to terms with his own inner darkness—they only made it worse.

Thus, it was with relief that I heard of Bendito Delacruz re-entering Jake's life.

It was one day in November when Jake saw him again. Despite the trouble it had gotten him in, Jake couldn't seem to stay away from the lure of the Library. And as it turned out, Ben was at work in the west wing. By now, he had finished with the demolition of the rotten and guano-covered timbers. He had finished removing the water-stained shelves. Thus, his task at the moment was the installation of brand-new cedar shelves. The subtle, pleasant odor of cedar filled the library as Ben worked, and a faint sheen of reddish sawdust drifted over everything in that wing.

It was the beginning of lunchtime when Jake saw Mr. Delacruz. He told me later that he hoped his friends—who were with him at the time—did not see him. Despite Jake's need for their companionship, Jake was not blind to his friends' baleful tendencies. Yet there was no such blessing; the group spotted Ben immediately.

Bendito Delacruz was sitting alone once more, seated on the top step of a small step-ladder, reading a book. Perhaps the crowd of ten boys who had come into the library with Jake thought that Ben looked comical, perched on the top of a ladder in guano and sawdust streaked garments, his black hair full of dust and in disarray after a morning of hard work. What added the edge of comedy to the scene, I suppose, is that Ben was wearing his day laborer's unwashed clothes, but was reading one of the largest and oldest books in the library. On his lap was unfolded one of our few antique bound manuscripts—I'm not sure how he got such a valuable book, or why he was reading it. The ten inches of the book were carefully balanced on his knees as he sat there reading through his lunch hour. Evidently, they thought an ignorant laborer was pretending an interest in education and antiques, making him an obvious target for their ridicule.

There was another boy with the group that day, a boy named Matt. He led the group towards Ben. When Jake related the events back to me later, I suppose I cringed when he talked about Matt leading them forward towards this quiet man sitting alone, for Jake had to tell me "C'mon Dad, Matt's not so bad—" in the middle of the story.

What I knew of the large boy who led them over to the ladder was that he was a bully. And I did not quite believe Jake's protestation of harmlessness, for already I knew I would not like to meet Matt the bully in a dark alley. In so many ways, he was that classic schoolyard enforcer: a little slow in the uptake, incurring the disdain of smarter boys, yet a little larger and meaner. In Matt's case, he went beyond the norm, being very large and very muscled and very mean. As he was growing to the age where being a bully was potentially litigious, Matt was beginning to augment his income by serving as 'protector' for several others—including Lev the thief—and by being quite good with his money, once he received it. He was known to tell boys that their grudging contributions would go towards a new bike or stereo he'd been saving for (he had at least one savings account that I knew of) and he had a knack for knowing just how much he could ask for, or how far he could push someone. His aptitude for money, and his ability to scent his prey would someday make him a fine venture capitalist.

Yet at this point in his life, instead of catching up to his fellows through intelligence, emotional insight or leveraged buyouts, he merely intimidated. In the classic form, he collected what he called "taxes" from his fellows—money that they had to pay in order not to be beaten within an inch of their lives. Either he had his weekly "tax" from them in the form of a substantial part of their allowances, or else they ended up with severe bruises to show for their recalcitrance. "Pay up or put up," he called it.

Matt was not a pleasant type. But he was the first one of the bunch to talk to Ben, and Mr. Delacruz won him over immediately.

Matt started out with his typical lack of subtlety. "Hey, check out the greaser readin' the English book—ya learning your ABCs, ya loser wet-back?"

Ben looked up slowly and smiled enigmatically. Jake said later it was as if he'd heard something nice—as if he'd seen an old friend.

"Hey Matt," said Ben gently. "How ya doing, man?"

Matt stepped back, for the first time in his life. "Woah—how do you know my name? You know me?"

"He knows me too," volunteered Jake.

"Shut up," said Matt.

Lev disregarded Matt's instruction and spoke to Jake. "He knows you? How?"

"Ah, we used to walk home from school together. Over by the Creek."

"What's he doing in here?"

"Oh, he's working on the wall—he's cool—he ripped off part of the library wall there, broke it up with his bare hands."

"With his bare hands, huh?" There was a murmur in the crowd of boys, as they looked at Ben's tanned and thickly muscled arms.

"Maybe he escaped from the Moolhouse or something," muttered Jimmy. Moolston State Treatment Facility was a local psychological care center with high-security, known for treating criminals who had pleaded not guilty by reason of insanity. Popularly, it was known as the Moolhouse.

"Can't we just leave him alone?" muttered Tom. "What if—"

"Shut up, Tom," commanded Matt. "He didn't escape from Moolston."

"So why's he sitting there reading?" said Andy.

"Yeah, what's he reading, anyway?" said Matt.

Ben closed his book and smiled again, looking down on the commotion from his perch atop the ladder.

"Shut up, you guys," said Matt. "I wanna find out how he knows 'bout me. Hey you—how you know my name?"

Ben spread his hands out. "I don't know," he said. "— it just came to me. You look like a Matt."

"No greaser knows me," said Matt, shaking his head. "You should get your dirty Mexican hands off that Rockhorn book."

"You want the book?" said Ben. "Okay, here." He picked up the nearly foot-thick tome in one hand and placed it gently in Matt's hands. Matt staggered under the weight.

"Hey—don't *give* it to me," complained Matt. "This thing is heavy, dammit. Give it to one of these other guys—one of these other losers. You friggin' greaseback, why'd you do that?"

"Matt, don't you get tired of it?"

"Whaddaya mean?"

"I mean, don't you get tired of having to be mean all the time—of having to pick on people? Doesn't it just wear you out sometimes?"

"Whaddaya mean?"

"Look at you—that thing you're holding is too heavy for you. It's like all that meanness you're spitting out—that's not you, man, it's not really like you, it's too much. It's too heavy for you. Doesn't it get old?"

Matt considered. "Yeah, I guess."

"Well, put it down for awhile. Rest, my man." Ben waved his hand through the air, as if brushing away years of sullen rage. "Let's leave it behind. You wanted to know what I was reading, right?"

"Yeah," said Matt, regaining himself. Heavily he upended the book on the floor, setting it down. "Yeah—what's in the book?"

"Stories," said Ben.

"Stories," echoed Symon. "I like stories."

"Stories are for little kids," sneered Lev.

"That's okay," said Jimmy. "You don't have to listen—I wanna hear this, about the made-up stories."

"Oh no—these aren't made-up stories," said Ben. "All the stories I tell are real. And the ones I've been reading—" he tapped the book. "—are real world stories too."

"You tell stories, huh?" said Matt. "Could you tell us a story—like right now, a made-to-order story?" Now that Matt had lost his bearing as a bully, the situation had turned entirely away from a confrontation into a boisterous, but not unfriendly, conversation.

About this time, a young assistant librarian intervened. "Mr. Delacruz," he said. "It's a little loud over here—are you teaching this group, these boys, or shall I ask them to leave?"

"Teaching us?" said Lev indignantly. "He's a dirty greaz—I mean, he's not a teacher. He's a worker."

The assistant librarian picked up Matt's heavy book from off the floor. "Done with this?" he asked Ben.

Mr. Delacruz nodded, and then the librarian addressed Lev. "Oh, he may be just a worker," he said. "But all that glitters is not gold. Mr. Delacruz is the only other reader of ancient languages here that I know of. We're lucky to have him at Rockhorn; he could teach me a few things. He's also quite a storyteller—you should hear him sometime."

"Yeah, tell us one," said Matt. "C'mon—tell us a story, huh?"

Ben stepped down from the ladder and grinned at the librarian. "I suppose I'm teaching now," he said. "Don't worry—I'll leave with them—just tell Bill I'm on lunch break." Then he walked out of the library with the boys. As was his wont, he was already beginning to tell a story.

That was the last the assistant librarian saw of Bendito Delacruz. He was released from employment by the Library a week later—I believe at the urging of Catherine Foss. As it turned out, Miss Foss had not taken kindly to the idea of carpenters and day laborers actually using the book stacks while employed on the renovation. After the young assistant struck up a friendship with Ben and found out about his unorthodox and autodidactic wealth of knowledge, Miss Foss' full wrath was revealed. The assistant librarian's encouragement of Ben, and his friendship with the man were seen as a direct betrayal of Herself. Thus, anything that particular assistant librarian learned about Ben, or from Ben, left with him. Soon after, Miss Foss brought on a new assistant, a Ms. Sandy Hedron, who was given firm instructions regarding the use of the books. There were also very particular instructions regarding the general public's access. In short, there would be no access to the book stacks by common laborers—no matter how well versed they were in arcane languages and ancient literature. Ms. Hedron carried out the letter and the spirit of the law rather well—in fact, after she came on board Jake stopped frequenting the library, frightened off, he said, by her chilly demeanor.

Ben Delacruz seemed to sense Miss Foss' and Ms. Hedron's hostility—perhaps they actually did confront him a time or two; I've never been clear on this point. In any event, even before Ms. Hedron was hired, Ben left the library with the group of boys and he never returned to the books. He moved on. After that day, he simply did his job, finishing the carpentry and wall repair that he'd begun, and never glanced at another old book again. The next phase of Ben's activity at Rockhorn had just begun.

The story Ben Delacruz told as the group of boys left the library and moved to the playground was an elaborate tale about a boy much like themselves who had run away from home, taking his parent's credit card with him and exploring life on the low side. It was compelling to Ben's audience, of course, for most of them were lifted far above the poor end of the class system. In Ben's description, the boy left without any clear destination—he simply left to be independent and to see if he could make it on the other side, in the mean streets of the city.

The concept, of course, was fascinating to these boys—few of whom had ever experienced real hardship—and it was made even more fascinating by Ben's (successful) attempts at verisimilitude. Although when I heard it later, I felt he went too far—Bendito gave very the clear descriptions of the boy doing drugs, and talked about the endless days of drug-induced haze, the food that was given up in order to satisfy the appetite for mind-altering substances. And there were other details that Ben told that made the story real: the exact amount of money the boy had taken from his parents, the color and fit of the clothes that gradually wore out on the boy's starving frame, detailed descriptions of high-living parties, and the capstone detail—Ben claimed that he had actually known this boy. Jake swallowed it all, of course, as I'm sure most of Bendito's young audience did.

According to Ben, the boy ran his father's credit to the point where the credit company called his father and cut off further expenditures. Ironically, said Ben, the boy's father wanted to keep it running, allowing his son's high living, but the bank wanted immediate payment of all outstanding debt—and I bet that would have meant cashing in a few of those hard won T bills. So the credit account stayed closed.

The boy, without other resources, didn't show the good sense that one would think and return home. Instead, embarrassed and destitute, he ended up in some god-forsaken trailer park, feeding laboratory animals and donating plasma for his basic sustenance.

At this point I would have ended the story with some high-minded moral—a lesson to the boys about the necessity of thinking ahead. Bendito did not stop here however—perhaps the demands of verisimilitude required him to keep going. He added gruesome detail on gruesome detail—as Jake related the story back to me I felt that even his graphic portrayal of the situation was going beyond the necessary and into the realm of horror. Yet Jake's version was most probably a lesser version of Ben's—a version without the bright pigments Ben was so skilled at using.

As I said, the story continued. In Ben's telling, in the course of injecting himself with drugs or endlessly donating the substances of his own body, the boy used a needle that had been left behind by other donors, and in some fashion contracted one of those horrific diseases that afflict so many of the less fortunate. Now the boy couldn't even donate his own body—it was poisoned. He continued to slop out the laboratory animals, but his income was much reduced, and he began to feel the effects of the disease as it raced through his body. The picture Ben painted was extreme, and compelling.

By the time Ben came close to the end, many other listeners on the playground had been drawn in. He had managed to hit on a narrative that was sufficiently interesting to Jake's friends and playmates that the group of children had grown completely silent. The crowd surrounded Ben; there was a hush all around.

Unfortunately, as Jake was finishing relating Ben's story to me, I interrupted him to take a business call, and I never quite heard how Bendito ended the narrative. When I came back to Jake after the call, he refused to tell me the ending again—perhaps he was irritated at the interruption. On the other hand, perhaps he thought I wouldn't empathize with the father's situation, or wouldn't agree with Ben's ending, but in any case, I imagine the boy got what he so richly deserved. From what I remember from half-hearing Jake tell me the ending as I was on the phone, the boy eventually realized the depths of his depravity and returned to his home. There, I imagine he was punished severely, becoming some type of a servant. I can't imagine any other type of ending, and as I came to know Bendito better, I realized that often he seemed to have a moral in his stories, although some of them were hard to figure out, and some—conversely—seemed quite subversive (but often I couldn't quite figure out how). I'd assume then that the ending of this first story that Ben told had a suitably direct ending, an ending designed to thrill and to instruct at the same time.

No doubt, the direction that Ben had aimed at all along with his audience was the moment of recognition of themselves in this boy, and the careful weighing of his choices in their own lives. That moment was where Ben's conversation excelled. This sense of direct empathy with mere children was what I most admired in him, and then as time went on, this was what I came to envy and then to fear.

4.

JAKE TOLD me later that as the story began—as they all began to walk with Bendito Delacruz towards the benches outside—he felt that peculiar sense of ownership that we feel when a person we know well is suddenly welcomed by a crowd of strangers. Jake had known Ben first, and he still felt as if he were wholly responsible for his group of friends discovering such an interesting—older—companion. (He had, of course, forgotten his initial urge to turn his friends away from seeing Ben.) Because he knew Ben better than they did, he felt that sense of proprietary knowledge that at times feels to us like the other person is a possession.

The story served—among other things—to immediately disabuse Jake of this notion. As they walked outside, Jake was chagrined to see a large group slowly coalesce around their table—a group that had many others that weren't part of the central core of his crew. Evidently, Ben had already established some contacts among other children on the playground. Many of these other boys seemed to know Ben well enough to call him by name. It occurred to Jake that each one of these students may have also once felt that they owned Ben. The sense Jake had of him as a tame possession disappeared.

When Jake first related the incident to me, I was certain that this incident was the first step in Ben becoming an informal member of Jake's loose-knit group of malcontents. Afterwards, as Jake told me more about his feeling of loss when he saw Ben surrounded by a crowd, I came to realize that Bendito didn't become a member of anything that day. Perhaps instead, Jake's friends simply became a part of Ben's larger group of adherents.

In the coming weeks, the lunchtime meetings continued. Jake's group of friends had previously gathered inside, where they could do a bit of mischief in the construction at the Library before lunch got underway outside. Ben's story changed their direction; now they congregated at the table he'd led them to on the first day. The lunch and story that day turned out not to be the first time Ben had eaten with students—some of the larger crowd of children had been there for some time—but it is the first I knew of—the first lunch that Jake was involved in.

I would think it was unusual for a laborer or maintenance man to eat lunch in the children's quarter of the outside yard. Who among us would choose to spend our lunch hour in the vicinity of a horde of milling children, risking bouncing balls colliding with our lunches, high-pitched squeals interrupting our thoughts, or the tedious juvenile conversations that we would have to put up with throughout the long hour?

Yet Ben seemed to look forward to spending a lunch hour outside, risking these dangers. From what Jake has told me, Ben seemed to have no other place that he'd rather be than in the company of children.

Although Ben, or anyone else for that matter, never formalized the lunchtime arrangements, this gathering at lunch time became a regular—if not daily—occurrence as the months went on. At some indeterminate time during the lunch hour, Ben would leave his maintenance or wood-working work in the library, or the basement, or the auditorium, or wherever his odd carpentry jobs took him around the school, and would join the group of boys at a table on the periphery of the playground. It wasn't always at the beginning of lunch, but Ben regularly managed to make it to the table before lunch ended, in time to exchange at least a quick story, a few words, a bit of humor or a witty remark with the children he so enjoyed before lunch came to a close.

The larger group of children around Ben at lunch began to coalesce into a regular bunch—the ones I heard Jake tell me about at home— along with the hangers-on and fellow travelers who came along for the stories, but didn't stay for the duration. Interestingly, the group that used to be around Jake changed composition as the weeks with Ben passed. The ones who were for one reason or another unimpressed by

Ben began to fade away, and the ones who were hard cases and had no use for stories or for adults also drifted from the scene.

Sadly though, most of the children who chose to stay with Ben did not seem like the right type at all. Evidently, Ben didn't share my opinion of them, but perhaps he didn't have my context, experience, or depth of observation.

I have observed that an expensive private school like Rockhorn generally attracts two types of students: the excellent achievers—the Young Republicans and gifted mathematicians—and on the other hand, the children whose parents know that they need help, and are willing to pay for it. Typically, this second type of student doesn't need remedial academic help (although some do). Instead, they usually need assistance in understanding remedial social skills. These are parents with money or pull who want to find the best possible therapy for their little misfits.

Thus, a private school is often an unbalanced society: a place composed of the upper cream and the absolute dregs of the cup—and mostly the dregs are made worse by exposure to money and to privilege. It spoils those who are already going bad, like fruit left in the sun. And sad to say, there is usually no middle ground—no middlebrow children who achieve slightly more than the minimum, being average students (yet not brilliant), good athletes (not extraordinary), and whose behavior fits a societal norm. No, here at Jake's school, I've observed that you have only the achievers and the dregs.

Unfortunately, Ben had scraped the very bottom of the barrel to come up with the assortment of losers, stoners, and maladjusted misfits that regularly surrounded him at lunch. His lunchtime stories and discussions were popular enough that it seemed to me that he could have chosen a better class of student to be associated with. He seemed to choose few that had excellent morals and reputations—although oddly, a few of them did choose to be around him, of their own accord.

Perhaps that was the key—he didn't choose you, you chose him. And perhaps the dregs, with nothing left to lose, were in a state of mind more ready to choose him, to choose anything, while the rest of us are too busy with our own obsessions, our own lives, to be distracted to the place where we could choose to be with Ben. I don't know if any of this makes sense—it just seems important to me to point out that Ben did no proselytizing for the daily lunches that so rapidly spilled over from the tables to cover the entire rounded greensward at the side of the square. And that, in the end, I would like to believe that he wasn't responsible for what happened, and wasn't responsible for the mass delusions that swept through this bunch—the dregs of Rockhorn—when he was gone. How could he be responsible for such things? He was only a day laborer.

But I am getting ahead of myself. Ben had established himself as a lunchtime presence in Jake's life, and although I continued to feel uncomfortable with Jake's choice of friends, they were—at the least— at the center of things in this small circle of Ben Delacruz. I suppose they did represent the dregs of Rockhorn rather well, after all.

As fate would have it, the prickly, disruptive personalities of Jake's acquaintances did not fade gently into the general mass of misfits. After their initial meeting, Ben seemed to have a special affection for characters like Matt the bully and Sym the thief, and they returned his attention, being closer to him than anyone else. Perhaps on some level, these obstreperous boys reminded Ben of his no-doubt misspent youth, recalling his younger self. For whatever reason, instead of drifting apart in the general attention that came Ben's way in the coming months, Ben became closer to the small core of Jake's friends.

As the weeks went on, and Jake continued to bring stories of Ben home to me, I found myself gaining respect for the man. It seemed Ben was not unaware of the negative tendencies of the group that surrounded him at lunch.

For example, Jake's friends Jimmy and Jon, the two siblings who always seemed to be fighting, were spotted quickly by Ben as potential trouble. According to Jake, it's hard to miss Jon in any circumstance—his anger flared on a moment's notice, pouring through him like lightning, animating him to punch holes through walls, curse loudly and kick any object in his vicinity. Usually, he seemed to explode for no particular reason, and his friends quickly learned not to be near him when he became enraged. Often, the person nearest him was Jimmy, who when pushed a little, was capable of similar blitzkrieg rages. When their fury brought them together, the fights were scar-inducing and frightening to watch.

One afternoon as lunch began, Ben calmly walked up to the roiling mass that was Jimmy and Jon fighting, and pulled them apart by the collars. He took a name for them from the comic books. "Hey, Thunderheads," he said. "I know this business of hurting each other is real important to you, but I got a story to tell. So knock off the eye gouging for right now—you can go back to it later." He received no response from the flailing boys. "Jon, Jonny, Jon," he said. "Jon." No response. Then Ben lifted him off the ground, "Hey, Thunderhead— you kapich?"

"Yeah, yeah, I hear ya." Jon looked up at him as if he'd seen him for the first time. Sulkily, he put his fists down.

After that initial incident, the name stuck. Everyone called them "Thunderheads" thereafter. There were other names that Ben gave too—names not to point out the obvious failings, but names that I believe were designed to change the identity of the recipient, much as a gang nick-name identifies a person as a member of a gang. Or perhaps that's simply my perspective, my jaded opinion of the whole fad of adding street-wise monikers to a legal name.

Jake's thieving friend Sym, the loudmouth coward, became "Stony" to Ben, which seemed to me to be an oddly conscious reversal of all of Sym's worst traits. Perhaps in Ben's shoes, I would have chosen a different name for the boy—Coward Kid, YellowBelly, or Irritating BigMouth Boy—but Ben didn't emphasize such traits, instead, choosing the opposite of what Symon was—giving him something to strive for. In the name itself, Ben told him he could become a solid person, a stony redoubt—"You'll be a leader someday," said Ben; and in that moment, perhaps Sym first believed in himself.

In any event, Ben gave them all new names—nick-names out of popular culture, names of his own making—and what was more interesting is that these boys took to these names, they wore them as badges of pride: Thunder-Boy, MoneyBags, Stony, and the like. Jake, for one, was very proud of his obscure nickname. *Rabbit*, he said it was, one of Ben's typically bizarre appellations, and of course I had no idea what it meant. Although Ben's naming seemed like nonsense to me, and although Jake's name had little of the coolness of a "Stony" or "Thunderhead" name in it, "Rabbit" changed Jake in some subtle way. I noticed it, at least, when the darkness lifted a bit. The day he was first called Rabbit was the day that I noticed that his sense of himself had subtly shifted, had moved away from the edge, further towards the center of life.

5.

ALL DURING the months that Bendito Delacruz was meeting at lunch with his juvenile friends, his contract as a maintenance worker at Rockhorn continued to be renewed. Before and after his lunchtime story sessions, Ben continued working his odd jobs here and there across the campus: moving from fixing the broken fountain in the ornamental pool in front of the old Administration building (built in 1926 by Mr. Solmonsson), to patching a hole in the roof of the Caper auditorium and adding new shingles that matched the old, to fixing a masonry fissure at the top of the venting tower near the bakery. During that time period, Ben also began and finished the complex job of replacing the two main timbers that crossed in the middle of the library ceiling.

Eventually, someone else at Rockhorn noticed his considerable skill with power drill, sanding block and paintbrush. One day in early January, it seems that Laszlo Lindbloom, Rockhorn's lifelong instructor for various Shop classes—automotive and woodworking shop among them—noticed the craftsmanship of the new timberwork on the ceiling of the old library. Fortunately for Ben, his handiwork was noticed by someone who could recognize and appreciate the careful precision that he brought to his work with stone and cement and most particularly—with wood.

When Laszlo looked upward on that afternoon in September, instead of seeing the disintegrating joint that had stained the center of the library ceiling previously, warped and rotten with water damage, gaping wider and wider with time's passing, he saw new and carefully trimmed cedar timbers forming a perfect joint. Although Ben had managed to recruit another laborer to carry and place the heavy timbers into the library, he had done the fine detail of joining the dove joints together himself. I know; I have been to the library, and seen Ben's handiwork myself. Perhaps at the moment he saw it, Laszlo stood frozen, transfixed by the site of the perfectly joined pieces, solidly crossing at the apex of the ceiling. Perhaps this is what happened—I don't know—is this what Shop teachers do when they see good carpentry?

In any case, Laszlo made inquiries. He'd had the job available to all comers ever since it was approved by the Board last year; it had been posted for nine months now:

"Assistant Shop Instructor needed. Skill in fine woodworking, construction practices, automotive maintenance required. Instructional experience a plus. Inquire at Administration Office of Rockhorn Academy or Mr. Laszlo Lindbloom, Office of Instructional Crafts. 1500 Shekinah Ave East, 206-767-0000."

But when it came to skilled laborers who also were articulate and could instruct students, it was a desert out there. Of course, I could note the obvious (Laszlo, as always, was quite exacting in his standards) but that is beside the point. Mr. Lindbloom wanted the best for Rockhorn, and thus, he had interviewed nearly 20 individuals in the last six months. None of them passed his muster, and at each Board meeting the small notice on the agenda was renewed: "The position of Assistant Shop Instructor remains open. Your references are kindly requested by Mr. Laszlo Lindbloom." Occasionally, someone made mention of perhaps closing the open position and moving on—obviously, Laszlo had made it this far on his own—but as fate would have it, the position was filled just when Laszlo needed it most.

By the time he came to hire Ben, Laszlo had tired of the everyday interview process. And perhaps he had grown suspicious of the claims of too many of his applicants. Thus, when it came to Bendito Delacruz, he didn't believe anything that was told him. He simply put Ben to the test as a carpenter. Lindbloom talked to him for only a few minutes—I would imagine learning in the process that Ben was well-spoken and forthright, direct with both adults and children—and then contacted the Maintenance Supervisor, Bill Girus, not to ask for Ben's time to help him as an assistant instructor, but merely to ask for a few weeks of Ben's construction contract to be extended to Laszlo, so that he could use him on a maintenance project in the Shop building.

Girus was agreeable, and Ben began to report to the Shop room every morning for work.

In Laszlo Lindbloom's classroom, he was originally tasked with fixing the timbers on the Shop ceiling—I would guess that Laszlo wanted a copy of those exquisite cedar dovetail joints he'd seen on the ceiling of the library. Ben was also charged with taking apart an antique chest and putting it back together, refinishing its crusted varnish and ancient fittings in the process. Lindbloom could probably do neither of these jobs himself; he had become quite corpulent over the years. At this juncture he weighed over 300 pounds, and had largely been reduced to teaching fine detail on carpentry projects with his students and trouble-shooting parts that the students brought from the cars they were working on.

As Ben worked on both of these tasks, Lindbloom asked him to talk to the students in his advanced Wood Shop class and to demonstrate the techniques he was using. Thus, by hiring Ben, Lindbloom killed two birds with one stone—he got someone to do the work he couldn't do, and he also got a new and different kind of instructor to help in one of his most demanding classes.

Perhaps Laszlo had plans to hire him on a more permanent basis—I don't know—I never thought to ask Laszlo after he came out of the hospital, but when Laszlo went into the hospital, Ben was still technically a laborer, blessed by no formal title, just doing another menial job—albeit this one for Rockhorn's Shop instructor—working on an interim contract before moving on to the next item in his long list of interim positions.

In fact, when I think of Ben, I think sometimes that all of his work was simply a restless temporary placement. It is as if each job he took was just an eddy in the current—a place where he was momentarily grounded on dry land, left behind for a moment in the inert world that stayed in place all around his perpetual movement.

Although there are many areas of academic excellence at Rockhorn, and all students are required to take some sort of craft or handiwork class at some point in their career through Rockhorn, Shop classes are uniformly not the place where nascent talent is nurtured at our school. This is demonstrated most clearly at Rockhorn by the fact that despite the generous endowment, very few of these millions are devoted to the Shop program. The Argurion trust was supposed to give some monies to Vocational Studies, but for some reason that was held up until spring. The Shop building itself has been falling apart for nearly twenty years; every year Lindbloom assigns a class or two to a repair project, and allows the rest to disintegrate further.

At Rockhorn, everyone takes their required unit of Shop and moves on to other avenues of study, leaving behind the students who naturally lean towards work that can be done with the hands instead of the brain. No one with a brain seems to care about Shop. It is an unfortunate stereotype, but everyone seems to have swallowed it. For example, when Jake was finally forced to take his one unit of Shop, he immediately burst out with the typical denunciation that "Shop is just for losers and stoners. Why do I have to take it?" Perhaps this is true; on the other hand, perhaps Jake was just brainwashed by the cliquish peer pressure all around him, and Shop class at Rockhorn is in fact, the domain of smart, well-groomed and socially well-adjusted young men.

Unfortunately, the facts as I know them demonstrate that Jake was probably right. Most damning, I believe, was the fact that a number of Ben's maladjusted group from lunch were already enrolled (perhaps permanently) in Shop. When he enrolled in Shop that semester, Jake was simply joining that asocial crowd once again, drifting down into what I saw as a spiral of destruction.

Ben Delacruz, of course, despite his interim status, connected with the students in his single Shop class immediately—and he moved beyond that single classroom. Many laborers, much less full-time teachers, would not have known what to make of the denizens of the lower Shop classes, but Ben had a wonderful time. He was everywhere at once: a prophet without a kingdom, a teacher without credentials, a minister without portfolio. Yet everything he touched turned meaningful, everything he touched turned into gold.

Ben spent the early morning carefully sanding away layers of dead discolored varnish and talking his group through their work on other pieces of the chest; late morning found him in some back corner of the automotive section, buried up to the waist in an engine well, while lunchtime often caught him outside, wiping grease off his hands while he conversed with the crowd around his lunchtime table. Afternoons, he spent teaching students to carve timbers to fit the dimensions of Laszlo's ceiling. Besides his old compatriots from lunch, Ben also began connecting with a larger group of students who had never heard of him or met him. By the time Ben had been there for a few weeks, instead of Shop consisting of a set of disconnected students who worked on projects that never touched each other, he had gradually welded his single class into cohesive group that wanted to discuss their projects with each other, wanted to hear each other talk, and wanted—most of all—to interact with the instructor about the work they were doing. From an outsider's perspective, the most dramatic shift was that they were proud of the craftsmanship they were learning, rather than ashamed of being in Shop.

Laszlo Lindbloom himself sensed the shift. Although it took a number of weeks, he soon joined the renewed spirit of success and accomplishment that seemed to have filled his decrepit building. As the ceiling beams were being completed, Laszlo even christened Ben with the nickname that we came to know him by.

Jake's story goes that Laszlo heard cheering from the main classroom, and came in with a scowl. All the students were looking up, and when Laszlo followed their gaze, he saw Ben dropping the last two cedar beams together. The sight of the new cedar was enough to cheer even dour Lindbloom up, and he blinked in the glare of the ceiling lights, grinning with pleasure. "He's quite a carpenter," Laszlo said. "Quite a Carpenter." Thus, Bendito received the nickname that would soon evolve into "Carp"—the name the boys called him, and the name he'd keep for the rest of his time at Rockhorn.

Ben helped Lindbloom bring the Summer Term classes to a close for the semester, and then after the break, helped organize the classes for the Fall semester. All of this was proceeding as one might expect when, out of the blue, Laszlo Lindbloom collapsed. He was, as I've mentioned, quite fat, which I believe endangers your heart, bringing on all manner of ailments—high blood pressure, asthma, diabetes, gout, and all the rest. They said it was a blood clot or an aneurysm in his head or something of that sort that took him down.

Laszlo Lindbloom went into a coma for four months. I went to see him once, and it was astonishing to see his rounded body gradually wasting away. It was as if a plug had been pulled somewhere. All of that delicious fat was draining out of him; the pale crescents of his cheekbones, and his ribs, and his hips gradually rose to the surface. When I went to see him, Laszlo never opened his eyes or varied his machine-induced breathing. He could move nothing; in fact, the doctors said that he had not moved or shown any sign of consciousness since he first entered the hospital. There was no brain activity, and after a month the doctors were sure he was merely a vegetable, holding onto the simulacrum of life. While at the hospital, I mentioned in passing to the doctors that someone should make arrangements to disconnect his feeding and breathing tubes, and to donate his organs after he had passed on, but they didn't seem comfortable discussing such things, perhaps because I wasn't a family member. In any event, it was a shock to see Laszlo brought so low, so quickly. He was out of commission within the first two weeks of the new school year.

My friend Joseph Matheson, the Headmaster of Rockhorn Academy, was caught quite off guard by Laszlo's unplanned collapse. After a few quick consultations with selected parents, and after interviewing Bendito Delacruz himself, Joe asked Ben if he'd mind staying in charge of all of the Shop classes on an interim basis—as a substitute teacher—until they could make some more permanent long-term arrangements. Ben also took over the management of various community projects and work-study activities that Lindbloom managed, and in stepping into Lindbloom's shoes, also began to supervise some of the grounds maintenance. As I was to discover later, Joe didn't offer Bendito any sort of a teaching contract—Ben didn't have a degree after all—and so technically Ben remained simply a carpenter at the school, working under the direction of the Grounds Supervisor, Bill Girus.

Despite the technical details of his employment, Ben's visibility and stature at Rockhorn Academy definitely increased. Before he stepped into Laszlo's shoes, he was a mere lunchbox bard—somehow a leader, yes, but without a mandate. Now that Joe had given him more formalized responsibility, Ben came into the role automatically, as if the Carpenter had been born to be teacher. He became a *de facto* leader, blessed by no tenure track appointment, no ordination or Ivy League degrees. Ben Delacruz was that rare thing in our world of hierarchies and carefully negotiated title inflation: he was a leader simply because he led.

When I first heard about Ben's transition, I was a trifle apprehensive. I am saddened to report that even in the best schools—even in places like Rockhorn—classroom management and discipline has become an inordinately large part of the teaching job. With disorganized, broadly distributed classes like Shop that contain a number of unruly types, it's courting disaster to throw an unproven substitute to the wolves. Yet all the really hardened cases had already been softened by Ben's entertaining stories and gentle wit. The toughest or most distracting boys in each class seemed to already be listening to him; they were the ones who had Ben's nicknames. And because the rest of the students couldn't figure out why boys like Jon and Jimmy (Thunderheads 1 and 2), Matt (Bags), Sym (Stony) and Jake (Rabbit) were attentive to Ben, the rest of the students were attentive as well. So because Ben had already gained the respect and friendship of the worst offenders, he did fine.

In fact, Jake reported that classes taught by Ben rapidly became quite popular. Yet just as he did no proselytizing for the lunch-time stories, so Ben also did no active recruiting for his simple Shop classes.

Despite this lack of advertisement, students began to transfer into his class from math, from science, from English, from music, from any class that they could get out of. The new semester had just begun, and students were allowed several weeks to make changes in their schedules.

I still don't understand what exactly Ben's appeal to students consisted of, but I can report that the number of children in Ben's shop class gradually rose until the period for official changes stopped. There was a pause then, a minor hiccup, yet soon after the exodus to Ben's building resumed. Now, instead of official changes, there were the official parent-approved "over-ride" change forms, and there were "medical" change forms, and there were even one or two faked "override" class change forms, discovered later in the school year when the Registrar combed through the files to find out how many of Rockhorn's finest Ben had taught. Even mid-way through the semester, when there could be no more official class changes, new students continued to show up in Ben's class, taking unapproved absences from their registered classes.

Ben didn't blink at this—perhaps he thought it was par for the course for a new teacher at Rockhorn—and welcomed each and every student into his class, even when the number of people in the room began to resemble an assembly of half the student body, rather than a small and tight-knit classroom. It is hard to blame him for this though—he was new to the teaching system, and perhaps he didn't realize that he did not have to automatically approve each class change request that came to him. Perhaps in his mind, such a mob of students was normal for a new and unproven teacher at Rockhorn. In any event, Ben simply continued teaching his straightforward Shop classes, focused on carpentry techniques. Occasionally, he'd intersperse the carpentry with anecdotes, stories, and witticisms, all of them precisely tuned to his audience, and all of which endeared him even more to the mass of students that filled the room.

I am getting ahead of the story though. At the beginning of the semester, there were other oddities.

I doubt if Ben had ever taught a class before in his life, or had any valid experience in teaching. Thus, he took a rather novel approach to curriculum. Rather than directly assigning a reading (I don't even know if they have 'readings' in Shop classes, having never taken one in my life), or providing a syllabus, or even outlining a project that the students would be building during the course of the semester, Ben asked for an unprecedented level of student participation. (Perhaps, since Ben had no prior experience to draw on, he simply threw his hands up.)

What Ben did to jump-start each of his Shop classes was that he asked each student to bring in items that needed to be fixed, and in Shop, they would spend the first part of the term fixing these items, and perhaps duplicating them to create a general project that everyone would make. It seemed that in this class, instead of making wood and stone products from scratch, the students would be making old things anew, re-making them, so to speak. This practice began at the start of the semester.

As I remember, it was a day near the end of September when I first heard of Ben's unorthodox proposal. At first, I didn't understand what he was doing. I was irritable with Jake that day—I'd lost a client to a long battle with brain cancer. Furthermore, despite my constant attention, it turned out that the client hadn't liked me enough to bother to enlist me as either a beneficiary or as the executor of his estate, leaving the executor task in the hands of his idiot sons, who were also accountants, and who had just recently returned from overseas. The bitterness was double, as I'd labored long and hard over the man's accounts, and although the first blow was having him gone—the second blow of not getting my due was almost as harsh. It seemed to me someone who had labored for years should be more rewarded than someone who had just showed up. When I arrived at the funeral home after his death and the sons directly asked me to leave, I lost my patience with the family and told them exactly how tight-fisted and selfish the old man was before he died. Perhaps I believed it a little myself, but perhaps I never understood the man, perhaps I never knew him. In any event, he probably didn't deserve to hear the words "He can go to hell!" said over his dead body; no one does. By the time I returned home, the frustration and bitterness overwhelmed me entirely. Thus, on the day when Jake first explained the fishing pole idea to me, I also took out some of my rage on him, telling him it was a very stupid idea.

Jake persevered through my evident frustration though—going on about Ben's idea of making old things new again. Then I told him that it would have been better for Ben simply to cut to the chase, and call the class "Antiquing: Techniques for Profitable Resale of Old Furniture," but again, perhaps I was imposing my own sensibility on boys whom God knows I don't understand.

After I'd had a stiff drink, I finally I gave Jake permission to bring in whatever broken thing around the house that he wanted to fix—I assumed he'd take an old toaster or something similarly practical, but in the rubbish heap out back Jake found an ancient fishing pole. It was a pole that I'd recently unearthed myself, from some back closet, an old snapped piece of wood that had once belonged to my father—a relic of a time gone by—and a relic that I'd decided would be better served by rotting in the ground with his ashes.

In retrospect, perhaps the whole story might have been different if Jake had simply taken a toaster—events might have taken a very different course, ending without incident. But there's no help for it now. Jake chose a broken fishing pole, and from my perspective, that made all the difference.

In the morning, I was still irritable and despondent over my lost client, and I suppose it showed.

When Jake brought out the broken pole, I asked "Why are you taking *that* thing in to school?" not realizing that Jake had chosen this as his project for Ben. "That thing is unusable– you won't catch anything in the creek with it, that's for sure."

"Maybe I will catch something after we fix it in class. It's my project," said Jake. "We can make it like brand-new."

Again, the enthusiasm with which Jake expressed his handyman ambitions caught me on a rough edge. In any event, I reacted out of my bitter moment.

"Brand-new?" I said. "Look, that old piece of junk will *never* be brand new. It's broken, and you know what broken is—it means something has become a piece of junk. You could throw it away, or you could use it some other way, maybe to stick in the ground and hold some clematis or something up."

I took the pole out of his hand and flicked the broken part of the pole back and forth, bending and snapping it further. "See that?" I said. "That means it will never be like my father had it. He broke it, and so now we can't use it. It'll never be anything but a piece of wood now."

Jake took the broken pole back, somewhat forcefully, I might add. "Carp said people might say stuff like that," he said.

"He did, did he? And Mr. Delacruz lets you call him Carp, even though he's your teacher now?"

"No, no, he doesn't. I just call him that outside of class. Like now. But in class, we all call him the Carp."

"I see," I said coldly. "So what else did 'Carp' say?"

"Oh, he said you guys wouldn't understand. But he said it's no big deal."

By this point I was becoming irritated. "Really?" I said coldly. "Pray tell, what part of my understanding did he describe?"

To my chagrin, Jake didn't appear to detect the level of my irritation. He proceeded to tell me everything Ben had said.

It appeared that Ben had given one of those teacherly lectures designed to inspire. At the time, as I've mentioned, I was on the edge of infuriation, and hearing Ben spout off about "making everything brand new" didn't help matters. In his go-for-broke style, Jake described him as saying all manner of foolish things, statements like: "We can fix anything. There's nothing we can't fix!" and "We can make everything in the world brand-new!"

There was more to this little inspirational speech. I was past caring by this point, but I could still hear well enough—and all over the place throughout his speech was this sense of revolutionary fervor, this touch of messianic ardor, this possibility of "changing the world." Probably it was merely good teaching—inspiring the student, and all that. But at that particular moment, it struck me as bitter medicine to a sad world.

Laced all through my week had been a realization of loss and now all I heard from Jake's mouth was false enthusiasm, manufactured hope, and impractical excitement. All of it put there by the machinations of the unschooled Ben Delacruz.

I was harsh with Jake. I told him to grow up—to throw the bent and twisted heirloom pole away. It would be better, I said, to simply let bygones be bygones. Despite all this, Jake kept referring back to Ben's maddening level of faith in the power of human beings to fix things. He seemed to believe like a child, that anything could become brand-new once again.

At this point, I felt an inexplicable anger slowly fill me, the gorge rising in me, a creeping surf that turned imperceptibly into the crashing surge of inarticulate rage. I told Jake out of my anger, as I am telling you here, that Ben was wrong—some things break beyond repair.

Toasters, CD players, microwaves, and cheap fishing poles are just the latest manifestation of the general breakage. And as I get older, there only seem to be more broken things around me. Someone technical might call it the inertia towards entropy, this trend towards being broken-beyond-repair. I don't know what it is; they didn't make this world to last.

I do know that the vagaries of life can't be fixed through simple faith and a bit of hard work. I've known too many things that break in the course of my life, this broken story I am telling not the least among them. This week had broken everything: my client's brain had been broken by cancer, and now my fee had been broken out among his sons, and finally, my relationship with the client's family was now irretrievably broken by my own bitterness. Yet it wasn't just this week.

In fact, I would venture to say that most men my age, in my circumstances, are good examples of their own particular broken-beyond-repair phenomenon. And there's no real explaining for most of it; I have broken enough important things to last me a lifetime of explanation. A broken marriage, incurring one of those trite broken hearts, broken ambitions (who sets out to be a minor league tax accountant, after all?), broken stupid meaningless friendships with people who want things from me, a few broken one-night-stands, and at the end of my long workday, I come home to a broken spineless child, always laboring under a dark cloud, and now enthralled by some uneducated roustabout's gruesome stories. If that's not broken, I'd like to ask you what is.

6.

IRONICALLY, THE fishing pole that I had so derided took on increasing importance in Jake's life as the semester lengthened. On the day that Jake went to class with his broken pole, it seemed that all other parents were successful in their arguments, because everyone else in the class brought toasters or defunct CD players, or something of the like.

But Jake brought an old wooden fishing pole, something of a bygone age, and as soon as Ben saw it, it seemed that he was enamored with its snapped and cracked length, its unraveling wrappings, and its warped and broken old-fashioned line-spooler. The broken pole that I had placed on the rubbish heap became the centerpiece of their classroom, as Ben made it the model for new poles that everyone in the class would construct. In a matter of hours, it had become the focal point—the first project of the new semester.

I am reconstructing the way that Ben took my father's old fishing pole as his example, for I didn't hear about the fate of the pole until a month later. I am not sure why Jake didn't tell me, but it fit the pattern of anger and silence that we were all too familiar with. Sometimes it was Jake who was upset and I who had to have the patience to let the waters settle back into calm, but more often it was me who brought the torrent of rage that made Jake tiptoe around the house until I came back to myself. After all, it was I who was so often distracted by work, overcome by the twin pressures of raising Jake and holding a job, weighed down by the grief of dealing with dead clients and insolvent ex-clients.

Perhaps Jake felt that it would be best to not tell me what had happened to it—to let me forget my irritation at the entire original incident of the pole before I heard more.It was our pattern, and we were both well used to it. Yet when they were almost done with the new versions of the poles, a moment of unguarded casual conversation from Jake revealed that in fact, the pole had not been burned the moment it hit the school campus, but instead, had been carefully dissected as a model for new poles of identical lineage for every one of Jake's classmates.

It was astonishing to me. I don't know why, but the idea of each one of Jake's classmates carrying around new fishing poles just like my father's was nearly shocking; it floored me.

"What right does he have to do that with my father's pole?" I began, but when Jake glanced at me, I saw that he had clammed up once more, and that I would get nothing further from him on the topic of Ben and the classroom fishing poles.

In between, I heard about the fishing poles again only because Jake was so excited after his first after-school fishing escapade that he forgot to keep his mouth shut.

This incident happened soon after Ben's class had put the first coats of varnish on their new poles. Instead of being content to let them sit in the darkness of the classroom and dry, Ben was like a child—he wanted to use them. Thus, he told the members of his class who didn't have sports or other extracurricular activities—and few did, in this room full of misfits—to meet him after school at the creek, the same creek where Jake had pushed him in when they'd first met, or into which he'd pushed Jake (I was never quite clear on who bumped into who). In any case, it was the creek where they'd first met, that small ribbon of water crossed by the footbridge near school.

It was like Ben to take his classroom instruction far outside the doors of the classroom, into territory that I would have thought would be prohibited as a dangerous liability for the school, but to which Ben didn't seem to give the slightest concern.

The next morning the story was all over the school, for every boy had brought home at least one fish—some of them had brought home a whole rack full of fresh-caught sunfish and catfish, and an assortment of different varieties and sizes of rainbow trout. Someone even claimed to have brought back a small salmon, caught on its way to a mountain pool.

No one had even thought of fishing in that trickle of a stream for years—I suppose we'd forgotten that it was deeper than it looked, the true depths concealed by mounds of overhanging bushes and steeply angled banks.

In any case, on the day they fished it out, Ben's boys spent a good two hours there. When Jake came home, breathless with excitement, carrying his rack of three catfish and four trout, he related how the boys would string fresh bait onto their hooks and the line would barely hit the water before the surface would boil with activity and multiple fish would strike for their lure, begging to be taken back home and be roasted for dinner.

It was another fascinating thing for me to think about—I hadn't gone fishing in years (certainly never in the populated Valley), and never with my son—but Ben had had the gumption to tell his boys to throw their hooks into a tiny suburban creek that they crossed every day, and as luck would have it, the suggestion didn't turn him into a laughingstock. He had tremendous luck, in that it was a smashing success. It wasn't just a success in the fishing department either—it was also very successful teaching. Every boy now had a capstone of excitement with which to crown his fishing pole creation experience, and every boy wanted desperately to finish his pole so that Ben would take them fishing again.

I went to chat with Mack Demson, the Dean of Students and fellow member of Rockhorn Board, the day after the fishing incident, and he agreed that their success in Albe Creek was remarkable. "Have you ever heard of anything like it?" said Mack to me. "I didn't know there was anything in that creek."

As usual, I found a reasonable explanation for their success. "Perhaps that's the reason they caught so many—no one knew, and no one has been near that creek for years, for decades perhaps. The fish have been undisturbed. They're probably also very hungry, and will strike at anything."

I mentioned the liability, the potential for drowning, or even with injury through the flinging of sharp hooks around, and Mack agreed with me. There was potential liability in such impromptu, unauthorized trips that took place after hours with a Rockhorn teacher in tacit control of the situation.

However, as Mack noted, there were no injuries, and thus no concerned parents—this time. I told him that I was concerned, and Mack laughed in my face. "If I had a dollar for each time that you were concerned," he told me, "I'd be a much richer lawyer."

Yet despite his laughter, Mack did listen to me. We shared information, discussing what he'd heard about the fishing expedition from other parents and what I'd heard from my son.

Mack and I ended the evening with a bottle of Scotch, and a promise to meet each other early the next morning

It was a Friday morning, and we spent several hours there before work, employing the best fishing gear that money could buy. Over and over again, we tried to equal the success of Ben's boys. First, in the early hour before the sun rose, we tried the tasty artificial bait—the pink blobs of false and puffy gel bait, dripping with toxic-looking aromatic oil. When that failed, we switched reels and line, and turned to fly-fishing with practiced poses, dropping perfect handmade replicas gently onto the slowly moving surface as the sun began to rise.

Eventually, as the hour for work approached, we gave up fly-fishing as well, and tried metallic lures, small enough to be intriguing, and then big enough that we could see the glimmer in the deep water all the way from the shore. Finally, we gave in, and used bread-ball bait, and then even live bait: crawfish, grasshoppers, and even worms.

Every now and then—especially on the grasshoppers—we would get a small strike, and even more rarely, we would pull in a very small and worn-out sunfish. But there was nothing like what Ben's class had found.

We were too late, we concluded. As the workday began, Mack and I went to a small café near Rockhorn. There, we drowned our sorrows in a big pot of black coffee, and concluded that the creek had all been fished out by a teacher and his intrepid middle-school fishermen.

Perhaps the next time Ben tried for an impromptu fishing lesson, he found the same, because soon after, each one of the parents of students in the class received a special permission slip to sign. One of the advantages of Rockhorn experience was the school's openness to non-traditional modes of learning, including off-campus weekend or weeklong jaunts, entirely funded by the school endowment. Perhaps a child suggested it—I don't know. But I suppose that once Ben found out about this characteristic of Rockhorn, he wanted to take immediate advantage of it. After all, I reasoned, his style of teaching didn't seem to fit very comfortably inside Rockhorn's hallowed walls.

Jake came home almost incoherent with excitement. He wanted to go on a weekend trip with Ben and other students, fishing up in the mountains.

That was how I came to hold in my hands a small yellow Rockhorn "Weekend Trip" form, and I was intrigued to see how carefully every detail had been filled out in advance—our name, our address, and my full name was already included. Only my signature remained to be added.

I assumed that Ben had instructed them to fill out the form with a maximum of detail, the better to draw their parents into signing it. I was not about to be taken in by such a transparent maneuver. In my mind, what possible benefit could there to Jake spending more time with this laborer-turned-teacher, and his gang of unruly juveniles?

The permission slip outlined the fact that a large group of students from Rockhorn would be going. It was not just Ben and his class, but I suppose all of the misfits who surrounded Ben at lunch, and other teachers who were also enamored of Ben. All arrangements had been made, said Jake, for adequate adult supervision. I told him it wasn't adequate enough for me. It was really unthinkable, sending my son up into the hills with this gang of Rockhorn's dregs and druggies. I told Jake that I wouldn't be at all surprised if one of them produced a weapon somewhere up in the mountains, or if the fire got out of control, and burned down the campsite.

My first instinct was to turn it down, to flatly tell Jake "no," and to then go about my business.

But then it struck me—this could make up for my frustration and for Mack's. Even though Mack didn't have a child in Ben's class, or even a child who spent time around Ben (I envied him that, let me tell you), he and I might both be able to push onto the entourage of the trip. Essentially, Mack and I had them over a barrel. If two members of Rockhorn Board—including me, the Treasurer—decided that the trip wasn't a good idea, we might conceivably be able to put a stop to it entirely, and they might know that.

I thought of calling Ben immediately, and telling him this, informing him that Mack and I wanted to go, but somehow I felt that he wouldn't care if we wanted to go or not. I didn't feel that he would understand. He didn't seem like a very political person; it would be most embarrassing to have to baldly explain political maneuvering to someone uninformed like him.

Oddly, I even felt like Ben might not like me to go. When the thought first occurred to me, it was with a flicker of worry. I had the bizarre sensation that he knew better than I did how I really felt about him.

Instead of calling him, I ended up signing the original permission slip. Then I had to negotiate with fellow Board member Sol Tharsen, who was supplying every camper with brand new 4-Season tents from his camping gear company. Tharsen apparently was helping Ben coordinate the trip, and even though I was an adult attendee, I had to confirm my arrival and departure times with him. Finally, I got both a tent from Tharsen and permission for both Mack and I to accompany them up into the mountains. Regardless of the times I'd committed to Tharsen, I had the idea that Mack and I would depart from the group, and find a concealed, much better fishing hole, from which we'd emerge the next day carrying armfuls of fish, enough to astound them all.

Sadly, though, this was not to be. Despite my best negotiating efforts, both Mack and I ended up with other things that we had to do that weekend—I had the first flicker of interest by several tax agents into a situation that would increasingly complicate my life in the months to come, and Mack had to finish some work at the office. There was a pile of paperwork to complete for the Argurion endowment grant, most of it time-critical. So neither one of us were able to go.

But at the time of first giving permission, it seemed like a reasonable compromise. Allow my son to spend more time around Ben—even extending to outside of school, on the weekend—in exchange for the opportunity to catch some monster fish in the mountains with Mack.

In the end, I had to hear about the fishing trip just as I'd heard about everything else involving Ben—vicariously, through Jake's eyes.

The first day in the mountains was uneventful, according to Jake. They drove in; they pitched camp. Ben and the other parents and teachers arranged a campsite that was tucked into a little cove in the woods, close enough to the river to hear its chuckling flow as they settled down to dinner. Overall, said Jake, the first day and evening were boring.

As the weekend progressed, the children became more excited about being up in the mountains. They fished for hours with their new poles, standing hip-deep in the swirling cold mountain water, watching their lures be dragged down-stream in the current. I can picture them in my mind's eye—the gang of boys (and some girls), wild in the woods, playing games with water and branches for hours every day, calming down only when they were exhausted, by the campfire. (After only a few days up there, Jake came back with the deepest suntan I've ever seen on him. It was as if he'd not been under shelter once during the weekend.) In retrospect, I suppose I should be glad that I didn't have to spend my weekend herding children away from deep spots in the river, and contending with endless childish games. The only thing that I wish I had gone for is the fishing.

It was marvelous fishing. On the first day, Ben spent quite a bit of time teaching them how to fish safely in the mountain streams. And by the end of the second day, they'd caught so many fish that it was obvious that if they kept pulling in fish at this rate—and if they kept eating fish with each meal—the majority of their food would be superfluous. Even with a herd of ravenous thirteen and fourteen year olds, the prodigious amounts of fish they were catching exceeded demand, and at each meal, they always had buckets of leftovers.

The fishing was tremendous. On the second evening, by the campfire that night, perhaps bored by the ease with which they were all catching fish, Ben proposed a contest—a fishing contest that would take them through the rest of the weekend. Ben further proposed two teams: the older boys (fourteen and up) against the younger boys (the first form at Rockhorn—twelve and thirteen). At first there were vocal protests from the younger ones that the matching was unfair, but then Ben clarified that he would be on the team composed of younger boys, along with some of the other adults. Then there were protests from the other side. In the end though, everyone agreed to the contest. It was simple—during the night and the day remaining, whoever caught the most fish (in number and poundage) would win.

That night after the campfire—the only remaining full night they would be spending on the mountain—the older boys went back out to fish. They planned to spend the night hours getting the jump on everyone else. Thus, they waited by the water for hours, faithfully plunging their hooks back into the water, over and over again, determined to win the contest.

Unfortunately for them, the night-fishing didn't pay off. Although they stayed out by the mountain river for hours into the darkness, until two or three in the morning, they only caught a few bottom-feeding, dark-dwelling carp, and several somnolent sunfish, and that was it, for all their effort. When the older boys staggered back to bed, they felt they had an edge, but only a small one.

If only Mack and I had been there, I wonder if we could have helped them to win a few more fish in the small hours. I wonder how we would have fared. No doubt, we would have bested them all. None of those boys (or Ben either, I suspect) knew to do anything more than fling a lure or a worm and hook into the water, and pray for fish to strike.

We knew better. We had underwater fish sensors, we had black-light lures, and more importantly, we had the knowledge and skill that comes with decades of high tech fishing.

It was a pity we couldn't be there. If Mack and I were fishing in the wee hours, we might have lowered a glow lantern into the water, to attract the fish. Or perhaps some of that toxic pink bait, the junk with the aromatic flavor, would have brought the fish in. In any case,

I am sure that with our equipment and our expertise, Mack and I could have brought the older boys ahead. I am sure that we would have joined them after all—Ben had his own methods of getting the younger boys ahead in the game.

Very early the last morning, only a few hours after the older boys had staggered frustrated to bed, Ben quietly roused the most dependable of the younger boys—including my son Jake—and took them further upstream.

Gradually, as the blue hours passed and light leaked into the sky, they filled their creels with rainbow trout. As the dawn struck, the fish rose in a body, and took their bait. It was as if they had merely been waiting at the surface to be hooked, and the desire of these fish to be taken out bent their poles to touch the surface of the water. At least one of those hand-built poles snapped under the weight of the striking fish, but this only urged the small boys onward. Soon, they were struggling to find a place to put all the fish. Someone—it was probably Jimmy's father, Zeb—snuck back to the campsite and retrieved an empty cooler. Stacked end over end, the fish nearly filled the cooler.

Although the older boys used the rest of the day to catch up to some degree, they only managed to get out of their sleeping bags at around mid-day. By the time they emerged and went back to the river, the fishing contest was essentially over. The younger boys had won.

Jake had another story though, one that he told only to me, and that he swore me to secrecy on before he told me (he didn't want to imperil any future fishing trips). It is a story that put the fishing of the night into perspective, and also made me admire Ben, if only during the time I was hearing Jake relate his story.

It seems that when the older boys were fishing, some of them became too zealous in their efforts. In the pitch darkness of the late hours, they felt with their bare feet for underwater rocks and inched their way gradually deeper and deeper into the dark pools, until they were in the water up to their chests. Gradually, all of them began urging each other deeper into the water, getting as close as they could to the fleeing fish.

Most of the older boys seemed fine doing this—many of them could swim extremely well, and there were no public reports of injuries, near drowning or even water inhalation among them. Unfortunately though, one of the older boys was Sym, who could not swim and had refused to tell anyone of this lack. I only knew of it because of my son; Jake was his closest friend on the field trip, and Jake knew.

In fact, Jake—one of the younger boys by a hairsbreadth—had snuck out of his tent and was with Sym that night, wading into the deep holes along with the older boys.

Jake said there was a moment of uncertainty before he was swept away, a moment of limbo in which his body hung between the moss-covered rock on the bottom of the river, and the roiling current that caught at him in the upper levels of the water. He was suspended for a moment, and then he was pushed suddenly, as if by a hand on his back, into the darker water. Jake flailed and held his head above water—I'd taught him that much at least—and soon he found himself several hundred feet further down the river, lodged between large rocks just on the safe side of a group of rapids. He knew he was close to the rapids because of the splashing white foam all around him. He was (relatively) safe there—all he had to do was to find a way out. But as he clung to the large rocks, he couldn't find a purchase with his feet. So he simply held on and waited, buoyed up by the splashing current, and wondering how many hours it would be until sunrise.

He didn't have to wait until dawn. Symon didn't know that Jake was safe. As Jake floated away, Sym valiantly threw himself into the water, struggling to catch at Jake's collar or his pole—anything with which he could rescue Jake. Unfortunately, he moved too fast and too furiously in trying to catch at Jake, and soon Sym found himself in the same precarious limbo, caught in the current between the rocks on the bottom and the waves on top. It was the worst possible fate for Sym the coward. He flailed much more vigorously, genuinely afraid of the deep water, and found himself caught in the current that much quicker, carried away into the darkness.

Jake said he heard Sym choking as he floated by: he said he could vaguely hear Sym's head splashing under as the current tossed him from side to side, and then when he'd splash out of the water, Jake could hear the hacking urge of the water coming back out of his mouth.

Sym was carried into more dangerous water than Jake. Instead of a safe lodging between two huge rocks, Sym was carried right past, into the rapids themselves, where he was bounced between sinkhole and churning water, down the course of the river. Jake could do nothing but listen to his increasingly weak and distant cries for help and the fading sounds of him choking on inhaled water. Then the sounds of Sym faded away, and Jake was left to wonder if that was his fate as well, to slip away from the safety of the rocks, and be caught in the rapids.

He sank a little lower in the black water. The churning rapids around him sprayed his face with water, and Jake began to hyperventilate. At that moment, he heard a voice.

It was Ben. "Don't worry," he said. "I have my own way of finding things in the river." He gestured down at his feet, no doubt indicating the concealed line of rocks he was standing on in the rapids. "Come up here," he said. "Where it's safe."

Jake took his hand, and was soon standing beside Ben, out of the deep water. Then they went searching for Symon.

They found him a good distance away downstream, waterlogged and frantic with fear. As the water dripped off his head and into his eyes, Sym looked up at them as if they were ghosts come to retrieve him in the night, the whites of his eyes wide as silver dollars. Ben spoke again.

"Be strong, Sym! It's only me—come here—you can do it."

Then Sym pushed himself upwards with frantic strength, propelling himself bodily out of the water, so that Jake said that for a moment, it was almost as if Sym were standing on the surface, a cartoon character spinning his legs, trying to run on top of water. He hadn't moved towards them at all though—certainly not to anywhere solid, and he sank again, almost screaming with frustration. "Help! Save me!"

Then Ben reached out from his firm spot, and lifted Sym out of the water. When Sym got to the place where Ben and Jake were standing, he was finally above the rapids. Sym's whole body shook with relief.

"I think I'll just call you my little Stony—my pebble—from now on," said Ben to Sym. "You were a little pebble caught in the current, not big enough to hold back the waves."

"Yeah, I was some stone all right," said Sym. "I was sinking like one. The current was pulling me down."

"Oh, you were just my man to catch in the current—I caught you instead of a fish. You would have been fine."

"Yeah, and I'm sure glad you did," said Sym. "We would have died if you hadn't found us."

Ben tapped him on the back, almost knocking him back into the water. "No, don't doubt yourself. You gotta listen to me—you gotta have faith."

Slowly, they walked back to camp together. Moonlight glimmered on the white rapids as the three of them splashed along in the night, walking along Ben's hidden path through the water.

When I heard Jake's private story of the night, and put it together with the rest of the stories about the older boys fishing late, and the younger boys fishing early, the night seemed full of action. Jake slept for only an hour or so after his adventure in the river, before Ben woke his tent full of younger boys, to go fishing before dawn. But I don't think Ben slept at all during that last night in the mountains. I think he was out there on the river, watching his charges, making sure they didn't drown, all night long. In the end, I had a certain grudging respect for the man. He didn't want to lose any of them.

Hearing Jake's version of the story later, I remembered that he'd had little sleep the night before. I thought he'd probably conflated it with all the other stories we hear—the endless rounds of mythic types on Superhero Saturday on TV—and had Ben as a bit more of a heroic figure than he really was.

In Jake's mind though, the weekend elevated Ben to the status of a superhero—a man who quietly told stories during the day, and then when night came, rescued those who fell into the current—it was the fervid stuff of any young boy's yearning imagination.

Just before they left the mountain streams though, Ben also made some decisions about how they would pack, and what they would do with what they packed out.

Because of all the fish the boys had caught, the adults found that there were whole buckets and coolers full of extra food and extra fish. On finding all this extra food, Ben took the odd stance that instead of simply packing all of their extra food (and extra fish that was on ice) back to their respective houses, they should donate it all to a shelter, to the poor. And in fact, that's what the entire group did when they returned.

I was sitting in my BMW in the parking lot, waiting for the car with Jake to arrive, and I heard the parents who had just returned discussing the decision.

"Fishing for homeless men," joked one of the parents. "We should all get T-shirts—I caught a fish this big and I gave it away to a man without a fish."

Then they all laughed, and I was left to find out what the story was behind their laughter later, when Jake told me all the details.

7.

ONLY A week or so later, after the excitement of the fishing trip had died down, I was surprised to hear from Jake an entirely different story about Bendito Delacruz. Once more, the story confounded what I'd come to expect from the man.

After the fishing trip, and Jake's endless stories about Ben, one theme had come clear. Ben had connected with my son in a way that I never had. I've always had a bit of distaste in my mouth for these types of men—the men that wear the ridiculous uniforms and play the ridiculous boyhood games, and are willing to spend an inordinate amount of time with a group of children twenty years younger than them.

Some time ago, I'd had a conversation with Joe in which I brought up my concerns about Ben's influence on the boys. "What's the harm in him?" Joe had said. "He's only a Shop teacher, trying to help a few of these losers out of their depressions."

Reluctantly, I concluded that Joe had been right. Ben was simply a glorified Boy Scout—a person who liked to work with boys, and liked to teach them how to channel their testosterone energies in productive directions.

I suppose the male mentor role is also attractive to some men because for a short time—for that time that they're in the classroom or with the Scout troop—they get to live in a wholly adolescent, masculine world, one that doesn't have the complications of women, of gender warfare, or the worries and ambiguity of sex. It seemed that although Ben was not necessarily predictable, he was basically harmless—he was only a motivator, the Ur-ScoutMaster, and as boyish as they come. I'd never really thought of it before, but until the day that Moira joined the lunchtime crowd, the group was entirely composed of young boys.

Ben was just yearning to re-experience boyhood; and now, he was in a job that allowed him to vicariously re-live his adolescence every week through his charges. In this role, Ben wasn't a threat to me anymore, and now I wondered why I'd ever felt so intimidated by him. I looked back now on my little investigation with a bit of shame.

The story that Jake told about his friendship with Moira then, was confounding. Why would a pseudo-Scoutmaster get involved with sexual politics, and why was he so knowledgeable about the sex lives of Rockhorn's athletes?

Perhaps I should begin with who Moira was, and why her inclusion in Ben's group was such a shock to me. The year before was the first year that Rockhorn had accepted girls into the school. Bound by some sort of legal decision that affected our funding, Rockhorn had finally made grudging efforts to both recruit and accommodate female students and teachers. Moira was one of the first girls to attend, and she came at the behest of her grandparents.

I am sure that under other circumstances, Moira would have never been permitted into the school. Moira herself had gone through various difficulties at other schools, and typically we did not admit anyone with a record of school expulsions. However, as her grandfather had attended Rockhorn himself and continued to be a major donor to the school foundation, she was admitted as a legacy, an experiment of sorts. Perhaps Rockhorn was the last place that would take her, or perhaps, for whatever reason, Moira's grandparents still had faith in Rockhorn way.

Moria was being raised by her grandparents at the time this all happened, but despite the advantages of her situation, she was still a girl with evident problems. Many of these stemmed from the sexual and emotional abuse of her early childhood living with her father—who was now institutionalized—but she carried the consequences of this with her everywhere like a red flag.

At this early stage in her life, her grandparents perhaps didn't realize that Moira was essentially beyond rescuing. They had seen how cruelly Moira had been treated in other schools, and perhaps they felt they were doing Moira a favor. They chose to remove her from the mocking company of other girls her age, by placing her in an exclusive nearly all-male society. Perhaps they assumed that she would be enriched by the challenge—perhaps they thought they were doing her a favor. Far from it. If anything, they were cursing her to a lower circle of hell.

Here, in this rarified and testosterone-thickened environment, her inappropriate sensuality blossomed into full flower. It was already rumored that she had managed to seduce various of the upper-level boys (always the misfits and outsiders even in the upper levels—these were the types that Moria gravitated towards, and the only types that would have her), and was now reaching her clutches towards those not exploited—her own peers, the ones in the mid-levels, the ones her own age.

I suppose one cannot resist the instinct to urge one's children to stay away from those who bear the stigma of abuse, no matter how well-intentioned her caretakers or how far along her healing had progressed. On some level, it would never heal –her early exposure to sexuality would forever be with her.

As she grew older, I imagine that she would seek to fill that wound in her being with far too many partners; one can't conceive that she would be able to survive very long here in the adult world of consequences and infectious body fluids.

Even in her adolescence, on meeting her at an open house, I saw it as a festering open wound, something that bled through her very being, in moments of inappropriate sensuality, displays of coquettish behavior inappropriate to her age. One urges one's children away from such a person, even though the abuse is not their fault, for fear their exposure might infect your own children like a virus, some airborne pathogen, repugnant and nasty, unable to be taken back once it has taken hold.

I felt, of course, a certain degree of pity for Moira. When I first heard that Moira was now part of Ben's group, I lay in bed that night, thinking of her, and gradually my pity was overwhelmed by fear. It was as if our more innocent children could be infected by her slightest contact, even a look: an expression of nasty glee, a whisper of illicit pornography. Perhaps, in the end, this is what I feared.

* * *

Like most damaged goods at Rockhorn, Moira soon drifted to the least challenging classes, and the classes on the outskirts—Theatre Set-Building, Sound-Mixing and other "Vocational Studies" (which course of study Rockhorn was required by the state to offer), along with the usual stoner stand-bys: Metal Shop and Wood Shop. I feared the worst because she had rapidly become part of the mix of dregs at the bottom of the cup where Jake spent his time.

Already, I had justification for my fears. I had already heard the odd rumor and bits of news about her. It seemed that on a day-to-day basis, Moira was alternatively abusive to younger children and seductive to older ones. She seduced by offering her body—a bruised and fragrant fruit—to the prurient interest of boys who otherwise would not have given her the time of day. It was all one transaction to Moira: either she controlled through fear, or she controlled through lust. Bargains of this type led only to hatred, and to retribution, and soon Moira was tortured anew by the boys of Rockhorn.

On that Friday when the confrontation happened—at the end of winter—Moira had just transferred into the entire series of Ben's classes. Perhaps she hoped to escape there the tormenting and the sexual jokes that followed her across the campus. Perhaps she hoped to escape the payback she was due for the nasty things she had done in return for being teased.

The confrontation occurred just outside Ben's afternoon Wood Shop class. Moira had arrived in Ben's classroom merely a half-hour before it happened; I am surprised he even knew her name. Yet he did; as it turned out, he knew much more than her name.

The students were scattered throughout the warehouse-like classroom, under the supporting beams Ben had replaced only a month before. The hiss of sandpaper and the delicate taps of finishing hammers were drowned out at regular intervals by the raucous buzz of saws and the crash of wood hitting the floor. People talked loudly, shouting to each other across the din, and half the students wore large headphones, to protect their hearing from the racket. Thus, perhaps it is not surprising that when the door to the classroom was first thrown open, no one noticed.

There were three of them at the door—although it is cliché, it also happens to be true that all three were graduating upperclassmen and star athletes, groomed by privilege and athletic success to consider themselves above the common law. Everyone knew their names—their pictures were in the local paper nearly every week for some athletic feat or other. Given my work with the Board, when Jake told me their descriptions, I recognized them all as members of the Student Advisory Board—thus, one might even say that they made the law of the school.

These three had come to the low-end of the Shop building, to a place they never frequented, in order to seek what they considered justice for a wrong done to them. As Jake heard the story, it seemed that all three of them, at different points throughout the baseball season, had managed to get their hands on that lithe and manipulative young girl, and now they felt violated by her.

When the rumors came home to roost, the reality was worse than I had imagined in my nighttime fears: Moira really did have a disease—not just a metaphorical virus made of perverted thoughts, but a real virus—one of those horribly infectious ones acquired through copulation. And now all three of these boys had been infected by it, and they were sure that Moira, manipulative as she was, had intended to infect them.

When the whole story came out later, I found that there was some justification for their accusation. Each of her trysts with the boys had begun with the boys referring to her in the hallway as a "bitch," and a "slut," and other epitaphs too obscene to repeat—it seems they took pleasure in degrading those they considered less than themselves. Instead of flinging vitriol back at them, Moira sweetly offered to sleep with them anytime, anywhere. In hatred and derision, the boys each took advantage of her poisonous offer, receiving in return a punishment far beyond their crime.

It seems absurd, but you would have to know Moira to realize how capable she was of such malevolence.

Jake was near the door, and he heard the commotion as the three athletes pushed inside. He looked around to see who else had heard it, and quite near to him, partially concealed behind a sawhorse, he saw Moira's pale and frightened face. In that moment, he knew they were there for her, and he could also see that she was trapped. She knew no one in this classroom, and there were no other exits, short of the windows. Moira was cornered.

I suppose they thought they could get away with it in the disorder of the Shop room—rush in, take care of the problem girl, and rush back out, without anyone really noticing. After all, I imagined they thought that down where the dregs sink, no one would really care. In fact, perhaps no one would even look up when they took a hammer or a baseball bat to Moira's face.

Yet Ben caught sight of Moira's frightened face, and he stopped them on the very threshold of the door. As they made to force their way in, Ben put his large and muscled arm across the doorway, and held them on the threshold. I suppose anyone could tell what they were up to—Jake said the violence in the air was almost palpable. Despite Ben's size, they made to push their way past him, cursing and shouting. Perhaps, in his non-descript work clothes, they did not realize that he was now the teacher in charge. Perhaps they did not care.

"Who are you?" they said impatiently. Jake said later that when they were stopped he could feel the temperature in the air rise, as it rises before a fire takes hold.

"I'm Ben," he said mildly. "The Carp."

"Well, *Carp*, where the hell is she?" said one of the boys.

"Who?"

"Moira. Moira the slut." The leader hefted a baseball bat. "I've got a home-run with her name on it."

"So you caught her little secret, did you?" said Ben, just as mildly.

"It wasn't no secret to her," they said. "The bitch wanted to get us infected."

"Your little appendages and Moira collaborated all on their own, huh?"

"Appendages?"

"Those little things between your legs—they just got up in the night after the game and went off and humped Moira on their own?"

"Screw you, *Carp*," they said. "We can take you anytime. You're just a substitute. Wait till Lindbloom comes back. We know all about you—we know where you go, we know where you live, we know who you are."

"Do you now?" said Ben quizzically. He looked at them for a long minute. Then, while Jake watched, Ben walked back in the classroom and picked up a sharp chisel from a bench. He winked at Moira, and walked back out in the hallway where the boys were. Straight across from the open doorway, he calmly began to scratch the paint off the wall.

There was a pause, while the saws whined in the background and the chisel scraped against concrete. The boys watched uncertainly.

After a moment, Ben spoke again. "I want you to see something."

"What?"

"This," said Ben. He stepped back from the wall, and revealed a large patch scraped clean of paint. Underneath the paint was a grotesquely exaggerated drawing of male genitalia, stained blackly by Sharpie marker into a patch of bare concrete.

They grunted in surprise. "What the hell is that for?" said the one with the bat.

"I painted over this when I moved into the classroom," said Ben. "I wanted you to see it again, now."

"Ah, screw you! We don't have to look at some big dick to get the point!" said the boy with the bat. "She asked for it—and then she screwed us over. She's gonna die."

"Yeah," added another. "What she did was wrong!"

Ben turned and began to scratch the chisel on the wall again. This time he scratched with the edge, etching something into the concrete. When he was done, he turned his head and called for my son.

"Rabbit," said Ben. "Can you bring me a hammer?"

As soon as Jake placed the hammer in his palm, Ben swung it around and slammed the head hard into the wall—BANG—loud enough to make them all jump.

After the sound was dead, Ben spoke again.

"You need to answer a question for me," he said to the boys in the hall. He punctuated his sentences with repeated blows of the hammer on the wall.—BANG—"You can have her"—BANG—"Yes, you can have her, if you can answer a question"—BANG—"This question I have for you"—BANG—"One little question"—BANG –

"What's that?" said the boys.

Ben flipped the hammer in his hand and used the handle to point at the crude picture on the wall.

Jake and the boys all looked at the wall again, where a list of three names was scratched inside the great round bulge of the drawing.

Ben spoke forcefully, but so softly that Jake could barely hear what he said.

"I want to ask you about what you did with this thing. What did you do?" he asked.

"But what she did was wrong!" whined the boy with the bat.

"What about screwing someone younger and less powerful than you are? What about stealing her clothes on the baseball stands after the game, and screwing her there, after everyone left, hard enough to make her cry? What about running off with her clothes afterwards?"

"How the hell do you know all that?"

"It doesn't matter. Answer the question. What about that—was any of it wrong?"

"She's a loser, a stoner bitch! She's a screw-up!"

"I know all that. I know she's a screw-up," said Ben. "I don't doubt it. But what have *you all* done? You can have her, if you didn't do anything wrong." Then Ben's voice grew louder, and louder still, until he was nearly shouting.

"Go in and get her, if you're so innocent. If you've done nothing wrong—if she's the only one who's ever done wrong—you can have her."

No one spoke up.

Ben turned the hammer around again, and began to slam the head against the wall, hard enough to make a hole, hard enough to crack the concrete. A long minute later, when Jake next ventured to peek into the hallway, the hammer in Ben's hand was still thudding away, pounding the picture and the names into nothingness. The hallway was empty.

* * *

No complaint was made at that time regarding Ben's behavior. These boys wouldn't tell their parents about Ben or about what they'd done—or what they were meaning to do, no not these types. I don't know where they went, or how Ben knew their names. Some weeks later, when I came to the same classroom to pick Jake up for a doctor's appointment, I glanced at the wall outside the door, and found the remnants of Ben's activities that day—a large patch of pockmarked broken concrete, riven and wrecked by heavy blows.

It seems that somehow, before Moira even stepped foot into his classroom, Ben had already known Moira's history, and the recent events, and made his judgment based on this private knowledge. However, the incident in the hallway was Moira's introduction to Ben, and it was a revolutionary change for her. Someone actually knew her side of the story, and believed it, and this same someone didn't entirely condemn her. After the incident with the upperclassmen in the hall, said Jake, Moira became nearly inseparable from Ben.

Jake said that it wasn't merely that Ben had defended her, but that he had defended her with all the facts in hand—he knew who Moira was, and what she did, he knew how badly she had wanted to hurt these boys. It seemed as if he knew what they had all done to each other, and saw both sides. He hadn't shut his eyes to the reality.

Yet Ben seemed to see these sordid realities without that layer of disgust that covered people's impressions of Moira, and he didn't sink to the sentimental pity that Rockhorn population reflexively used when referring to her. I suppose it was almost a shock to her, in the hothouse environment of Rockhorn, simply to hear someone state the facts, good and bad, without pleasure and without condemnation.

Moira made her decision where she belonged—and it was not out with the crowd, it was with Ben. Oddly enough, after she began to spend her time with Ben's little gang, I heard very few reports of Moira as a disruptive force. My friend Mack the Dean said that he almost missed her sneering face in his door, missed finding out how she'd tormented some younger boy or seduced some moneyed upperclassman, whose parents would sue the school if their boy was infected, or if she were pregnant. No, Mack never saw her again after she came to Ben's classroom.

Ben's group closed ranks around Moira, and suddenly, she had found a home. She was safe.

The entire story about Moira, of course, was captured through the earnest, frightened filter of Jake's eyes. I wondered aloud what it was like to see Ben react to people like Moira in a manner that seemingly demonstrated no condemnation, no anger or disgust, and—what is most impressive to me—no fear of contamination.

"It's like he knew who she was," explained Jake. "Like someone finally knew her."

"What do you mean?" I said. "Does she tell him everything now?"

"Nah," said Jake. "It's not like that. You don't get it."

"What do they talk about?" I asked. "Is Moira upset? Is it like she's in therapy, telling him everything she's done? Making up for it?" (I still couldn't shake out of my head the image of Ben as a role model, as a ScoutMaster.)

"No," said Jake. "They laugh a lot, and talk. It's like she liked him saying she was a screw-up, like he got her—he understood her—the same way he got me."

The truly odd thing about all this is that in the end, I actually did understand what Jake meant. And for a moment, Jake's story stilled the aversion and disgust towards Moira in me—just as I'd seen Ben through new eyes, I saw Moira anew as well. I think each of us longs for someone like this—someone who understands all of us, both the good and the bad.

Later that night, I thought of Moira again. I saw her in my mind's eye, before she met Ben, trapped in her perversion and manipulation; back then, it was as if she were isolated in her own wilderness the same way that Jake has always been isolated in his wilderness of darkness and despondency. And it struck me how odd it was that they both found peace being with Ben—how strange it was that he was always with the decrepit, the crippled, the broken. He never chose someone normal like me, or someone like I was when I was a boy.

Why couldn't he choose some clean-cut Boy Scout to be his friend, and his charge? Why did he always have to choose the most decrepit, the most broken of us all?

Oddly enough, there was a coda to the story.

The next day, the upperclassmen came back. This time they weren't there for Moira. They were there for themselves.

It seems that Ben's frank talk about "screwing" had led them to conclude that Ben would understand their problem. Perhaps even the compassion that he'd shown to Moira made an impression, because I can't imagine anyone else at Rockhorn being so frank or so sympathetic with any student caught *in flagrante delicto* on the baseball stands.

The second time they came to Ben's classroom, they were quiet. The door slid open an inch, and one of them put his head inside. Softly, attempting not to draw attention, he asked for Ben.

Ben came to the door, and went out in the hall. He closed the door behind him, as if he knew what the topic of discussion would be. Jake said that they were out there, talking, for some time. For a few moments, he was concerned for Ben's safety—he thought perhaps that their quiet plea was a ploy, that these boys had come back with more baseball bats, but this time aimed at Ben.

Jake left his woodworking bench and crept to the door. He put his ear to it, and heard nothing untoward out in the hallway. Surprisingly, he heard a boy's agonized voice, just at the edge of hearing, a voice that broke into sobs and inarticulate pleas for help. Then Jake heard Ben's deeper baritone, saying something that stopped the sobs. There was more: little of it Jake could understand.

But at the end, Ben began to open the door again. Jake jumped back towards the bench. Ben went to his desk and retrieved a pen and began to scribble information on a piece of paper. Ben stood in the doorway writing. Then he handed the paper to the boys, saying "Now, here's the number of a free clinic. They won't even ask your names."

Ben stepped back inside and for a moment Jake caught sight of the older boys outside the door, grateful and shame-faced. One of them rubbed furiously at his face and his eyes with the back of his hand, scrubbing away the signs of his tears.

Ben said nothing to Jake about what had happened, but he must have known Jake was listening, for moments after they'd left, he closed the door and came to Jake's bench. Quietly, he said, "Don't tell people about this. They don't need to know."

"But why did you do that?" Jake asked. "Why did you help them?"

Ben shrugged. "They're sick. They need a doctor."

He stood and patted Jake on the back. Then without further ado, he went back to carving the decorative nameplate he'd begun earlier that hour.

In the end, the way Ben kept changing was the most confusing part of him. He always slipped out of simple categorization. I couldn't make out, week to week, if he was a vagabond, a wild cult leader, a clean-cut role model, an iconoclast, a sexual fiend, or simply a thoughtful teacher and motivator. He kept slipping out of my grasp, changing my vision of what he could be.

All of this mutability made me uncomfortable. If I couldn't tame him, if I couldn't understand what he was about, what his motivations were, I certainly didn't want him teaching my child, or being part of the school whose endowment I had helped to build. And why didn't he want Jake to tell anyone? Why did Jake insist on making me swear I wouldn't tell Mack or Joe about Ben's encounter with the boys? It was almost as if he were afraid of being unmasked—but what lay beneath the mask, what was he really?

As events would later prove, all of my apprehensions were well founded, but when I heard the story of Moira, all I had to go on was a vague feeling of uncomfortable incomprehension and fear—fear of the unknown.

8.

DESPITE BEN'S classroom duties, he continued to meet at the lunch-time table with a group of his young friends—a group that now included Moira. I was worried that Moira had just exchanged one kind of anti-social lifestyle for another, but this one seemed to cause less harm, and bother less people at Rockhorn, so I decided to let it go, and to keep my promise to Jake not to tell the Dean or the Board. From Jake's perspective, the group now seemed tighter-knit than ever before; now they had their own classes, their own trips, their own stories, their own conversational shorthand, and—of course—their own gang-style nicknames that Ben encouraged them to use.

The only aspect of Moira's story that continued to bother me was a little thing, an event of no significance other than the fact that it kept recurring, and each time it recurred, it was like a burr itching into my skin. I hated it.

The nickname was what bothered me. Every time I heard Jake addressed as "Rabbit" either by his friends, or in one of the stories he told about Ben, or even by himself on the phone to his friends (*"hey man, it's* Rabbit. *Howzit going?"*), it felt like a further insult. I had named my son Jacob after my paternal grandfather, and Jake was the same appellation that my grandfather had used. For me, using "Jake" was shortening a classic name far enough. I had no intention of allowing my son to be known by a gang-style "handle" instead of my grandfather's name.

At first, I teased Jake gently about the name, in the hopes that as was typical of his soft backbone, he would melt under the pressure, and stop using it. Then, when it became clear that he keep it despite my objections, I began to needle him about it out of simple frustration. Although I knew he didn't want to tell me—no doubt due to one of Ben's stupid secrecy mandates—I kept asking Jake how he got the name, what he did to acquire it. I wanted him to feel the results of his obstinacy. Of course, each time I asked him, Jake seemed to pull back further into his shell, retreating from me into his inner darkness.

After the Moira incident, I needled him anew about the name. Then, one day, out of the blue, Jake demonstrated some new resolve, some new backbone that I'd never seen before. He told me. And it was nothing like I'd expected.

Weeks ago, around the time when the nicknames first emerged, it seems that Ben had told the group a simplistic children's story as an illustration of a point he was making. Ben told the story because his group had begun a debate—a sort of metaphysical debate about teenage social values. The debate centered around how "fake" and "cool" everyone outside of their insular group seemed to them, and how "real" the ones in Carp's group seemed to each other.

Personally, I would have ignored the whole topic: why indulge the gossip of children? Yet I suppose it would be typical of Ben to take them seriously, and to have the courage to re-tell a fantastical children's story to a group of toughened adolescents, in order to illustrate a larger point about their discussion. The story stuck—I'm not sure whether or not the point did.

The story he told wasn't much in the way of stories, and I was frankly surprised that Ben used it at all. It was the children's story found in the *Velveteen Rabbit*, that classic that describes an animated toydom where the animals speak to each other while the children are away. The saccharine story was re-told at lunch one day with all of the relevant plot points in place:

The young plush Rabbit awakes on Christmas morning, stuffed in a stocking at an old-fashioned fireplace. He meets other toys—wooden toys, and stuffed dolls, and mechanical things, Gameboys and the like—and they all feel they are more "real" and more valuable than he is. Then the Rabbit meets the HorseSkin Horse, a decrepit old thing gradually breaking down, and on the verge of being thrown out.

The Rabbit looks up to this old Horse, despite his obvious decrepitude. The Rabbit believes what he says. And the salient point the Horse makes is that he himself is "real"—a toy that had become "real" through a long process of being coddled and loved by human beings.

Gradually, the Rabbit is also coddled enough by a Boy to have various patches of fur and accessories worn off of him, and in time this Rabbit is loved by the Boy in much the same way Jake used to love and long for his old stuffed things long after I'd thrown them out.

Eventually, of course, the family notices how worn down the Rabbit is, and once when the Boy isn't paying attention, the Rabbit is naturally enough thrown on the rubbish heap. Jake took pleasure in telling me that instead of ending up like his old toys—being burned on the pyre of flame that the rubbish heap became—the story of this Rabbit depends on a *deus ex machina* plot where a "Nursery Magic Fairy" comes down at the last moment, rescues this bedraggled sack of stuffing and turns it into a real-world rabbit who can hop on his hind legs and eat carrots along with the rest of the rabbits in the world.

I remembered it well—it had been one of Jake's favorite tales as a child. I had, in fact, grown quite tired of reading it over and over to him. Now, re-hearing it from his lips again, I once again tired quickly of the maudlin sentiments, the saccharine moral, and the emphasis on mawkish "love" for inanimate things that the story endorsed.

This tale, Jake told me, had been the inspiration for his nickname. For at the conclusion of Ben's re-telling of the *Rabbit* story, Jake had burst out with the exclamation that he wanted "to become real." Again, I was at a loss for what it meant, and in fact, was at a loss for what the whole discussion meant. But again, Ben took him seriously, and laughingly asked him if he wanted to be called "Rabbit"—for the Rabbit from the story. Jake latched onto it, and soon all the boys and Ben were calling him by that name.

It seems that Jake was not the only one who was affected by the story. There was no derision from Ben's audience at the conclusion. All of them instead seemed to take the story quite seriously. Emphasized in their post-story discussion, said Jake, was the fact that the rabbit had to sacrifice most of what he was for the sake of being transformed into reality. To me, this was an odd thing for the group to focus on.

In any event, said Jake, the group took the concept of "being Real" as their own, and began to use the phrase "the real world" in their everyday argot, until it was part of the nearly unconscious sarcasm and parody of adolescence. This explained the repetition of the phrase "the real world" in the conversations I had overheard on the phone and in the car. According to Jake, it was all tied back to that story of the toy Rabbit.

Of course, I found it hard to believe when I first heard it. Why would a bunch of junior hoodlums, borderline delinquents, and abuse victims find such a story interesting or engaging? I suspected Jake was pulling my leg.

On the next available golf date then, I discussed the whole thing with Mack Demson. Strangely enough, I found that he swallowed it all.

Mack pointed out that although adolescents like to declaim loudly that they are grown up and that they want to be treated as adults, often these loud statements are merely a cover for a longing for their disappearing childhood—the childhood that is swiftly fading away behind them, receding into the past. Often, they want to hold onto childhood, and tie their childhood memories to the new memories they are making as nascent adults.

In any case, this is what Mack said, and he seemed so convinced of its veracity that I decided to believe him. Jake got his nickname 'Rabbit' from the children's book, because he wanted to be "real." I suppose I should have been thankful that he didn't take the name "Velveteen" instead.

Once Jake started talking to me about "being Real" though, he couldn't stop. It seemed that for months now—ever since Jake had met Ben Delacruz—one of the primary topics Ben harped on had been this concept of "the real world."

The original distinction was an obvious one. Being near-teenagers, the group felt that they were hemmed in by the rules and the mores of Rockhorn experience. They were sure that outside the walls of the school existed a "real world" with activities and choices more compelling and more exciting than anything inside the safety of the school. The world of jobs and responsibility, of grown girls and the freedom to choose their own bedtimes, their own homework, their own friends and activities—this world was "the real world" to them.

In contrast, the unreality of their school-based world was all around them—in the endless video games they played that made their jaws slack and their eyes bloodshot, in the price of the sports shoes they bought—the ones that Ben told them (correctly) equaled a month's wages for many who lived our same city—in the dead languages they studied that no one ever used outside of school, in the difference between the carefully modulated eighteenth and nineteenth century novels that they studied in school that seemed to have no relation to the violence and disruption they saw every evening on the news. Unreality surrounded them—it is only understandable that these children wanted to escape the fakery, wanted to know what the real world was like.

Ben, of course, was a natural source of "real" information for them. He was older than they were, so he was no longer a child. Yet he'd never been seen in a suit, and he spent every lunch with them instead of inside, in the faculty lounge, and thus on some level he wasn't to them completely an adult. As Ben often did, he existed on the borderline. To them, he was a connoisseur of reality—someone who had lived with poverty, and had known various stations in life—and was the ultimate reporter on life for them. When the group asked him, "What's the real world like?" Ben always did his best to answer with a story—something drawn from real experience. For all I knew, Ben was making each of the stories up on the spot, and giving them enough of the sheen of reality for credulous adolescents to believe they were true.

Yet as they heard more about the "real world" over the months Ben was in their lives, the term itself became iconic, a symbol of all that they still had to learn. Soon they were applying the term to all kinds of situations. Just as in my day the popular idiom had it that our friends could be "cool" or "uncool," the group at Rockhorn had their terms of derision or approbation—a situation or a circumstance could be "real" or "unreal." They'd ask each other, "You in the real world?" or "were you being real?" Hearing Jake tell it, being "real" was the ultimate symbol of acceptance by their little clique of misfits. According to this group, most of the rest of Rockhorn wasn't acting "real"—and in contrast, they would take off the masks, they would represent reality to the masses. If no one else would, they themselves would be citizens of the "real world" here in this place of unreality and falsity.

The phrase soon reverberated far beyond the terms of the initial inquiry. The real world ended up being a continual discussion, a metaphysical inquiry about the composition of their lives and where their choices would take them. Given their privileged situation, and their lack of exposure to some of the difficult truths of the world beyond Rockhorn's walls, it was a particularly apt term. "The real world" did await them someday not too far in the future—but they wanted to get there sooner than later.

Ben, of course, attempted to disabuse them of the notion that Rockhorn was "un-real" at its core. One time in particular, he told them that the real world "starts here, it starts today, right here at Rockhorn," but they took this to mean, I suppose, that the revolution began at that moment, because from then on their rhetoric regarding making the world "real" became even more strident. Yet Ben told them that to a great extant they were already living in the real world, that it was part and parcel of their reality, and that they needn't wait until they were seventeen or eighteen to begin to make choices that had "real world" consequences. I'm sure many of the parents would have disagreed with Ben—they would like to shelter their boys as long as possible from the consequences of the real world—but I found it refreshing. At last, there was someone who would trust my child with the statement that the real world had rules that Jake should already begin to follow.

Once I heard the drift of Ben's conversation with his group, I grew much happier with its logical conclusions. I suppose I thought it would naturally follow from that lesson that Jake should do a "real" budget for his money, so that he knew where it went; that Jake should begin to organize his possessions, because in the "real world" you were often judged on how neat or how slovenly your appearance was, and finally, I thought perhaps that Ben would explore other pertinent facts about reality—the fact that those who did not make good grades were also the ones who lost jobs in the "real world" interview process, and that the "real world" was full of the unfairness that adolescents continually raged against, and that this unjust "reality" would be theirs as well—how they acclimated themselves to it was all a matter of your attitude, and your willingness to take responsibility. In my view, these lessons of reality weren't bad lessons to teach those just growing towards adolescence.

Throughout the coming weeks, Jake continued to tell me every one of Ben's stories. Soon, however, I saw that Ben was not promulgating an adult vision of reality. Ben did tell stories about businessmen and the world of money and responsibility, but they were hardly the kinds of stories I'd anticipated. He confounded me at every turn.

Instead of telling stories about responsible money managers who were able to profitably manage portfolios and build up hedge funds, he told strange stories about money managers who keeled over dead the day before their retirement party. I'm not sure what lesson that one was designed to teach, but in my mind's eye, I could already see Jake earnestly asking for a trust fund because he didn't want to go into a lucrative career like portfolio management.

Ben didn't seem to understand how financial institutions really worked either. He said that he had once known a bank president—in the real world—whose line of credit was on the verge of being canceled. After some negotiation and pleading, the loan holders elected to allow him to stay in business. Naturally enough then, the president began squeezing his small creditors to pay back his own loan. However, instead of valuing his commitment to financial management, the lending institution turned against him at this point, revoking all his credit. Ben said that they were disgusted to hear how he was treating his smallest creditors. In my view, this was all backwards. As I attempted to explain to Jake, the president was simply exercising good financial policy in trying to get his money back. Jake though, said that the president told Ben after he was disgraced that he should have shown mercy, that mercy was owed to even the smallest creditor.

The next day though, oddly enough, Ben told the more straightforward story of a business manager entrusted with a large percentage of his bank's profits, who invested it all in speculative stocks, and lost most of it. Consequently, of course, the man lost his job and was held responsible by stockholders for the bank's losses, eventually losing all he had because he had too much pride to declare bankruptcy. That was all there was to the story, yet it was one of the only Ben stories that I could take to heart.

Unfortunately, more often than not, Ben's stories reversed the proper roles of financial institutions and their patrons. Responsibility was turned on its head; it always seemed like the losers won in these strange stories. For example, instead of telling about the rewards of real world business, Ben told a strange story about a real estate mogul who stopped inviting his chief investors to the society balls with which he always celebrated the openings of his new buildings. Instead he opened the doors to the workers who built the place, and to others, even worse—drug addicts, street people, and bums—to come in and enjoy his architectural feats. The thought of Joe SixPack or Joe Homeless taking in the Donald Trump Towers' gold leaf floors with a beer in their grimy hands turned my stomach. After that one, I hesitated to ask Jake what other stories were told. But Jake didn't need any prompting. He just kept repeating the stories he heard from Ben.

Ben's conversations with his group seemed to address all aspects of life as he saw it in the "real world," yet he too seldom told the stories of success that I had experienced. For example, on the topic of dressing well and working out, Ben failed to communicate the essential lessons that keeping a fit body and a fitting wardrobe are important to success. Instead, he told stories about people who were perfect specimens of physical health and had the best wardrobes, who were randomly struck dead in the street. I'm not sure what the lesson was for that one—"life is short," perhaps?

If he were truly trying to prepare adolescents for the "real world," it seemed to me that he should have talked more about college and exams, peer pressure and drugs—the usual things. He could have taught them a few pragmatic lessons that could help them after they graduated and went off to places like Swarthmore and Princeton, Harvard and Berkeley. Yet instead of describing the real world as it was—a place of pragmatic choices, without the sentimentality of childhood—Ben often attached all sorts of untoward emotion to moments in his reality.

For example, there was the day that Jake and Sym were debating the cost of a pair of athletic shoes. Obviously, these shoes were far overpriced—one bought them for the brand name and the styling, not for any intrinsic value that they carried. Ben came up to the group as this juvenile debate over money was raging.

Immediately, he launched into a story about a poor woman who lost a cheap stone out of a little ring that her fiancé had given her. Perhaps it was a remnant of poverty, but instead of simply telling her fiancé, and getting the stone replaced, Ben said that she spent the entire day searching for the stone, so that the ring was complete when the bridegroom came. I would have thought there were better uses for her time, and I told Jake so. Once again though, Ben had anticipated me. This time, he'd explained the story.

According to Jake, Ben said that she had searched for the stone not because of what it cost, but because of what it meant to her. It seems that the unspoken advice that Ben was giving to his boys was that there was much that was meaningful beyond money. It was an oblique way of addressing the boys' concerns over money and status, but an effective one—the conversation over shoes was never resumed.

Soon, nearly every story Ben told concerned itself with the real world, in one way or another. Yet Ben never seemed answer their questions straight on. Like a good teacher, he answered questions with metaphors or with other questions, urging his students to find out for themselves the truth about the real world.

9.

IT IS extraordinary to me how simple it is to communicate with one's children when one is simply present for them. During the height of the quarterly tax season in the Fall, when I was away from home every evening for several weeks, all manner of things happened to Jake: he found his group of disreputable friends, he broke into the Library after hours, he transferred out of most of his high-achieving classes into variants of Shop, he took to relying on Ben for parental direction, and he stopped communicating with me except through grunts and random scheduling directions. For several weeks after tax season, just as we did every year, we continued to communicate mostly through barbed comments and sniping remarks directed at each other's obvious failings.

But now that the quarter's tax season had been over for a month, the old relationship between Jake and I gradually emerged from the ashes. There was affection now, humor—and genuine communication. Every day, now that I was there after school to see him, Jake would tell me about the important events of his day. Typically a few accomplishments or experiences lifted the day above the norm—he'd cover these first—and then the rest was about Mr. Delacruz. All stories, all Ben, all the time.

For a time, the stories about the "real world" seemed to be relevant to what Jake and his compatriots were going through. Ben was painting life-lessons: "be kind," "be generous," "don't take the world for granted," "be wise, not hasty," "people matter more than money," "love your neighbor as yourself," and the rest of the common platitudes we know all too well.

Gradually though, I was distressed to hear that Ben was adding a distinctly counter-cultural bent to the stories. Increasingly, he seemed to celebrate the rebellious, the anti-social, the transgressive. Although he still began his lunchtime stories with the stock phrase "The real world is like—", he'd recently began adding elements of the fantastical and the bizarre.

One of the first I heard along these lines—and one of the most graphic—concerned a wealthy stockbroker and his homeless cousin. Ben described both of their lives in great detail—detail sufficient to imagine them to be real people. For example, Ben said the homeless man had AIDS and was afflicted with Karposi's sarcoma all over his face. Untreated, the sarcoma bled into ulcerated sores. This kind of description was borderline appropriate for a juvenile audience. Yet Ben went on.

Repulsively, in detail entirely beyond the pale, Ben added descriptions of the man asleep in the street, tossing and turning as passers-by kicked him, and dogs licking the puss from his sores. Of course, Ben's young audience loved the graphic content. When Jake began to describe rats eating the man's scabs, I had had enough, and demanded that my son get to the point of the story.

After grotesque descriptions like these, Ben launched into what sounded to my ears like the first lines of an old joke. The two characters in his story died and went, respectively, to hell and heaven. I'm sure you can guess who was in hell in Ben's story. (Why was it that he always had it in for the rich?) The homeless man was, appropriately enough, also a religious fanatic, and thus, went to heaven. However, Ben didn't treat the old ideas of 'heaven' and 'hell' as a joke—he kept describing their experience with enormous detail, as if he expected his audience to actually believe in these fictional mainstays. Thus, the pain of the flames of hell was described with equally horrific detail, and the people met in heaven were described as well.

The bizarre level of otherworldly detail in the story got to be a bit too much for me, and I cut Jake off again. I didn't need to hear this kind of mythological clap-trap. Jake protested—he was in mid-explanation, talking about how this, too, was "the real world"—but I didn't really care to hear more nonsense. It was evident to me that the story would have the same tired moral as any number of Disney cartoons—the poor man with the heart of gold, the rich man who learned his lesson. I'd heard it all before, and in my experience the old canard had little to do with the "real world" I knew—poor men in this world were usually conniving sods who couldn't keep a job, and the rich men I knew did their best to keep a philanthropic eye out. What more could one ask for?

Yet the reality I lived in seemed to have less and less to do with the "real world" storyland that Ben talked about. Increasingly, Ben was asking his charges to live in the little utopia—a fantasy realm full of the vivid characters he dreamed up, and populated mostly by people who were part of their little clique and acted as they did. Ben was preparing them for some kind of world, but this kind of egalitarian counter-cultural world certainly wasn't the same reality I had groomed my son to expect from his education, his upbringing, and his privileged environment.

It also worried me that Ben was separating his group more and more from the rest of Rockhorn. Instead of being inclusive, as I thought he'd once been, he almost scared people away now. To one boy, an upperclassman who tried to break into their clique, he said "Take off all your Abercrombie and Fitch—and give it to all the kids in the school over on Underverk Street—then you can come join us."

"What—what school?" asked the boy. "What kids?"

"The ones you call the 'Tards—the kids in the Development Disability school. You know, the Ihme School. Give them all of your expensive shirts—and your letterman jacket too. Then come back to us—come back naked, or don't come back at all."

Of course, the boy never returned. Who would?

Ben's stories became more and more strange, and his images more and more threatening. "Tie a skyscraper around your neck and jump in a lake," he once told a listener who misunderstood him. And to others, he talked about dead bodies and vultures. To the group he even thought out loud about drinking blood. These were gruesome changes—changes that definitely concerned me—yet I had no verification. All I had to go on were the stories that Jake told.

More oddly, Ben's stories were becoming repetitive. Themes were emerging. For example, I would have thought that once was enough on the "losing and finding" theme, but like clockwork, every week Ben seemed to come up with a new variant on the theme of people losing things of sentimental value, of meaning only to them.

And on top of the repetitive themes, Ben soon began asking questions of his audience, drilling them as if in preparation for an exam— "who was more generous?", "who do think I was talking about?", "who was the good man?" and strange metaphysical questions—"who are we?", "who am I?"

To me, it was nonsensical. Yet Jake was enthused.

"Being real is the ultimate, man," Jake said to me. "Some people search their whole lives to be real—heck, Ben says people give up everything they have to be real."

"Indeed?" I said. "And what in the world did Ben mean by that?"

"Well, Ben said he knew this guy in Hollywood, a rich guy who had everything, he was a movie producer, he had the big cars, the parties, everything. And then one day, when he realized that he'd lost a certain little thing, he left it all behind and searched for that thing. That thing, for him, was like who he 'really' was, it was the only part of the 'real world' he had left. He gave up everything for it. He threw it all away, just for that little part of the real world. You've got to stay real, and if you don't, you're dead."

"That's good," I teased Jake gently. "So I take it you want to live in the real world, and you'll do anything for it? Fly to the moon to make it real?"

"Yup, anything," replied Jake.

The fact that Jake didn't pick up on my sarcastic humor worried me anew—Ben was encouraging these children to take their gruesome little lunchtime discussions all too seriously.

What brought me to the point of true alarm was another story, one in which all the normal morals that we raise our children to expect were turned upside down. It concerned a young woman going home from school, a young woman who had a secret and a horrible act to perform, several members of the faculty and staff, and another of Ben's favorite maladjusted characters—a transvestite crack-whore.

I swear it was a story designed to induce nightmares, sexual anxiety, and complete moral uncertainty in his charges. Why would he introduce such charged sexual content to his students? Why would anyone want to listen to such a horrific story?

Ben made this story all the more vivid for beginning with a description of a seemingly normal student like themselves—this one happened to be a young girl. On her way home from school, this pubescent girl took a detour into the East side of town—the side where the drugs and the graffiti come from. Ben built suspense in this part of the story, never quite telling why she was there, but dropping hints along the way.

She went to a doctor's office, a run-down place sandwiched between a pornography shop and a drug house (both of which were described by Ben). Inside, she disrobed, and was examined. Then, she was put under by anesthesia—still Ben hadn't revealed why she was there—and then the doctor began his operation. Rapidly, it became clear that this young student from a private school remarkably like Rockhorn was there for an abortion—not a legal one. This would be one doctor'sappointment that she would never think of again, and that would never be reported.

In the inevitable course of events in stories like this, the abortion of course went badly. The girl, although alive, was left bloody and alone in the street. The task was done, as far as the unlicensed doctor saw it. She could fend for herself now. Unfortunately, the doctor had failed to stop the blood loss after the abortion. He sent her out to the street, where she continued to hemorrhage.

In the street, she was weak and light-headed from loss of blood. Yet in short order a gang of street toughs stopped her. They pushed her into an alley, took all the money that she had remaining, including her identification and her coat, and abused her further. They could tell she was weak, but this seemed to urge them on. After they'd used their steel-toed shoes to kick her nearly to death, they marked the alley with their graffiti and left her in a filthy doorway to die.

Vaguely she knew she would die if she did not get help. She dragged herself as close as she could to the entrance of the alley and blearily began to watch passers-by for signs of hope. No one stopped for her—some looked on with pity, but no one would come into that alley. She dragged herself further, away from the East Side, to a bus stop with a bus arriving that said "Downtown / Moolston" on it—it was a bus that would take her closer to her home and her school. She begged a free fare from the bus driver, and took it as far as she could.

When she got off near the downtown mall, she collapsed, unable to move any further. The blood flow had increased, and her memory was fading. There, in the midst of her delirium, she saw a few people she seemed to recognize. Members of the school faculty and fellow students passed by. Occasionally they'd pass her, and pause in horror, thinking they had recognized her for a moment, before they glanced at the blood dripping through her pants and hurried away. One or two stayed a moment longer, wondering if she was that person they knew. Yet she could not seem to speak, to reassure them, to tell them it was really she. Then they would glance at the bus stop, and realize what part of town she had to have traveled from, and they would hurry away, suddenly aware of where they were and who they were, and what kind of police report they'd have to fill out—all that knowledge would overcome them. Each one hurried onwards.

In and out of consciousness the girl drifted, seeing the phantoms of her past life pass by him forever. The fever dream of her last few heartbeats brought her other visions—he saw political candidates, pastors, prominent lawyers (her father's friends), and other important figures from her life—all of them seemingly walked through the doors of the buildings she lay near, glanced at the bus stop, and passed her bleeding body, shuddering at her condition.

Then she awoke. The blood had stopped flowing, the wounds she'd incurred from the beating had been bandaged repeatedly, and a broken leg had been set and was on the mend. Unfortunately, she found that her long-term memory was gone—she couldn't tell anyone who she was, or where she should be returned to—but she was alive, and no longer hemorrhaging. She was safe.

As best she could, she looked around at the apartment she was in. It was not only a grungy hole of poverty and meanness, but half the place was also filled with the paraphernalia of street-life: used crack-pipes, stacks of pornographic materials, strange clothes and odd paraphernalia (the latter looked as if were used to tie people up against their wills).

The girl was overcome with fear. She thought of serial killers and sexual perversity. Perhaps she'd been taken in as some sort of pervert's slave? But just as she'd worked herself into a state of true anxiety, the door opened, and her benefactor appeared. The girl recoiled—the person wore thick makeup, as if to conceal their identity, and their clothes were an outlandish sexual costume.

Yet there was no reason to fear—this person genuinely had her interests at heart. Although Jake wasn't entirely clear on the details— I doubt Jake understood them—I worked out from the descriptions embedded in the horrific story that the grimy apartment was the home of a transvestite prostitute, and that the paraphernalia was simply the materials that he used in the perverse work of catering to the twisted sexual longings of the city's lower classes. This strange creature had no interest in the girl other than as a fellow human being in trouble, and as much as was within his power, he had shown her every kindness.

He or perhaps I should say *she*—had rescued the girl, for no other reason than the fact that she felt pity for her, and because it was the right thing to do. He'd called a doctor in while she was unconscious— a doctor who successfully staunched the hemorrhage—and also had continued to care for her. According to the story, this transvestite worked as an occasional nurse during the day, and was able to care for her wounds himself—with the occasional intervention of a doctor (paid under the table by the man).

Weeks passed while he nursed her back to health. Finally, one afternoon her memory returned. The transvestite prostitute hired a cab for her, and she returned home.

Later, when she confronted some of the people she'd imagined passing her by at the bus stop, and asked if they were really there on that day, they were surprised to see her alive. At least a few of them were actually there on that day, and simply didn't want to get involved in a strange situation, even if it involved someone they knew.

The destruction of innocence Ben intended by telling this story was obvious, and was disgusting. I wasn't sure why Ben had recounted such a harrowing story of his "real world," but I was sure that I didn't want my child anywhere near these kinds of realities. The fact that the story turned out positively was to me pure happenstance—or pure make-believe on Ben's part. I had no trust that Ben's intentions were good. In fact, the story's elements of abortion, transvestitism, prostitution, and drugs nauseated and infuriated me. Who was Ben to presume that students at Rockhorn would want to identify with such disgusting characters, those who took lives out of their bodies, and those who sold their own bodies?

Unfortunately, this was one of Ben's most popular stories; the students asked for it again and again. Perhaps there was more identification with the characters than I had first guessed. Yet this too frustrated me—Ben's cavalier story-telling was beginning to infuriate me. As a member of the School Board, I had a certain responsibility to keep our children from this kind of garbage—to keep them from confusion.

I began to write down what I could remember of every one of Ben's various reprehensible stories—in fact, part of what I wrote then forms the body of this narrative—and I also wrote down everything I knew about him, which wasn't much.

As I wrote, a cold logic came over me. It occurred to me that in simply describing the type of delinquent students that Ben encouraged to join his class, and in describing incidents like the one surrounding Moira, I had enough information to seriously damage Ben Delacruz's future at Rockhorn. And at this juncture, although I was sure that Ben was an entirely corrupting influence at our school, I wasn't sure that the Board or the rest of the parents would support me. Because of the positive influence he'd had on the worst of his crowd, Ben had grown increasingly popular among desperate parents and faculty.

Therefore, I decided to keep the damning details of the most recent story concealed until I really needed it. My goal was to evict Ben from our school, and stop his polluting influence. If Ben was not immediately kicked out of Rockhorn, this story could be further evidence. It would be my trump card.

The first person I talked to was Joe Matheson, the Headmaster of Rockhorn. At first I didn't list my complaints against Ben: I simply asked questions. How did Ben end up here? What were the circumstances under which Ben had been brought into a Rockhorn classroom?

Joe simply told me the truth, one friend to another. At the beginning of the semester, when Laszlo was unexpectedly stricken down,

Joe had few options. He was already beset with classroom curriculum, hiring, and fundraising problems (I was helping him on the fundraising accounting). Thus, he briefly interviewed Ben, and then without further review of his qualifications, simply placed him in the classroom. Joe had forgotten to even ask Ben about accreditation, and assumed Mack Demson would cover that part. Although Ben seemed to be a natural at it, Joe didn't even know if Ben was certified for teaching at any level. He was teaching—as far as we knew—without a license.

Unfortunately, when I tried to outline the case against Ben, Joe didn't understand the obvious failings I was describing. I talked about the bizarre, neo-utopian bent of Ben's stories, and Joe said Ben was a good teacher. I talked about his encouragement of silence and secrecy among students, and the cliquish nature of that group of delinquents and asocial outcasts, and Joe said "they're a tight bunch." I outlined every way in which I thought that Ben could be a danger to the group that followed him, a danger to the school. And Joe missed the point entirely.

I suppose because he didn't have a child in the school, Joe didn't receive the disturbing reports that I received. It was the only explanation I could think of for Joe's willful ignorance.

"You've got to be kidding," he said at the end of it all. "Ben is about the furthest thing from a danger to these boys and to Moira. He's made their lives meaningful."

"How do you know that?" I said.

Joe sputtered for a minute. "Well, there's all sorts—all sorts of things. For example, I haven't received one report of vandalism in the Shop building—except that a wall was smashed in the hallway up a little."

"That was Ben himself. He took a hammer to the wall—I've told you about that thing with Moira, when he threatened the baseball players. That's damaging school property—that's damage he directly did."

"Well, yes, maybe it is. A hammer, you said? You have a point. The wall will take some work to repair."

"See?" I said. "Mr. Delacruz is basically enforcing his gang rules through force, through intimidation and fear. He's turning these kids into little gang members—into foul-mouthed little degenerates. It's the dregs from the bottom of the gene-pool: thieves, pornographers, all the rest of that type."

"No, no, I disagree. Look, a few weeks ago I heard—directly from Ben, mind you, and he didn't have to tell me—he said that when he was using his lunch hours to work on that big heater shaft in the auditorium, the central tower shaft, that some of his 'gang' (as you call them) actually asked to help him work there. He sets such an example of hard work and reliability that they wanted to join him."

"I bet they had other ideas. They probably planted a bomb there, to blow up the whole school."

Joe clenched his fists and leaned towards me. "No, look, they missed Ben at lunch. They wanted to help him out."

"Why? Why don't they have something else to do at lunch besides follow a migrant worker around?"

"Listen to me. He's not a migrant worker. Look, they wanted to help Ben work so badly that some of them actually—and I'll admit that this was out of bounds, but I let it go, I let it go—some of them actually got up on the roof, and lowered a smaller boy and a crescent wrench down to Ben, surprising Ben with a helper in the middle of lunch. I mean, what kind of man does it take for kids to want to be with him that badly? To want to help him that badly? They sure weren't committing acts of vandalism that day."

"Ah, but you already admitted that it was breaking the rules. Come on, Mack, kids on the roof? Kids on ropes in the heating shaft? Is this the kind of school you want to run?"

"But you know what? Ben didn't get upset at them. He didn't kick them out. He simply allowed them to help him. That takes a certain type of man, that's all I'm saying. Someone who understands the good intentions in kids' hearts—and he understands it, better than anyone I've ever met. The maladjusted kids just melt around him. He understands them—he cares about them. Why else would kids like him the way they do?"

"That's just my point though, Joe. What kind of attraction leads kids to break the rules? To cower in fear while he takes a hammer and breaks a wall down? What kind of charisma is he wielding here? I don't think it's healthy, to start with. It's unnatural."

"Look," said Joe. "It's just a total trust in him. They know that he's going to—"

"It could be drugs, you know. Hard drugs. Maybe he's doping them up in the bathroom."

Joe laughed. He actually leaned back in his chair and began to laugh out loud. "Hey, I'm sorry," he said when he was done. He wiped tears out of his eyes and composed his face. "It's just that those would have to be some heavy drugs, to inspire that kind of trust. And you know what, if I found any drugs like that, I'd take them myself, and I'd make sure you took them."

I was nonplussed. "What do you mean?"

"Wouldn't it be nice to trust someone?" said Joe. "I mean, look at yourself. Just man to man here for a minute, you don't trust anyone, you know that."

"I trust my spreadsheets, my numbers. I trust my clients."

"My point exactly. Wouldn't it be nice to trust someone—someone who's a friend?"

"Sure it would. But that's not the real world."

Joe spread his hands out, as if he'd lost an argument. "Well, it's sure Ben's real world. That's the world he lives in. Trust. That's all it takes."

"Dammit Joe. Let's take some action. I can go ask someone—hell, I'll go get the police to arrest that Mexican drug dealer who works downtown. They can get it out of him—he'll point his finger at Ben. He'll know about his own type—he'll know Ben, he'll know if he's dealing."

Joe sighed. He leaned back in his chair and looked at the ceiling.

"What?" I said. "What's wrong with that?"

"You really think Ben's dealing? You really think he's capable of that?"

"Yes, I do, and furthermo—"

"Well, I don't. And if you're going to go in front of the Board with an accusation, I think that's the least credible one. Jeezus, listen to yourself—you're going to go talk to your Mexican drug dealer and report that conversation to the Board? I don't think so."

"Well, it just seemed a likely source to me."

"But frankly, we don't even know if Ben's Hispanic at all, or where he comes from, or anything. Just between you and me, it doesn't seem like he is Hispanic—not that it matters one way or the other."

"That's part of the problem—we don't know anything about Ben, we don't know what he's about. That's why I'm worried."

Joe stood up and leaned on his desk. "Great, that's honest at least," he said. "Good for you—meet the guy. Find out about him, learn what he's like. I'll tell you in one word what he's about. It's Trust. He comes through for these kids. He's faithful. When he says he's going to do something, he does it. He's decided that what's important to him is spending real time with kids this age. He's there for them, in the flesh."

"Well, so are we, all of us parents, parents and teachers. And we don't get that level of attention, that kind of adulation."

"No, we really *aren't* there. We're always foisting them off on Gameboys or PocketPCs or MTV or God knows what-all. Kids are a marketing category to most of us: they take in entertainment and spit out homework. Do you know how many hours of TV most families watch? Do you know how many hours of TV most kids this age watch?"

"Well, I don't think that Ben is some kind of answer to our cultural ills. If you think that, then you've got—"

Joe waved me off. "You know," he said. "The more parents I talk to, the more I'm convinced that most parents would prefer that kids this age just grow up, and stop bugging us with their little maturation process, their questions, their confusions. We don't want to know—we're blind and deaf to where our kids are really at. I talked to one set of parents who had no idea their son couldn't read—they had no idea that their son was failing, or was taking drugs or any of that. They had no idea that their kid had never done a day's work in his life. And you know what?" Mack leaned across the table to look me in the eye. "They thought they were involved in their kid's life. They thought they were connected to their kid. They weren't. You know where that kid is now?"

"With Ben?"

"Damn straight. He was the kid on the rope—the one that cared so much that he went down there to help Ben out."

I stood up. It seemed to me the discussion was over. "This has been a waste of time, Joe," I said. "What am I supposed to do with all this now?"

Joe shook my hand. "Meet the guy. Find out what he's like, where he comes from. Do what you must—but I would prefer that you not take unproven and unfounded accusations to the Board. All you're going to do if you go through with that is cause trouble for Ben, and trouble for the school. And I don't think that anyone, frankly— anyone at all—would benefit by it."

"Thanks, Joe," I said. "I know you have the best interests of Rockhorn at heart."

"Yes I do. I really do." Joe showed me to the door. "And I know that while I'm on vacation in the next several weeks, you're probably going to come to the Board with some sort of report on Ben Delacruz. I'd just ask that while I'm gone, you don't make some wild accusations where you end up embarrassing yourself. Can I ask you for that?"

"Well, I'm going to tell the Board the truth."

"That's good," said Joe. "Just don't go making anything up. Don't fabricate any charges. I think the facts speak for themselves, loud and clear."

"Right," I said. "The facts can speak for themselves."

10.

TAKING IT to the Board was not in any way a betrayal of my friend. Joe simply didn't have any idea what he'd gotten himself into when he hired Ben. In fact, that's what I told the Board when I met with them:

"Although Joe Matheson has met with Bendito Delacruz regularly as part of his teacher-review process, and although he has continued to observe Ben in the classroom and at the lunchtime tables, I don't believe Mr. Matheson has any idea of the extent of the problems and potential problems that Ben had introduced to Rockhorn community.

"Ben Delacruz is serving as a *de facto* instructor without any accreditation and also without any background information on file—no references, no transcripts. The Board has not even reviewed his resume and training; the Headmaster of Rockhorn has not conducted a formal interview with him. Now Mr. Matheson has admitted his fault in not reviewing qualifications more formally, but he says he had little other recourse at the time. Be that as it may, I believe it's now far past time to take stock of the situation.

"Mr. Delacruz has been working at our school in one capacity or another for nearly six months now, and these are the results that I've seen: the children who really need help, the ones that Rockhorn often takes in out of the goodness of our hearts—these children and adolescents haven't been allowed to disperse across the campus as they usually do, finding mentors and role models across the school. Instead, they've been gathered together—segregated—into a small clique of antisocial misfits, a group that merely encourages their antisocial tendencies, and does nothing to further integrate them into the life of Rockhorn student body.

"I am sad to say that my son has been lured into association with this group, and in fact, this is why I first became concerned. Mr.

Delacruz is directly responsible for creating this group of delinquent children. Furthermore, he encourages their destructive tendencies. He also gives them sexual information. In fact, several of these children have at one time or another engaged in acts of prostitution or solicitation on or near the school grounds. Some of them have also destroyed Rockhorn property, defaced property surrounding the school, sold and purchased drugs at Rockhorn."

There was a loud "harrumph" from Bartimus Santos, the Chairman of the Board. Bartimus had been re-elected Chairman for years now, and was greatly respected among Rockhorn community. At one time he'd been a prominent judge; he'd only retired recently. All through his years in the courtroom and now at Rockhorn, he had kept an unlit pipe in his mouth while listening. He took it out to talk.

I glanced over at him, but the pipe hadn't moved from his mouth. His mane of white hair was growing thin, and his face deeply lined. He did not look at me. After a long moment, I made to continue. It seemed his noise was merely a sign that he didn't believe me yet. I would have to prove my case.

Before I could begin again though, I was interrupted by Sol Tharsen, whom I hadn't liked ever since he forced me to negotiate with him to get permission to go on the fishing trip. Tharsen spoke up in the pause I'd reserved for Bartimus.

"Isn't it true—" began Tharsen. "Isn't it true that these adolescents did these things before Ben Delacruz got involved? Didn't he get them in his classroom after the fact? Is he really responsible for these kinds of delinquent criminal acts?"

"You know, you might be right," I replied disingenuously. "I don't know what he's responsible for. We should ask him. I do know that Mr. Delacruz is responsible for several children going up onto the roof of the school during school hours and lowering one of their number down the main auditorium heating shaft. I also have it on good authority that Mr. Delacruz has directed students to sexual education clinics. And Mr. Delacruz himself is in the habit of swinging a hammer around his classroom—"

Tharsen spoke up again. "He teaches Shop. They use hammers, you know."

"Right," I said. I was getting impatient with Sol Tharsen. "But Mr. Delacruz swings his hammer into walls. Outside the door of his Wood Shop class, there's a large section of Rockhorn wall that's been entirely destroyed by Mr. Delacruz's hammer."

Bartimus harrumphed again.

Someone else made a sound, and then spoke. "Just for your information," said a woman's voice. "That could be criminal. Willful and malicious destruction of property."

I paused, happily surprised to find this woman agreeing with me. I had thought I would be on my own. She continued, speaking calmly, but forcefully. "I believe there may be more incidents of destructive, manic behavior that we don't know about yet. We should be concerned about this man—he is responsible for acts of violence, of—of sedition, and of solicitation of youth, at our very school. He is already a real threat."

I wasn't sure what to do with her unproven new information. Instead of addressing her allegations, I simply tried to carry on with my original argument.

"Well, I appreciate your support and understanding of the issue. But the real area that I want to address though is not whether or not Mr. Delacruz is responsible for one or more incidents of violence and property destruction at Rockhorn. Frankly, I would be surprised if he was—he is an instructor here, after all, despite the fact that he has no accreditation and no teaching license. The real issue I am concerned about is the content of Mr. Delacruz's teaching, and as the directors of Rockhorn's destiny, the actual content in each Rockhorn classroom is, of course, our primary concern. What kind of an education are Rockhorn students getting? What is Mr. Delacruz doing in the classroom, and under whose direction is he doing it? Our direction, and the dictates of Rockhorn teaching guidelines, or his own, or even someone else's?"

I paused again, giving them time to consider.

One of the Board members sighed. "Why don't you tell us? What exactly is Delacruz doing in the classroom that's so upsetting?"

"To start with," I said. "He tells stories. Endless stories. The stories he tells are purported to come from his own life experience, and they are graphic, disturbing, and nihilistic. He tells stories about children—children like our own—who are criminals, who are vagabonds, and who are counter-cultural misfits."

"Sounds like the group that he has in his Shop classes."

"Yes, it does. But instead of encouraging these children with role models or uplifting stories, he brings other unsavory characters into his stories. Drug transactions, transvestite prostitutes, abortionists, dying AIDS patients, and religious fanatics—all manner of social malformations. This is the world that Ben Delacruz is preparing our children to expect outside of Rockhorn."

The woman's voice spoke up again, and I leaned forward to see who she was. "Perhaps this world of perversion and criminal activity is the world that he comes from, the world that he lives in. It's clear this is the unsavory world that he is bringing home to our hearths, to the very bosom of Rockhorn."

"But Miss Foss—" said Tharsen. He knew who she was, and now I recognized her as well. It was Catherine Foss, the Librarian. "What about the fishing trips? The sense of accomplishment these boys got from that long weekend fishing trip—I think they were mostly boys—the confidence-building was incredible."

He turned to look at me, and I nodded vaguely. I was thinking about who this person was who had agreed with me. From what Mack Demson had told me, Catherine Foss had the ear of the Board, and often controlled their dealings. And with the Argurion family fully releasing their Grant to her this spring, she had the clout to do just about whatever she wanted.

Now that the cards were on the table though, I couldn't decide which way I should go. Should I throw my weight behind Catherine Foss, even though she went so much further than I was willing to go? Or should I defend Ben, even though I was unsure whether or not he was good for Rockhorn, good for my child?

Tharsen was still talking. In his Pollyanna way, he was defending Ben Delacruz.

"Right then, just as the gentleman here told us, the man has been a positive influence," said Tharsen. "I heard fabulous things about that fishing trip. There's never been anything like it, I don't believe, not for

Rockhorn students. Wasn't that a successful thing that he did, a good thing?"

"Yes, I suppose it was," I replied. I decided to follow Mack's advice, and let the facts speak for themselves. "But I must tell you that I have it on good authority that several boys engaged in extremely unsafe behavior. Swimming in deep water in the middle of the night—things like that."

Miss Foss jumped in immediately. "In fact, isn't it true that several young children almost drowned on that fishing trip? He exposed them to danger. All of this, of course, has been kept secret by Mr. Delacruz. It has been intentionally covered up."

"Covered up?" Bartimus leaned forward.

"Well, perhaps," I admitted. "He does encourage his students to be secretive, and to conceal what happens outside of the classroom." I glanced at my notes. "One of the students was asked not to tell people that he was studying with Ben at all."

Catherine Foss spoke softly this time, musing aloud in her calm insinuating voice. "I've wondered if he is an escaped criminal, a drug dealer, a fugitive from justice—"

She was derailing my point entirely, caught up in her own obsessions with Ben.

I interrupted. "Please, pardon me, but let me return to the beginning of my discussion. I don't know whether or not Mr. Delacruz is responsible for a number of different incidents. Perhaps Miss Foss can inform us more about this later." I gestured in her direction. "For myself, I'd simply like to ask him about what he's saying in the classroom—to find out what all this stuff he's telling our children *means*."

"You want to know what his stories mean?" asked Miss Foss.

"Yes, I do. I care about what he's saying."

"It's just a bunch of mythologically-derived claptrap. Entertaining fantasies. Who cares about them? I want more than explanations for his stories. I want to know what *he* is—is he a gang-leader, a criminal? You might have a point, sir, that Mr. Delacruz *isn't*, in fact, responsible for everything that's attributed to him. But there's a lot more distasteful activity that's attributed to him." She picked up a small notebook from her lap, and shook it, as if it contained all the evidence she would ever need against Ben Delacruz. "And there are even more acts of defiance and destruction attributed to the student group that is always around him."

"Well," said someone else in the crowd. "Perhaps we should investigate a bit, and bring a few incidents—perhaps a single important incident—to Mr. Delacruz's attention, with a view to sanctioning him for that one incident. I've met him, and I find it hard to believe that all of this is actually his fault. I don't know about his classroom rhetoric. I wouldn't know good rhetoric from bad, anyway." They laughed. "Perhaps he doesn't realize that what he's doing is inappropriate. In any case, is there a particular incident that people would like to, that you'd recommend for further discussion—"

I interrupted. "I appreciate your interest. All of your interest. I really do. What I believe we should concentrate on though, as the first area of investigation for the Board, is *not* a specific incident, but instead the destructive rhetorical pattern. I know, this is harder to investigate, harder to prove. But at Rockhorn, we don't use massive amounts of outside field trips and enrichment activities to help our children grow. We hire the best, and ask them to teach as traditional teachers, to use rhetoric and curriculum planning skills to fill our children's minds with uplifting, educational, and ennobling words. At Rockhorn, it's all about the words our teachers use. Am I right?"

There were murmurs of assent. The Board had already been over this ground before, when we narrowly approved Ben's unusual and unorthodox fishing trip.

"And this is what most concerns me. Ben Delacruz's words aren't the words that we want coming out of a Rockhorn instructor's mouth. He is telling our children stories about the criminal world, and he is also inciting them to destructive behavior, rebellious and criminal behavior with revolutionary slogans and gang-type nicknames, gang terminology, and even gang paraphernalia. There are also religious overtones to what he does—perhaps he's converting our children to some new cult. I don't know—I'd just like to find out what he's teaching, and why."

"I'd like to add to that statement," said Catherine Foss. "I believe that Mr. Delacruz's way is *not* the Rockhorn way, and I believe that he should be released from employment by Rockhorn. Perhaps, if events warrant, he should even be prosecuted."

The room broke out in an uproar. "Sir? Can you tell us—" started the same person as before, while someone else called out "He hasn't done anything—nothing at all."

And I could hear Catherine Foss, speaking above the many voices, saying loudly, "We should prosecute at once."

In the middle of the commotion, Bartimus Santos laboriously rose to his feet. That was all it took. When they saw him, the room quieted. Then Bartimus sat down again.

Once there was silence, Bartimus took his unlit pipe out of the corner of his mouth and spoke. He talked quietly, but forcefully. "This is disgraceful. Such a hubbub over one man, one teacher here at Rockhorn. With all manner of unproven allegations."

He pointed his pipe at me.

"Sir, I thank you for bringing this to our attention. However, we must proceed in a thoughtful manner. I have also received numerous reports of Mr. Delacruz being an inspiration. It seems that despite his rhetoric, he is a source of encouragement to many of our—ah, ah-um—less accomplished students here at Rockhorn. We might be removing a real source of hope. He might be removed to the detriment of Rockhorn."

He pointed his pipe around the room again. "Instead of going in a thousand directions, perhaps we can begin by simply asking the man about his work in the classroom, and what his intentions are in telling these kinds of disturbing stories. I don't believe anyone would object to meeting Mr. Delacruz. Perhaps once you all meet him, and question him a bit, we can come to a more reasoned agreement on whether or not his behavior is appropriate or detrimental to Rockhorn way. I don't believe it's necessary to conduct a formal investigation or a formal censoring review. At least, not at this point in time." He pointed the pipe at me. "Do you agree?"

"Yes, well, sort of," I said. "I think that's a good start. That would begin to prove the parent's trust in us."

Bartimus sighed. "Yes, the parent's trust. That's what we're given, isn't it? Their trust. I think we'll begin here—maybe we'll even stop here, if nothing else is proven beyond a reasonable doubt. Do I hear a motion?"

"If that's as far as we can go tonight, I so move," said Catherine Foss.

"Seconded," I responded.

"Any further discussion? No? All right—is there anyone opposed?"

Mr. Tharsen began to raise his hand, and then, considering, dropped it again.

Bartimus sighed. "Moved, seconded, and passed. Discussion? No? All right then..." Bartimus slowly brought his hands together, bringing the matter to a close. "Well, Secretary, please review these notes with Mack Demson. I trust the Dean can make the necessary arrangements for this body to talk with Mr. Delacruz." He sighed again, as if this was all making him very weary. "Next item on the agenda, Secretary?"

Afterwards, we wrapped up with the usual catered late evening snack—coffee and French Madelines. The murmur of conversation filled the room, but as usual, I stood alone, off to the side like Jake, watching the rest of the people in the room. I hadn't know she was there when she first spoke to me.

"You know, he's insane," she said. "I'm glad you see who he really is. That was a brave thing to do."

I turned, mildly started to find Catherine Foss herself at my elbow.

"I'm not sure how brave it was," I said. "I attacked an unarmed carpenter who happens to be keeping our delinquents out of trouble." Then I paused, wondered if she would take offense to anything I'd said. I decided to take a different, less confrontational tack. I shifted my coffee to my other hand and began again.

"I'm sorry," I said. "I think we've met, but I'm not quite sure." Then I introduced myself.

"Yes, yes, I remember," she said, giving my hand a desultory grasp. "Catherine Foss. We met when your son was caught inside the Library. I do hope you've kept better track of him lately."

"Um, well, yes, as a matter of fact, I have," I said. Frantically, I wondered where Jake was right now, and hoped that she wasn't about to ask me for his exact whereabouts.

We stood there together for a minute, watching the people move animatedly in their endless politicking dance.

Then Catherine Foss spoke up again. "You wouldn't think really think that a man like this could cause such commotion."

"Oh?"

"Well, all he does is teach Shop classes, you know. It's not as if he can be taken seriously to start with."

"Just Shop classes," I reiterated. "The place where all the losers, the dregs of the classrooms, drain down to. No one important in those classes—no one worth saving."

"Right," said Catherine Foss. "Well, sort of. Except your son of course."

"That might explain why there's no formal investigation. I get the feeling the Board didn't take me very seriously."

"Oh, if I have anything to do with it, the Board will take your concerns very seriously indeed. This is an investigation now. Bartimus passed it. You just have to be patient—Rockhorn takes care of—and disposes of—its own."

"But there's no formal process in place. No police inquiry or anything like that. No one putting Mr. Delacruz on administrative leave and interviewing his students."

"Don't worry," she said. She touched my arm. "At our next meeting the investigation will start. He will be coming here to explain himself. Next time." She paused and then spoke again. I'm not sure why her next sentences alarmed me, but it did. "I'll be there too. And we will have carte blanche to do as we will."

Catherine Foss retrieved a cookie from the table, and took a long drink of her coffee. Then she spoke again.

"He's a fundamentalist, you know. Attacking our liberal culture in every way he can. Taking away our children's freedom in any way he can."

"He is? Ben?" I said.

"Well, in a manner of speaking," she said. "Of course, I haven't talked to him much. Perhaps I should. Perhaps he's more pliable than I give him credit for."

"More pliable?"

"Well, like anyone—" she slid her eyes toward me, and I distinctively felt she was about to say 'any man.' "—Like anyone, he could probably be persuaded to do something for the greater good." She took a long drink of coffee and stared at the crowd. They were beginning to thin out.

"Of course I'd probably be unsuccessful. God knows I usually am." She glared at her watch. "I mean, where the hell is Wallace—when is he arriving, for God's sake?"

"Wallace?"

"Wallace Steg—you know him. He runs Moolston Psychiatric Facility."

"Oh yes," I said. "I think I do know him. I thought he was a judge."

"Not any more—he's a former judge, like Bart Santos," said Catherine. She put her coffee cup down. "Anyway, Wallace is my escort for the evening. He was supposed to pick me up here." She waved a waiter over and got him to refill her cup. "You know, for this character, I think that it's all about religious nonsense. It really is."

"For who?" I said.

"For the man in question—Mr. Delacruz. That's why he was in the Library all the time."

"Oh," I said numbly. "I thought he was working there. Rebuilding, making it all new."

"He was working there all right. And that should have been all that he was doing there. What was that phrase you used just now?"

"Um, which one? Making it all new?"

"Yes. See, you've heard it too. 'Making it all new.' You must understand by now that he has an obsession with destroying what we are. Ripping it all down and changing it all. He's trying to create something unearthly, something that speaks to humanity's shared delusions in mythology. It's a religion for him. Religion is not a healthy obsession to have around impressionable children. He's very conscious about it, I think."

"I wouldn't know," I took a sip of my coffee. It was rapidly growing cold. "All I care about is my child, and I was just concerned about the quality of the classroom instruction he's getting. It seems to have changed in the last few months."

"You're damn right it's changed." She drained her coffee cup and set it down on a credenza. "If no one else does, I at least take your concerns very seriously. I see what he's carrying as a new plague—some disease, a bug in the lower classes, a poison that that man is carrying, trying to release into our school."

"What?" I said. She'd lost me with her sudden descent into disease.

"Well think of it like this. Our children aren't inoculated against the infection of belief, of faith in the supernatural, of the religious fanaticism that Delacruz carries."

"Yes, I suppose you're right." I drank my cold coffee, swallowing the harsh taste down. All around us, the room was emptying out. "From what I've heard, Ben does talk a bit more about his own private beliefs than I'm comfortable with."

"He shouldn't be talking about his private beliefs at all," Catherine Foss snapped. "He's created a utopian fairytale, and now he's leading them towards it, hoping that they'd jump off the precipice of some sort of revolutionary, counter-culture vision."

A gentleman approached us, carrying two coats. Apparently, this was Wallace. A white-haired distinguished gentleman, about Bartimus' age.

"How did the Board meeting go?" He nodded at me. "Good to see you."

Catherine took his hand and then turned to look me in the eye. "Read a few books in the religion section, and you'll see what I mean. You'll see the dangers of belief."

Catherine Foss stepped towards the gentleman holding her coat. "Thank you, Wallace. You took long enough." she said to him. Then to me, she added, "It was good to meet you again. If not before, I'll see you at the next Board meeting."

"Thank you. Have a pleasant evening," I replied.

Then she was gone and I was left alone with my thoughts. I was beginning to understand her concern. Why would Ben lead us back to an age where we had to believe there was more than this bone and blood, more than flesh? Why would we need to be deluded into chasing dreams and figments, the spirits and phantoms of a bygone age?

Yet perhaps there was a connection between Ben and religion. I'd just never thought of it before. For me, religion was one of those crutches you keep in the closet until your life breaks, and you desperately need it. I didn't keep a spiritual closet, and I had no crutches in it.

I'd venture to say that most of Rockhorn community agreed with me—why would we need a crutch?—we are the elite of our society, our children the next generation of leaders. Even if our lives broke, we would turn to our everyday saviors for damage control and breakage repair: a good therapist or a dose of Prozac or something more prosaic: a nice divorce or vacation to set our lives in order, and our minds free from worry or from guilt.

11.

BEN DITO DELACRUZ wasn't present at eight in the evening, when the next Board meeting began. This month, Mack Demson was there in place of Joe Matheson, and Mack wanted a complete explanation of the minutes from the last meeting. Bartimus, in his droning voice, began to review the actions we'd taken, explain the complaints made, and outline the line-by-line approval of the budgets that had taken place. Instantly, I was bored.

What I wanted more than anything this evening was a complete explanation from Ben: I wanted to know the truth. Unfortunately, we might get nowhere near the truth; already there were too many people with their own agendas. As always, those people seemed to be the most vocal. A few of them had called me already with fully formed opinions and little knowledge. They were the ones who concerned me.

Yet there some who shared my open-ended approach to the inquiry—parents who called me this week to find out if we were, in fact, going to question Ben tonight, and who were genuinely curious about what he taught, and what his intent was. I'd been quite encouraged by the interest shown in their calls.

I looked around the room and tried to count the heads of those I was sure would honestly question Ben. There were less than I would have liked. It seemed as if Tharsen was knowledgeable about the events of the last few months, but he was too overtly supportive of Ben to contribute much that was not biased. Then there were those like Catherine Foss, who I was beginning to feel was too overtly negative to honestly find out whether or not Ben Delacruz's teaching was beneficial to our children.

Along with several sets of parents who had heard stories, and had come to the Board meeting to find out more, there were a few people I felt could ask questions whose answers they didn't already know.

Mack Demson would be intellectually honest—that I was sure of—yet I was divided about Bartimus Santos—I couldn't tell where he was on the topic. But one never could tell with Bartimus; it was part of his strength, and part of his mystery.

After Mack received his comprehensive explanation and review of the minutes, Bartimus reviewed the agenda for the meeting on this night. Before we got to talk to Mr. Delacruz, there was a discussion of the Library, the Argurion endowment, the long-term Library expansion plan and a complete review of their budget. It seemed that there were a variety stipulations in the Trust documents that outlined suitable ways we could spend the rest of the money. Perhaps this was the reason that Ben was late; perhaps the Secretary had told him that he came at the very end of a two-hour agenda.

Last week's minutes were accepted by Mack, seconded, and passed. Finally, tonight's meeting began. Bartimus introduced Catherine Foss with a flourish and explained that Foss would be reviewing the budget for the endowment with us. Catherine stood to acknowledge Bartimus' introduction and then baldly stated that she would be making specific proposals that she would like passed this evening. It didn't seem as if she expected any opposition, although no doubt her plans would include spending millions out of the endowment fund. At the end of her short speech, she glanced over at me with a tired wink before she took her seat again. The communication was nearly instantaneous; it was as if she was saying that she had enough on her mind this evening, and that she was counting on me to interview Ben. It looked to be an interesting evening.

Late in the meeting, the Secretary asked me if I'd step into the foyer outside the Boardroom and check to see if Ben Delacruz was there yet. We weren't quite done with the endowment budget yet, but I'd had no interest in it to start with. I decided that regardless of whether or not he was out there, I'd wait in the hallway until they introduced the agenda item and called us in.

My timing was impeccable. I waited in the foyer for only a few minutes before I saw a man come to the door of the Administration building. He looked up at the stone façade above the door where the name and function of the building was carved, staring as if he'd never seen the building before. From inside, on the couch in the hallway, I could see him. He looked lost and a little bewildered, as if he'd just been out for a stroll, and got turned around in a city he knew well. In spite of it all, he didn't appear to be anxious. When I walked to the door and opened it, inviting him inside, there wasn't a hint of apprehension in his greeting.

I'd never met him before, and somehow, although I knew it was Ben, he wasn't as impressive as I'd expected. He was, in so many ways, non-descript. He was not too tall, and he was not short; he didn't need a haircut, but I think he'd forgotten to shave that day. Other than his eyes—which somehow struck me as penetrating, or at the least, memorable—he was like any other lower class immigrant day laborer: clothes that were well worn and only vaguely clean, shoes that had seen better days, hands roughened by work, face a little wearied by the churn of life. When he spoke to me, I was surprised by how calm and soft-spoken he was, and yet contradictorily, how authoritative he seemed. He spoke more directly, and with more genuine humor, than most of the people that I knew. What I was most struck by was how true it all seemed; none of what he said seemed to carry a false front. Unlike a politician, nothing he did was an act. This must have been why Laszlo and then Joe hired him to teach—children can see falsity quicker than any adult. He was, if I can use his own vernacular, "real."

Although he was here for an inquiry, Ben also didn't act as if he were worried. I said a few words, to let him know that I didn't condemn him outright, but immediately, I could see that it wasn't necessary. In that moment, it was as if he'd been through all of this before, and I was the one who needed reassuring. As far as I knew, this was the man's first chance at a job with great responsibility and good compensation, and now it was in peril. Yet he acted as if, in the end, the position didn't really matter to him. He wanted it—you could tell that—but that desire didn't define him.

While we waited we talked, for what seemed to me to be a long while. He gave no sign of knowing that it was I who had originally raised the complaint with the Board. We talked about Jake, and we talked about other students he was working with; we talked about Rockhorn; and in the end, we talked about our lives.

He told me a little about his early years. It was a difficult life: he was born with no advantages. In fact, he said that his parents were essentially homeless, and it had taken a number of years for him to begin to be a teacher.

"But you weren't a teacher when you came here, were you?" I said. "You mean, working like this, in the classroom at Rockhorn, this was your goal?"

"Oh, no," he laughed. "I was a teacher a long time before I came to Rockhorn."

This was the first I'd heard about him teaching in a previous career. Immediately, I was reassured. He wasn't just a day laborer who was now unaccountably in charge of my son and twenty other paying students. He had teaching experience.

Ben went on. "I've done just about everything." He ticked his experiences off on his fingers. "I've been in the fields with the farmers, I've worked in the hospitals, I've even been on battlefields, I've worked on a boat, a fishing boat. You might say I've been in nearly every job. And of course I've taught people—adults and children."

"Heck, I've only been an accountant. For taxes," I said. "What did you enjoy most? What would you recommend if I were to leave taxes?"

"Oh, you could follow me around the world, I guess. Doing every other odd job." He laughed again. "But I guess in the end, what I've enjoyed most is telling a story. I've been a teller of tales, a drama guy with a good story." He grinned at me.

"What about the teaching?" I said.

Yet that was the last I heard of his many careers that evening. Gently, he turned the subject to me. "No, no, tell me more about what you do. What's accounting like?" he asked.

And soon we were off and running on the topic of tax collection and tax management. Ben was quick on the uptake, and demonstrated an evident interest in tax management, hedge funds, and my work as an accountant. He told me a few stories he'd heard somewhere about accounting practices that can get you into trouble, and laughed with me at my own anecdotes. In fact, he was more interested in my work than my ex-wife had been. It was as if he'd done this job too, once before, and was reviewing it again, with pleasure.

I've become rather good at sensing hidden agendas and sniffing out buried political knives. Yet instinctively, despite myself, I liked him. I felt he was simply telling the truth as he saw it. I sensed no agenda in his questions to me, no politics in his simple story of raising himself up from poverty to learning. He'd been everywhere in life, and enjoyed it all. I was the one who was conflicted about my life—not him. It was as if he were the calmest rock in the water, and I were something on the surface whirling by, something frantic and nervous, incapable of slowing down.

For a long moment, there in the foyer, I felt that I would have enjoyed going deeper with him, into that calm under the surface, into the quiet water that was his soul. But there wasn't time. The Board called us in.

Bartimus Santos began the session. As soon as we were seated, the whispers around the room died down. Bartimus carefully took a pair of reading glasses out of his suit pocket and glanced at the notes on his lap. The gentle solicitude of his questions laid the boundaries for all of us, and demonstrated that he expected this to be a polite inquiry.

"Mr. Delacruz, welcome," he said. "I do apologize for being the bearer of this news, but as our Secretary may have noted over the phone, we have received a variety of complaints about your teaching style. The complaints seem to be related, so instead of separating each one of them out, I thought I'd simply outline several of the areas of concern. Then, if you feel up to it, I'd like us—all of us, the Board and you—to hear your perspective on your career thus far at Rockhorn, and ask if you can explain your actions a bit, thereby helping us to better understand your intentions."

After this news, I felt that Ben was surprisingly gracious. "Thank you. I thank all of you. I do appreciate the opportunity to talk with you. To take the bull by the horns, I guess I should tell you that one of the sacred cows that I regularly skewer in my classroom is hypocrisy. I have no patience for it, or for the pride that comes merely from privilege and inheritance. You can see how hitting both of these points could lead to some disliking me. I would imagine—I would hope—that some *would* dislike my teaching and my work with students outside the class. I'm not doing something right if everyone agrees with me. Yet for less mature students, my work also has the tendency to encourage them to see hypocrisy everywhere—even in the Dean, and at the Board level."

There was a modest chuckle of appreciation around the room. Then Ben resumed. "But I do tell them that it's not for them to judge, that it's not for them to take action. I guess another thing that might rub feathers the wrong way is the fact that I do tell them that there will be a judgment that will take care of things like that."

"A judgment?" repeated one elderly Board member in a high, horrified tone.

"Well, yes," said Ben. "I don't think our actions live in a vacuum, or have no moral weight. There are consequences. I think it's useful to tell students who are on the edge the truth about the world—that there are consequences to drugs, to sexual activity, to missing class. The real world has consequences."

There was a murmur of approval from around the room.

"And there are also consequences for those things we take for granted—for power over those weaker than us, for pride in our own self-worth. I think there are some very negative consequences for wealth and for self-satisfied privilege—there may be consequences for Rockhorn itself. We need to understand our purpose for being here, and I'm pretty sure it's not to collect the most money in our children's trust funds."

This time the murmur was not nearly so positive. Yet Ben waved off the sounds of concern.

"All I'm saying is that for everything we do, it's obvious that somewhere there is a balance that must be paid. I must admit that I do believe in a higher power—call Him God or what have you—but I think that we should be working to understand what that's about. And if we're thinking about higher meaning, I think one of the primary things we're put here to do is to love each other—love our classmates, love our neighbors. We need to care about even the unfortunates, the ones who don't fit in—what I teach is that the world doesn't turn around caring for the standard accomplishments of money, success, power. It turns on love. We need to care about the misfits, the outcasts. It's trite, but true. 'Love your neighbor as yourself' is one of the founding principles of our society, and one that we should begin to take seriously."

"That's an interesting way to phrase it," said Bartimus. "I must admit that I hadn't heard it put quite that way before. What you're saying is that we work to be in tune with a higher power, and that most of your work as a teacher aims at morality—at the basic principles. Love, truth, honesty, justice. Love, at the root of it all. Most appropriate for students, of all ages—more important than a lot of degrees I see on people's walls." Bartimus replaced the pipe in his mouth, chewing on it slightly. Ben seemed to have given him something to think about.

"Yes," said Ben. "Thank you, Judge Santos. You might have heard the phrase 'the real world' that I use when I'm trying to explain this concept to the students in my classes. What you've just said, Judge Santos, is the essence of this 'real world'—you've grasped the essential concept. You're in it, right now."

"Well, you don't have to call me 'Judge' anymore. I've retired, you know," said Bartimus, but I could tell that he was secretly pleased with Ben. Bartimus glanced around the room, at the faces all intent on Ben. "Are there other areas? Ah, Miss Samari, you have an opening question?"

"Yes, I do," said Meredith Samari. Miss Samari was the school secretary, and also the Secretary at our meetings. Typically she didn't make any observations or interjections into our meetings—she simply took notes. This time, though, she had something to say.

"It's something I've observed," said Miss Samari. "Since I'm always on the school campus, unlike many of the rest of you, who work elsewhere. In every day life around the school, especially outside of the classroom, after school and at lunch, it seems to me that you've gathered the misfits of the school around you. You've started to do things with them. What's your goal in drawing these misfits—these drug-prone children and juvenile delinquents—around you? Why them?"

Ben leaned forward to address her, speaking immediately after her question was done. "Frankly, Miss Samari, I don't think it's the good kids who need a good teacher. They're going to prosper anyway. Kids who I might describe as 'sick' need one. I mean, to stretch the metaphor, well people don't need a doctor, do they?"

"No, I guess not, not when you put it that way."

At this point, I broke in. "Well, I object to your characterization of any students of Rockhorn as 'sick,' particularly my son, as he does spend time around you, and I'd hardly think of him as mentally 'sick'."

Ben spread his hands out, admitting nothing, yet somehow taking responsibility, taking blame for everything. "All I'm saying is that all of the over-achieving kids already have people pushing them on, helping them succeed. They have all of you urging them forward. The boys I work with, and girls like Moira, have little or next to nothing. And with the exception of your son, sir, they often have no one. They're the ones who need some help. I figure that's something I can do."

Bartimus sighed. "So what I'm hearing is that you don't have any particular plans with them. You're just trying to help out, in and out of the classroom. Fair enough. Other questions?"

"Yes," said Wallace Steg. He was wearing a perfectly pressed wool suit, and looked displeased with Ben and with Bartimus, as if he did in fact have a good amount of money in his children's trust funds, and a number of degrees on his wall, and he didn't appreciate them being denigrated.

"Yes, I have a question. You talk about our duty to a higher power. But what about our students' duties to the school itself? I haven't noticed a lot of school participation by your students, and I believe your work hasn't exactly been supportive of the school. There are some specific complaints in this area. What do you have to say to that?"

"Thank you for the question," said Ben. "Well, obviously, my students are students of the school, and I have told them time and time again that they should give back to the school as much as the school has given to them."

There was a pause while the room worked out the meaning of Ben's reply. At first blush it was a standard exhortation—any teacher could have given it to any class of high-achieving honor students. However, when I thought about it, most every one of Ben's students had received the rough end of the stick from Rockhorn. What was he saying, really? What would these types of students 'give back' to Rockhorn— anger, retribution, rejection?

It seemed that others in the room may have come to the same conclusion—Bartimus quicker than most. When he spoke again, he seemed slightly nervous, as if he'd found a sharper lawyer than himself.

"Now that's all well and good, sir." Bartimus rolled his pipe back and forth between his palms. "Well and good, sir," he repeated. "But perhaps we should move on to the particulars of the complaints we've heard, and ask—perhaps—if you have any explanation for them."

"The first is that you've gathered a bunch of children—the misfits and delinquent members of our school—around you. I know you've said that we should 'love' students like this, and in fact, with Miss Samari's question, I believe you've already addressed this sufficiently. I gather though that there are some outstanding concerns in this area—that perhaps you've brought gang *terminology* onto Rockhorn Academy campus."

Bartimus lifted his reading glasses from his lap and put them on the end of his nose. He squinted down at the notes on his lap—some of which were mine, and some of which seemed to have come from a different source. "The second complaint is somewhat related, but not directly," said Bartimus. "It's said that your statements are designed to incite, that you use a lot of revolutionary rhetoric—not all of it positive. Now I know that you've said that you're, um, 'spiritual' in some sense, but I do hope that doesn't mean that you're religious in any way." Bartimus looked over the top of his glasses at Ben, and in that moment, I realized that Bartimus was taking this inquiry very personally. "I imagine that I don't need to tell you, sir, that proselytizing our children with religious garbage is unacceptable, do I?"

Ben said nothing, and Bartimus went on. "I'm not sure I should even dignify this complaint about your rhetoric with a comment, but it seems necessary for me to point out to you that although Rockhorn was founded, nearly a century ago, by a minister, Rockhorn Academy *has* worked hard over the years at being non-sectarian, and at not endorsing any particular, ah, religious 'brand-name' or even religion in general. The parents expect this—many parents send their children here specifically because we are non-sectarian. This policy also allows Rockhorn to receive significant federal funds. And we produce students who aren't religious bigots—who don't hold any particular belief. This is, of essence—"

"You mean, there's no religion allowed at Rockhorn," said Ben. "No faith, no belief."

Bartimus wasn't used to being interrupted. He stumbled in his reply. "Um, ah, well, in a manner of speaking, I suppose you're right. There is no endorsement of religion here. Rockhorn is not a religious establishment."

"You don't know what benefits you're depriving them of, do you?"

"Now then, sir, that's debatable. It's debatable whether or not there are any benefits to that sort of thing." There was a murmur of agreement around the room, and Bartimus paused as he considered whether or not to pursue the topic right now, in front of us all.

"Harrumph," he grunted finally. "Let's move on, shall we?" Evidently, he had decided he did not want to continue in this vein. Bartimus glanced around at the other Board members for reassurance, and received in return solemn nods and a few murmurs of affirmation.

"The third charge that we've heard is that you're taking classroom instruction outside of the classroom. You continue class lessons outside—at lunchtime, talking to your students for hours about topics that were first begun in the classroom.

"Those are, in brief, the issues that people have brought before us, and I hope that you, sir, can adequately address them. Address them in such a way as to set our minds at ease, and allow you to... ah... *continue* your tenure as a Rockhorn instructor."

A long pause, while people shuffled their papers. Perhaps they expected Ben to be nervous, or to have papers of his own to shuffle. He was not. He had no papers, and no shuffling. He simply looked around, as if the atmosphere were not heating up at all. For all his face showed, he could have been in a tranquil glade beside a pool on a quiet day in summer.

"In fact," said Bartimus. "Let's begin at the last item, and then circle back. Partially because I don't really understand the issue. Is it one of Mr. Delacruz using the school facilities in an unauthorized manner? Or is it that classroom teaching is going on outside of the classroom?"

"It's the latter, sir," I heard my voice saying. "There is classroom-style teaching going on outside of class. It's not an approved class."

"I see." Bartimus took off his glasses and rubbed them slowly with a handkerchief. He addressed Ben. "I'm not sure what the problem could be, other than the fact that you might not be using approved curriculum. What do you have to say on this topic, sir?"

"Let me address that question with another question," said Ben. "Say, for example, sir, that you are a father."

"As indeed I am," said Bartimus.

"Say, for the sake of the example, that your child, when quite young, comes to you hungry. Would you give them something to eat? Or would you give them something inedible? Stones, sand, dirt—things like that?"

"I'm not sure I understand how this relates to the question, sir."

"I don't either." Catherine Foss spoke up in an unnaturally loud tone of voice, as if she'd been waiting for an entrance to the conversation all evening. "I don't see how these clever, but irrelevant answers from Mr. Delacruz are helping us understand anything. I don't see how any of these, um… stories and stock phrases are relevant.""Let's clarify the question on this one," she said. "At Rockhorn, we believe it's important for the children to have adequate recreation. To have a chance to ease their minds, to relax. You're violating that central tenant of Rockhorn Academy. You're making it impossible for a child to leave your side, without thinking they've missed something. You're making it hard for a child to relax for a while, before entering back into academics. It may not seem like a big deal to you, but believe me, with the pressure our students are under, it's not right to take away their only time to stretch their minds in non-academic ways."

"Oh, I firmly agree that the world is not entirely academics. I'd be the first to send them out to go fishing," said Ben. There was a pause, and then Catherine seemed to realize that that was all—that was the entire substance of Ben's response. Frustrated, she continued.

"Well, what do you mean by that? Why do you take away their lunchtime recreation then?"

"Allow me to ask a question in return?" said Ben.

"Yes, please go ahead," said Catherine Foss. "You always do, anyway."

"If I were to ask if the Library doors were nearly always open, you would of course tell me that they are."

Catherine nodded quietly. She seemed to be struck now, by the politeness of Ben's replies.

"It's closed at night, of course, but I've been very pleased to see the Library open at all sorts of hours. And in fact, the Library should be open all the time. The words in those books help us to understand ourselves—they tell us our history, our ancestors, our origins. Without a Library like the one we have, it would be difficult to have meaning. I need it, to understand myself, where I come from."

Catherine Foss sounded vaguely astonished. "You think a Library is essential to understand yourself?"

"Yes, essential. And furthermore, I think it's interesting that along with an excellent Library, on the school grounds is also a small Chapel."

"There is? Where's that?" said Bartimus.

"Oh," explained Catherine. "There's this little old church-type-thing that looks like it was built in the same period as the Library—out on the grounds. Been there for years. I'd forgotten about it—probably a holdover from decades ago."

"Well, that little Chapel speaks volumes to me," said Ben. "It says to me that this school once understood that the source of our meaning is found there. And there's more meaning in that Library—the two are tied together. In fact, I believe the Library is where your son—" he gestured in my direction "—first found me."

With a certain eagerness, Catherine Foss spoke up. "I hadn't realized you felt that way about the Library," she said. "You and I should talk afterwards. There are some plans—some plans that you might be interested in."

"Ah-hmmm," said Bartimus. "I believe we're a bit side-tracked here."

There was a pause. Bartimus waited for the noise in the room to die down, and then he continued. "The issue of lunchtime instruction is still open. It seems that despite the several classes that some of your students have signed up for in your building, you have kept the students throughout the day—" He squinted down at his notes. "—I believe the question and the concern was whether or not you were requiring your students to use their lunch hours to get further instruction from you?"

"Let me be clear," said Ben. "I am not requiring them to do anything. I don't enforce laws and timetables on my students. But just as the Library is open, and doesn't turn people away, neither do I. A good comparison is this: for those of you who are parents—haven't you helped your child with homework at odd hours before? If your child comes to you on a weekend, and wants to understand something in their homework, don't you explain it to them, or do you say—'oh no, wait until Monday. That's when school is'."

"Well, quite right, one would hardly do that," said Bartimus.

"In the same way, just as you'd want to answer the question, there are no limits on my availability. There are no boundaries on learning, just as there are no limitations on God, and God's love." Ben spread his hands out in the air on either side of his chair.

"Now, sir, that type of language is exactly what we're concerned about," said Bartimus. "I hardly find appropriate the invocation of God in an environment where you simply want your students to learn carpentry and car repair, and perhaps—in their spare time—to learn about morality."

"I take your point, Judge Bartimus. The way in which it's said doesn't matter at all to me. However, what's easier to say? To tell my students, do something because God made you a higher being? Or to tell them, stop doing that bad habit—just because you might feel like it? Which explains the choice better?"

This time, Bartimus looked down at the floor for a long moment. He didn't seem to have an answer to this strange question. His pipe rolled quietly back and forth between his palms.

"Well, sir," said Bartimus finally. "I don't know if there's a lot more to cover here. Perhaps the Board should convene separately and discuss these matters, and decide if it is worth our time to move forward. More questions?" He looked around the room, and seemed relieved to find no one.

"Do you have anything else to say for yourself, sir?"

Ben spread his hands out again, in a gesture that I was beginning to find irritating. Bartimus wrapped up with a few desultory follow-up questions and the meeting concluded rapidly.

"Until next month then." Bartimus put the pipe in his mouth, and mumbled the next words. "Do I hear a motion?"

"Move to close the meeting."

"Seconded."

Moments later, we were all swilling down coffee and talking at once. The atmosphere, although somewhat festive as always, seemed almost somber this time, as if no one was quite sure what we'd just gone through.

After a few long minutes of avoiding Ben entirely, I saw a few people begin to go up and introduce themselves to him, as if he had somehow furthered his reputation and status in their eyes. I too was drawn to him—I wanted to continue the conversation we'd begun before the meeting—but as I was the one who had brought the original complaint, I thought that the rest of the crowd would probably consider it unseemly. This evening, no one was mobbing me with questions and comments.

Catherine Foss was one of those who surprised me. She moved quite rapidly to Ben's side, and was soon laughing at his comments, and leaning close to talk rapidly and intimately to him. No doubt they were discussing the library and her building plans—the future of her endowment.

Remembering the last meeting, when it seemed that we'd shared a common purpose, I was saddened at how quickly the tide had changed. It was as if I'd been replaced overnight in her affections. I was surprised to find myself vaguely jealous.

I looked around the room and found little reason to stay. I was, in fact, on the point of leaving, when I saw Joe Matheson across the room, headed my way.

I looked at Joe's pleasant, determined face, and then I realized anew that Joe hadn't been there during the course of the entire inquiry. Perhaps he knew that Ben could hold his own. Joe had a lot to say to me.

"How are you?" said Joe. "Sorry I couldn't make it. I had a conflict at home. Came for the aftermath."

"Glad you could make it." I hoisted my drink towards him in salute.

"Well, how did it go?" asked Joe. He picked up a cup of coffee. "Did it end up in the direction you'd hoped?"

"Well, not quite," I replied. "But then again, I wasn't sure where I wanted it to go."

Joe lifted a handful of cookies, the chocolate-chip variety, from a credenza. "Cookie?" he said. "I hope that you feel a little bit better about your son hanging around with Ben now. I mean, he's passed your test."

"Well, he can certainly hold his own in a conversation like this—an inquiry," I said ruefully. "I thought he'd be a little bit more subdued. It's almost like he's been through this kind of thing before. He didn't have any straight answers."

"Oh, I kind of knew how it would go," said Joe. "I've spent quite a bit of time talking to Ben myself."

"But what about all that religion stuff—he really is religious," I said. "It's like someone who doesn't want to ride in an airplane, or refuses to use a computer. I can't believe it—I've met a walking anachronism. No one believes in that stuff anymore."

"Well," said Joe, patting my arm. "Just don't call him a Neanderthal, and I don't think anyone will take offense. I think he's a good guy."

"Yeah, despite myself, I guess I do too."

"Right," said Joe. "He doesn't mean any harm—and what do a few phrases and ideas about God do to us? He's not harming the kids, that's for sure. You should get to know him. You'd see he's really pretty modern in his ideas. It was a surprise to me too."

"But I do know him. I know all about him," I said. "I hear about him every day through Jake and Jake's stories."

"No, that's not quite the same," said Joe. "You and Ben should actually spend some time together. Once you actually talk with him, at length, you'll see that he doesn't mean any harm." Joe took a long swallow of his coffee. "Look," he said. "I've got just the thing for you. Why don't you come see me in my office tomorrow?"

"Why?"

"Oh, indulge me." He drained his coffee and put his empty cup on top of the credenza. "Come see me. I need some help."

Then he was gone.

* * *

In the morning, after a client meeting, I went to Joe's office. "So, I still haven't decided about Ben," I said. "Want to tell me why you've made up your mind?"

Joe lifted his eyes from the stack of papers on his desk and waved me to one of the comfortable Wedgwood chairs on the other side of his desk. "You're getting ahead of yourself," he said. "I'm not saying that I've made up my mind at all. And I'm certainly not going to tell you anything that will change your mind."

He looked back at the papers on his desk and began to shuffle through them, looking for something. "And besides," he said. "I don't want you getting involved in all the political stuff that's going on here. There's too much to worry about as it is. Hang on a sec—let me finish this up." Joe found what he was looking for—a page near the end with a blank signature line. The page had been helpfully marked by Meredith with a yellow sticky note. With a flourish, Joe signed, and reshuffled the papers together. Then he walked to the door and leaned out to hand the stack to Meredith. When he came back, he'd shut the door firmly behind him.

"You know," he said. "The staff changes have been really hard in the last few months. You have no idea how much you rely on the status quo until it changes. Just provides a lot of day-to-day consistency. But how's your business?"

"Oh, business is fine," I said. "Tax season is mostly over."

"So for this year at least, you're already done helping corporate crooks escape the long arm of the law?"

I grinned. "Oh, the good fight is never done. They never let up."

"I bet they don't."

Joe sounded preoccupied. I waited while he went to the window and gazed out at the long green lawn behind Rockhorn. "I wish that you and Mack both had the opportunity to go on the fishing trip," he said. "You would have enjoyed the time together, and the time with the boys. It was incredibly relaxing—tranquil, in fact. And Ben was a big part of that."

"So, we're back to Ben now?" I said.

Joe turned and walked over to me. He sat down in the chair next to me, and put his feet up on the desk. "Look," he said. "I really think you should put your mind at ease. I've got just the thing for you. See,

I've got to send someone over to Shiloh Hospital this week, someone from the Board, to check on Laszlo."

"Laszlo?" I asked.

"You know, Lindbloom, Rockhorn's Shop teacher—how quickly you forget that we actually have one. We've heard that his condition is deteriorating, and I want to make sure the Board has given all the support and comfort it can to his family."

"Who are you going to send over there? How can I help?"

"Well, Catherine Foss wants to go to the hospital." He sighed. "God knows why."

"Catherine Foss? I just met her. Why don't you send her? Fascinating woman—very intelligent."

"Yes, I know," said Joe. "She's incredibly driven. And too damn political for her own good."

"What do you mean?"

"Catherine Foss shouldn't go see Laszlo. She'd give him a heart attack." He sighed. "She's always hated him. If he's in a bad way, the last person I think he'd want to see is Catherine."

"Lindbloom dislikes her?"

"Oh, no, it's not Lindbloom disliking *her* that is the problem. I mean, you've met him—he's a pretty mild-mannered old coot. Heck, I don't think he has an emotional bone in his body. It's Catherine that's the problem—she hates *him*."

"Why?"

"Well, it's complicated. I think it starts with the fact that the Vocational Studies program here at Rockhorn was also named in the Argurion endowment, along with Catherine and the Library. She's got most of the money she needs, but if he would have come through for her—if he would have approved something—before he went into the hospital, she would have had a lot more."

"I was wondering what happened to the Vocational Studies money."

"Yes, well, there's quite a bit more that's supposed to be disbursed. Laszlo is supposed to work with Catherine to disseminate an extra three to four million, but he refused to go along with all her plans, and started a feud with her which held up almost all endowment funds until the dispute could be resolved."

"What was the dispute over?"

"Oh, it doesn't matter now," said Joe. He waved his hand through the air, as if brushing away years of complicated politics. "All that matters to her now is that his roadblock is still there, and he's out of commission—he can't lift the roadblock, even if he wanted to. Catherine's stuck. I think secretly she hopes that Laszlo will wake up on his deathbed, say the magic words that release the entirety of the trust to her, and then die with no further disagreements. Frankly, I think if she got in the room, she'd want to strangle him, and try again with someone else."

"Those are strong words."

"Well, Catherine believes that she should have been given full control over the endowment, instead of some untutored Vocational Studies instructor. She's the one that speaks multiple languages, she's the one with the PhD –she thinks she's the only one who knows how to spend money like this. She's the only one who is qualified."

"On that note, I heard a rumor that some of the workers on campus were restricted from checking out books—older books?"

"Oh, don't get started on that issue. There's nothing I can do." Joe turned away from me. "There's nothing I can do," he repeated in an undertone, as if to himself. He took his feet down and stood up. Then he walked to the window, to gaze out at the great expanse of greensward acreage.

"Look," he said finally. "Catherine Foss is a power in her own right. The majority of the endowment—the part that she directly controls—is bigger than the rest of the school's entire budget. I may not have any power over how she spends the Argurion money, but I at least have some limited power left. I'm not sending Catherine over to the hospital. I'm not starting that hell."

"Who are you going to send over instead?"

Joe walked towards me. "I think I should send you," he said. "You should go over there. You don't hate Laszlo, after all. And you have a compassionate face." He clapped the side of my cheek with his hand.

"The reason I'm sending you over is that Ben Delacruz wants to go to the hospital to see Laszlo as well—he used to work for Laszlo. And I think it's only appropriate that a member of the Board and the teaching staff go together to see Laszlo."

Joe chuckled dryly. "You'll be great." He shook my hand. "You'll see—it'll be fine. You guys can go over there together, and share a few moments with Laszlo, and with each other. You'll see—you'll come back the best of friends, and Laszlo will benefit from your visit."

"Okay. Right. Whatever." I shook hands numbly with Joe.

"Great!" said Joe. He checked the master calendar on his desk. "Why don't you go tomorrow afternoon—Mr. Delacruz has a study-hall in the late afternoon that I can get covered for him. Just pick him up after his three o'clock class. Can you do that? Can you make it?"

"Sure," I said. "Um, thanks."

Instead of me using Joe to get rid of Ben, Joe was using me to baby-sit his teachers. It hardly seemed fair.

12.

WHEN I arrived at Room 177 the following afternoon, the children had already departed for their next class, and the hallways were mostly clear. No one was waiting for me. I checked the hall, and found the nameplate outside: Mr. Delacruz, it said. I was on the point of simply opening the door and walking in, when I heard voices inside. I listened for a moment and realized that I'd come upon what was no doubt a very private conversation.

I glanced up and down the nearly empty hallway, checking to see if anyone would notice me standing nonchalantly beside the door, head bent as close as possible to the frosted glass. The few last tardy students were hurrying to class, and had no time to glance at a stranger. Gradually, they all disappeared, until I was left alone.

Inside, there was a woman's voice talking very rapidly and forcefully. In response, I very rarely heard a man's voice respond. I was nearly certain that the man's voice was Ben's, but I couldn't place the woman's voice although I was sure that I had heard it before.

At first, I didn't catch the drift of the conversation, but soon the aim became apparent. Someone was promising Ben things that I doubted they had the power to give. She was promising him a guaranteed future at Rockhorn, a place in the sun, respect, admiration, success. Whoever she was was so convincing and persuasive that I found myself almost desiring to be her target, almost believing that if I merely did her a small favor, that I could be the recipient of the generosity she was promising.

Ben also seemed to be enthralled by her voice. He was complacent, barely answering her entreaties with a sound. It was as if he was sinking under the mellifluous current of her voice.

She made her request for a favor from Ben at the beginning, and then she moved away from it, without waiting for commentary from him. Instead, she assumed he'd accede with her request and began to talk about his successes, in the past and the in future.

"After all, you have an assured position, I could even help you get some degrees—there are ways of getting them without years of schooling, you know, it could happen overnight. One day, you're Ben, the uneducated carpenter. The next, you're a tenured professor here, one of the few with a PhD. You just concealed it when you first came to Rockhorn, because you didn't want to make people feel bad about all your accomplishments."

"That would work?"

"Of course it would work. And hell, with a few good words said in the right places, you could eventually become Dean. No one would question you, not with your natural charisma, your charm, your articulate knowledge. Why should anyone? And as long as you don't do anything really out of line, no one will ever think to ask. Just don't run for politics."

"Politics?" said Ben. He sounded vaguely astonished.

"No, wait, it's not out of the question." She laughed again. "I could help you do that as well, we could do it together. And there's no reason why you wouldn't be able to run for almost any office, especially with the supportive base you would have built up at Rockhorn."

These heady offers must have been a big temptation for an uneducated man. To my eyes, Ben was a man with native smarts and ambition, and drive, but without the connections, the networking skills, the degrees to be able to do it. And here all of those things were being offered to him on a silver platter—it was a future full of possibilities.

Yet there was the small matter of the favor she wanted done. As she described it in her beautiful voice, it became a small thing, a thing of no account really, nothing anyone need ever know about, or care about.

"Just do something about Laszlo," her voice whispered. "Disconnect him—I don't care what you do. But he's never going to wake up from this—this fugue state he's in, and there's no other recourse."

"It would be a mercy killing," said Ben. "That's what you're saying."

"Well, I'd hardly even think of it as a killing. I mean, if you go in there, I bet you can already smell him rotting away. There's nothing left to kill. It's just pulling a plug, a little plug out of the wall."

"And what do you get?"

"Well, we all get to improve Rockhorn. We all get to move forward, instead of back, into the past, where his rotting corpse wants to take us. We all get to work together, and that can include you—you are going to be a vital part of that vision."

She didn't dwell on the idea of Laszlo too long. Instead, she moved back to the topic of Ben's personality, and the success that he could realize at Rockhorn. She must have been at the Board meeting, because she used that as the basis for her flattery.

"You have real talent, Ben," she said. "You have true gifts—I really liked the way you kept turning the questions around into other questions, making people question themselves. That was so clever, you know—doing that makes people feel so smart."

"Well, that wasn't really my intention," said Ben.

"Oh, but it worked!" the woman's voice said, in a breathless giggle. "I especially liked the questions that challenged the way people think about things. Talking about sick children needing doctors, about parents giving their children stones."

"It was bread, food. That's what I was talking about. About feeding your children."

The woman giggled, as if at her own foolishness. "Oh, stones, sand, bread. It's all the same thing."

"But we live on bread, not stones, not dirt. I mean what parent.... I mean, that was my point. If you can't remember it, I can tell you again—"

"Oh, words, words, words. You're just so good with words. I just wish you'd be good through action. Be good to me—be good by doing something. You could do this, you know. It wouldn't be hard."

"I don't think it's right," he said.

"Oh come on," she said. "You're getting that stuff from being religious, aren't you?"

There was a pause, but he didn't reply.

"Look, if you're so perfectly religious, think of the angels. Afterwards, he'll be an angel, and he'll be a grateful angel. You think Laszlo is happy like this? Make him an angel."

"Actually, that's not really theologically correct."

"Get off the high horse—there's something in those old books about angels rescuing people, isn't there? Taking care of us?"

"Perhaps. I don't know if he's happy right now. But your theology is all wrong."

"Oh, Ben." She laughed. "The-ology?" It was a little girl's laugh, a coquettish giggle that made light of the whole situation, that negated anything he'd said. Ultimately, her laugh said, it didn't matter. None of this banter seemed to matter to her, at all, except as a means to an end.

"I don't know," Ben repeated.

"Well, there you have it," she said. "You can't be sure. None of us can be sure—of anything! But once he's done, then you can do the religious thing, and ask the angels, or whatever you do. Once he's done, then you'll have an angel on your side. And you'll have more than that, you know. You'll have it all. You and I will be together, and we can do anything—anything your heart desires."

"Yes, you've said that," said Ben. "You've told me enough about this. I don't need to hear anymore to make up my mind."

She giggled again. "Oh good," she said. "At least you're tempted by it."

"No, I'm really not," Ben said. "I think you should leave—"

At this, I moved back from the door. Someone could be coming out soon. Thus, I heard only tones of voice after that. There was the woman's voice, soft and sweet in reply, perhaps adding more flattery to the fire. Then Ben's voice came back, louder and firmer. Perhaps he was, in the end, agreeing to her proposition, whatever it was.

In any event, the conversation was concluding. I expected someone to come through the door at any minute. I moved down the hall, away from the classroom, so that I could pretend to just be arriving. Consequently, I missed the last exchange between them. I can't imagine it was very positive though—she came out of the door rather quickly. Perhaps Ben hadn't acceded to her demands after all. Moments after I last heard Ben's voice, Catherine Foss herself came barreling out of the door moments later, her face livid with rage.

Unconsciously, my mouth dropped open. I had supposed it could be any number of women in that room with Ben, convincing him to do something—I couldn't really understand what—in exchange for dubious honors and false degrees. But I had never counted on Catherine Foss being the voice promoting the logic of euthanasia, the self-aggrandizing 'vision,' and most of all—I never thought she was capable of that seductive giggle. But it was she.

One would think that the moment I saw Catherine Foss, I would have put two and two together, and realized that Joe Matheson was not simply being cute or metaphorical when he told me about Catherine's hatred. I should have understood that in fact, she did want to get rid of Laszlo, if not by strangling him, then by other means. But these thoughts did not occur to me until much later. At the time, I was much too worried about her seeing me in the hallway, and about whether or not she realized that I'd been eavesdropping.

She brushed past furiously as she made for the stairs, hardly seeming to recognize that there was a person in the hallway with her. After Catherine was gone, I shifted my briefcase from one hand to the other, not so subtly dropping it to the floor and picking it back up, generating some noise as I approached the classroom, so that Ben would think that I had just approached.

Inside his classroom, I was surprised to discover Ben calmly watering the plants in the window box of the classroom. Apparently, the storm had passed by him, leaving no evidence behind. His blood pressure didn't seem to have even been affected whatsoever. It was as if it had taken place somewhere else, as if it had never happened at all.

Ben nodded and smiled at me, and said hello. For a moment, the dissonance between the rage I'd seen in the hallway and the calm inside was too great. I couldn't easily reply. As best I could, I nodded and smiled back. A few moments later, he closed up the room and we were on our way to the Shiloh Hospital.

The admitting nurse at the hospital was very talkative. She had comments to offer on the weather, my briefcase, the length of Ben's hair (it needed a haircut), the length of my hair (already short), the color of my tie, her tenure on the ICU ward, the doctors who worked there (a detailed case history of each one), and every one of the patients under her care at Shiloh Hospital. It was when she got to Lindbloom's case that I began to actually listen. She seemed to notice my attention, and thus detailed every item she could remember about Laszlo. On the long hallway march from the front desk to the room in the far corner of the eighteenth floor, the monotonous sound of her voice filled me with despair. I couldn't escape her endless narration, and I began to feel as if I had lived and died every day of Lindbloom's life for the past three months, since the day he was brought in with sawdust on his back from the floor of his classroom, to the recent gradual downhill slide of his lungs, his heart, and his entire body.

By the time we were left in silence and peace in Laszlo Lindbloom's room, it was a relief to be quiet. We looked around at the dusty walls and the worn bedclothes. The room was filled only with the sound of his slow and labored breathing.

It was worse than I'd thought. Mr. Lindbloom looked like the wax mummy of some preserved Egyptian corpse. His fat had melted away, yet it had left all this loose skin around his neck and his face, which hung in flaps and wrinkles against his bones, as if they'd been molded there, extruded like a disgusting white plastic. His skin had various abrasions, especially around his mouth and the tubes that went into him, as if there were careless care here, or as if he'd been nibbled by rats.

Ben looked down at the thinning body on the bed of the man he'd replaced in Shop. "I've been here before," he said.

"Here in this hospital?" I replied.

"Oh, no," said Ben. "I mean, I used to work in a nursing home, you know, taking care of sick people."

"Really?" I said, amazed again, at the variety of life experiences that Ben seemed to dredge up at every occasion. Not for the first time, I wondered what it would have been like, living like he did, moving from position to position, shaking the dust off my feet every time I left a place, never looking back with regret.

"Really?" I said again. "Where was that?"

"Oh, it was in the high desert," said Ben. He waved his hand in a generally westward direction, towards the Pacific Coast.

"What was it like?" I asked. I didn't want to look at Lindbloom's breathing husk on the bed anymore. I glanced at the monitors; every green line was even and nearly flat. The heart monitor showed a tiny blip from time to time, as regular and unremarkable as an electric engine on low batteries. I went to the small window and traced my finger in the dust on the pane. I was ready to leave.

"Well, there were many sick people there, many injured people—all in need of my care," said Ben.

"Overloaded, where you? I've heard nursing homes are about the worst place to really get adequate care."

Ben didn't seem to hear me though. Perhaps being here in this hospital had brought up bad memories for Ben; perhaps there were ghosts he couldn't leave behind. He was still looking directly at Lindbloom, and he responded to me in *sotto voice,* as if he were concentrating so deeply that he couldn't spare the energy to talk out loud.

"People would come to the place I was," he muttered. "They'd come in. They'd need a lot of help. And then they'd leave the home, healthy again. Well."

It struck me that this was not necessarily the normal course of events in a nursing home. Usually people left there in a pinewood box, not healthy and well, but far be it from me to tell Ben this. I just hoped he didn't have any expectation that we'd be leaving with the aspirating corpse that was all that was left of Laszlo Lindbloom.

Ben seemed interested in looking at him, at communing with him on some level, but I knew that Lindbloom had no use for us in this room. Propriety, I assumed, meant that we had to stay in the presence of the artificially breathing body for a period of time, but I didn't have to sentimentalize his remains by conducting any such foolishness as touching his flesh or holding his hand.

I continued the conversation. "Hard work there, huh?"

"Yes," said Ben distractedly. He was looking at Lindbloom. "Very hard work. I used to help people take these tubes out when they needed them out."

I glanced at Lindbloom, and grimaced at the way his face was distorted by the lines that ran in and out of his mouth and nose.

"Ah, that would be something I'd avoid doing, myself. Ugh."

"But taking care of people is satisfying work. You should try it sometime."

I laughed hollowly. "Ah, not me. I don't do that sort of thing."

There was a long pause. I looked away from the body, around the room. It was as if the room and Lindbloom had both been abandoned here in some way station to hell—I looked at the faded cards sent a month or more ago, the old bedclothes, the heavy dust that floated in the light through the room, the cobwebs on the outsides of the windows. It was hard to believe there was anything living in this room at all. In a sense, I suppose, there wasn't. Ben looked away from Lindbloom and glanced up at me.

"What's his name?" he said. "His full name."

"Laszlo," I said. "Laszlo P. Lindbloom."

I went out in the hallway to get a soft drink. Ben didn't want anything, but he didn't want to leave either. So I killed some time, and then came back to the room, hoping that Ben was ready to leave.

When I came in, I was drinking my soft drink, and so at first I didn't hear what he was doing. Then I heard it. He was whispering Laszlo Lindbloom's name, over and over again, leaning close to the head on the bed and simply whispering his name.

I watched for a minute, and felt a certain horror creep over me. It was like watching the people who fling themselves down on top of fresh graves, wanting desperately to be with their departed loved ones. I took a long swallow of my drink, and prepared to leave the room.

When Laszlo blinked, I didn't believe my eyes at first. I leaned closer, to see the rheum that covered his eyelashes shift and move as his eyelids opened and closed. Perhaps it was a reflex, perhaps these were death throes, perhaps we were going to witness his actual expiration.

"Nurse?" I called tremulously. "Nurse? He's blinking - hey, nurse, he's blinking, could you get someone in here? Is this normal? Can he hear us?" I turned towards the call buttons, the microphone, looking at the green glowing lines on the monitors that were now moving all over the place, jumping like so many rock rhythms. I stared stupidly at the equipment, looking for what one should do in a circumstance like this.

Then I put my head out of the room, hoping beyond hope to see medical personnel running towards the room down the long hallway. There was no one there, but I looked for a long time.

While I was looking for help, I had no idea what was happening behind me on the patient's bed. There was no great commotion to hear, no disturbance in the Force. In fact, there was nothing extraordinary happening at all, except that Ben had changed his tone of voice and he was gently talking to a very wide-awake Laszlo Lindbloom, eyes now fully open and alert.

I turned back towards the bed in time to see Laszlo grow animated and attempt to speak. With that, he found the feeding tube in his throat and began to choke on it. He reached up and feebly grasped the tube. Ben then leaned over and gently helped him pull out the tube. Then, in a rasping croak, Laszlo spoke.

Sometime after that, the nurses and doctors finally came rushing in the door. By the time they arrived, Laszlo Lindbloom was sitting up in the bed, blinking like a newborn bird at the dust motes floating in the air all around him.

Even an hour later, Ben and Laszlo seemed caught up in their own world. I'd remembered Laszlo as dour and fairly mean-spirited. Yet at this moment, Laszlo wanted to thank someone—anyone—for this gift of life. And despite every test the doctors ran, Laszlo didn't thank them. He thanked Ben, with trembling hands, with tears streaming down his face, as if he actually believed that Ben had something to do with this.

Momentarily, I was frustrated with him. I thought that it could have just as easily have been me that Laszlo woke up to. Then I didn't think that anymore. And at the time, for a long moment afterwards, the raw faith on Laszlo's sunken face disturbed me. The level of belief that was suddenly there worried me. That also didn't worry me after a minute or so.

In fact, for a long time afterwards, I wasn't disturbed by Ben at all, or by anything he did.

Laszlo just kept saying "Thank God."

I was spellbound. The concept of God for me is bound up in a lot of old superstitions—primitive things, not worth my attention. I suppose I always left the door open for some sort of watchmaker behind the scenes—a *Spiritus Mundi* that animated the world beyond the reaches of science or of reason. Yet the mythology and superstition of deities here and present in our daily lives, on some personal level, have always been essentially useless ideas.

Yet now I was struggling, in a room full of scientists—doctors and nurses—with Laszlo's gratitude. I'm not sure what else Laszlo did after he finished thanking Ben, but despite myself, I know that I breathed a small prayer of appreciation to whatever antiquated deity had manifested itself in that dusty room at Shiloh Hospital.

13.

AFTERWARDS, FOR a long per iod of weeks, nothing was quite the same for me. I found that I couldn't concentrate on my work or really connect with the tasks of organizing my client's tax records for next quarter's filings. The economy was roaring along, and it looked like business would be booming for me next quarter. Yet even this didn't engage my attention.

I was now beginning to understand the behavior of the children in Jake's group. They were enthralled by Ben—entranced by his seeming ability to touch something deeper in reality, something perhaps that we had lost. For better or for worse, it seemed that I had now caught a mild version of what had fascinated them. But if Ben was a disease, they had the full-blown flu, while I only had a touch of a cold.

I thought more about them, and about their reactions to Ben in the weeks after the incident at the hospital. Every time I went to see Laszlo—I couldn't keep away now, after I was there on the day he woke up—I was reminded of my reaction on the day of his waking. Laszlo went through a considerable recovery period, but eventually he came back to full capacity, and was able to return to teaching. In fact, now that Ben is no longer with us, Laszlo is our Shop Teacher once again as I write this.

Yet long after Laszlo's recovery was a surety, I was still distracted by Ben. Obviously, my experience was precisely the same as his students' response to him. And that fact, in itself, helped me to understand my own behavior better.

When one looked dispassionately at the group of children around Ben, it would be evident to any outsider that to a man, they were each misfits in their own way, divided among themselves. In fact, it's a misnomer to call them a group—they weren't a distinct and unified unit at all. The only unifying purpose is that they each one of them shared the individual, desperate desire to be someone else. They all yearned for some kind of acceptance, and the acceptance that they'd receive among their own group of misfits never could still that yearning. In essence, that's the characteristic that makes a child a misfit, a social oddball—the inability to be at peace with themselves as a person, their discomfort with their own identity.

As I saw more and more of them in the coming weeks, I saw that being with Ben took away that longing to escape from themselves. Interestingly, Ben did not unify them as a group at all; they were not a better fit with each other after their time with Ben. Each one of them as individuals though, seemed to fit better into their own skin, their own sense of self. I watched the adolescents in the group change and grow over the months, and saw them become themselves, become more aware of just who they were. This was, perhaps, also what had happened to me for a few weeks after Laszlo woke.

It seemed that I was preternaturally aware of who I was, and what I was doing with my life. Sol diers in battle, and midwives in the birthing room describe the sensation. Being close to death, or to the experience of new birth, can do that to you. And I suppose, in being there with Laszlo on that day, I had come through a type of both death and birth. Thus, I was experiencing that same sense of heightened awareness, that same radical caesura that happens on the battlefield and at the first cry of new life.

It occurred to me that perhaps this was what the boys meant when they talked about the "real world" and tried to describe "living in the real." Suddenly, my choices mattered; I felt so alive. Yet it only took stories and descriptions for Ben's young students to get the concept—for me, it took Laszlo.

I even began to find excuses to come by the school right after classes. I had to drop off Jake's medical records with the health office, I'd say, or I had to check on something in the Administration building. At first, I made motions towards actually doing these things while I was there, before I came by the table where Ben held forth. Then I began simply to drop by, no excuse in hand.

There was an allure to being there after school with him. I felt as if I was drinking from a fire hose of knowledge about life. I got to meet most of the players in Jake's endless stories—Sym (whom I'd met once before), and Matt, who still couldn't keep a strident tone out of his voice. I met Tom, who stuttered through nearly every sentence; and the Thunderheads, resplendent in their rages; and finally, cowed Moira, blossoming awkwardly into adulthood.

And I wasn't the only adult there after school. Other parents were there, and increasingly we were joined by several staff members who left their desks as early as they could to be able to spend some time with Ben before the group dispersed and they all drifted home. For the first time, I was making friends with other parents of children at Rockhorn. In the early days, Sol Tharsen was a constant presence in Ben's group—he had a lot to say, but he was also very articulate. And I met Zeb, the large and intimidating father of Jimmy and Jon. In contrast to Sol, Zeb was as silent as his children were hyperactive, but underneath his stoicism, I sensed that he concealed the same capacity for rage. I also got to know a quiet woman named Martha who worked in the records and administration office. She turned out to be the mother of one of the few upperclassmen who found Ben intriguing. Finally, I met the talkative and domineering mother and father of Tom. Their behavior explained a lot about Tom to me. These may not have been the parents I would have chosen as my companions, but nevertheless, they were the parents of my son's peers, and they were there for the same reason I was.

For me, the change between being in a business meeting or enmeshed in a client's spreadsheet versus choosing freely to be with the informal group of children and adults on the playground in the late afternoon was astronomical. The principal difference, perhaps, was that level of respect that Ben showed toward everyone. In business meetings at my firm, I think that all of us were constantly watching over our shoulders for who was driving the firm forward, and who was dragging it down. Thus, we were often resentful of another's attempted power grab, or frustrated because one of our colleagues had either screwed up—or was about to screw up—a long-standing client's account. It wasn't that we didn't work well together—we did—it was that we all wanted to move ahead, and we didn't want someone else's weakness to slow us down. I suppose most of us lived by the maxim that we only have so much time to make managing partner before retirement. A career in business, as some wit has observed, cannot be anything but "nasty, brutish, and short." Thus, the anticipation of weakness worried us. Ben, on the other hand, seemed to know that everyone was weak to start with, and he didn't run away from it.

There was Moira, for example. Every day that I dropped by the playground, Ben sat near her, who was about the most unpleasant person I could imagine. The girl alternated constantly between a sneering cynicism and a falsely simpering flattery. The edge of attractiveness that remained in her was concealed under a washed-up world-weariness, and the jaded quality of any conversation with her was disgusting in one so young. To me, the fact that high school boys would even consider sleeping with someone so transparently needy simply demonstrated how desperate for sex boys their age were. Moira's very mannerisms—the tick at her mouth, the way she held her hands, the sneer in her eyes—all of these things irritated me.

Yet it was almost as if Ben saw a very different person sitting beside him. It was almost as if he didn't know the Moira that we all knew and disliked—or knowing, did not care.

I asked him about this one day, as the group was dispersing. I had just seen him patiently listen to a long stuttering question from Tom, and respond with never a flicker of disgust or impatience. The children were wandering away, towards their rides or after-school activities. I watched them go until I thought they were out of earshot. Then, carefully, I intimated that some of the children in his group acted in ways that were distasteful or frustrating, and I wondered how he could force himself to spend time with them every day. Quite honestly, I was curious.

Ben responded in a way that made me think he knew exactly what I'd been avoiding by being here at my son's school in the late afternoon.

"At work, you spend time with clients and business people whom you dislike, don't you?" Ben asked.

"Of course—their time is worth money to me."

"Do you think they know that they're unlikable? That they aren't pleasant people?"

"Why no, I wouldn't think so," I said. "I would think most of them think that they're God's gift to the human race. That's partly what makes them so unlikeable. They don't get the fact that they're a jerk, or else they just don't give a damn. The fact that they're bastards has gotten them ahead in life. And they've had it good for so long, they don't get that they aren't God's gift to the universe."

"So, look around you," he said. "How many of these children here do you think realize that they're social rejects—that they don't fit, and that no one likes them? How many of them know that they sometimes act like jerks? Or that they do things no one likes?"

"Even Moira?"

"Oh, especially Moira." He pointed at her back in the distance. She always walked away from the group with a peculiar staggering walk, bent over as if to avoid a blow. "Look at her—do you think she imagines people like her?"

"I hadn't thought of that," I said. "I always thought children thought they were the center of the universe. That's what immaturity is, isn't it?"

"No, children mostly know they're on the periphery. They are often the most honest about their own failings. ? Tom stutters, for example, because he knows his own failings far too well. All too often we adults actually believe that we have no failings. So you asked why I spend time with this kind of child?"

"Yes, I did."

"For better or for worse, these children are living a real life. They know what's really happening, and they're up front about it. I don't have dig through many layers at all to discover the truth. Try doing that with your business colleagues—they're like an onion, made of layers of lies to themselves. And they usually believe their own press."

I didn't quite know how to respond to this. I'd never thought in terms of a child's needs being on the same level as an adult's needs. Yet in this new and strangely altered reality I was living in, the children mattered more than anything else. Who was more important, more "real"?

After we'd made our departure from the group that day, I thought about the conversation from various angles. The importance of choices had stayed with me. What were my choices? It had come back to me—who was I choosing to be. Was I being real?

* * *

The idea of being more honest with myself haunted me—it was like a recurring dream of a person I had once met. I found myself idly examining my calendar in the late afternoon. Then, one day, I picked up the phone to call my secretary to cancel my appointments around the time school let out. I could justify it by saying that Jake needed me after school.

I dialed, the phone started ringing, and then I caught myself. It alarmed me how close I'd come to the edge—I was on the verge of giving up several hundred dollars worth of income per day, simply to waste some of those hours of precious time with my benighted child—Jake—and his uneducated Shop teacher, Ben. What was I thinking?

It were almost as if Ben were a magnet, something I couldn't avoid turning towards. But I was leery of being this tied into him yet.

So I took refuge in analysis. The approach came to me one day as I waiting in the lounge outside Jake's therapist's office. As I waited, I found it difficult to concentrate on the papers I'd brought from the office. Instead, I found myself trying to psychoanalyze Ben. Why did he care so much about children? What had his childhood been like? What was he really about?

To start with, I was reasonably sure that I could assume a country upbringing for Ben. Given his name and his obvious ethnic heritage, it wasn't a stretch to imagine him to be the child of migrant farm workers—many of the Hispanic types I knew in this city came from that stock. To back up my assumption, there were also a few random comments Ben had made.

There was Ben's comment to Zak, for example. Zak was one of the more surly kids in the group. He was sitting on top of the table when Ben arrived for lunch one day. Ben teased him by saying: "You know, when I was up on the table, my Mom always used to say *Were you born in a barn?* And you know what the funny part of that story is? My folks were homeless—you know, farm workers—and I *was* born in a cowshed. So I ask you, were you born in a barn too?"

"Nah," said Zak, and got down and joined them.

Thus I knew that Ben came from a place with cows and barns,

someplace tolerant of nomadic fruit-pickers and itinerate farm work-ers. Yet most of the farm workers I'd met weren't as obviously intel-ligent, well spoken, or purposeful as Ben. Who had educated him? Where did he get his self-assurance from? Despite my depth of ex-perience and understanding of our pluralistic culture, I had no idea how to fit Ben into my world-view. My limited knowledge of the lower Hispanic elements in our city indicated a level of character and type that were quite the opposite of Ben.

I suppose I could play to the stereotype, but the stereotype is in fact my entire experience: these people were generally obnoxious loud-mouths shouting drunkenly to each other in a slurred foreign lan-guage, playing ugly mariachi music far too loud for my ears, driving back and forth from construction sites in their fume-belching cars, and generally confirming how low humanity could sink.

Many of them worked illegally, deriving their income in back alleys or under the table. Often, one read in the papers about someone with a name like Ben's being arrested for being connected in some poorly defined way with a drug cartel.

Ben was evidently illegal in some sense of the word—despite his obvious learning, erudition, and poise, as a child he had been pursued by the law before the incidents that happened at our school. The stories Jake had told me about this illegal side of Ben's life were confusing.

"When he was real little," said Jake. "He was running away all the time."

"Ben was running away from home?" I asked.

"No, no," said Jake. "The cops were chasing his family, and so his family ran out and got over the border. Then later, when he got older, they came back."

I personally doubted that a family with small children would leave the country, cross the border, and then easily come back—braving the guards and the journey several times with a young child—but this was the story that Ben told to the group.

Perhaps it was drugs his family was involved in—more than like-ly—or perhaps it was less harmful, and just as illegal. Perhaps his family transported human cargo back and forth, taking illegals to a new life, re-birthing them as citizens, angels to those destitutes, and criminals to the border guard. That would explain the apparent ease with which Ben told Jake that they moved back and forth—an ability to re-invent themselves. This was certainly a facility Ben demonstrated at Rockhorn school, re-inventing himself and re-inventing others.

At Rockhorn, Ben had at the least invented his way out of poverty and deprivation. Ben told Jake that his parents were two unmarried homeless youths, but it just didn't fit with his auto-didactic knowledge, and his erudition.

After he was gone I was startled to learn from Jonathon, the Assistant in the Library, that Ben could speak several languages with near-fluency, yet of course I know his name—the name he told us—was a standard proletariat Hispanic name. In point of fact, despite his name, I still don't know for sure whether or not Ben came from a particular national origin or culture. I never got around to asking him.

In retrospect, I wish I'd been at the school on the day that his family came to see him at work. I would have learned a lot more about Ben. Unfortunately, though, they came out of the blue—with so little warning that even Ben seemed taken by surprise.

He sent them away empty-handed, without inviting them into his classroom. He refused to see them. I suppose his behavior would make sense if his family was connected with drugs, or was in some manner criminal. It would make sense to me that Ben would want nothing to do with them. However, Meredith—the Secretary—said that during the time they sat in her office waiting, they seemed like a perfectly nice group of people. Perhaps a slight Hispanic caste to their skin—she didn't really look at them closely—but she said that they didn't seem like a 'criminal family,' whatever that means.

Perhaps, I speculated to Meredith, his family had come to see him about an inheritance the family had just received. In my money-conscious view of the world, why else would a family come to see a wayward son at his place of work?

Yet if there was an inheritance, Ben didn't take it. The encounter with his family was another incident that I had little explanation for—it was another mystery. Perhaps I was obsessed—perhaps I couldn't help it—but I wanted to understand some of these mysteries.

My therapist didn't have many answers, so I stopped going to my appointments. Instead, I began to ask my acquaintances around Rockhorn community for what they knew about Ben.

Joe Matheson told me that he'd been quietly cashing Ben's checks for him and giving him the money directly, as Ben told Joe that he did not have a bank account. There were other oddities with money. In fact, said Joe, Ben seemed to sometimes forget his paycheck entirely—going for several weeks without picking it up, and without seeming to notice the lack of ready cash.

He didn't seem to own anything—but he didn't seem to want to own much, either. Then it occurred to me that he had to, at the least, own tools, to make a living as a laborer. Tools, then, were my next line of inquiry. I asked about the equipment that Ben used on his various projects around the campus. But this too, was a dead end. It turned out that Bill Girus, the grounds supervisor, had been loaning him tools since the first day he had arrived on Rockhorn campus.

Girus said simply that he loaned Ben tools because he liked the work that Ben was capable of doing. As far as Girus knew, Ben owned absolutely nothing except the clothes on his back.

During the first week of my inquiry, I was fortunate enough to be invited to a blacktie event downtown. I say I was fortunate, because at the party I happened to run into someone who said he was a detective. I painted Ben as a hypothetical case, telling him I was curious about the identity of a client who paid only cash. The detective was happy to speculate, but in the end it came down to the paucity of my information.

Missing persons or people without clear records are usually tracked down through their purchases, through credit card receipts and the like, said the man at the party. Cash purchases would destroy a trail like that, and without a bank account, the scent was even colder. With Ben, there was little to track in the way of possessions; I might as well be trying to discover the origin of air.

Yet Ben's ideas haunted me still. I wanted to be closer to who he was, but I had decided that I would find my own way to him. Somehow, I felt that if I understood him better—if I had more knowledge—then I would be able to approach him anew, with the upper hand this time, not as a supplicant or needy person, but perhaps as an equal. I wasn't a misfit, and I didn't need to be part of that after-school group of children and hangers-on; but I wanted that indefinable quality that drew me to him. I didn't want to take the risk yet of changing my schedule, the risk of commitment—I would find out more first—I would be removed from it all, and I would make a rational decision before flinging myself wildly off the cliff.

Thus, I took the only helpful advice the detective was able to give me.

"If you've got nothing else to go on—there's only one other way," he had said. "You've got no information, no credit card records, nothin'—I'd go for the old reliable."

"What's that?" I asked.

"It means that you put on your walking shoes, and you follow him home one day. Maybe you even follow him around for a couple days—over a weekend, maybe. If you do it well, without him knowing that you're doing it, then you find out where he lives, where he goes, what he does, who he knows. You find out a lot by following someone."

"Isn't that illegal?"

"Actually, it's not unless you're close enough to harass them. And if you follow them and *let* them know you're doing it, by calling their name, that's also harassment."

As he spoke, I could just picture myself, running down the sidewalk after Ben, shouting his name: "Ben—Teacher! Hey, Teach, Carp!"

I chuckled aloud. "Yeah, like I'd be shouting his name."

"Right, pretty stupid," said the detective. "But if you can do it circumspectly, you have more information than you started with. And you haven't paid anyone for the information."

The idea excited me. I could be part of Ben's world after school without him even knowing it. I could be close to Ben, yet not have to answer awkward questions. I could pursue him without being obvious.

I determined that I'd follow him on a Friday evening, after school, when it was most possible that Ben would do more than just go straight back to his home. He might go out, and I would discover who his friends were, who he spent time with after work. I might discover that he had twelve children of his own, or none at all.

14.

ON THAT Friday, I made arrangements for my secretary to take care of Jake after school. Then I left my firm a little early—around the time school let out. Outside the school, I waited in my car until almost everyone else had left. The school janitors came and went. The sun dropped lower in the sky. For a moment I wondered if I'd missed him.

As I waited in the car, I thought further about why I was there. Being around Ben had forced me into some uncomfortable moments of moral self-examination, and perhaps some part of me hoped for some sort of cynical unveiling of Ben's life. What if I discovered that Ben purchased reams of child pornography from a sleazy shop in old town? What if he loved to visit neo-Nazi bookstores or frequented neighborhoods where drugs were sold? Those would be among the most disappointing of discoveries about him, but in retrospect I know that I secretly hoped for something like this. It would reduce Ben down to my level. It would make him answerable to me—not the other way around—and I was already feeling that it would be a relief to no longer continue the introspection that I'd undertaken recently. So many possibilities occurred to me in those moments when I waited outside the school—but what didn't occur to me is what actually happened.

Just as I was on the verge of leaving, Ben came out. He didn't look tired at all, despite a very long day within the confines of Rockhorn classrooms. Instead, he looked refreshed, invigorated. He began walking with a purposeful stride, traveling ten to twelve blocks at a rapid pace. Carefully, I followed in my car, edging my way through traffic, driving slowly in the outside lane, and at various times taking small detours into parallel streets, so as not to draw too much attention to myself. After a time I glanced at my speedometer, and was surprised to discover that he had walked nearly two miles at this point. When I glanced back up, it appeared that Ben had stopped—I couldn't see his striding figure anymore. I sped up, hoping to pass him wherever he had stopped, and then circle back around.

We were on the outskirts of one of the most expensive residential districts in town. Two major roads crossed here—one heading out from an upscale neighborhood towards the expressway, and the other leading into downtown. Here beside the road was only an open patch of concrete beside the merging traffic flows, a place without character or personality. Only a convenience store graced the curb beside the bus stop and the moving traffic. Why would he come here—there was a bus stop right in front of Rockhorn? As I sped by, I caught sight of what I thought was Ben's standing figure in a crowd of people. There was a bus stop here also—but I hadn't expected to see a crowd in such a respectable neighborhood. Involuntarily, I slowed, surprised to see so many standing here in the middle of nowhere on a Friday evening. Then the similarity of the clothing and the skin color of those who were waiting resolved itself into something familiar. The women were wearing white uniforms; these were all the domestic laborers from the expensive mansions up the hill, all headed home for the evening. And all around them were men who shared their race—Hispanic day laborers, dusty and muddy from working on construction sites and posh home remodels. This spot was also where these unemployed men waited in the morning for a contractor who needed an extra pair of hands. If they got in the contractor's truck, they were worked until they dropped, but they were also paid in cash, no questions asked. Perhaps I had once passed this way before, taking the long way around on my way to downtown or to work, but I had never thought to pause to watch the men waiting for someone who might offer them a day of work. It had also never occurred to me that the domestic help I was familiar with came from the same class and heritage as these dirty men. My own home was only a few miles away; perhaps even our domestic help was here, chattering away with the rest of them, waiting for a bus late in the evening.

I glanced to the right, wondering if I'd see any familiar faces, and there in the middle of the crowd I saw him. Ben was holding forth—I recognized the stance and the group's rapt attention from so many sessions at the lunchtime table. All around him, men in dirty overalls and women in pristine household costumes were watching him, and whispering from time to time.

I drove around the block several times, watching him. He was more jocular here, more relaxed, and the crowd laughed with him at regular intervals, as if he was one of their own. For a moment, I was struck by the fact that he was probably speaking in Spanish, and that he was connected with these people too, perhaps even more deeply than he was connected with the children at the lunch table. More so than at lunch, it was a conversation he was holding with old friends, not a lecture. And here too, he came to bring hope. Each time I passed on my circuit around the block, I saw the day's weariness lift from the faces around him. His vitality was contagious to the crowd around him. By the time the bus came to take them all back to where they'd come from, I could see grins on most of the faces. Obviously, Ben had told an entertaining story. Uncomfortably, I thought it could be about me, the *gringo* who was following him in the nice car—the one they could barely see circling them in the distance.

The bus that came was an express for the south side of town. It stopped only a few times before heading directly for the outskirts of the city. This was a route for household help and construction workers who needed to get from the expensive neighborhoods—like those around Rockhorn—back to their homes in the more disadvantaged districts. Thus, the bus skipped the downtown and the shopping districts entirely. What could they afford down there?

Down on the south side, even the billboards were in Spanish, and my stereotype of Hispanic life was simply reinforced—at each bus stop, it seemed someone was playing mariachi music from their open window. Each time the bus stopped here, hordes of domestic help and migrant men came out. By the time it left the Spanish billboards behind, the bus was mostly empty. The bus still had a few people in it, but it was headed now for a mile of drug-ridden projects; Ben would have no business in the drugs and guns zone. I was thinking of turning around, to check back on the mariachi streets—perhaps I had missed him—when I saw him emerge at a bus stop.

All around us, the walls and sidewalks were covered with the scrawling curlicues and jagged lines of spray painted graffiti. Loud music poured out of houses and cars—not mariachi, something more strident and destructive. The jagged sounds and beats of the music competed in volume for the air. On the street corners, young men loitered in baggy pants, no doubt holding hundreds of dollars worth of drugs inside their clothes, along with guns and other weapons. I had rolled up my car windows and had my cell phone handy on the seat beside me. I could feel sweat under my collar. Perhaps following Ben into the evening hadn't been such a good idea.

When I saw him walking quietly up the street, nodding in a respectful way to the tattooed young men on the corner, I cursed under my breath. Perhaps he actually lived here. Why did he have to live in such a horrendous part of town? If I kept moving the car slowly, I'd soon be offered drugs, and if I refused, no doubt I'd be taken for a police officer. Neither were scenarios I wanted to encourage. I whipped the car around the corner and parked a block ahead of Ben, hoping against hope that he'd stop somewhere between the bus stop and the next block, or else I'd have to move the car again.

I kept my window rolled up, and for anonymity I relied on the time-honored tradition of reading a newspaper. I pulled it up in front of my face as he went by; he never seemed to notice. With such close proximity, I could observe him here in what I supposed to be his natural element.

Oddly though, just as his clothes and his mannerisms didn't really fit at Rockhorn, neither did they fit seamlessly this neighborhood. He wasn't dressed in the current style—his clothes were very nondescript and still dirty from the Shop—and he didn't bounce along with the music, the way half the people on the street were doing. He was the perpetual outsider: never fitting in entirely. He sat down on a stoop a few doors down, yet no one seemed to resent his presence. Quite the opposite, in fact.

As I watched him, I was struck by a sense of déjà vu. Once one looked past the changes in clothing and surroundings—and skin color—it was clear that the way the people acted towards Ben was just like they acted at the bus stop, and just as they acted at Rockhorn.

Here, in this god-forsaken neighborhood, young men came up to him and pounded fists with him—a peculiar gang-like greeting, in my opinion—while gradually a group of children gathered. I could see Ben's mouth moving. Obviously, he was talking to them. But through the closed window glass, I couldn't hear a word he was saying. I wondered if he was talking about his experience at Rockhorn that day—if he was telling stories about the rich kids he worked with. On the other hand, it occurred to me that he might just be telling the same kinds of stories and ideas that I had heard at the school. I ran through a few of the ones I'd heard from Jake as I watched Ben's hand gestures, trying to place which rote story he was telling. I couldn't seem to lock his expressions and his gestures to a particular story I'd heard. Perhaps he had changed them, or added elements that would appeal to this class of listeners. Then it struck me that none of his stories really constrained themselves to a particular social class. In fact, the objections that many parents at Rockhorn had had to his style of teaching would be unobjectionable here, in the projects. I watched him talk and move his hands. I watched the people collect around him.

It seemed that Ben had built up a certain street respect in this neighborhood. No one threatened him; no one spoke to him in derogatory tones (as I was sure would happen to me, were I to get out of my car). So the thought occurred to me that there were few ways a person might gain the respect of a neighborhood full of gangsters. What neighborhood drug dealer had Ben killed in order to be left alone? What blood had covered his hands in order to find a way to survive this environment?

Yet despite these disturbing questions, I gradually found myself relaxing. Even the incessant pounding beat of the music seemed less intrusive. I glanced around at the young men making their living on the corner, at an older man stumbling up the street, at the street urchins gathered at Ben's feet. What had changed? Why did I catch the edge of a smile or two between these people—why were the intimidating young men on the corner so calm? I swear I saw them telling an older woman to watch for traffic before crossing and I watched one of them take a drug vial away from a child. No one seemed to fear being shot—yet a few moments ago, the air was full of that unbearable tension that is present just before a fight. Something had cleared the air of that implicit threat of violence. In some odd fashion, Ben had brought peace to the most unlikely place.

The crowd here almost had the same regard for him as the students at Rockhorn. It was clear to me already that that school yard adulation wasn't simply the result of Ben's school audience being young and impressionable—here in the projects, all manner of ages and types surrounded him.

His lack of overt power made me wonder how he'd held his own in these harsh environs. Closely, I watched the young men approach him, waiting to see a knife in a hand, a gun held as a threat. Or failing that, a sign of obeisance, of fear towards a powerful character who had forcibly won their respect. There was none. I'd been mistaken—there was no death-debt from these gangsters to Ben, no blood oath that had been taken to incur fear and artificially still the wrath that lay like a fog all through these abandoned streets.

I watched Ben on the stoop, and I thought back to when I met him for the first time. Although intriguing in some hard-to-define way, he was no pillar of charisma, no overwhelming presence. In fact, if he hadn't spoken to me, I may not have really noticed him—I may never have noticed him at all. There was that curious humility about him, something that effaced his own self even as he spoke to you, even as he made himself known, as you were absorbing his words, he seemed to fade away. Even now, I am left only with a certain vagueness, a blurring of memory that makes up all I can grasp of Ben Delacruz.

If there was no blood that had been spilled, and no overt power that he held, what was it that held his audience here to him? Why did the money and the drugs not matter for this one evening?

In this neighborhood, it seemed to me that they lived in like characters in some trite gang-banging Hollywood action movie, where every wrong move could bring a bullet, and every cop would turn away, thinking that whoever caught the hit probably deserved it. Although it's not politically correct to say so in our era of affirmative action and multicultural sensitivity, just as the old man with his liquor wandering down the street or the young woman with her tight clothes and the puncture marks on her arm seemed like trite caricatures to me, they also weren't real people to the majority of the population. Just another statistic on a graph—inner-city violence, gang-related deaths, neglect, abandonment and crime—they have all become just numbers to us. What's a few more or a few less people with the wrong color skin who have problems? I'd venture to guess that's why a few hundred thousand deaths in a place like Bangladesh or Mogadishu don't really stay in the headlines for very long. No one cares; they're just numbers.

Of course, in our defense, it's a little hard to grasp the sheer magnitude of those dead and downtrodden every year. Unless, of course, we have a face we recognize in the crowd. How can we understand or identify with thousands of people we've never seen, and never cared about before? It's a human impossibility.

That's what was always odd about Ben. Everyone seemed recognizable to him—each person had a face. In fact, on this Friday evening, I was struck to see how closely he paid attention to every single person who encountered him. Just as he paid attention to every face he saw in the crowded halls of Rockhorn, even the misfit faces, the faces no one sees, he also paid attention to the faces here, and he paid attention to me.

He saw my face—perhaps, in the end, that's it after all—he saw my face as I really am. It took me unaware. Perhaps it was as simple as that. Instead of seeing me in all the ways I project myself into the world, he just saw me. For him, there was no powerful Political Player or paycheck-holding Accounting Manager, no intimidating Partner in the Firm, no Board Member, no Trust Fund Consolidator, and even no Useful Contact, Potential Client or Source of Revenue. He just saw me, and perhaps, in the end, that was enough for me, and enough for all of the misfits at Rockhorn, and enough for each of the domestic laborers at the bus stop, enough for each of the criminal statistics who surrounded him on the stoop here in this neighborhood of instant death and slow decay.

I watched Ben speak, as the composition of the crowd around him shifted and changed. Sometime in there, someone shared some pretzels with him, sometime in there, someone handed him a can of soda. Unfortunately, I had no such sustenance, and the hours were drifting longer and longer. As the color in the sky changed and the evening light came and went, the few remaining streetlights here gradually glowed awake. But there was no change for Ben—he continued on the stoop, talking and laughing with the people he paid attention to.

I had turned the car on and I was on the point of departing when I realized that Ben was leaving as well. He had made his farewells and was wandering purposefully up the street towards the next block. Perhaps this wasn't where he lived after all. Or on the other hand, perhaps he was simply turning the corner towards his own dilapidated brownstone or broken-down tenement, where he'd find rest for the night.

Slowly, I followed him in the car. He walked quickly, traveling in less than half an hour out of the neighborhood of gang-bangers into a place that—if I could believe my eyes—seemed immeasurably worse than the graffiti-covered projects where the bus had first stopped. We had moved far away from the places where there was room for a story-teller. In this late night nightmare, I couldn't imagine anyone would care to escape into a story. You only came to a place like this to kill yourself, in my estimation.

Here, instead of young men with guns and drugs, there were shaking, washed-up junkies who waited languidly on the street corners, waiting for someone who would pay for their burned and punctured flesh, providing them drug money to wake to another purposeless day. I could well imagine that half the people here had spent some part of their lives in the Moolston Psychological Facility. There was a morbid, fleshly radiance in ground-floor windows—red neon that lured passing drivers to the living wares inside. Fog was beginning to cover the city streets, lending a strange unearthly glow to the neon-lit windows and the made-up faces that passed me in the street.

Here in this place, as the clock moved towards late evening, Ben stopped again. His routine was making me tired. Neither of us had eaten yet; I was beginning to wonder what fuel sustained him.

At the next street light, Ben had stopped to talk with people near a closing bar. Flashing lights strobed over the sidewalk, intermittently illuminating the faces and gestures of those around him. In the gathering fog and the flashing lights, it was hard to tell who these people were—or even what they were. Were they particularly hard-faced women? Women dressed as men? Then it came to me: they were neither, and both. They were men who had chosen to be like women, perhaps even to modify their bodies—as I could tell with at least one near to Ben—to blur their gender and pervert their sex. I looked at the people filling the sidewalks on both sides of the intersection. There were men here who acted as women, women here who acted as men—it seemed clear to me that regardless of natural gender, most were simply interested in selling themselves as expensively as they could to any warm pot of walking flesh.

These were the types of perversities that Ben had described in that one story that infuriated me, the one with the injured boy and the transvestite. It occurred to me that that story—the one I had considered to have pedophilic leanings—could have based on one of the characters whom Ben was currently talking to. I was nauseous at the thought of a street filled with these sexually-charged creatures, nauseous at the thought that my son spent time with someone who might know more than I wanted to know about this type of freakish lifestyle. Here were the true dregs of humanity. Despite their celebratory makeup, the faces I could see here looked desperate and lonely—it was as if their self-worth had been shot into orbit, along with their natural-born identity.

I determined to wait only a few minutes longer before I'd drive home and abandon my investigation. I'd already gotten one curious knock on my car window—one flash of a nasty 'come-hither' smile that was beyond disgusting, coming as it did from a masculine face covered in feminine makeup and bad hair, doing its six-foot best to act coquettish. I didn't need to put up with any more of this filth.

I forced myself to think like an investigator. It was a Friday night, after all. All the freaks were out on parade. Perhaps Ben retreated here after a hard week of school to release his frustration by renting one of these perverse creatures. Perhaps this was the direction his sexual compass swung. Far be it from me to judge someone else's sexual desires. Even as I tried to think clearly though, other thoughts shook me with rage. For what if this was, in fact, the place where Ben lived—in a land of violated sexual mores, where all the rules are broken, all the time—renting a hunk of new flesh every night? What if Ben was secretly a pedophile? What if he, himself, was a transvestite? Would I still be so comfortable with him teaching my child?

Yet I also recalled remembered conversations from Rockhorn playground, in which Ben demonstrated the fact that he wasn't a sex-fiend. Just as with the story of the girl raped and left for dead, he told stories

with characters who had made sexual choices and faced the consequences. But for his students, that usually wasn't satisfying enough.
They wanted to know the details. The children pressed him to talk
about 'real world' sex more than once—there was, for example, the
time when they were all talking about origins, and he volunteered
information that gave rise to prurient discussion. Ben had just explained that his parents—the two homeless youths—weren't married
when he was conceived. After he was conceived, his father almost
left his mother, and she also considered an abortion. In the end, they
stuck to their life together, and gave birth to Ben. His students immediately wanted more information. They wanted to talk about exactly
what it took to make someone pregnant, and what your options were
if your girlfriend got pregnant. Most of the crowd, one must remember, were boys just on the verge of puberty, and without much in the
way of information beyond their parents' instructions on morality
and standard animal behavior (the birds and the bears, or something
like that). But to Ben's credit, instead of entertaining the speculation,
he simply re-stated the bald facts, and moved to other topics.

There were also other indications of Ben's uncomplicated and un-
involved approach to sex. Although some of the boys in his group
seemed to have difficulty connecting the act of sex and the result of
pregnancy, a few of the jaded girls in Ben's crowd didn't had any problem understanding it. Rumor has it that more than once, he was prop-
ositioned by an underage tart who was infatuated with him. From a
reliable source—Jake again—I heard that Ben had flatly turned her
down, without even glancing at her twice.

Watching Ben's face in the crowd on the sidewalk, I could well
imagine that he was similarly turning down the perverse propositions
that floated towards him in the night. He smiled at those who gave
him sexual signals, as if at a joke, and made them smile back before
they drifted away, looking for other, hungrier, prey. As I watched Ben
through the gathering fog, I gradually realized that one or two of the
people on the street with him weren't drifting away. One of the types
he was talking to was festooned with tattoos and multiple piercings
and wore a grim sneer—my basic vision of a criminal—and the other
was made-up beyond recognition. S/he was wearing a dirty white
dress, as if to emulate some long-forgotten bridal night. I watched as

the criminal type spoke into Ben's ear for a moment. Ben listened, and seemed to commiserate, and then gave advice that seemed to cheer both the pierced one and the soiled bride. They took Ben's hand, thanking him, and wandered away.

The thought of actually conversing with such bizarre creatures—of having one of them actually speak close enough to me that I could feel their perfumed breath against my ear—this disgusted me anew. I drove around the corner, trying to still my nausea. When I came back to the front of the building, I'd lost Ben in the crowd. I scanned the make-up covered faces for a moment, and was about to drive away when my eye caught a glimpse of him. Once more, he was sitting on a stoop. This time, the landing above him was crowded with johns about to go inside for their evening of pleasure. Below him, in the street, were the freaks and hangers-on that Ben was evidently addressing. This time though, instead of holding forth like a storyteller, Ben seemed to speaking very intimately to one person at a time, just as he'd spoken to the two freaks I'd seen earlier. Repeatedly, I watched as the whores and their clients came close to him to chat for a moment, and then moved away. The same listening scene recurred over and over that night.

I'd observed the late night madhouse for a half-hour, and didn't really understand what was going on until one person passed quite near to me. I watched one slight transvestite approach Ben and coyly, nervously, ask an unheard question. Ben nodded at him—her?—and without blanching, leaned close to her glittering ear to whisper some word of reassurance. Moments later, the person hugged Ben and wandered away. She passed my car quite closely, so I took the opportunity to glance at her face, and was surprised to see tears were streaming down her made-up cheeks. But they didn't seem to be tears of sadness. Something in her had lifted, some weight was gone. Watching the pantomime conversation from this far distance, it was almost as if she had called home, and heard—after years of distance and derision—the voice of her mother or father, telling her that there was some small sliver of hope in her strange world.

Ben was treating them, all of them, tricks and whores alike, as if they were actually worth paying attention to. I was taken aback—did his attention stretch even this far into the depths of depravity?

Yet the evidence before me told a clear story. I could see in the failing light the pose that Ben had struck there on the stoop, the way that he was listening to someone; this was identical to the way he sat at a table at Rockhorn, listening to Jake or Moira talk with him, listening to their concerns. There was that same attentive expression, the same quiet intensity, and the same empathy for their confusion. Ben was once more sitting with a friend, talking with someone he knew well, telling them he trusted them, and telling them the secrets of being real. He acted as if he had all the time in the world.

Then, quite a bit later, I watched a gray-haired person approach Ben without speaking to him. Heavy and solid, yet mincing down the sidewalk on light feet, the person shared the sexual indeterminacy of half the crowd. Whatever her original gender, I saw that she was a powerful figure, a madame, the keeper of some sort of inn of ill repute. I caught a glimpse of something metallic in her hand, and flinched back for a moment, thinking it was a weapon. Perhaps Ben was now going to pay the price for distracting customers from her wares.

Yet as I watched, the person leaned over to him and handed Ben a package of tin-foil covered food: a hunk of roasted lamb from the Greek place around the corner. I could clearly see it with my binoculars. My first reaction was one of horror: he was actually going to eat something given to him by one of these streetcorner types? Who knew what diseases they carried? Yet this was Ben's dinner that night, and it wasn't necessarily something he had planned on –he was surprised, and then, visibly grateful. But it was the only dinner he received, and on some level, it was the kind of meal he'd expected to get—something out of the blue, something given to him.

I watched Ben eat. The crowd was thinning, but he still took the time in between bites to say hello to passing transvestites, and hold a quick conversation with those he seemed to know. My own stomach was growling, but I kept the binoculars trained on him. I was beginning to realize that for Ben, Rockhorn Academy was only part of his day—perhaps a very small part—and all of it, including Rockhorn, was part of something else for him, something bigger. I couldn't really put my finger on it, but he seemed to take it all so seriously. This wasn't just a Friday night on the town for him: he treated this like work, as a labor. Everything was so deliberate, even the happenstance things like his meal.

When I stepped back and thought about it, I realized that I was treating Ben like a paranoiac treats their tormentor or a novelist treats a character—giving meaning to their every little action, not allowing them to do anything without imbuing it with larger intent. Yet despite all these deliberate actions, I'd seen him do very little that was typical of a person in their off-hours. I still hadn't seen him purchase anything—no new stereo for Ben, no toilet articles, no fancy suits, nothing so far. I didn't know where he got his clothes from, or where he did his shopping. Perhaps he did none—perhaps it was all given to him, like his meal this evening?

I thought back through the course of the evening, and wondered about each decision. Why had Ben walked down that street, or made that decision in who to talk to? Why did he pass that grocery store, and stop at that one? Who was he talking to here, and why? What decision led him to take Johnson Avenue instead of Paulsen? I wondered about every footstep, every block he passed, because it seemed to me that everything in his path had a purpose.

The night was getting very old indeed, and the crowds were thinning out, when I made my decision to leave. Ben might be here all night, and I'd never see where he actually slept. For all I knew, he did rent a room in one of these flophouses, most probably not sharing a bed with anyone at all.

Just as before, when I started the engine, it was almost as if Ben sensed my departure. He stood to leave also. Slowly, he moved on from this neighborhood of red neon and transvestite junkies. I followed, driving far back from him. I hoped that my car was at least a little concealed by the heavy fog and the thick darkness. I felt compelled now to find out where he went next.

I drove down a parallel street, keeping Ben in sight at the intersections. He walked for a long hour out of the city limits and into the suburbs. Slowly, the streets dwindled. Soon, I couldn't use the dodge of driving on parallel streets, or of hoping that the traffic would obscure me. I was forced to follow him only a few blocks back, with my lights dimmed. Then, much later, at about the time when I feared that he'd turn around and realize that a slow car had been following him for many blocks, he turned off the road into a forested area. It was a national forest, or something of the like.

In order to follow him now, I couldn't watch from a distance anymore. I turned off the car's engine, and waited for my eyes to adjust to the level of uncertainty in the complete darkness. While I waited, I tried to come to the point of decision, of commitment to this endeavor. If I were to follow him on foot, I thought, it could involve possible danger; I didn't know what I was getting into.

Slowly, I got out of my car and quietly closed the door. I began to follow him on foot. Far ahead, I could see his shape, walking along some off-road path.

For some time, I followed him along the path into the woods. I watched his back moving ahead of me, and carefully, I tried to stay close enough to the trees that I could duck behind them if the need arose. As I watched, I saw him step off the path and out of my sight. He didn't appear on the path again. Perhaps this was where he actually lived. I stood in the trees for a long moment, watching the spot where he had gone to ground, but I couldn't make him out.

I walked in the opposite direction, back towards the car. I'll admit I was nervous about following Ben into a place he knew well. For all I knew, he could have circled back around me, and could pop out from behind a tree at any minute and hold a gun to my head. He would definitely be within his rights to question me then, to ask me why I was following him. Yet I really didn't know why I was following him—it had taken far more time and commitment than I had ever I was capable of—but I still didn't know; I just felt compelled.

And finally, that was what drove me onward, back towards the spot on the path where Ben had disappeared. I forced myself back up the path to the very spot where he'd left it. I peered into the murk. Were I to step off the path, I could lose my way in these dark woods almost immediately. I watched the shadows of the leaves, the fog drift through the trees, and listened to the creak of wood and branches.

Finally, after long minutes of staring into that darkness, I saw what had happened. Ben was lying on the ground, almost directly at my feet, fast asleep. He was already snoring lightly, as if he didn't have a care in the world. In fact, the whole time I was debating whether or not to step off the path, he was within five feet of me, sleeping as peacefully as any child.

I crouched down on the path and looked at him. It was obvious to me that this was utterly natural for him; he didn't look around and worry about where he would sleep, or search frantically for a spot. Perhaps he came back to the same next of straw and leaves on the ground each night, or perhaps he moved from place to place. In the end, it really didn't matter—as the night's events had proved, he was comfortable anywhere you put him.

Ben probably had a long morning as well. I could imagine it—I would not follow him on his route. He probably rose early, and went to talk to other friends on the route back to school, used a public bathroom to wash his hair, brush his teeth, and do his basic grooming. Everyone said that he was well-groomed, but he did all this without a bathroom. He never really looked disheveled, and now I wondered why.

It wasn't as if he was like any other homeless man I'd ever encountered. No alcohol helped him to drift to sleep, no drugs soothed him as the rocks dug into his back. He took no pains or precautions to protect himself from the uncertain events of the night.

Instead, he laid down as unconcerned as your average plant, and seemed to sink, under the weight of sleep, into the darkness of the forest.

I could hardly tell he was there, myself, and I knew where to look.

The passing thought occurred to me that anyone could have killed him here, on many of the nights that he'd slept here. But I couldn't imagine why anyone would. Ben had done nothing to anyone that I could see. All the crimes I had imagined for him in his off-hours were beyond him, or beneath him; he was innocent.

I thought of my typical Friday evening, without Ben. Instead of traveling through every dead and decaying place in the city, I would have probably dropped by an after-hours place for a cocktail with a colleague, or maybe would have treated my assistant to a drink. My dinner would be nearly prepared at home by the time I came in the door. Then, after dinner with Jake, if Jake was going to a friend's house and I had a free evening, I probably would have taken a quick spin through the LakeStrand district, hitting all the chic shops and buying a few things for the house or for our cabin. I might while an hour away in the rare books store, or take in a movie (especially if I was accompanied by a friend), and would probably cap off the evening with a coffee and some dessert out on the town.

Obviously, I rarely really required most of what I bought at these stores. In point of fact, I probably "needed" very little of it—amusingly, I once left all my Friday night purchases in a shopping bag in an upscale LakeStrand store. I didn't notice that I hadn't brought them home until a week later. Fortunately, they were still being held for me by the store when I returned—I wouldn't want a Friday night's work to go to waste.

My evening tonight would have been very different if I had not followed Ben. Ironically, of course, I had somehow expected Ben to do some shopping tonight. And now, I almost wished he had. Right now, I could have desperately used the coffee. But I didn't depart yet. Something kept me there.

For a long hour, I crouched on the ground, watching him sleep. There was no traffic out here, no shoppers, no television, no radio, nothing to disturb we two alone in the woods, the sleeper and the watcher. Instead of seeming smaller—the way I'd expected him to, after I'd seen his after-school routine—he seemed more impressive somehow. He was a real person to me now, reduced from a mystery to just an everyday man who ate in a poor district, spent time sitting on neighborhood stoops in good districts and bad, and slept homeless, outside in the forest.

Looking down at him on the forest floor, I could feel fatigue seep into me—Ben must be even more tired than me. All day long, he'd traveled a circuit of the dispossessed. In all those broken-down places, he was the one who was supposed to bring energy and hope—he was the one people looked to for succor. I hadn't done that—why was I tired?

Instead of letting my new knowledge diminishing my admiration for him, it was quite the opposite. I found that I had a greater respect for him now. Despite the nothing that he possessed, he was somehow larger.

Ben turned in his sleep as I watched; he was like a child—utterly at peace in his sleep. My breath steamed in the night air; it was cold here, this autumn night, but Ben didn't seem to feel it. He was perfectly comfortable here in the forest, in this holy darkness. I felt as if I had invaded his privacy, as if I were on the verge of disrupting the quiet. Perhaps no one else disturbed the forest this late at night. Watching him, I felt at peace too, as if I myself might lie down too. Perhaps I was simply bone-tired.

I stood, unbending my cramped legs, and walked silently back to my car.

15.

A MONTH later, it began to snow. I don't know where Ben Delacruz slept when it snowed. But I soon began to know all about how he spent his days. I wanted more of that peace I'd felt in the woods with him. After all this time, if I reach far enough down inside, it's still there, something renewed at the core of my self. Despite all that has come since, and despite the distance I have traveled, it's still undeniably present, a residue remaining from the month I spent in Ben's company.

Every day, after school, Ben's young friends congregated in an abandoned shed on the school grounds—or, if it was a nice day, outside at the old school yard picnic table. But as I discovered when I joined them, the group that gathered after school wasn't there just to hear stories and commit vandalism. They came together to talk with each other, and to play games, and to work on their studies. Rapidly, I became part of that group.

Ben was nothing like I'd expected. In spending time with him after school, I suppose I had expected to unravel a more straightforward puzzle, to unveil a man who would be more similar to me, who would share a few of my compulsions. At Rockhorn, I'd begun to find people on my level, but for a variety of reasons, I had not gained many friends: there was Mack Demson, of course, a former college professor and a good discussion partner, and there was Catherine Foss, who I was beginning to respect and to admire. Above me, there were obviously Joe Matheson and Bartimus Santos, but after all a long period of not having any close friends, I wanted someone on my level. I suppose I wanted to discover a friend who inwardly shared my penchant for making money and for conservative economic policies. Failing that, I would have settled for a compatriot that I could argue with—someone who was respectably on the left, identifiably a flaming liberal like Mack, and proud of it. I wanted to be able to feel that if our lives had taken different turns, Ben could have taken my path. Ideally, I wanted to discover someone who wasn't so extraordinary after all—someone with whom, under the right circumstances, I could share a round of golf or an evening in the LakeStrand shops. By this point, I wanted a friend who fit a mold—any mold.

On his long walk, of course, Ben had shown me someone who broke molds. And as our acquaintance lengthened, he continued to be hard to pin down. He never gave me that ease of friendship. Instead, he pushed me in directions that had been unfamiliar for so many years that I thought they were unnatural.

Yet after the incident with Laszlo, I had begun to listen to Ben. I can do no better than to say that during the winter season that year, I began to wake up. I was waking from a life that I'd been sleep-walking through, and it's hard to put my finger on exactly why I felt the way I did—a nascent mid-life crisis, perhaps?—but the change was there, indelibly there. Instead of being some charismatic thrill-ride from a politician or a preacher, my time spent becoming closer to Ben was a simple season—only a few weeks long—during which time I found that I was no longer lying as much to myself.

As the days grew darker and colder in the weeks to come, I found the weight of the world lighter, rather than heavier. We were snowed in for a week, yet I hardly seemed to feel it. Ironic, isn't it, that as the darkest part of the year came, I was feeling my life renewed and meaningful once more? Yet instead of the death of the old year in this deep midwinter, I felt that new things were being born, deep under the snow and the ice. Some of them were ideas that had been there for years, my own old ideas and ambitions that I had thought gone forever.

Yet Ben found these things in me. At the risk of sounding trite, I tell you that it was as if Ben saw the true self that I had buried so deep that I'd forgotten it was there.

There were others who were spending increasing time with Ben's little group as well. Recently, Ben had received a special dispensation from Joe Matheson to spend some of his time working with the children at a neighboring school—the Ihme School for disabled and retarded children. Jimmy and Jon's father, Zeb, had committed to help Ben in this endeavor, and was spending an inordinate amount of time retrofitting the shed and the neighboring Chapel building with facilities for the handicapped. After that initial project was complete, Zeb elected to cut in half the hours he'd dedicated to running a very successful construction business so that he could help Ben with Rockhorn Shop curriculum. This made it possible for Ben to increase the time he was spending with the Ihme students.

In fact, every week, a few more of the severely needy Ihme children were joining our little group after school. Despite Ben's work to integrate them into his group, I felt that they were disruptive to the tight-knit unit of Rockhorn children I'd come to know very well. When they first started coming, others felt the same way I did. Sol Tharsen was even so put off by their disabilities that he stopped spending time with the group. In fact, I soon heard negative comments from him about the group experience in general—by all accounts, he had rapidly turned from being an advocate of Ben into a vocal critic.

Obviously my perspective wasn't as negatively colored by the Ihme children—I definitely did not feel it necessary to challenge Ben over the issue. Mostly I simply felt intimidated and overwhelmed by their differences. I didn't know how to interact with them, or how to help them with homework, or even how to converse with them.

Fortunately, I wasn't the only adult who stayed involved. Zeb was committed to the endeavor and remained a calm presence. One of the other Rockhorn mothers—Martha—also continued to be a regular attendee. And because of Ben's involvement with their students, we now had several Ihme faculty members who had drifted into our circle as well. In that little shed on the edge of Rockhorn's football field, there was a real sense of community involvement in working together tutoring children from several schools in the same building. I felt as if being there meant something in the larger picture.

So when Ben asked me to spend my time focusing on the needs of a particular child—one of the children who came in a wheelchair—I said I'd give it a try. Every day, it seemed that this boy named Steven struggled with his basic homework until he was in tears. Someone needed to help him, and Ben had chosen me. At first it was an honor, and then I was confounded by the difficulty of the task he'd given me.

Watching Steven grow increasingly frustrated with his work, I was taken aback. I didn't know how to deal with him; simple matters like his colostomy bag made me acutely uncomfortable. I asked Ben if I was really the right person—besides the obvious disabilities, Steven seemed to have serious difficulties with this work. It was clear that he had a serious learning disability. He also seemed to be grappling with a disproportionate self-hatred and frustration that alarmed me. Every day after school it was the same—every time he failed to figure out a problem, Steven scratched himself deeply down his arm with his pencil, and then rapidly pulled up his sleeve again, concealing the wounds. I'd caught more than one glance at his arm; the flesh was welted and covered with old scabs. It bled when Steven scratched fresh wounds into the skin.

How could I help someone like this? I was no social worker or psychologist; if anything, I was known as the opposite—I was the one that caused people to have breakdowns, not the one to heal them. I mean, not to put too fine a point on it, but I was known at work for having little patience with secretaries who were slow filing papers, and for shrieking at lawyers and clients who caused a miscommunication. I can't tell you how many people I've had fired at my firm, on firm and shaky grounds. There are good reasons that I'd never been a teacher, an advisor, or any type of mentor. My patience couldn't tolerate it; that was why I'd always hired a nanny for Jake, even before his mother left us.

I made all these excuses to Ben, and although he listened to me, he also seemed to be listening to something else, something I couldn't hear. Perhaps he wasn't taking my protestations seriously. So I pulled Ben away from the group, and put it to him more forcefully.

"Ben, you can't be serious," I said. "That boy has problems. Steven isn't just bad at math, he's bad to himself—he hates himself. Something is seriously wrong with him."

"I know," said Ben. "But his disability in itself is a minor issue. Do you know what Steven's real problem is?"

"What?"

"He has no patience—no patience with himself, no patience with anyone else. None whatsoever. That's why you're going to help him."

"Why me? I'd prefer to just stay here—listen to you, work with some of Rockhorn upperclassmen, talk about life, take Jake home afterwards. Not worry about people with no patience. People like that."

"No, you're perfect—you have no patience either. You're a vulture with no patience, and you're the only one who will fully understand this little sparrow hawk who's ripping himself apart. The only way to reach a bird is to send another bird. That's what I did, after all."

And with this inexplicable phrase, Ben turned back to the group. Moments later, he sent Steven over to me. In looking at the boy as a younger version of myself, I found a reservoir of patience and kindness I didn't know was there. At first, Steven and I were both stranded, not knowing what to say to each other, but as my time with him increased, it grew easier. Oddly enough, even Ben's enigmatic stories were beginning to come together for me, in some sort of sensible pattern.

It seemed to me that instead of just random tales, he told stories to make a point about the incidents of that day, and the discussion the group had already begun. This was the context that I'd formerly been missing when I first took my concerns to the Board. The stories he told made more sense when they grew naturally out of the day's events.

There was one conversation—a conversation about time—that I will always remember. It was near the end of his attempts to organize a relationship with the Ihme School—and it came at the most inopportune time imaginable.

The way that Ben had become involved with the Ihme School was the same way he became involved with most of us—informally, through the happy circumstance of being interested in our lives. Apparently for about the same amount of time that Ben had been walking home from Rockhorn with Jake, he'd been also walking to the Ihme School in the morning with one or more of the wheelchair-bound students.

Several weeks ago, the news had come out that the Ihme School was nearly bankrupt. I couldn't see every reason for the place to go bankrupt—it was a special school for children with severe learning and development disabilities, and many of the parents at the school had already used most of their savings to cover the cost of medical care.

Furthermore, it's a lot easier to garner philanthropic interest in your school when you have National Merit scholars who will shake your hand and thank you instead of autistic children who stare blankly through your donors. Due to this chronic shortage of funds and a recent shortfall in their admissions, the school was soon to dissolve.

Ben knew the students—in fact, we all knew them by now through Ben's influence. And we knew how distressed they were at the possibility that their school would disband, their teachers disperse, and the special care and attention they were used to having would disappear entirely. Many of the teachers at Ihme agreed with the students' assessment that it would take many months—possibly years—to recover from this loss of the investment that had been made in helping them to communicate and get along in the world.

For several months, Ben had been promoting the idea that Rockhorn Academy should take over the running of the Ihme School and should undertake to revitalize its programs. He did have some unforeseen advocates at Rockhorn for this idea, as Bartimus Santos' nephew (and namesake) was enrolled there, along with Bill Girus' daughter. Santos' nephew was blind, while Girus' daughter suffered from a particularly hard to control form of epilepsy. There were other supporters on various Committees at Rockhorn as well, but overwhelmingly the Board was opposed to such a risky change in Rockhorn's core mission.

For Ben was not simply seeking to "rescue" a few students—he was seeking to change the entire focus of our school. Instead of simply being an excellent private school, Ben's vision was along with its own nationally-renowned academic programs, Rockhorn could also become a magnet school for special needs children with academic potential.

It would be an uphill struggle. As I pointed out to Ben, everyone knew that the Ihme School had been unprofitable every year of its existence. The school catered to children with the most worrisome maladies: Tourette's Syndrome, autism, deafness combined with blindness or other problems, retardation, and partial or complete paralysis of the limbs. Rockhorn students who encountered these children on their route to school called them the 'Tard kids and other more unsavory epithets that probably aren't worth repeating. As the nicknames testified, these were not very pleasant problems to deal with, and the students afflicted with these problems required an enormous investment in time, services, and money. Personally, I had always wondered why there was so much effort expended on children who were obviously such lost causes.

Of course, the community around us—including many of those well-heeled enough to send their children to Rockhorn—did what we could for those less fortunate. I myself had once contributed towards an Ihme fundraising drive; charitable acts were not beyond us. However, I doubt if anyone other than Ben really cared enough to visit the place. Now that I think of it, that was almost a hallmark of Ben—he went where no one cared. He went to the Ihme School and made the place his own.

As a first step towards saving the Ihme School from extinction, Ben had been attempting to get permission from the Administration to allow several faculty members—including himself—to spend several class periods a week working with the Ihme children. In that way, we could evaluate if it would be possible to integrate some of them into Rockhorn's excellent academic curriculum. Separately, Ben had been pushing Joe Matheson to gain approval for part of the extensive Rockhorn endowment to be used to purchase the Ihme campus and extend the teaching contracts of the teachers, but this was much more of a commitment. It would require a vote of the entire Rockhorn faculty, and consequently would be a much longer-term effort.

Despite my own doubts about the viability of acquiring Ihme or working with these children, I encouraged him to pursue the idea. It was incredible to see that although the idea was rejected multiple times by members of the Board, Ben didn't give up. He didn't accept the easy brush-offs ("Rockhorn isn't designed for that kind of student") or the platitudes ("We really care for them too, but let the State take on the responsibility"). Instead, Ben kept pushing for Rockhorn to become more involved with rescuing Ihme. In fact, I was surprised to discover that on some level he seemed to enjoy conflict—he used it as a way to force people to make the choices he considered right. It was an uncomfortable side to Ben, but a side you couldn't avoid.

Ben kept pushing, but by the end of the semester there was quite a stonewall of resistance. There were continuing rumblings from the Board about Ben over-stepping his boundaries, some of the complaints precipitated by the remarks I'd made before I knew better.

That negative impression of Ben had remained, despite anything I might say now. It was impossible now to take back what I'd said.

Instead, I tried to make up for what I'd done in the past. I managed to arrange a hearing for the idea before a Board Committee that I happened to be a member of—the Long-Term Planning Committee. Because it contained several student members, there was a random element on the Committee. In my experience, this made it possible to get things approved that the Board itself would never have allowed to see the light of day. It was a wild card, but I hoped that the Committee might approve his idea despite the Board. Though if he didn't get the Committee's endorsement though, it was the end of the road. If this seems like a lot of political maneuvering for a small commitment of time from a few teachers—it was. Ben's reputation was just emerging then, and anything out of the ordinary had an uphill battle at Rockhorn. As we all knew too, this initial commitment from Rockhorn faculty was just part of Ben's larger agenda of merging the unhealthy children of Ihme and the healthy children of Rockhorn into one student body—a ludicrous idea, according to many of the well-to-do families who, at some expense, had chosen Rockhorn for their children. Thus, in so many ways, the Committee meeting would be Ben's last chance. If the idea went before the entire Board, I was quite sure that they'd reject it, and Ben's hopes with it.

On the day of the Committee meeting, I got there early, and put a copy of Ben's very well-written proposal on every chair, along with last weeks' minutes and the Proposed Budget for Spring Quarter Activities, which we'd be reviewing at the end of the meeting. Gradually, all the Committee members filtered into the room. I felt it would be a good introduction to the ideas and the presence that Ben brought into a room, so I'd invited some other people as well. I'd even invited Mack Demson, as a representative of the School Administration, to observe our little meeting, and I was hoping that Ben made a positive impression.

There was small talk, and then we sat and waited for Ben to appear. After a quarter of an hour, I changed the agenda. Instead of covering Ben's proposal first, we would cover next quarter's Budget and

Planning process at the beginning. While they began with the Budget, I excused myself and went to find Ben.

At first, I thought I'd let myself into the shed where his group met during the winter months, and find out if anyone had seen Ben. I was sure he wouldn't be in the shed with the children on such an important day. In fact, I wondered what the group would be like without Ben around.

So when I opened the door of the dilapidated shed, I was surprised to see him. After I closed the door, and looked around, it seemed almost like any other day. Ben was holding forth in the corner, talking to three or four students, while others were talking and laughing. Gradually, the small group that Ben was speaking with broke up and moved into the crowd. I approached Ben, but before I could get there, someone else approached him. A young girl, talking as softly and haltingly as Tom.

I watched Ben speak to her for a long moment. I knew the Committee was still waiting, wondering if Ben was going to join them. After a time, I couldn't hold myself back anymore.

"Why are you here? Why—", I interrupted, "What are you doing? You're going to miss this Committee Meeting!" Did he not know that people had spent valuable time putting this together? Perhaps he had forgotten it? Perhaps it had slipped his mind, or it had failed to end up on his calendar?

"Sorry," he said. "I don't wear a watch." Then he returned to his slow conversation with the stuttering girl.

"Ben!" I said loudly. "You should get a watch—you're going to miss this Committee Meeting!"

Instead of immediately answering, Ben looked up at me from his conversation. He stared at me until I was uncomfortable. Then he asked a question.

"You see that book?" He gestured at the things I was holding.

"Which one?" I glanced down at the pile under my arm. There was a legal pad, a scattered assortment of tax notes and forms, a handheld computer, a file with Jake's doctor's records, and my day-planner. I hefted the day planner to my other hand. That was the only true book in the stack. "This one—the planner?"

Ben nodded. "How much time do you have in there?"

"What do you mean 'how much time'?" I opened the book to a random page, scrawled with appointments. "Look—we've got to get going—the Committee—"

Ben reached over and flipped to a page months in the future—the slots were mostly white and unmarked. "How many hours in a week can you choose what you are doing? How many hours are yours to make of as you will?"

"Oh, I don't know," I said. "I've got obligations—I've got some regular running appointments. Some long-term financial management clients. I don't really know. But the Committee, the Committee is waiting—"

Ben tapped the nearly empty page, months in the future. "I know, I know, but I'm trying to make a point here. Look at the book page—"

I didn't look down. "The Committee—" I began.

"No, look," said Ben. "This is important—you have a wealth of time to make of as you will. If you choose to make money with some of these hours, you can do so. If you choose to take a business lunch on one day, and not on another, you can do so. Or if you decide to take a day off, you simply block it on your schedule. You have thirty, forty, sixty hours that you work with, this far out. Am I right? Your time is valuable, but it is also your own, am I right?"

"Yes," I said. I gritted my teeth. "Yes, you are right. I make my own schedule."

"You control your destiny." He nodded at me, as if something had been decided.

Ben gestured at the crowd of children behind him, all talking amongst themselves. "All of these here—they don't make their own schedules—they don't control their lives. In fact, you'd be amazed at how much their parents, their school, their caretakers schedule their time."

"Well, time is money." I glanced at my watch. "And we're wasting it."

Ben shook his head. "Right, all of their parents have money, or they wouldn't be here at Rockhorn. And like you, each one of these parents consider money to be time. They want to invest in the time. They want to spend it wisely."

He pointed at a small group of boys in school uniform, who had lounged across the grass at the edge. "Do you know how much time one of those little guys has? Guess."

"Oh, I don't know," I said. "A couple hours for television, a few before school, after school? Five hours a day free? Three?"

"Well, there are the regulated hours of the school classes—" Ben ticked them off on his fingers "– morning physical education starts at seven o'clock, with first period at eight, and those hours carry through the day until four p.m. Then there's a formal tutor, sometimes a counselor, depending on the home situation, and soccer practice, or la crosse, or rugby, or whatever the sport *de jur* is for the parents this month. In the evenings, the nanny for the younger ones, and a formal tutor for the older ones, and bed at a regulated hour. There are maybe a few minutes before bedtime when Mom or Dad, or more likely the Nanny, reads them a story. If there's something else—a doctor's appointment or something—it comes out of one of the other formal activities." He sighed. "I guess most parents really do think that time is money—they don't waste a penny."

"Oh, you have to be exaggerating a little bit. They have time to hang out here."

"Yes, they do," said Ben. "They have about a half hour after school, before the evening schedule commences. Sometimes an hour. This is their *only* truly free time. Do you know where they choose to spend it?"

"Here, with you."

"You're right. They aren't choosing to spend it anywhere else. Those other people: the Committees, the Boards—" Ben gestured at the administration building, where the Committee meeting was underway. "They'll be fine without me. They've given an hour they had to schedule anyway. They don't need me to be there to have their meeting."

"Actually, Ben, today they do. This is the day you're going to present the Ihme School to them."

He put his hand on my shoulder, as if to calm me. "I know, friend. But it's not such a big deal. Don't worry yourself."

"But what happens if you don't get approval—there won't be any future for the Ihme kids, and there won't be anything else that you can do. You'll be stuck doing this forever."

He raised an eyebrow at me. "Well, and unfortunately, that's not going to be the worst they can do to me. They'll knock this place down, you know. Knock it flat."

"What are you talking about? Don't you want to do more than just talk to children? Don't you want a whole program—something to run, something to be in charge of? A real building, a real classroom—some real power?"

I swear that Ben nearly yawned. It was infuriating. "Oh, it's not so bad doing this—working with children like these, this is real, this is the real world. I don't need something else to be satisfied."

"But, but—" I sputtered. "I think you can make a difference here at Rockhorn. I think you can really have an impact. And I have faith that this could help. This could do it."

"I think I've made my point though. I don't need some other program, some other power to make a difference here."

My head hurt. I sat down on a chair and sighed, resigning myself to explaining to the Committee why Ben had never showed up. I would look like a fool, but Ben would look like an even greater one.

There was a long pause while Ben sat back down and finished the conversation I'd interrupted. Then he sent the girl off and moved across the room. He picked up our coats and came back to where I was sitting on my chair, holding my head in my hands.

"Are you okay?" he said to me at last. He pulled on his coat. "Let's get going. We've got a Committee Meeting to catch."

"I thought we weren't going," I said. "I thought it didn't matter to you."

"Oh, it matters. But they can read the proposal. I'm not in it because I want to be in charge of anything—I wanted you to understand that. But I'll go—you have faith, after all. And the Committee will have faith. And we'll work with the Ihme kids. It'll all be okay." Then he grinned at me.

Despite the fact that we were half an hour late to the meeting, it was a great success. Perhaps the anticipation of Ben's appearance carried us through the discussion, a wave that buoyed us up. The discussion was spirited, and overwhelmingly positive. The central point of contention was not Rockhorn's participation with the Ihme school—surprisingly enough, approving Ben's proposal seemed to be a given—but whether the idea would be funded through our monies or if Ben would have to get additional funds from the Executive Committee. The fact was that Ben's proposal for using Rockhorn faculty to shore up the Ihme program was overwhelmingly accepted by the Committee members. The Committee wanted to avoid complications at Rockhorn that would delay the program from being implemented, but they absolutely seemed to take Ben at his word that this work would be hugely effective in saving the reputation and services of the Ihme school as they began to cut staff. In fact, the Committee seemed to take Ben seriously in all respects.

Or perhaps the presence of Mack stopped the Committee from unilaterally rejecting the idea. Perhaps the Committee wanted to show off their debating skills. I don't know. In any event, Ben had ample time to present his ideas, his plans, and his camping trip. He seemed very relaxed, as if he went from dirty Shop sheds to Budget approval planning meetings every day. After the initial awkwardness of shuffling into the meeting late, kicking snow off our boots, I also found myself relaxing.

Last time I'd been in a meeting with him, I had opposed him, and it had not been a pleasant experience. That time, I had felt as if I were trying to catch a fish that was constantly twisting and turning out of my grasp. It was frustrating. This time, however, I was on Ben's side, and it was an entirely different experience. Even when he was telling the Committee unpleasant truths about Rockhorn student body, he said things in such a way that people had to listen to him. Ben could say nothing wrong. I felt almost as if we were being carried on a warm tide, towards an inevitable landing on a dry shore. When we finally landed on that distant shoreline—when they approved the initial relationship with the Ihme School—I was so assured it was coming that I didn't even bother to glance around the room, to verify that our supporters were all present and accounted for. The moment came, the approval was given, and the meeting concluded rapidly.

Afterwards, I'd arranged for coffee and cookies to be delivered and I had hoped that he would stay for refreshments. That way, he could have met a few more of the adults at the school. But it was not to be. Ben immediately recused himself to go back to the shed with the children, while I found my way over to the Committee secretary and reviewed the notes. The Committee had approved a variety of flexible schedules for Rockhorn faculty who wished to participate in this endeavor, with the caveat that their current classes had to be covered in some fashion and the innovative allowance that Ben and other teachers whose curriculums weren't academically rigorous could hire part-time assistants who did not have to be fully accredited.

Overall, it was a satisfactory compromise.

Afterwards, the topic of conversation on everyone's lips was Ben. Mack nearly collided with me at the coffee table, he was so anxious to talk about him. As he ran into my elbow and jostled my coffee, he was already talking. "That man—I want to meet that man,"

"Which one?" I said dryly. I took a sip of my coffee and pretended to scan the room.

"You know," said Mack. "That Ben Delacruz—he was really something. I should have met him before—he could have really helped my grant work this year."

"Impressed, are you?" I said. "Yeah, Ben has that effect on some people."

A short woman, the Athletics Coordinator, interrupted. "No, I think he has that effect on people in general. We're all pretty interested in what he has to say. You should bring him back. Find something else he needs approved—we'll do it."

I choked on my coffee and spluttered for a moment. When I recovered, I said, "I'll tell him you said so. I certainly will."

"Well, you do that," said the Athletics Coordinator. "He certainly has great ideas on motivating young adults and furthering community involvement!"

"I think his ideas are interesting," said Mack. "But there's more than that—his personality is fascinating. What if I created a position for him? What if I made him a School Ambassador? Gave him a real job, with real responsibilities and real power? Do you think he'd be interested?"

"No," I said. "I don't think he would be."

"Oh, pshaw. Of course he would be," said the Athletics Coordinator.

"Yes, who wouldn't be interested?" said Mack. "What a great position that would be—School Ambassador for Special Funds. Instead of working with disabled children, he could recruit gifted students at the better private elementary schools. He could work with parents, and with funding boards. He'd have some real influence here."

"Yeah—I didn't think of that. He would be great at fund-raising, too," added Athletics. "He could go to grant committees, financial organizations, banks."

I thought back to the conversation with Ben before the meeting. Perhaps this was precisely why he'd told me how he valued his time. Perhaps he saw this coming.

"No," I said politely. "I don't think he'd be interested." Then I moved across the room, leaving them to be entertained by the web of ideas they were spinning.

16.

ONCE THE post-Meeting drinks were over though, Mack wouldn't leave me alone.

As the sun slowly set outside the room, and the hubbub of conversation died away, I found Mack Demson once more beside me, asking about Ben.

"Where did he come from?" Mack asked. "Do you know anything about him?"

"As a matter of fact, I do. I know he sleeps in the woods, he talks to the homeless, he walks to school with retarded children. He—"

"Yeah, yeah, you already told me all about your little spying expedition." Mack waved his hand. "But I don't mean that—what do you know about his classes, his work with the kids? What does he tell them about himself?"

"You know, he's been here on campus for months now. He's no secret. You've been in a Board meeting about him. You've heard all about him, from parents, from children, from me."

"Well, yes," said Mack. "But I've never met him, and I guess I thought he was some kind of—of—yogi, or mystic, muttering weird stuff about drug trips that the stoner kids would get into. You know, from my office window, I'd see him at his picnic table at lunch, and I thought he was just telling them stories."

"He probably was. That's mostly what he does."

"Yes, but I never went out there to hear him. I had no idea he was so—so—vibrant, so alive. He's full of heart. He's a real guy, someone that my parents, my classes could really relate to."

"Yes, that's what I've been trying to tell you about him. He's harmless."

"Harmless?" said Mack. "I doubt it—he could get anyone to do something they'd never thought about. I mean, look at the Committee:

they had expected to turn down his proposal, am I right? And we approved it, after all, am I right?"

"Yes, I suppose you are. Ben is persuasive."

"See, he's not harmless."

"All right," I admitted. "But at least, he's not harmful—"

"Ah, but not harmless." Mack pointed his finger at me. "Anything that spends money is not harmless. But not bad for me, you know. I need to meet him. Talk to him. Spend some quality time. Put it together for us, will you?"

I felt a curious reluctance to introduce Mack to Ben Delacruz—the reluctance had grown with Mack's evident interest. It was as if Ben was my possession, and my knowledge of him was something that would be diminished if I shared it. I'd like to think it was merely an impulse to keep Ben unsullied, but admittedly, it was ultimately selfish in its instincts. I gulped down the dregs of my drink and shook off the feeling.

"I'll see what I can do," I muttered.

"Good, good," Mack rubbed his hands together. "Maybe we can do lunch. So, where is he most of the time lately? Where have you been hiding him?"

Then an older woman tapped Mack's elbow, and he turned to greet her. Soon, he had his day-planner out, and he was scheduling her in, chatting away as if she was an old friend—or at least an endowment grantor with a big checkbook.

Over his shoulder, he glanced at me. He leaned forward and spoke in an undertone to me. "Come on," he muttered. "Come on, get me out of here."

"All right." I shrugged and resigned myself to Mack's enthusiasm. I went to the coat-room and searched for my things and for Mack's coat.

When I came back in, I saw Mack putting away his schedule and bidding good-bye to the older woman. I handed over his coat.

"You really want to meet him?" I asked.

"Yes, yes, of course I do," he said. "Just get me away from here before someone else decides that their idea for selling cookies will change Rockhorn's students forever. Where are we going to find Mr. Delacruz this time of day?"

"Come on, you've known where to find Ben for weeks. Spends most of his time in the classroom, or after school he's at his table, with that group of kids."

"I haven't seen him at the picnic table in a month or more."

"Well, during the winter, over the last month, he's been spending time in some sort of shed near the Back Forty. That's usually where he is this time of year, I guess."

Mack glanced at his watch. "Is he there after school usually?"

"Yes," I admitted.

"Well, I've got the rest of the evening free. It's not too late, is it? He might still be here."

"Yes, he might."

Despite myself, I felt drawn in by Mack. The cloud that had come over me with Mack's interest in Ben faded away. In the end, I could see this going in a positive direction. Finally, there was someone else at my level—an adult, wise in the ways of the world—who saw what I saw in Ben, who could appreciate why I'd felt so drawn to him, someone else who would understand.

We stepped outside. The edge of the sun was disappearing behind the Auditorium. The last rays faded into the snow that covered the campus, giving a thin glow to the heaped drifts. I shivered.

On the way to the building that I'd already started thinking of as Ben's Shed, I told Mack about the group who might still be there with Ben. Despite Ben's descriptions of their schedules, it was the end of the week, after all. I would hope that some of their scheduled activities would be curtailed in favor of some Friday afternoon free time. I described how they worked together, helped each other with their homework, and talked incessantly.

Mack had questions. "What do they talk about? What kinds of kids are they? Would I know any of these kids?" Mack, of course, would know many of the ones in the group on sight or by reputation—his job was to know every troublemaker Rockhorn had ever produced.

So I avoided telling Mack about the backgrounds of the kids in the group. I didn't want him to be prejudiced, as I had been, by the reputations of those he'd meet. It had taken me too long to see past the disreputable reputations and the tarnished history to the silver that Ben had found buried inside Rockhorn dregs. Instead, I told him about their most frequent topic of conversation—Ben's stories— how surreal and disturbing they were at times, yet how realistic they seemed as well. I described the way the children spent hours puzzling out their meanings, and how their terms had become part of their vernacular almost overnight. Mack seemed very interested in Ben's notion of "the real world," and asked me to describe the concept.

When I actually began to tell one of Ben's "real world" stories by way of explanation, Mack interrupted me.

"Wait, wait," he said. "I feel a story coming on here from you." He held up his hand. "It's Friday afternoon—" he checked his watch "— it's after work. The school day is done. It's cold and snowy outside here, and someone is about to tell a story. But something's missing..." he said.

"Oh, really? What would that be?"

"Ah, glad you asked, my dear man—glad you asked. I think we're missing the brandy, wouldn't you say? It's cold, after all."

I played along. "Sure," I said. "We're missing the brandy."

"Ah, but we're not!" said Mack. He reached inside his coat and produced a slim hip flask. He uncorked it, waved it under his nose and took a sip before passing it to me.

I held it critically in my hand. "You carry this around with you all day long?"

"No, of course not. It was waiting in my office all day, behind the bookcase where it always waits, and I grabbed it on my way to this last meeting, hoping that I would be able to waylay you, and maybe grab an after-work Manhattan or something. But brandy will do in a pinch. Come on, drink up!"

I drank, and the hot rush of brandy was a brisk counterpoint to the cold outside.

"So, you were saying?"

"Well, I was about to tell a story," I said. I went on to outline the basics of Ben's story about the young girl who went to the east side of town, and her adventures there, being rescued by the transgender person, and finding her way back home.

"Very dramatic," said Mack, taking another swig from the flask.

"What do you think he meant by it all? Or was it someone he knew, do you think?"

But there wasn't time to ponder the story—we were almost at the Shed. I opened the door with a flourish, expecting to see Ben's students scattered around the room, talking in small groups, laughing and talking as Ben regaled them with another anecdote. It was Friday afternoon after all, and most of the students would have more free time to spend after school.

However, the room was largely empty when I opened the door. In one corner were two boys whom I didn't know well, slightly older stoner-types. They were crouched close to each other, talking or something of the like. Although they glanced nervously over at us as we came into the room, they didn't get to their feet or change their position at all. Even that made them look guilty; I asked them a question and their voices crackled with anxiety as they answered. Then I saw one of them glance at Mack, and I realized that it wasn't everyday that the Dean of Students wanders around the outbuildings late on a Friday afternoon.

I felt embarrassed—I'd told Mack all about the energy of the group, and instead we'd merely surprised two stoners skulking in the corner of a dark room. Under the circumstances, they couldn't help looking guilty. It was as if we'd caught them doing drugs.

The two boys said that Ben and the rest of the group had taken a walk down to the Creek to explore possible spots for an on-campus ice-fishing expedition. They said that Ben had taken a hatchet with him, and a pole. He said he was planning on checking the thickness of the ice and the depth of the water. Maybe they'd light a fire in the firepit before they called it a night.

Mack looked around the empty room and then stepped outside with me. "That's a great idea," he said. "Let's go ice-fishing with him. Come on, it's not too late in the day."

"But we didn't bring anything," I said. "We don't have poles or bait or anything to sit on—we can't sit on the ice."

Mack took another swig from the flask. "Oh, who needs all that stuff? We aren't actually *going* fishing—we're just going to watch a man fish. That's the fun part anyway."

"But we don't know where he is out there in the Back Forty."

"Ah, here, have some." Mack handed me the flask. "Get into the spirit of the evening—all we have to do is to follow Albe Creek downstream. He has to be somewhere along there."

So we went down towards Albe Creek. In our dress shoes, ties, and office overcoats, we pushed our way through light drifts and slipping across spots of ice and sludge. To our left was the cleared expanse of the football field and the soccer field. To the right were more heaped drifts and snow-covered brush. Every now and then, there was a clump of trees—a remainder of the forest that had once covered the acreage the school was built on.

On the way there, we kept sipping from Mack's hip flask and I teased him about his sudden impulse to meet Ben.

"Ah, c'mon," he said. "I don't need to hear about all the reasons I should have met him before now. Tell me about the group that hangs around him—who are these kids? You still haven't told me if I know any of them or not."

So as we approached the Creek, I told Mack about the students who made up the after-school group. Of the ones who Ben had particularly taken under his wing, there was Matt the bully and Sym the coward, along with lonely José, and of course, Moira, who had remained close to Ben ever since that day he had dissuaded the upperclassmen from taking revenge. Mack nodded and listened as I described these characters, but when I came to the rest—my adopted son Jake, out-of-control Jimmy and Jon, Lev with the sticky fingers, and lost little Andy—then he laughed out loud.

At first I thought that he was laughing because I'd painted such a colorful picture of the group. I came to the nick-names, and Mack began laughing even harder. "Stop, stop!" he said.

"They're pretty crazy kids, aren't they?" I said. "Is that what's so funny?"

"No, I just can't believe it," said Mack. "That's where they've been?"

"What do you mean?"

"This bunch can be in a room together?"

"Well, yeah, they're at lunch together nearly everyday, they're in class together with Ben for as many classes as they can get away with—they're there after school with him all the time. Yes, they're always together."

Mack chuckled again, a little more thoughtfully. "How do you think I know these kids in Ben's crowd so well?"

"Well, I can only imagine that it's because they're the ones that should be expelled—" I said dryly. "The dregs of Rockhorn, and they've probably visited your office a lot of times for a lot of things, drugs, soliciting, vandalism—"

"– for fighting."

"Right—for fighting too."

"No, the rest of it went away mostly when I came down hard on it. But they continued to come to my office for fighting—especially Jimmy and Jon." Mack scratched his head, as if he were puzzled. "And now they sit together, happily listening to Mr. Delacruz. No fighting?"

"No, no fighting, usually. But Ben knows about the fighting—that's how they got their nick-names, after all. Thunderheads, Stoneheads, whatever you want to call them."

"It's from a comic book—Thunderheads—I wouldn't let children watch it. Too much blood and gore."

"Well, obviously Ben's seen it. He named them that, from the show."

Mack shook his head. "He has no idea. The show is a perfect description of them. These boys never fought like children—this is ferocious: eye-gouging, nose-busting, bone-crunching street-fighting. Jimmy and Jon—and Andy too—can be very unpleasant characters. I wouldn't want to meet them in a dark alley after they graduate—if they manage to graduate."

"Why haven't they been expelled?"

"Oh, the problem is the same as with that boy Matt you mentioned. Parents are alumni, and they give."

"That shouldn't matter."

Mack held up his hand. "Ah, but it does. You know it does, and there are no two ways around it." He shook his head sorrowfully. "And also the boys are just smart enough to not be caught doing the really bad things. Do you know how many times I've suspended Jimmy and Andy for fighting?"

"No, I don't."

Mack looked down the long snow-covered path ahead of us, to where the sun was setting in the distance. He mumbled to himself, as if he were counting. Then he shook his head and looked back at me, apparently giving up the counting effort.

"Oh, never mind," he said. "Look, I was laughing earlier just because I really can't believe they're happily hanging out together, without bludgeoning each other to death. But it does explain a lot. My work has changed this quarter, and now I see it's because of Ben Delacruz."

"What does this explain? I'm not following you."

"These are the kids I'm not seeing anymore in my office. I wondered where they'd gone, what they were doing with themselves. I gotta tell you, it really sets my mind at ease to know they're with Ben. I thought... I don't know what I'd thought. But it sounds like Ben has really made a difference in their lives. Seems a shame to waste him on the Ihme children."

"What do you mean?"

"He's probably just waiting to get his hands on a real class—not Shop. He's probably just hankering to work with upperclassmen. Instead, now that the Committee has approved it, he's going to be spending a lot of time trying to teach a spastic to talk correctly, and teaching retarded children their alphabet. I mean, come on, do you think that's a good use of someone of Ben's caliber? He should have some real power, some real influence."

"I don't know," I said.

"Oh come on, everyone else who teaches easy classes wants that, why not him?"

"But he humiliated one of the upperclassmen who came to spend time with the group."

"He did?"

"Told him to take his clothes off and clear out, or something like that."

Mack admitted that that was odd. "But still," he said. "Those kids are going to take so much work, I think Ben's wasting his time. Already, the students he has take a disproportionate amount of time and effort. I can tell you this much—if their parents weren't really active alumni, I would have expelled several some time ago. Right now, though, we need the alumni funds, and that's why I want to talk to Ben. We need someone who can lead the school in Spirit, and can take us to the next level, make us really a force to be reckoned with in our state. Perhaps even drive the Athletics program forward—that always produces a higher profile for a school, higher than academics, of course. I think he could be the man for it."

"You have a plan for Ben?"

"Yes—if Ben can do what he's done with the stoners and bullies in our school, just imagine what he could do with the best, the high-achievers, the National Merit scholars, the ones we should be proud-est of. Just imagine, if he spent time with me, what he could learn."

"That's possible," I said warily. Something bothered me about the scenario. "But I'm not sure Ben would do it. After all, he *chose* to spend time with these dregs, instead of picking out the brightest and best. And now he's *choosing* to spend time with the Ihme children."

"Yeah well," sneered Mack. "Who would really choose to spend time with them?"

By this time, we had reached the Creek and were following its frozen course further into the woods. Every now and then the edge of the Creek disappeared under a partial drift and we stumbled into the muddy unfrozen edge, our feet sinking through the slough ice. The Creek wasn't yet frozen solid and my feet were soaked through before long. The wind out here was cold and soon I was shivering.

But we kept following the Creek and sipping from Mack's flask as the evening lengthened. And the movement and the alcohol combined to keep us warm enough. After an hour or more, it became obvious that we weren't going to find Ben easily. Perhaps we'd started too far down in the Back Forty. Perhaps he was further up, closer to campus. We crossed the Creek at the lower footpath bridge and turned around, headed back towards campus as darkness came. The wind threw up a scrim of ice particles and grainy snow off the surface of the Creek. Through that snowy fog, I could see a tiny flicker of fire through the trees—someone had lit a bonfire in the firepit on this cold night. I was beginning to shake from the cold, and the thought of a fire comforted me. I motioned to Mack and he headed in that direction as well.

Unfortunately, we focused on the fire in the distance, and forgot to watch our feet. The wind was blowing very hard by then, and it was hard to see anything. So it only took a moment of lost concentration before Mack and I stumbled through the slough ice and into the Creek. I lunged back towards the bank before sliding down into the water, but a gust of wind caught at Mack. If he hadn't already been mildly drunk, he probably would have been fine. But as it was, he only scrabbled faintly at the frozen cattails on the steep bank before sliding through the thin ice and into the water.

I held onto a clump of frozen brush as the wind continued to blow, and I watched as he clambered onto a piece of thicker ice—something that seemed solid. But the ice floe only carried him deeper into the water before breaking apart also and stranding him in the middle of the Creek.

He came to the surface quickly enough, sputtering and floundering as he smashed a ragged hole in the ice around him. The ice wasn't heavy enough to hold his weight, but it was thick enough to impede him in getting back to the bank. I reached out for him. But he couldn't seem to swim closer to me, even though he was flailing his arms wildly.

Now Mack was moving with the water, being forced downstream with the ice. I watched, but now I could barely see him in the black water. The wind was gusting strongly and from moment to moment his head appeared and disappeared under the water. Through my inebriation, it penetrated that this was a very bad situation.

"Help!" I called towards the fire that we'd seen upstream. I tried to follow Mack along the bank, but the bank on this side was steeper than I'd remembered. I reached out towards him and could feel myself beginning to slip down the icy bank myself. "– God, someone help us! –" Then I stepped back and held on tight.

I shouted again. "Help!"

There wasn't a voice in answer, but I heard brush moving along the streambank, as if someone were forcing their way through. Then vaguely I could see the shape of a man reflected in the black water of the Creek. In the darkness, he was like a solid shadow—something moving into the water, something unreal in the icy night. Fluidly, he pushed into the water, retrieved Mack, and brought him back shivering to our side of the shore.

When I made my way across the frozen ground to them, I saw Mack's rescuer stripping his Mack's sodden coat off of him and feeling for the pulse in his neck.

"What can I do? What should I do?" I said. I didn't even look at him—all of my attention was focused on Mack. The moonlight showed him pale and gray, as white as the snow around us. Chunks of ice were stuck in his hair and on his coat.

Then I looked at the man for the first time. With great relief I saw it was Ben. He grinned at me in recognition.

"We found you," I said stupidly. "But the wind blew us in the water."

"It's easy to get confused by the wind," he said. "The wind blows where it wants. You can hear it, but you can't tell where it's blowing you to, or where it's coming from."

Ben looked as if he were going to continue, but then he just shook his head. He half-lifted Mack and began to haul him to the fire. I did my best to keep up. As we approached the fire, someone brought up a warm sleeping bag and wrapped Mack in it. I saw Jake in the crowd around Ben, and was gratified when he ran towards me, helping to wrap me in another sleeping bag. Soon we were basking in the warmth of a large bonfire. After a time—after I stopped shivering—I saw that some of the older children from the group at school were here, along with some parents who were friendly to Ben.

By way of explanation, Ben didn't mention the brandy flask or my inane remarks at all. "Look at the size of the one I caught in the deep water! Get another sleeping bag for him!" Ben shouted, and then he simply told the group that Mack and I had been on our way to join them, to celebrate the Committee's approval for more camping trips. He said that we had gotten confused in the darkness and the wind, which I suppose was true.

After Zeb helped settle us into the group by the fire, and put hot cocoa in our hands and wrapped sleeping bags around our shoulders, Ben picked up the thread of something that had apparently been underway before we interrupted the fireside conversation.

"I'm almost done people, but there's one more thing I have to say," said Ben. "Let's finish talking about light. Light has come into the world, but men love darkness more—because evil is exposed by light."

I was comfortable in the sleeping bag, and I could feel the fire and the chocolate sending warmth coursing through me, but I was uncomfortable to hear Ben talk like this, especially in front of Mack, who didn't know him from Adam. I looked around, but no one else seemed disturbed by this. Zeb grinned at me and went back to quietly carving something in the firelight.

Yet Ben sounded more mystical than I'd ever heard him be. And for another, I wasn't sure how comfortable I was with the concept of 'evil.' People could be irresponsible, even careless with other people. But 'evil'? The term itself was archaic—something out of a children's story, a fairy tale of 'good and evil,' light and darkness. Who believed in this anymore?

But Ben continued, unperturbed by my cynical glance. "On the other hand... if you do good, you like light, you want people to know about it. Come into the light."

"Yeah, come into the light," echoed several voices around the fire.

There was a pause, and then conversations broke out all around me, with everyone began talking at once. It seemed that we'd come for the end of the story—the concluding stanzas, such as they were. I yawned and moved a little closer to the firelight. Mack, to my right side, had a big grin on his face, and was happily swilling his hot chocolate. On this long winter evening, he had found exactly what he'd wanted. I leaned over to find out how Jake was doing, and found that my son was curled next to me, snugly asleep. Just then it didn't matter that I'd just been knee-deep in icy water or that my feet still shivered with the cold. And right then it didn't matter to me at all that I didn't understand some of what was being said, or that I found it difficult to tutor Steven, or even that I had very little in common with the children in this circle. I looked around at the faces of all the people I knew in the circle of firelight, and felt at peace. I had this moment in common with them. It was the happiest I can remember being in a long, long time.

17.

IN THE end, I suppose I am writing all this down because I still feel some of that peace in myself. Even after all this time, if I reach far enough down inside, it remains there, something renewed at the core of my self. Despite all that took place, despite what was done to him, and my participation in it, those moments with Ben and with his group are still undeniably present in me. And I suppose part of me would like to reclaim—even at this late date—a memory of that night when I first followed him, of that moment in the forest when I left Ben alone to do his strange and solitary work.

Perhaps my first error was being unable to leave him alone. I'd like to think he forced the issue—that by demanding our attention, he was the cause of all of his own difficulties—but somewhere in me, I know that's not the case. He didn't bring it on himself, just as he didn't bring our adulation on himself. He didn't ask anything of us, much less demand it. We brought it all to him, unbidden, good and bad alike.

I admired him for his care for all the unfortunates of the world— God knows I didn't have that kind of altruism in me—but when it came to my own life, I couldn't stomach his solicitude, his kindness. His knowledge of who I was, and who I could be, was too much to bear. This was the root of my frustration with him.

I was drawn to him, it seems, not simply because of who he was, but because of who I wasn't. In truth, perhaps I wasn't the model father, the caring community leader, the perfectly moral businessman I'd like to think I am. We all have our failings—the fact that mine were made public for a time only makes the obvious more painful. But this is what drew me to him. The hollow in myself, that evident lack of purpose, of truth, of peace in myself is what led me to look for fulfillment in him. He never promised such a thing of course, but I looked to him for it. And when it turned out that he couldn't give me what I wanted, I suppose one might say that I reacted badly. In the worst way.

During that period—while Ben was at Rockhorn—I experienced a difficult time, the events of which rapidly became public knowledge. Everyone close to me was affected by it—including my ex-wife, my son Jake, and all of my business and personal associates. I'd venture to guess that my business colleagues and my friends at Jake's school— Joe Matheson, Mack Demson, Meredith among them—were probably affected the most by the circumstances of what happened. That was where the bonds of trust I'd built up over the years were tested the most, and where I had the most to lose.

It all began simply enough, during the previous Fall's Budget Planning sessions. As a senior member of Rockhorn's Executive Committee, and the designated Accountant for the school, I had determined on my own that the school's financial status could be temporarily changed, affording the school certain tax advantages. Because I informed the State Revenue department on a quarterly schedule and the national Revenue Service on a yearly schedule, I was able to change the status of the school for a few quarters and then change it back, profiting both the school and myself. I was also able to award myself the benefit of the extra income that derived from the transactions, and continue to accrue interest for the school. At the time, it made a great deal of sense to me, especially in light of the new Mercedes which came my way through the various transactions I created to reflect the changes of status, and the consequent billings to Rockhorn that came with each of those transactions. Thus, it was most unfortunate that the national Revenue department saw fit to conduct a random audit in the middle of this cycle, and at a time when the profits were accruing at a remarkable pace in my account—unfortunately I had not yet passed on the benefits to the school account. Also unfortunate was the fact that the Revenue department did not see the situation in the same way as I did, although I argued vigorously that I had indeed intended to move large sums back into the school account. It also didn't help that my first lawyer left my case—for moral reasons, he claimed, but I continue to believe that an argument over his fee precipitated his departure. Thus, although my second lawyer submitted numerous briefs, it was all to no avail. The Mercedes was returned to the dealership—at a substantial loss, I might add—and there were other penalties more odious. In fact, I am still in debt to this day, paying the Revenue agents whose obstinate stupidity our tax dollars fund.

That should have been the end of it, but it was merely the beginning. The worst consequence of the entire episode came out of the fact that several years before, the school's inane "open records" policy on the activities of Board members, faculty, and staff (so that the Board could read staff meeting notes and the staff could read our notes) had been gratuitously extended to the school's student media services—the school newspaper, yearbook, and nascent radio station. Although I argued at the time with the Board that this policy might have very negative consequences, I never dreamed that the consequences would be demonstrated on my own life. So now I made new pleas to the Board. I argued that the detailed justification for these types of financial transactions would escape the understanding of juvenile reporters and their equally junior editors. Unfortunately, once again the Board refused to listen to reason. The policy was not waived, despite my extenuating circumstances.

Thus, the entire embarrassing series of events was covered in great detail in the student newspaper and discussed in even greater detail among the faculty and students. After the initial reports of "financial impropriety" appeared in this juvenile rag, the mass market local newspapers and even television stations had *carte blanche* to cover my own personal affairs in sordid detail—they had been reported in an organ of the free press, after all, and now were in the public domain. Unfortunately, even these senior news organizations didn't get it right, skipping over the complex and quite legal transactions that led to the current debacle. They simply focused on the profits I'd accrued—the ones that should have been in the school account, that ended up in mine.

For a matter of weeks I dreaded turning on the television for fear of seeing my own face as the subject of this ongoing investigation. It was not resolved quickly. In fact, I had to face the crowds and the reporters for months after the initial investigation. And the investigation itself seemed to drag on for an interminable time—all during which time my fate, and my son's fate, hung in the balance.

This entire sordid tale is related here not to further explain my actions (my very sensible defense and detailed objections to the criminal proceedings are on file in the courthouse under RW 140256.29), but simply to outline the background for Ben's behavior during the entire incident.

In the first painful weeks when the situation was gradually revealed, it was amazing to me that I still had Ben's support. Why should he not turn away from me—according to all the newspapers, I had stolen from the poor to give to the rich (myself being the chief beneficiary). And I must admit that early on, I appreciated his support. Despite the ongoing press attention, I continued to be drawn to Ben's little group in the late afternoons. Each week, I spent an hour or two there, and often I discussed the situation with him. Ben did his best to put me at ease, but understandably I was a little embarrassed about being seen at the school. For one thing, I detested the unthinking reaction that most members of the faculty had when they saw me. When one is convicted in the court of public opinion, it does not matter if the legal decision is still pending—everyone is judge and jury, and everyone's judgement is transparent on their face. There is the passing glance of recognition, and then a sneer, or a look of shock or horror, and then it is gone. The faces go blank—they all look away, not wanting to meet your eyes, not wanting to acknowledge your existence.

My lawyer told me that it is like being homeless—no one will look you in the eye. For the dispossessed, he didn't tell me why this happens. Perhaps people look away out of embarrassment or perhaps fear of the same happening to them, and I suppose it is the same for my situation. Even people who knew me well didn't seem to want to see my own face anymore. When they glanced at me, they simply chose to see the same wickedly grimacing caricature of me that had been plastered all over the evening news and in every local newspaper. (Some local reporter had managed to snag the worst picture of me, coming out of the courtroom on a cold day and squinting into the sun. In black and white, the expression looks quite malicious). I suppose it is much the same thing as the experience of living on the streets: you are objectified, treated as an object of shame, not as a person.

So it was astonishing to me that I still had Ben's support. Why did he keep defending me? Why didn't he just walk away, like so many of my erstwhile friends did in that time of difficulty? Why didn't he just cast his anchor off, and sail away from Jake and from me? In fact, when it comes to that, why didn't he just leave behind all of Rockhorn's minor obsessions, monetary indulgences and small neuroses? He obviously had more needy people to listen to him on the street. I couldn't understand it.

But since it was there, I even had some faint hope that Ben's acceptance of me could turn the mass of public opinion, redeeming me in the eyes of Rockhorn community. Of course, I wasn't sure how seriously that community took Ben. Perhaps I was overreacting though. In fact probably, no one else at Rockhorn had spent the time I had thinking about Ben, and thinking about the implications of Ben's work. Did anyone even notice when Ben embraced some person, or proclaimed the innocence of an accused person? Perhaps no one else knew, or cared.

This was my working theory, and I determined to test it on Meredith in the morning. She would know how Ben was perceived, and how I was perceived, and if anyone else had put the two together yet. She always had her finger firmly on the pulse of Rockhorn's social heart. In fact, I'm always amazed by Meredith's frank reactions – when you go talk to someone without vested interests, and without the power to change things, to influence events, they are often directly honest. It always amazes me. More often than not, people who don't have any power to influence anything—people like my domestic help, or at Rockhorn, people like Meredith –just tell you what they think is the truth, for better or for worse.

Unfortunately, Meredith's "truth" wasn't one I wanted to hear.

I began by asking a few questions about how Ben was perceived, and tested the waters with some new information.

"You know what I found out recently," I began. "Mr. del Mondo spends a great deal of time outside school with transvestites."

Meredith shuffled the papers she was trying to file. "I don't know what that is," said Meredith. "Trans...?"

"You know," I said. "Transgendered people—perverts on the south side of town."

"Oh those," she said. She smirked at me. Then I swear she almost yawned. "You know, that kind of black mark against him isn't what people have been talking about lately."

"Oh really," I said.

"Nah," she said. She stuffed a stack of papers in a folder and slammed the drawer shut. "They've been talking about you and him spending time together."

I laughed and hoped she'd laugh with me. Then I mocked a look of surprise as I leaned over and spoke to her in *sotto voice*. "You mean— *we've been seen together?*" I chuckled again.

Meredith did not laugh with me. She shuffled more papers and then looked up at me, again without humor. "Look, Mister Accountant," she said. "He's been talking all about maybe you're not guilty until proven innocent, and people are thinking maybe you did it for him—that maybe he helped you skim off the top for the Shop program or something. You know, competing with Catherine Foss, with all her millions."

"Oh." I simply stared at Meredith.

"Look, it's not something to laugh about," she added primly. "You're going to be in trouble."

"I'm already in trouble," I said.

"Yeah, but I mean both of you. He could get in trouble with you. He's going around telling people not to *condemn* you and all that. He could be an accessory, getting a payoff. He could get investigated too—and be in big trouble if it's true."

With a sinking feeling I realized that I was more of a liability right now to Ben than anything he might do in his off hours. He was endangering his whole career here as a teacher, simply by espousing my cause.

What would Ben gain from supporting me? Didn't he realize he was only hurting himself?

Why did he do it? I suppose I should explain all that happened first before delving into the answers to that question. But there is another question that plagues me even before I get to the question of motive— the question of "why" proceeds out of another question, the question of what his overall goal was—what motivated him?

What did Ben himself want? That is the largest puzzle. I would have thought, for example, given his upbringing and evident poverty, that he would have jumped at Catherine Foss' offer to split power with him, to share the endowment with her. (If I understood correctly what I heard in the hallway that day.) But he seemed to care more about small things—about people that none of the rest of us ever bothered about. Laszlo Lindbloom's wasting life and frustrated ambitions, for example. As I saw at the hospital, Ben cared about this man—he did something nearly unexplainable for him. By the same token, he spent all his valuable time outside of the classroom with the same group of failing juvenile drug fiends. And even though the faculty at Rockhorn were beginning to accept him, he did nothing to curry favor with them. Why did he care so little for those who could give him nothing?

Even my son was wise enough to know that he would gain nothing by standing by his father in a moment of misdeed. Jake reverted to his old habits of voicing regrets about being adopted. He came up with such helpful witticisms as "my real parents wouldn't have done such a stupid thing," and "my real parents aren't criminals like you, I bet." I imagine that Jake's reaction largely came out of the fact that because of the incident, he himself had been made a pariah at Rockhorn, and even an outcast among his misfit friends. Like most juvenile afflictions, I knew that it was only temporary and would pass as events passed, but I couldn't help but feel that I'd simply tapped a reservoir of hatred that had been there inside of everyone I knew, including my son—something malevolent that had been there all along. No doubt Jake felt the same sense of an overwhelming flood of rejection; yet I couldn't comfort him. No, not I.

* * *

Ben did that. He comforted both of us. When all the whispers and the muttering were taking place, Ben took me aside and plainly told me "It's what's inside that counts—not what people put on the outside—not what people think of you, what you know is inside you."

Then when Jake was being teased about it, Ben brought it out into the public, defending me directly, despite the absence of any clear facts from the case as of yet. Jake had already been ostracized, so Ben grabbed him that day, and stood him up in front of the crowd. Then he said "Hey, if anyone here has never, and I mean, *never*, screwed up, you can call him a creep. But I want to see a note from your priest, man, saying how you're so perfect." Someone mockingly handed him a slip of paper. "Why thank you," said Ben. "And you know what I'm going to do with that very useful piece of paper?" He took a lighter out of his hip pocket, and burned it in a moment to nothing. Then, parodying the boy who had handed him the note, Ben bowed and gave the handful of ash to Jake. "Very important note, your honor," he said.

The whole crowd laughed. The ice was broken; my son was no longer a pariah. Instead of allowing Jake to become another outskirter excluded from another in-crowd, Ben claimed him as integral to the group. He also—and this is what astonished me anew, every day—he also claimed me.

When I appeared on the playground after school, he did not treat me any different. Despite the fact that my face was a lurid news icon at the moment, he didn't seem to blink at looking me in the eye. He shook my hand every day, greeting me as if nothing had changed. It was almost as if he didn't know—or knowing, didn't care. It seemed to make no difference to him that I might be a criminal. He treated me like a person. In the beginning, this didn't bother me. Perhaps it even helped.

I have always been profoundly grateful to him for these unasked acts of kindness. Yet my feelings towards him didn't change the bald reality of my later actions. It doesn't excuse or explain them; they were two different things entirely. I just happened to get caught up in one thing while the tidal wave of another crashed over me. What I did in the midst of that tidal wave wasn't my fault—it was never my fault.

As I've said, I appreciated Ben's initial support. But later on, as the tide began to turn in my favor, it began to irritate me. Then, as I saw what Ben was about—what he was doing to me, and to my reputation—his actions infuriated me. I suppose the first moment I realized that Ben's support wasn't necessarily benefiting me was when I saw that he was taking pity on me.

It was after school again. I was there to pick up Jake, and to spend time in the only group where I was supported and accepted lately. I had just come from a lengthy meeting with my lawyer, a meeting at which we'd both had to raise our voices to make our points, and I was admittedly weary and short-tempered. I hadn't told Jake I was there yet—instead I was chatting with some upper-classman who had applied for a transfer to Eton—the one and only Eton in England. Then I heard Ben quietly say something in the background. I let my attention drift over to him, even while I was ostensibly listening to the upper-classman. This was what I heard Ben say:

"It's not the nice guy who need support—it's the friendless, the jerk. Those are the people who really need a friend. He has a problem—people don't need to make it worse by spitting on him now."

Then Jake's voice replied. Jake said: "You're saying he has a problem."

"Yeah, I guess I am. Does that bother you?"

Jake pondered for a moment, and then "Well, like you said before with those other guys—he's sick, huh?"

"Yes, I guess that's one way you could put it. He's sick, he needs a doctor."

There was not a doubt in my mind that they were talking about me. Why else would Jake be so serious? What other person's life would Jake analyze and ask questions about? The anger at Ben's sanctimony rose in me like a fountain. I muttered a good-bye to the upperclassman, approached Jake, interrupting their conversation, said a terse farewell to Ben and the group, and took Jake out to the car without another word.

In the car on the way home, I began to realize what Ben had done to me by including me in the group. By supporting me, he had identified me as another misfit, another outcast. I drummed my fingers on the wheel and thought of all the other outcasts he welcomed. The strange group of children who didn't fit in at Rockhorn were the first group. A selection of the socially maladept and uncontrollable. The butt of endless jokes, every one of them, from Tom to Moira. Then there were the household domestics and the day laborers, but perhaps they didn't count, perhaps they were simply part of Ben's ethnicity. But after them were the gangsters in the projects, the ones I'd seen on that long evening—the hard cases with only their weapons and their wits for a means of support. I recalled more damning details now that I was focused, trying to analyze who he welcomed and supported. There were drug-dealers who approached Ben that evening, after all. Young men obviously packing heavy guns and loads of heroin or cocaine. Now, most recently, there were the spitting spastic children of Ihme, all with their rolling eyes and their uncontrollable obscenities, their self-punishment and their laborious speech. These were the types he welcomed.

Belatedly, I then recalled the worst—the nauseating ones. There were also the ones he hugged and comforted in the late evening, the ones who had to drag themselves out of a drug-induced haze to find a sexual partner. The addicted ones who were almost walking corpses, and the ones who cried mascara tears over their infected male skin, looking for a sexual fix.

It came in a blinding moment of clarity—he was trying to drag me down to that level of scum and societal rejection. He thought I was a misfit, and he had decided that I therefore now into fit his group of equally deluded rejects. How dare he make me a misfit—lumping me with all my accomplishments into a bunch of socially maladept children and drug-dependent delinquents? I was no delinquent or common criminal with needle-tracks on his arms—my problem right now was a simple tax difficulty. The next thing he'd want me to do would be to admit some sort of fault or failing. I refused to be dumped into the refuse heap where he'd found the rest of his twisted heroes. How could he equate me with those pariahs? It was enraging; how dare he champion my cause?

18.

IN THE weeks that followed, I tried to avoid spending time around Ben. I suppose I should have liked him for what he did—perhaps he even thought I would—but given his circumstances, and given who he was to the lower tier of students at our school, I felt that it was so clear what he was doing, that there was no way of even confronting him about it, or explaining, much less forgiving him for it. I just couldn't bring myself to be near him any longer. The sad thing was that he simply didn't live in the politics that I lived in—he didn't know about them. Like a child, he just thought that what he was doing was a kindness.

But the reality of the situation is that Ben's simple approach to problems obviously didn't fit my needs, because his solution was to take me down further. A child's faith and a child's ability to forgive and to seek some sort of reconciliation wouldn't get me out of this mess. If one went with the childlike urge to admit fault, with it would come an equally unreasonable urge to give some of this money back. And what was it worth if I had to give something up—if I had to leave Rockhorn Board, or if my business was damaged by all this? Obviously, something like this couldn't be summed up into a child's easy summation of right and wrong. It couldn't be that simple. I would choose a more adult approach to complications.

I think any adult would do it. I would begin by leaning on my friends for favors, regardless of what they thought of me, and then would move on confusing the issues, until no one would be quite sure what had happened, or if I'd actually done anything anyway. The key to everything I did to clear myself was that I did in fact have powerful friends, and there were many ways of putting them to use. With my contacts, there were plenty of ways of complicating the situation, instead of simplifying it.

Of course, there are a few things one loses when you go with the adult way of solving moral problems. You give up the child's genuine feeling of sympathy, of understanding, and even a child's sense of clear forgiveness. What's to forgive when no one can be sure that you really did anything wrong? By the same token, what "goodness" are you reclaiming if the "wrong" that you did can just be equivocated away? It is true, after all, that you do give up a certain amount of moral clarity when you grow up—as adults, after all, we live in worlds of indeterminacy. What's real? What's right? Who cares?

In my class of people, after all, money and good connections go a long way towards mending past misdeeds. Now that I thought of it, I was astonished to realize that in my time with Ben, I'd forgotten how easily forgiveness could be bought. After all, I had not exhausted all my powers of political maneuvering. Although there was talk at the school of forcibly removing me from the Board, and of removing my son from the school, that hadn't happened yet. I considered my options.

Now I suppose in leaving behind Ben's childlike approach to the problem, I was also leaving behind the possibility of eventually getting some honest sympathy from people, and of some sort of genuine forgiveness from others at Rockhorn. The ersatz kind of forgiveness and sympathy would do me just fine—and I could get it without all the emotional entanglements of actually admitting fault, or of actually having to atone for anything. I wanted the easy way out of this mess.

The first thing I did was to get the Board on my side. At the next formal Board meeting, I explained how convoluted the financial plan had become—so complicated that I myself didn't even know if I'd done anything wrong. I produced endless papers and files and pointed to numbers and columns of numbers. Then I begged them for patience and understanding, prevailing upon their good sense and their knowledge of the vagaries of the financial world. In fact, reasonable men and women who seek profits like I did—people like each one of them—could easily become embroiled in a similar series of unfortunate events.

"Bear in mind," I said to them. "Something like this could happen to anyone. It's a complicated situation. And if I did something unethical—something wrong… " I spread my hands out in front of them, concealing nothing, like a supplicant. "…I feel deep regret for the school, and for my reputation, for all of our reputations." I folded my hands and looked up at them all, daring them to contradict me. "But as far as I know, I didn't do anything wrong, and the court case, I believe, will prove this. It was complicated, and I need your support, ladies and gentlemen of the Board. I need you to stand with me." My aim was to level the playing field: it wouldn't be them against me, but all of us who acted as adults against those who didn't understand complicated, adult issues.

Finally, they acquiesced. The tide turned in my direction. The Board agreed to forbear from punitive actions until such a time as the whole situation was resolved and they had the legal opinion in front of them.

Following this victory, minor as it was, I worked with Joe Matheson over the following weeks to make some arrangements prior to my appearance in court. Mack Demson, for some reason, wouldn't go along with the arrangements, although—thank God—he did agree to keep his mouth shut. The arrangements with Joe and the school accounting books allowed me to reasonably claim ignorance in the case of where the school funds would eventually end up—I believe in presidential cases, they call such a gambit "plausible deniability." In any case, I had now for all technical purposes wiped my memory clean. With Joe's help, we could both now deny complicity. Of course, from the funds I'd managed to hide before the Revenue department froze the accounts, I was able to compensate Joe quite well for his assistance—so we both came out ahead. I don't believe the school suffered unreasonably from the events either: what's a few million of the general fund when the school's endowment will eventually be worth a hundred million?

In the evidentiary hearings, I also managed to blame the majority of it on the incompetence of my personal assistant, who a short time afterwards I unceremoniously fired. He'd been mostly ignorant of my activities in Rockhorn area, but for several months he had been lightly skimming the petty cash. And as I've always said, one bad turn deserves another.

* * *

The thaw had come, in more ways than one. All around town, the snows were melting, leaving heaped mounds of frozen sludge that covered the sidewalks and deep puddles of muddy ice in the roads. I had to get out of town.

Jake would be with his mother for the holidays, and so I was free for the duration. I contrived a trip to one of those palmy climes, for a conference and golf. Fortunately, I could bill the conference to business, but still play the requisite holes each day. Because Joe had been such a help to me in resolving this situation, I asked if he would like to join me for a few days on the firm's dime. The first day there, we toasted our victory over the forces of financial propriety with a celebratory round of golf.

That is how we came to be discussing a new position for me on the fifth hole, just after I'd neatly placed myself in the middle of a large sand trap. Even with my tarnished reputation, Joe seemed to feel that I could help the school in a practical way.

"Besides," said Joe. "You should do a good turn for the school—something hands-on—as a way of demonstrating your good intentions to the Board." Reading between the lines, Joe was saying that I should make up to the Board for the various headaches that had been caused by my ineptitude or malfeasance.

"What do you have in mind?" I asked cautiously.

"A business class," said Joe. "I want you to teach a business class to graduating students. Something practical, but memorable."

"For the senior students?"

"Kind of a senior project—some hands-on training for the real world, as only you could provide."

I chuckled hollowly and took an awkward swing at my ball. "You don't think I'd be a liability? You don't think it'll feel strange for the kids—knowing my recent history?"

"Ah, no," said Joe. "Come on—these kids are used to their parents, who aren't saints, let me tell you. You'll do fine—just keep your head up, and be proud of the good work you do."

"Well, I might be able to," I said. "I could teach something about how financial statements work, and how to bill a client, and so forth. How much time would it take, and what do you want to accomplish? I mean, what would my goals be?"

"Well, I think the key here is not really the classroom work, but the work you do beyond the classroom," said Joe. "I think that might help prove who you are to the Board too—I want a real-world experience. Not just the books. See, I want us to think of it in terms of some preparation for life. Bring in businessmen who are familiar with Rockhorn, people like Norman Foss and Martin Waite, to speak to them. You know, prepare our students a little bit for an MBA someday—make them remember us when they graduate from business school and run Fortune 500 companies." (It was a continuing source of frustration for Joe, for Mack and for the Alumni Committee, that several of our graduates had gone on to Ivy League schools, and subsequently succeeded brilliantly in business, but had never thought to compensate Rockhorn for their success. Apparently, they sent all their money to their colleges and MBA programs—not their old junior and senior high school.)

"I don't know." I wasn't so sure this would work—he was talking about me running a miniature business school. "What do you mean by 'the work outside the classroom'?"

"Business—real world profits and all," said Joe. "I want them to have the real experience of running a business, of being entrepreneurs." Joe also had ideas about what kind of entrepreneurial venture he wanted me to help fund, and how he felt it could best succeed. "You know how public schools get Title IX and Title IV funds, and they also get funding from companies to allow them to promote different snack foods and drinks on campus?"

"Oh yes—that's been hugely controversial. I'm glad we've avoided it."

"Well, yes," said Joe. He took a leisurely swing at his ball, and struck it far into the greensward around the sixth hole. "I'm glad we don't have to worry about those issues. But there's another side to the coin on this one. And it's related to the snack issue. We have all of these Ihme students now—and they traditionally have had some sort of training. Not just academic training, but vocational training."

"Vocational training—but other than Shop, Rockhorn isn't set up for that."

"Right—so we're stuck with the expensive and money-losing operations that are already going over on the Ihme campus."

"I think I can see where you're headed."

"Of course you do," said Joe. "You have your upperclassmen, your Rockhorn seniors who have taken the business class run the business, and then you have the Ihme kids as your labor. You end up training them in food services, and we've accomplished our goal. And made a bit of a profit at the same time."

I was still stuck in the sand. "So, I'm still not clear on what we're selling."

"Well, over the years I've let neighborhood groups set up a little snack bar in the back by the bleachers—bake sale goods, some soda pop cans, coffee, things like that. But I think there's a real need there— you could fill that gap."

"You want me to set up a card table and have the wheelchair students sell cookies? This is why you asked me to teach at Rockhorn?"

Joe looked at me significantly. "No, I asked you to teach because I thought you needed it."

"Right, right, I know," I waved Joe off and scraped at my ball with my foot. "But besides that—selling cookies and such?"

"I think it would meet a real need. You would bring together both Rockhorn kids and the Ihme kids, and teach them both a little about each other. And it's so straight-forward that I think you'd be a popular thinker in no time. This is a real world experience, building up business experience."

"Real experience," I sneered. I laughed and took a swing at my ball, burying it deeper in the trap. "It's a little protected bubble of experience. Selling cookies to their friends."

"But don't think of it just in terms of what you'd sell—I mean, look at Proctor & Gamble, or GE—their wares aren't very appealing on the surface, but they're profitable. And besides, some of these Ihme kids really need the work experience, and you could provide it. You should think of it as a compassionate act."

Joe's idea was beginning to intrigue me. After what I'd been through recently, running a business in a microcosm, in a place where I had some control over the market forces—this was somehow appealing.

"Well," I said. "If it's a real world business, tell me how we'd get the funds to start the business? We don't want to start under-capitalized."

"Ah, now you're talking," said Joe. "Here's the plan. I would propose the concept at the next Board meeting—once the Board indicates that it's a good idea, you volunteer for it without pay, thereby earning yourself brownie points for taking an unpaid 'volunteer' position, and then I propose a stipend, and a fund for the project. Once the Board has approved the concept, they won't hedge too long before approving the fund."

I looked around at the empty golf course, checking if there were any other golfers in range. I gestured at the ball, which was now nearly buried in the sand.

"I don't mind," said Joe.

I reached down and picked up the ball. I lifted it out of the trap and placed it on the side of the sand nearest to the hole. I was on the green once more. "Okay," I said. "So who gets the money we make?"

Joe and I had one more day in the palm-strewn golf paradise. Although we'd spent a late night in the hotel bar the night before, the next day we were up bright and early to catch as much golf as we could before we had to fly home that evening.

Once we were back on the links, the conversation soon got back into the well-worn track of Rockhorn volunteer project. The concept was increasingly attractive to me. I could continue to spend time around Jake during the day, but I would do it in a venue that demonstrated my strengths in business, rather than by doing useless things like listening to stories and tutoring drug-addled teens. But if I was going to do it, I wanted to do the business class with some panache.

"So," I said. "What about a facility? If it's just a card table with cookies and pop, I don't want anything to do with it."

"Trust me on this," responded Joe. "I'm miles ahead of you. Ben and I were thinking that we could get an entirely new building created specifically for this."

"Really? Ben's involved?"

"Oh, it was just something he helped me think up. It's a great dream, isn't it? Five stories tall—with a new cooking range, refrigerator, cash register, and all the rest. Maybe even a lecture hall on the second floor, just for you and your guest speakers. All of it wheelchair-accessible. You know what the kicker is? At the top of the building, we'll put your name. You'll have to contribute a little for it—maybe we'll get that out of the same funds you helped me out with— but you'll have a building named after you at Rockhorn Academy."

"That does sound nice," I said. "But I'm not going to pay for most of that building, you know. This was your idea. Where is the majority of the money going to come from? You already have a special fund earmarked for projects with me?"

"No, I don't need to earmark anything. I was just thinking that we'd just take it out of the Argurion Grant. I mean, there's 30 million dollars there. They don't need it all for bookshelves."

"But isn't that money already allocated to the Permanent Collections and Library improvements? Aren't there legal constraints on it?"

"Ah, but I do have some influence over the Grant process," said Joe. "Sure, I've worked with the family to make sure that there are some constraints on how the money can be spent at Rockhorn—what can be built, and so forth. But those constraints were added by me and by Catherine Foss. I added them, and I can change them. And a worthy volunteer project like this gives me an opening to slip some other changes into the allocation of the money."

I swung at my ball, punching it over a hillock and onto the green at the third hole. "So this is all part of a scheme, isn't it? Me too, I'm just part of the plan."

"Well, yes," he said. He walked a few yards towards his distant ball. "But it's a pretty good plan. I figured I'd take a million or so out of the Argurion Grant, get new lights for the field, new goalposts and audience seating, and throw in this new vocational training building— your idea, remember, it was your idea—and on top of the vocational building I'd put in a genuine announcer's box. On the ground level would be the coffee and snack facility. I need you to have this brilliant idea though to train the Ihme students: in order to take the funds out, I need a worthy volunteer project that needs funding. With a worthy volunteer—you."

"I don't know, Joe—football and food services seems a bit far from the Library Permanent Collections and such. Doesn't Catherine Foss have to approve it?"

"Well, sure she does," sputtered Joe. He pointed his golf club at me.

"But in point of fact, the Argurion Grant will go nowhere without my approval. Ultimately, I have to approve all gifts to the school—and Catherine knows this. She'll greenlight a few changes in the fund allocation if I ask her to. And I'm going to ask her to add this one, understand?"

"If you say so."

"Well, I do." Joe turned back to face me. "I'm going to add this. I can't see how Catherine Foss would object to only a million or so, for improvements to the physical plant. After all, it would lift the value of the whole school. I figure it would bring more people to her Library. She can justify it to the family somehow. Hell, we'll just slip the new football lights and the building into the fine print when the Grant is signed."

I putted into the fourth hole, and retrieved my ball. After Joe was done, we moved on to the fairway at the fifth hole. This game was going so much more smoothly than the previous day's; the warm sun only helped improve our mood. Under such balmy skies, it seemed a shame to bring up Catherine Foss, but there was no way around it.

"She doesn't have any idea about this plan?" I asked.

"Oh, yes," said Joe. "She's aware of it all, and she knows that I will never be able to sell it to the Argurion family, and to the Board, without a volunteer instructional project to fund. If I were to just propose new football lights, they'd go over like a ton of lead bricks. And even if I walk in with you in my pocket, she's going to have a counter-proposal of what we can do with the snack bar thing."

Joe sent his ball soaring down the fairway. I sent my ball after his, and then asked another question as we dragged the club-bag down the green.

"And what's her counter-proposal?"

"Oh, she thinks that if we have new volunteer projects that they should use existing structures. According to her, we should put a couple of thousand into re-furbishing some of the old outbuildings instead of spending millions on new ones. And that way, she could kill the new seats and the lighting. She's just too high-minded to see the benefits of lighting a football game correctly."

"Well, we do have some old buildings out there."

Joe reached his ball and looked ahead at the sixth hole. This was the one where I'd run into the sand trap yesterday. He selected a solid eight-iron from the bag and took a swing.

"Yes," he said after his swing. "There are two old buildings, but I wouldn't feel comfortable using either one as a snack-bar."

"Why not?"

Joe pointed the handle of his club on either side of the golf green. "There's the one on the right side of the field, and the one on the left. The one on the right side is that Chapel building, and it's used by some people like the Ihme kids and others."

"What's this Chapel?" I said cautiously.

Joe coughed, as if he were embarrassed. "Well, once upon a time people at Rockhorn went there to worship."

"Worship—as in church?"

"Yes, believe it or not," he said. Joe leaned on his club and looked down at the ground. Then he looked up at me again, as if a thought had just occurred to him. "You know, it's still kept open though. I think Laszlo used to keep it unlocked in the evenings, because some of our migrant workers—the ones who clean up the football field after games and pick fruit in the summer—they like to go in there for some reason. I guess I'm just not comfortable selling things out of there." He laughed nervously. "Superstitious, I guess."

I laughed. "Well, it's just used by the laborers and the Ihme kids then. No big deal."

Joe coughed again. "Well, anyway. It just kind of doesn't seem right to me to use it for this. It's one of the oldest places on campus. I know no one uses it now—but I don't know, it just wouldn't feel right."

"So what's the other building?" I pointed my club at the left side of the green, where the imaginary building from Rockhorn stood.

"That's the Shed. It's used from time to time by the kids from the Ihme School as well. There are bathrooms in there that someone worked on, so they're handicapped accessible. As we move towards acquiring Ihme, we'll need those facilities to be compliant with federal law. That way we get all the money for the field—the lights and all—and we don't have to contend with putting any new facilities."

"But did Rockhorn pay for those facilities?"

"Well, no," admitted Joe. "Zeb and Ben put them on their own expense, but we can certainly take advantage of them to claim compliance." Joe waved his hand. "Anyway—you don't need to worry about it. Right now, I'm just hoping the homeless aren't using the building—that would be a problem."

I laughed and took a swing at my ball, burying it once more in the sand trap at the sixth hole. "Well, you've already got a homeless problem. You've got Ben teaching at Rockhorn. As near as I can tell, he's homeless."

I glanced up at Joe, and saw his face blanch.

"What?" I said. "Is Ben Delacruz sleeping in that Shed? And you let him? Is that it?"

Joe chuckled uncomfortably. "Well, maybe," he said. "But I don't really think it's anyone's business where he sleeps. I just wouldn't feel comfortable taking those buildings away from Ben, if you know what I mean."

"So neither building will work for you, is that right?"

Joe hit his ball into the sand trap too, and then as I dug mine deeper into the grit, he just as easily hit his out of the trap and into the hole.

"Well, they won't work because they don't get me what I want," he said. "If you end up using another building for the snack sales, then what's the point in building a whole new vocational facility? What's the point in adding a whole line item? Then, all we need is a couple of thousand for re-furbishing—instead of a million for a better football program. She has her own ideas about the Argurion Grant, but if we stick to our guns, I expect to win the money I want."

I surreptitiously reached down and lifted my ball out of the trap a second time. At that moment, my ankle twisted under me in the soft sand, and I landed on my rear in the trap.

Joe laughed and reached down to help me. "Serves you right," he laughed. "Touching a ball instead of hitting it."

When he pulled me up, I realized that I couldn't stand easily on my ankle. It was really quite sore, but I hobbled on to finish the sixth hole, and there we stopped.

"You know," I said. "I really don't want to limp around the rest of the course. Why don't we just stop here?"

"Fine with me," said Joe. So instead of going back to the clubhouse or getting a cart, we just sat on the grass. On this side of the green, few people could see us. We put our clubs down and lay back, gazing up at the balmy sky. I waited for my ankle to heal a little, to the point where we could walk back to the clubhouse. In the meantime, we watched the beautiful blue sky and we watched other golf games pass us by. We talked.

The idea of the business class and the building with my name on it was becoming more and more appealing. It was definitely something that would improve my standing in the eyes of Rockhorn. Joe told me about other things at the Academy that would be changing as well in the new term. Evidently, while I'd been dealing with the stupidity of Revenue service agents, Ben had been having some remarkable success in getting Rockhorn establishment to embrace the Ihme School's needs.

"I was skeptical at first," said Joe. "But then Sol Tharsen came in and walked through the state forms for the kids from Ihme. He showed me how much money each of those special students brings with them. Then I was sold on the idea. Hook, line, and sinker."

"What do you mean?"

"Well, as you know, each child in our charter system brings with them a certain amount of funding, provided by our taxes."

"Right. And Rockhorn gets those funds if we accept a child."

"Correct," said Joe. "And for most of our students it's kind of a piddling amount. That's why we charge so much more for Rockhorn—we have an excellent program, and the state covers a tiny amount of it.

"However, if you happen to have a disabled child of some sort, according to the Office of the Superintendent of Public Instruction, you get a much larger allotment. One of these Ihme children would be worth nearly twice or three times as much to us as a regularly matriculated student. These children are worth gold!"

"So you've decided to work with the Ihme School because the children bring you more money?"

"Oh, that was decided months ago—back when you first got in trouble with the Feds. Six weeks ago, while you were staying away from Board meetings because you still didn't have this thing worked out, I pushed through the first approvals for Rockhorn to acquire Ihme. We've already made an initial investment in them—to keep their heads above water—and I've been working with Ben to coordinate the members of our faculty who are working there part-time. He's there nearly three-quarters time now."

"I had no idea."

"Oh yes," said Joe. "It's been a great success. And you know what's even better about this entire arrangement? Rockhorn has been under the gun in the last few years—ever since the I.D.E.A. was passed by Congress."

"Eye-Dee-Ee-Yay?"

"The Individuals with Disabilities Education Act. Basically, it says that if you're a school, and you get a qualified applicant, you have to provide services. No ifs, ands, or buts. Now that's a problem for Rockhorn—we aren't going to retrofit our classic building with those ugly handicapped access ramps or add Braille markers all over those brass plaques that date back to the turn of the century. I mean, what were they thinking making these rules apply to private schools with our kind of heritage to protect?"

"But Joe, back to the story—what about the Ihme School and this IDEA thing?"

"Right." Joe sighed. "Well, we've had to put up with various fines, and with the feds threatening to close us down for failing to comply with their rules for disabled children—not that we've ever had any disabled students. But now that the Ihme School will be a part of Rockhorn, we can simply send any child who has a disability over there—and that part of our campus is now in full compliance. They have all the little things that those kids need—the ramps and wheelchair lifts and such—and those students will still get full access to our programs, our faculty, and our Library."

"Really?"

"You bet—within a few months, the Ihme School will just be another name for Rockhorn's South Facility."

Joe went on to tell me the rest of the news from the Board meetings. Apparently, there had been many sweeping changes while I'd been out of action. The Argurion grant had been approved to move forward, and a ceremonial "Granting Celebration" would be held this spring, complete with a philanthropic ball. Laszlo had returned from the hospital, and he would soon be coming back as full-time Shop teacher. Joe said that his convalescence seemed to have been therapeutic, because his attitude and his health had improved remarkably. Laszlo would be keeping Zeb on as his assistant, and Ben would be moving to some sort of expanded position. It sounded as though Mack had big plans for Ben. At the next Board Meeting, a new outreach and fundraising program would be announced, and at the center of the program would be Ben, shepherding wealthy patrons into Rockhorn's Endowment Campaign. Although he didn't know it yet, his new job would be fleecing alumni of their charitable donations.

"A lot has changed since you went on your unofficial 'sabbatical'," said Joe. "But we've just got to have you back in commission so we can make sure the books all balance out in the end."

I laughed. "I don't know, Joe," I said. "In my absence you've managed to double the size of the campus, solidify your endowment base, find new funding sources and incorporate them into the charter of the school. What do you need a Treasurer for?"

"No, no," Joe protested. "We really need you analyzing the money again—just try not to cook the books this time."

"Sounds like you've been doing just fine without an accounting firm or an auditor. Besides, it might not look so good for me to be doing Rockhorn's books again so soon. Maybe I should take a break—I can recommend another firm."

"I can't tell you how much I've missed having you around," said Joe. "We need you back at Rockhorn—and if there are any doubters at the next morning, I'll be happy to set them straight for you."

It was good to hear this assurance of support from Joe, but going back to Rockhorn seemed unreal as a warm tropical breeze blew over the golf course. I looked around at the bright green grass and the tall palm trees. Under a summery setting sun, it was hard to imagine the thick gray clouds of winter at home. It was wonderful to be here, instead of stumbling through a snowdrift on the way through the parking lot, or waiting impatiently for a tardy client to show up for a meeting, or helping slow, stupid Steven solve a math problem in his wheelchair.

When we returned though, it was good to know that I was home free. Now both Joe and I were a little more beholden to each other than we were before. Our golf dates were closer together now, so perhaps out of all of this, I have at least proved that money can buy friendship, and at the time I was quite sure that this particular friend-ship with Joe would obviously be more useful to me in the long term than Ben's would ever have been.

The light was going, and down the way—near the end of the long green—we could see other golfers packing it in. Outside the course, on the road, we could see the headlights of evening commuters, on their way home. It was refreshing to watch other people come home from work.

Soon we'd retire to the bar for a few tropical drinks before we got on the plane for home. Joe and I were definitely enjoying being here—and now that I had the entrepreneurial venture to anticipate, I was also looking forward to going back home. We had a lot to do.

19.

I RETURNED to the most ironic situation I could have conceived. Upon my return, the department of Revenue and the government were both grasping at straws, unable to prosecute. Apparently, they couldn't find where the purportedly embezzled funds were. Soon, I would be free to go back to my old life and to the clients that remained in my portfolio. However, the morning after my return the newspaper did not proclaim my victory. The headlines on Page 1 of the Education section in every local paper—and one National newspaper as well—trumpeted the achievements of a singular teacher named Ben Delacruz.

It seems that while I'd been gone, Ben's work helping disabled children from the Ihme School participate in some of Rockhorn's academically rigorous programs had garnered some success. Evidently, several of the children who worked under Ben's supervision had received extraordinarily high scores in the National achievement rankings. In fact, they had out-performed the majority of Rockhorn's finest graduating seniors. Some of these children had formerly thought that they'd be lucky to have state assistance for the rest of their lives. Now they were now receiving letters of interest from prestigious universities. To the Ihme staff who had known them for years, it was as close to a miracle as they could expect.

The newspapers caught wind of the test scores because there was an actual congratulatory telegram from the National Merit Scholars Society. The news spread like wildfire through the Valley. Even now, I couldn't get through to Joe Matheson's office to find out his perspective. Meredith told me that he'd been besieged with phone calls from media publications ever since we returned. Next week, in fact, he was supposed to do a cover story with Ben for a national magazine.

The same rabid media coverage that had consumed my world was now being applied to Ben's activities—only this time, their spotlight was aimed in a positive direction. Now that I had concluded my struggle, it hardly seemed fair.

Furthermore, because of my recent difficulties, I was getting none of the credit for helping Ben gain approval for Rockhorn's relationship with the Ihme School. Everyone seemed to forget that it was the Committee which I chaired that had given the first green light for Ben's activities with these children. In fact, I'd like to think that without my involvement, none of this would have happened. No one other than Ben himself acknowledged this fact though. It was a bitter pill to swallow.

When I finally did manage to reach Joe, all he wanted to talk about were the headlines he was posting on the wall of his office. This week's favorite ones included: "Rockhorn Success Story" (in a regional magazine), "Special Needs = Special Achievement" (a follow-up story in the local paper) and "Revival of the Private School in America" (an editorial in a nationally-ranked paper). But today's press clippings had yet to top Joe's all-time favorite, posted on his office door, the one entitled simply "Rockhorn Academy: The Future of American Education?"

I wasn't interested in hearing the headlines though. I had called Joe to discuss the fact that people around Rockhorn continued to look away from me, instead of looking me in the eye. Although I'd resolved my situation, and would soon be back in good standing insofar as the legal community was concerned, I continued to be treated as an outsider at Rockhorn, and by many of my business clientele. Despite the coming legal opinion, my business had suffered. I made many calls that were never returned. To be blunt, I was being left out in the cold.

Joe made the appropriate sounds of sympathy, but I didn't feel he was really listening. He pointed out that a few properly placed financial grants to different departments and individuals within Rockhorn community could go a long way to restoring my standing there. Of course, I would have to wait until the interest built back up in the account before I could give on the level necessary to restore some measure of respect and friendship from other people here at the school.

I knew that there would be a lingering taint around me for some time—rumors and the like—but what could anyone do now that the Revenue department and the government prosecutors had stepped away from the case? And furthermore, why should anyone care? I'd done all the right things—all the adult things—but despite them, I was being ostracized.

After I concluded my short and unsatisfying conversation with Joe, I spent some time considering how involved I wished to stay with Rockhorn Academy. The Academy had been one of my largest and most lucrative clients, but much of my pleasure at being on the school campus was now sullied by my memories of Ben's strange little group, and by my experience of having gone through Rockhorn's own little media mill.

And Rockhorn was changing before my eyes. Instead of the tight little enclave of privilege, respect, and entitlement that I had enjoyed on first bringing Jake to the campus, I found a variety of other influences now at work there. Essentially, Ben's vision of Rockhorn as a magnet school for children with problems had now been achieved, and I didn't like the results at all.

Instead of a generally Caucasian campus with the children of the Valley's elite strolling happily in all directions, there were now all sorts of colors, types, and problems to be seen in our halls. The best place we could create for our children had been polluted by all kinds of bizarre additions. Everything we'd been trying to escape was now here with us. Children with severe physical difficulties and special requirements were making demands on Rockhorn faculty and staff. And instead of keeping to its own heritage and standards of behavior, Rockhorn was bending and changing in every direction to accommodate them.

Although I suppose I should be ashamed to admit it, I'd guess that many of the long-term faculty felt this way now when they walked down the hallowed halls of our school: instead of polite seniors in letterman jackets and well-groomed underclassmen, you had to contend with a variety of languages and dress, not to mention an assortment of wheelchairs. Mechanical voices emanated from several children who could not talk normally, and one was lucky to avoid the occasional pool of spittle or other unmentionables on the marble floors. In short, all sorts of human detritus were landing on our shores. The experience disgusted me. As I saw it, there was one person to blame for all of these changes: Ben Delacruz.

When I confidentially mentioned my impressions to other faculty and staff at Rockhorn, most of them gave me the wide-eyed stare typical of the confronted liberal with a full heart and an empty head. They simply did not respond in any useful way.

However, I did find a kindred spirit in one other person at Rockhorn.

Several weeks after my return, I ran into Catherine Foss in a coffee shop. Just as Joe had intimated, Catherine Foss had her own ideas about the Library endowment and the relevance of vocational training to the future of Rockhorn, and was not shy about letting me know she wanted to share them.

"Ah, Mr.… it's good to see you," she said as she caught sight of me. Obviously, she'd forgotten my name.

"Miss Foss," I said cordially enough. "How are you?"

"Oh, I'm doing fine—it's been hard dealing with this Ihme merger though." She waved her hands in frazzled way. "It's so much extra work."

"Yes, I can imagine," I said. "I don't know if this merger is a good thing for Rockhorn."

"Well, I've had my doubts all along. Rockhorn isn't set up to help these kind of children."

"Really?" I exclaimed, happy to finally find someone who agreed with me. "I'm curious then why the deal was made."

"Oh, Ben did it," Catherine spit out. "He has these grandiose ideas."

"Ben did all this? Isn't a deal like this a bit beyond his charter?"

Catherine picked her coffee up from the barista and smiled grimly at me. "Oh yes. Ben's definitely reached beyond his place," she said. "He needs to be taken down a notch."

"Grande Latte! Triple-shot!" the barista called, and I picked up my coffee as well.

"I'm glad to see you. Shall we sit together?" Catherine gestured at a small table near the window. "I hear you'll be part-time at Rockhorn soon. It sounds like we have a lot to discuss."

* * *

So it was that I heard Catherine Foss' counter-proposal well before the Board meeting at which all of the Argurion Grant money was divided. She didn't waste any time jumping into the topic.

"I'm glad I ran into you," she said. "I'm aware that Joe Matheson is floating some sort of a proposal involving ideas that you have in helping our food service to be more profitable, and also provide some vocational training. And although it's laudable, I'm not sure that you're headed in the right direction."

"Oh really?"

"Well, as I understand it, your plans include building a brand-new structure that would include a vocational kitchen. I believe you've even proposed that the funds from the Argurion Grant be used—the fund that I will supervise."

She took the lid off her coffee, and steam rose, clouding my glasses.

"Well, put that bluntly, I suppose that's close to the mark," I said.

She began to stir honey into her coffee. There was a long pause. "It's a delicate subject, of course," she said finally.

"What's that?"

"How far to go in accommodating the disabled. I mean, no one really wants to be on the record as turning down services for children like these, do they now?"

"No, I suppose not."

"I for one am in no wise suggesting that we do such a thing. But it does seem important to note that the Ihme children already have two buildings they use. The buildings have facilities for them, and essentially they use them as a base from which to access all of Rockhorn's programs. I believe they have some sort of an after-school homework group there as well."

"You're talking about the shed and that other building."

"Yes. That other one is known as the Chapel."

"Well, but…" I hesitated. "If they're already being used, I'm not sure I can simply take them over."

"Ah, but ask yourself who are they being used by?"

"Right," I said slowly. She seemed to have this all put together already. Finally, I spoke up again. "The person who is mostly using them is Ben, and his after-school group of students. He uses them everyday."

"You're correct. And goody for him, using those buildings to help those poor children." Catherine put her hands together in a little half-mockery of applause.

She took a long drink of her coffee before she continued speaking. "And what do you think his role at Rockhorn will be in the future?"

"I would imagine he'll still be here—I haven't heard he's leaving," I said cautiously. "Have you heard differently?"

"Oh no," laughed Catherine. "You misunderstand me. Ben has done amazing things with the children he's helped. But most of the work that's he's done in those buildings right now is outside of school hours—they aren't used during the day much at all—am I right?"

"Yes," I admitted.

"So back to the question of Ben. What's to be done with him? Let me tell you about his future here."

Catherine then began to speak in glowing tones about Ben. She described the extraordinary work he'd done in leading Rockhorn to acquire the Ihme School. The endless hours of tutoring and relationship building that he'd put in were about to culminate in a merger of the two schools. This achievement had truly lifted Ben's profile in the Valley's philanthropic community.

In order to reward him, Catherine told me that the new position I'd heard about from Joe was being finalized even now. As a senior member of the Argurion Grant Administrative staff, Ben would report to both Mack Demson and Catherine Foss. He would have much greater responsibility and would work directly with alumni and graduating students, rather than having to spend much of his time in the outbuildings and the grimy, greasy Shop. "We'll get him out of those dusty places, and away from the more difficult students—we'll put him with the cream of the crop," said Catherine.

It sounded as if Ben would have little time for his old pursuits of working with the Ihme children in the outbuildings. He might not even have time to lead long story sessions with the dregs of Rockhorn after school, and talk kids like Jimmy and Andy out of their homicidal urges. After all, Ben would now be wearing a suit and a watch. He'd be influential at Rockhorn and in the surrounding business community;

he wouldn't have time to spend in the Shed. "I can't even see him having the time to go back to the Chapel for a few hours a week either," said Catherine. "He'll have a very expansive charter, you know. A lot of power—and he'll be quite busy."

The fact that Ben would no longer need the Shed or use the Chapel was a compelling reason to use them myself. After all, we already had these buildings. But why was Catherine Foss telling me all this detail? The concept of a hands-on business for Rockhorn students wasn't my idea, after all.

"Ah," responded Catherine. "That's a very good question. Joe has been talking you up to the Board members ever since you two returned from your little trip. He's mentioned that *you'll* be requesting part of the Grant money for a new vocational training and food service building. I thought that you wanted this new building."

"Oh," I gulped. "I do—I do. I'm just... I'm just not sure if I'm the right person to carry it off, you know."

"Well, it's a fabulous idea—to give these students some real world experience in business. And I think it's great that we may have funds available to help them. I mean, it's something the public schools might do."

This did not particularly commend the idea to me. In fact, in the private school circles I moved in what she said was almost a curse, and I suspect she knew that.

But she went on. "Now, you do know that the public school superintendent is very happy with Rockhorn for not suddenly releasing all of these children with special needs into the already-overloaded public system. However, we're doing it at some cost. Our Comptroller is far from happy. You should be back as Treasurer, and properly evaluate the toll these services are taking on our long-term endowment."

"Well, I hope to be back in that role soon," I said. "I also hope to be putting into practice this vocational studies idea."

"Wonderful!" said Catherine. "As I said, I think it's a fabulous idea—I'm just not sure whether you need to build an entirely new structure. I mean, is this absolutely necessary to make *your* idea come to life?"

"Perhaps not," I admitted.

"I rather think that it makes a lot more sense to use the existing buildings, rather than build a new one just for these students and their needs. Why lock Rockhorn into a state where we're constantly attracting more people with special needs? Has anyone thought about where that takes us? Where does it all end?"

"You make a good point."

"Thank you." Catherine smiled. "Of course, I'd also like it if the Argurion Grant remained largely dedicated for use in the Library remodeling and new construction. Now you know where I stand. But just to sweeten the deal, let me tell what I'm prepared to do in order to work with you."

It was then that Catherine Foss made an offer to me. Now since that time, gossip has circulated which has inflated the value of the offer. For some reason, people have said that on that day, Catherine offered me—in cash—30% of the money that would have been spent on the new vocational facility and the field lights, if I would agree to simply request the use of the old buildings—refurbished, of course—instead of advocating the creation of a million dollar special fund to be carved out of the Argurion Grant.

Somehow, this rumor that I was directly offered an astronomical sum made the rounds immediately. Obviously, it wasn't true. It is true that Catherine Foss offered to reimburse me some of the money that I would spend on establishing the business, and also that she offered some additional monies as a good-will gesture. But 30% of Joe's funding target would have been an absurd figure to offer someone like me. It was an offer, but I will have you know that it was less than rumor has made it.

Now despite the fact that it was somewhat less than rumored, I did spend nearly a month seriously considering the offer.

In the next week, I was pleased to discover that all the charges against me had been dismissed. Evidently, no one had been able to trace the funds I'd transferred. There was no case left for the prosecution. The city attorney's office was forced to let the filing lapse. Now I was free to continue where I'd left off with all my old clients—if they would have me. The first client whose books I looked over was, of course, Rockhorn Academy.

As soon as I opened the spreedsheet with all the data for the last fiscal quarter, I could see the massive drain on Rockhorn's resource that the Ihme acquisition had taken. For a profitable school, Ihme was not a good investment. I blamed only myself. The deluded and fatuous support that I'd given to Ben's idea was already beginning to cripple Rockhorn's financial projections.

It's important to note that in seeing these facts in black and white, I was in no wise influenced by my own feelings about where Rockhorn was headed. Truly, the only thing that mattered to me was the evident disarray of our finances. There was, of course, a satisfying serendipity in the discovery of just how badly the Ihme acquisition would hurt Rockhorn's wealth, but the two were not connected.

The facts were alarming enough in and of themselves. Because of all these new demands on our programs, I projected that the school would slip in revenues up to 15%, and 5% in profits year over year, which would definitely affect our long-term capital planning. I looked for areas where we could economize.

Nearly every department's budget would be impacted, if we wanted to continue to be a profitable institution. The endowment, for example, could not be touched for the next few years until the interest built up enough to fund special projects, meaning that the cuts would cascade into long-term budget planning. The unkindest cut, for me personally, was the cut I saw coming in the food service and vocational training center with my name on it. Now that Catherine had expressed her displeasure with using money from the Argurion Grant, I had planned to ask the Board to allow me to use money from the existing endowment to remodel the existing cafeteria and to build this new vocational training and food service building out near the football field. I saw this building gradually fading away into a pipedream—and my name on Rockhorn's campus fading with it.

Obviously, a variety of programs and services would have to be scaled back if we were to continue to meet the needs of Rockhorn's academic program and to carry on with assisting the great variety of disabled children that the Ihme School had traditionally seen fit to assist.

There had to be some other options. Along with the quarterly accounts, I spent some time reviewing the most recent Board meeting notes to see if they planned to sell off any of the Ihme assets in order to recoup their investment. But it seemed that no one had anticipated had thought of contingencies. Unfortunately, the Ihme acquisition had apparently moved into its final phases: both the Executive Board and the Long-Term Planning Committee had approved the merger of the two schools. Carefully, I looked for loopholes.

Afterwards, I made a few phone calls. There might not be a way to put the brakes on an acquisition—Rockhorn would have to meet the letter of the contracts that Joe Matheson and Bartimus Santos had already signed. The merger would go through. However, other than a tacit understanding that the Ihme programs would be kept going, it appeared to me that many of the binding clauses in the written contracts could be finessed. I needed the opinions of other Board members before I could be sure, but there might be a way to save a large amount of money once the schools were merged: there were always redundancies.

I called Catherine Foss, and then I scheduled time with Joe Matheson. Yet I needed more back-up. I could not count on Board members who had too-liberal sensibilities. People were needed who had a mind for facts and figures. Only the ones with a long-term investment in Rockhorn's future would understand the importance of these decisions. Someone needed to help me influence Joe Matheson and the entire Board in the appropriate direction.

Regrettably, I could not call on Bartimus Santos or others who had demonstrated a potential conflict of interest. Yet I did find at least one other Board member who would be supportive—in fact, as I read the meeting notes, he had expressed his displeasure with the Ihme acquisition well before the papers were drawn up, presented, or signed. Sol Tharsen sounded as if he'd be a sure ally in the coming discussion.

One evening in late February, we met in a corner of Joe's office. The lights were low and the aroma of fresh coffee filled the room; we gathered around a round orange Tiffany lamp on the coffee table at the center of his leather sofa set. Although the weather was freezing outside, inside the building it was very cozy. Joe's suede leather furniture had kept the warmth of the day, and it was easy to sink into them.

The coffee was served up by Meredith, who then left for the night. I said hello to Meredith, but I begged off the coffee. Even though it was an informal discussion, I was nervous. Besides my invitees—Catherine Foss and Sol Tharsen—Joe had also asked Bartimus Santos to attend, and I had no insight into Bartimus' perspective on all these issues.

After some initial small talk—Catherine asked after our golf trip, and Joe passed around the pictures we'd taken—there was an uncomfortable pause. There was nothing to do but watch Bartimus light his pipe.

Soon, he was puffing away. He waved the match until it went out and looked around at us all quietly watching him.

"Well," he said. "So we're here to get a preview of the Treasurer's report, aren't we? Thank you for inviting me, Mr. Matheson." He nodded at Joe, and then he looked at me. "And our Treasurer has returned from exile. Welcome back, sir, it's good to have you in our midst once more. What do you have to tell us?"

Awkwardly, I ventured into an explanation of what I'd found in the books. Then I outlined the areas where I saw immediate cuts necessary. All of these areas had been traditionally covered by Rockhorn's general fund or our endowment, and all of them would suffer if we continued forward with further enrollment of children with Ihme-level disabilities.

The Bentley automobiles leased by the Academy for the Headmaster and Dean would have to be let go. There were other cuts for the Headmaster: there would be no more catered lunches for large donors in his office, and Joe's travel budget would have to be cut back substantially if we proceeded along this path—something I felt he'd be unhappy to learn. Guest lecturers in literature, contemporary theatre, and applied fine arts would have to be released from their contracts. Furthermore, an instructor we'd hired to teach special extra-credit courses on the College Admissions game would either have to take a substantial pay cut or not teach the class at all. I was pretty sure this woman wouldn't take the pay cut—she was formerly a prized professor and admission essay reviewer in the Ivy League, and we'd only got her after a great deal salary negotiation.

Under the circumstances, a constrained budget would also make it difficult to carry off all the details that went into the Endowment Party every spring. We had planned to add a formal ball for the Argurion Grant to the Party, with music and a parquet ballroom floor. These cuts would make it difficult to carry off. We would even have to cut some of the catering and many of the philanthropic gifts we were planning on rewarding our donors with. And of course, my building would never be constructed; leaving us short space for any new vocational training or handicapped students.

I capped my little presentation by asking if the Board, perhaps, had anticipated these revenue shortfalls? Were there other sources of income of which I was unaware?

Joe, however, seemed to be focused on keeping all of the Ihme services intact. I was surprised to find that he didn't even comment on my proposed cuts of his car, his lunches, and his travel.

"All right," he said. "Most of these things I don't see a problem dropping. But what about the programs for the kids that we've gotten from Ihme? And what about the possibility of building more bridges between those kids and our traditional high-achieving Rockhorn student? Will cuts be made there as well?"

"Let's step back a moment, shall we?" said Catherine. "Before we come to the long-term plan for how to make our budget and our profit with this amount of revenue, I'd like to review it again. Would you mind running through the list of immediate proposed cuts?"

I politely stepped through the entire list once more.

At the end, Catherine spoke again. "On the surface, it may appear that few of these are substantive cuts. Yet look closely at them—these items define Rockhorn experience. We are not a public facility, and our donors expect catered lunches, for example. Our students expect guest lecturers."

"Well, Rockhorn has always traditionally done these things," admitted Bartimus.

"Oh come on," said Joe. "Some of these things are negligible. I mean, pure luxury."

"She does have a point though," said Sol. "These are traditional things Rockhorn provides—I think if we begin to make cuts here, there's no telling where it will end."

"But what about the handicapped allotment?" said Joe. "There's an excess cost allocation from the state for each child in our charter program who has a handicap. That was part of the reason that I went ahead with the merger—we could get all these extra funds."

"No, it doesn't really make up for the shortfall," I said. "It's sufficient to cover the basic day-to-day care needs of most of the children, but not the cost of instructors, facilities, or all the special perks that Rockhorn provides. And the Ihme tuition has traditionally been not at the level of Rockhorn tuition."

"See, there you have it," said Sol. "That's why they were going bankrupt."

"Well, what is the Ihme tuition per student?" asked Joe. "Can we raise it gradually, over the next five years, say? And thus, go into a deficit in the short term, but keep our programs intact for the long term?"

"Let me check." I flipped through the stack of file folders I'd brought with me. Then, as I remembered the inconsistencies, I hesitated.

"Unfortunately, when you signed the papers, you allowed their tuition arrangements to remain the same," I said.

"Which are?"

"Well, essentially, a great number of the students have individual tuition arrangements based on income and whatever they can pay. They have a very flexible tuition arrangement, unlike Rockhorn's rigid fee."

Joe whistled. "So even if we raise tuition, it's not going to be the same increase across the board. Everyone has their own arrangement."

Catherine shook her head. "What a rat's nest. It's inconceivable that we could make a profit on the school at this rate."

"Well, that's a good question," said Joe. "We might not make our traditional profit, but could we keep the school open and running, even with this revenue drop?"

"Oh, of course we could," I said. "And I'm not proposing that you declare bankruptcy or something like that. I'm just saying that cuts should be made if you expect to keep these tuition arrangements and keep your doors open to children with special needs."

"Great." Joe rubbed his hands together. He picked up a file folder.

"Let's figure out where we're going to propose cuts."

"Yes, we could keep it open," said Catherine. "But I argue that the school would no longer be *Rockhorn* Academy we've all read about in the papers in the last few weeks. And I doubt that many of our elite students would remain, paying our tuition for an educational experience that seems primarily geared for the benefit of the disabled."

"But it wouldn't just be for the disabled," said Joe. "They would gain immeasurable benefits—our students are already gaining immeasurably—from the experience of working with and alongside students who don't have their innate abilities."

Bartimus spoke up. "My nephew, for example, contributes a great deal to Rockhorn. I'm glad he's now here."

"Yes," said Joe. "Our school would still have all Rockhorn academic potential, all of Rockhorn sports and most of the well-known lecturers. Those things have been here for decades: that's our reputation, not the fluff. And it would still have the students—that great caliber of students."

"To speak for myself—and probably for others—I would be withdrawing my son," said Tharsen. "I pay for a certain type of educational experience, and as far as I can tell, you've just told me that you care more about keeping these children with problems than you about getting students whose parents choose to—and can afford to—pay the high tuition. You apparently value some sort of 'immeasurable' benefit over my son's test scores and the everyday perks that I pay for."

"But Ben has just proven that we can get students—of all types—into good universities," said Joe.

"The test scores this year are just a fluke," said Catherine. "Everyone knows that Ihme wasn't successful at turning children like these into mainstream college students or successful adults."

"And Ben is not accredited," I pointed out. "I understood that was part of the reason you were moving him into the endowment program—so that scrutiny wouldn't be placed on him and his qualifications, as the school receives more national attention."

"All right," said Joe. He threw up his hands. "So it's not going to work long-term to have all the Ihme students, with their wacky tuition arrangements, stay at Rockhorn. Ben was wrong. And it was an unwise investment. My bad."

"Well," said Bartimus slowly. A long stream of smoke came out of his pipe as he sighed. "If it was an unwise investment, it was also my responsibility as well. But let us not cast blame. Where do we go from here?"

"Right," said Joe. "What do you propose we do?"

"I don't know," I said.

I honestly hadn't any idea what to propose next. I wanted what was best for Rockhorn, and although I felt that the halls were too crowded with wheelchairs right now, it did bother me on some level that we were talking so dispassionately about the lives of children who had the misfortune to have a disability. I suppose I was thinking especially of little Steven in his chair: despite myself, it seemed that I'd grown a soft spot for him. While I thought of Steven and his friends, Bartimus smoked and Joe looked at the ceiling. Sol Tharsen nervously drummed his fingers on the arm of his chair.

Quietly, Catherine Foss spoke up. "I would suggest first of all that despite our good intentions, the Ihme assets are not a good investment long term."

"Well, it doesn't take a rocket scientist," said Joe glumly.

"Yeah, the Ihme School is a money-losing boat anchor," said Sol.

Catherine carried on though. "In that light, perhaps we should consider divestment."

"We signed papers," said Joe.

"Yes, but if we do it quietly enough, we won't cause an undue disturbance in the community. By and large, these parents will find other means. I mean, really, these children take extraordinary efforts. And Rockhorn faculty really shouldn't be asked to do something that at heart should be a charitable act."

"By and large, I'm in agreement," said Bartimus. "But what about my nephew? I believe he's an asset and—"

"Of course," went on Catherine. "We should cherry-pick the few really high achievers—the ones who got our teacher Ben in the headlines this month."

"There should be some criteria that we use for making these choices," said Bartimus. "Say, we take only the top 10% of the Ihme students, whether or not they can pay. My nephew and others of that caliber can stay then. The rest must find other arrangements within the year."

"The top 10% sounds reasonable to me," said Catherine. "Some time in the next year, we can divest ourselves of the real estate, and the more difficult and troublesome students who remain from Ihme."

"Right," said Tharsen. "The ones who take a lot of time and expense, yet don't return adequately on our investment."

"That's correct," finished Catherine.

Bartimus took his pipe out of his mouth. "You know. There is one consideration we haven't touched on."

"What's that?" said Joe.

"Who's going to tell them?"

"What do you mean?" I said.

"Just that—" said Bartimus. "Who's going to tell the parents and the faculty to leave Rockhorn? If Joe and I tell them, then it will look duplicitous, or at the least underhanded. We signed the papers and we made the decisions. Instead, someone from the Board should tell the parents that at the Board vote both the Headmaster and the Chairman of the Board were overruled. Despite our strident objections, of course." He pointed his pipe at me. "And you, sir, should probably *not* be the person to give the parents these ill tidings."

"I'll tell them," said Tharsen. "I don't have any problem telling each and every parent that we can't afford to host their kids *gratis*. I'll be proud to do it."

"All right," I said hesitantly. "But what about some of the worse-off Ihme students who have endeared themselves to Rockhorn's student body? For example, what about Steven—that boy in a wheelchair with the learning disability—what about him?"

"Yes," said Joe. "Steven's a good example of the kind of student I'm concerned about, the ones who could really benefit from the special enrichment we have at Rockhorn. I think some of them have made a lot of progress this semester: Steven among them."

"Well," said Catherine Foss, looking closely at me. "Let's see what the records tell us. Is he in the upper 10% of the Ihme students or does he fail that test?"

Joe Matheson paged through the stack of Ihme student records on his desk, and produced an updated grading spreadsheet for the boy Steven. He looked it over, and then reluctantly handed it to Tharsen.

Tharsen required no more than a glance before he gave the printout to Bartimus for review.

"Well," said Bartimus after a moment. "I'm afraid by the criteria we've discussed, Steven here will be one of the first to go."

Joe and I both must have looked somewhat despondent over this news, for Tharsen spoke up immediately.

"Don't worry, you won't have to talk to him about it," he said. "He really will be one of the first to go. I will tell his parents as soon as I can. You won't have to see him around very much longer at all, or be reminded of him."

"Thank you," I said with relief. "Thank you."

Joe stood from his chair. "Well," he said. "This calls for a break. I think we're almost done here—I'd like to wrap up with a review of our decisions and a plan of action—and I think Mr. Tharsen has begun to lead us in that regard. But a break for everyone, and then drinks all around! Ten minutes? Back in this office?"

The five of us stood and stretched. I had to pull myself up from Joe's comfortable leather chairs and loveseat; it was hard not to fall asleep there. Already, it had been a long evening. I think we truly did feel good about our decisions, but there was also much weariness in the room. I poured myself a quick cup of cold coffee and swallowed it down. Then I went to visit the men's room down the hall.

I found Joe standing at the next urinal. He glanced around at the brass fixtures and the empty room and then leaned close to me. "Look," he said quietly. "I don't want you to get the wrong idea. I still want your building to be built."

"My building?"

"Yeah—the one with your name on it. I think the purpose may change slightly. No wheelchair ramps and all that—we aren't taking in any more Ihme children, not if we can help it."

"Really?" I said. "I just kind of assumed it was kibboshed."

Joe finished up and met me at the sink. Now he looked at me in the mirror, and he spoke aloud.

"No, your building is still alive—at least in my mind. It was never just for those handicapped kids—you and I both knew that, and so did Catherine. We want a new announcer's box, a press booth, and a snack facility out by the sports fields. Not to mention the football stadium lights. If we can get a fund designated for your building, we can get all these things. And besides, you've still got to have a really professional place to teach your business classes in. I mean, if you have Martin Waites or Norman Alan Foss, or other prominent businessmen like them as guest lecturers, you need a real place for them to speak."

I turned on the water at my sink and thought for a moment. "That's all very well," I said. "But in amongst all these cuts, where is the money supposed to come from?"

"Well, the Argurion Grant isn't going to be touched by these events. I still think that we should force Catherine to request that an even million be allocated to a special construction fund—for your building, the business classes, and things like that. The Board will still approve it—we can push it through."

At that moment, the door swung open and Bartimus Santos walked into the bathroom. He nodded at the two of us and headed for the urinals.

Joe dried his hands. He leaned over to me and whispered. "For the moment though, we should just get the money allocated and lie low. We can break ground for the building next year—after the flap over our finances dies down."

"I'll think it over," I said. "I have to consider my options."

Joe clapped his hand to my shoulder. "It will be fine. Don't stress about the project. Don't worry—you won't have to use those old buildings for your class," he said. "We'll knock 'em flat—I promise." Then he strode purposefully out of the bathroom. I dried my hands and followed him.

I wasn't making any snappy decisions that evening. Although Joe's idea was intriguing, Catherine's offer (and the remuneration she proffered) remained very attractive. Yet it's not as if I was entirely motivated by financial gain. After all, I had to take care of my family. And I still had legal bills to pay from the last time I had worked with large sums of money. I wanted to weigh my options.

* * *

After we all returned to the office, Joe unearthed a bottle of port from the small safe where we kept the accounts and the permanent grading records. He managed to find several empty glasses on top of the little refrigerator in Meredith's office, and we poured ourselves a complete round of drinks.

"I keep this for special occasions," he said. "And I think tonight counts as one."

We raised our glasses over the warm Tiffany lamp in the center of the coffee table. A rich ruby light came through the thick port in our glasses and spilled over the table. Incongruously, I was reminded of sunset light in a window, seen from far away. I glanced over my glass at Sol Tharsen and he smiled back. I felt satisfaction rise in me: we had accomplished a great deal this evening.

"Here's to the future of Rockhorn," said Joe, and each of us took a drink. Joe nodded at me next and I nodded my head. "And to our Treasurer, who had returned. Long may he keep our books."

There was a polite chuckle, and a round of sips.

"And to the students of Rockhorn. Long may they grace our halls," said Sol Tharsen, and we added another quick swallow.

Catherine spoke up next. "To the Argurion Grant, and our grantors."

"And to our many other benefactors," added Bartimus in a deep growl, and we all drank again.

"So, there is some business to cover here at the end," said Joe, as we all sat down heavily, our port glasses in our hands. "Let's review what we've done. We will mainstream the best of them. And if we do things right, we'll keep getting the good press for keeping those few. As soon as possible we'll rent out the Ihme campus. If it doesn't go soon as a complete campus, we'll raze it and put up condominiums. Hopefully, it will soon be a profitable real estate investment—yet more property in our portfolio. If this keeps up, we'll own most of the East Side of town!"

Everyone laughed.

"I don't think we should lose sight of the fact that we want Rockhorn to keep growing though—this just doesn't seem like the right direction for a school with our high standards, our costs, and our reputation to preserve. But we should keep growing in the kinds of services and programs we can offer."

"Oh, I quite agree," said Bartimus.

"So keep in mind that there may be some new construction at Rockhorn in the next few years," added Joe. He waggled his eyebrows in my direction. "For all of us here this evening, this is only the beginning of a revitalized Rockhorn."

At this point, Catherine Foss jumped in. "And keep in mind," she said. "That we still have unused space on campus—let's not forget to use all our space wisely." Joe nodded, but didn't he didn't accede the point. Instead, he winked at me.

Joe continued speaking, but Catherine leaned over to me and muttered a message to me: "Perhaps we can chat about your plans at a later time—call me next week. I'll make myself available any time to talk."

I didn't respond though. I was trying to give the impression of listening to Joe.

"—In the next few months I'm sure you'll agree that to keep up appearances, we should maintain the same level of expenditure for our annual Endowment Party, especially since this year we have the Argurion Grant, for which we'll conduct a little ceremony. I'm sure our donors will rise to the occasion, and I know our Librarian will thank us."

"I do appreciate it," murmured Catherine.

"But in the near term, I'm going to authorize our Treasurer here to make the other cuts he's suggested. I think I can put up without a school car or catered meals until the end of the term. I think we all understand that once we divest ourselves of the most expensive holdovers from Ihme—who are only liabilities to us now—we can plan to be back on a firm financial footing in the next school year. Thank you, to all of you, for making these difficult but necessary decisions."

Everyone finished off our glasses on this declaration, and then Catherine Foss gave hugs and cheek pecks all around the room. That evening in Joe's office was a truly forward-looking moment for Rockhorn. Our endowment, prestige and perks are several of the reasons we're rated so highly with parents, alumni, and prominent universities. Without these things, we'd receive a much lesser caliber of student, and we couldn't allow that to happen. Our reputation was too important.

20.

ON SATURDAY, I purchased a new tuxedo shirt and prepared myself for the best formal party Rockhorn community had ever seen. Carefully, I tied an exquisite hand-knotted silk bowtie I'd purchased that day and fastened the solid gold cufflinks inherited from my grandfather.

I was excited about this event on many levels. There was the pleasure of seeing philanthropy on a grand scale, and the accompanying pomp and ceremony that would go with such largesse. Then there was the obvious satisfaction in seeing one of my largest accounting clients—Rockhorn Academy itself—receive additional funds to increase their operating budget and their fiscal planning. This party would be even bigger and grander than usual since we were inviting past donors to both Rockhorn Academy and the Ihme School. And finally there was the anticipation of all the changes underway at the school, not least among them a potential building with my name on it, and a new high profile role for Ben Delacruz.

As I strolled onto campus, it was gratifying to see the Jaguars and the Mercedes gleaming in the parking lot and to contemplate the wealth and position that I'd soon see represented in main hall of the library—completely changed for this evening into a formal ballroom. The mayor would certainly be there (Rod Harper was an alum), along with various City Council members and the Chief of Police, Philip Avecet. They would be joined by many executives from my own corporate clients, several of whom sat on Rockhorn Board. Rumor had it that the governor might even make an appearance.

We were seeing the tail end of winter now. It was an unseasonably balmy evening. In fact, I almost left my heavy great coat in the car for the short walk across campus. But I was glad I hadn't, for I was out in the cold longer than I'd expected. On my way to the library hall, I detoured from the straight path, and wandered past Ben's old classroom in the Shop building. After this week, he wouldn't be in that room anymore. Laszlo Lindbloom would be coming back, and although he might need help, they would probably encourage Mr. Lindbloom to hire another laborer to support his Shop work. Ben himself would have new responsibilities. So I went past the classroom because I suppose I wanted to contemplate the end of an era, and the beginning of a new one. It was pleasant to realize that instead of being treated like an itinerant substitute, Ben was about to be accepted with open arms by Rockhorn community, and given a position of honor and respect.

My spirits were also considerably lighter that evening because I was walking into this party unencumbered by my past. I had just paid my lawyer the final bill for the tax case and wiped my hands of it. I was happy to note that there was no clause to restart the case; it had been entirely dropped for lack of clear and compelling evidence, due only to my own hard work.

Now I wouldn't feel nervous anymore passing out business cards at occasions like this. I felt quite vindicated by the series of events, and even if I couldn't say it directly to Ben, on some level I wanted him to know that I'd done it without his help. I didn't expect to see him this evening, except at a distance, surrounded by throngs of admirers, in the midst of the crush of Rockhorn's Endowment Party.

Therefore, when I turned the old corner past the Shop, I was surprised to see him in the flesh, bent over outside his classroom door. He was standing over a pair of sawhorses and sawing away at a huge piece of timber with an archaic manual saw. The sound of it was muffled by the heft of the wood, but still the faint shriek of the saw being pulled back and forth bit at my nerves.

It was awkward to see him—but not entirely so. After all, he knew where I was headed, and that would be a topic of conversation. My only question was why he wasn't also dressed up and already inside the library's simulacrum of a grand ballroom. Some of the announcements this evening, and the divestment of the Argurion money, directly affected him and his future. And I supposed we both knew that the announcements regarding Ben promised to be quite laudatory.

As I approached him, one or two young men came out of the building, carrying additional timbers to be cut. One of them remained behind and began to paint a piece of timber with dark wood stain—apparently a task that had been halted to carry more wood outside. Ben stopped sawing and took a bite of something he'd laid on top of the timber. Then he called inside. Three or four more faces appeared at the door. He handed one of them the remainder of what he'd been eating, and gave them some direction that I could not hear. There were chuckles and laughter as they went inside again. What kind of a teacher spent his Saturdays at the school? I suppose only a teacher who could still prevail on his students to be at the school on a Saturday. I thought I had gotten used to the Carpenter's oddities, but here he was, surprising me again.

It was a bizarre sight—instead of being dressed in a suit, sipping a glass of Chardonnay and preparing to introduce his himself and his ideas to the larger Rockhorn philanthropic community, Ben was outside in the yard, wearing a shirt that had been stained and torn that day, holding forth with his juvenile friends, and sharing a dirty candy bar with some child. He was liberally dusted with sawdust and streaked with mahogany stain.

I greeted Ben warmly. He shook my hand, leaving a gritty residue on my skin. Gently, I raised the topic of the party we were both about to miss. Inside, I knew, the Endowment Committee from the Board and many of the teachers were talking and wondering if Ben was going to join them. I tried to tell him that missing this sort of thing did ruffle a few feathers, but of course, he didn't see it. It seemed clear that instead of coming to the meeting and socializing on an adult level, Ben intended to stay out there the entire time, leading another impromptu bull session with the misfits and loners that filtered down to him through his Shop classes.

There were even gifts inside for Ben—although I didn't tell him this—tokens of the Administration's esteem for him, and of their hopes for his future as an alumni booster and a fundraiser for Rockhorn. I knew that Meredith had coordinated a card signed by the entire faculty, welcoming him to his new role, and Mack and Joe had personally contributed to a beautiful silver-embossed fly rod for 'the Carp'.

One or two students came outside while Ben and I were talking, and Ben turned from me immediately to engage them in a different conversation, one regarding the number of paint coats on a piece of wood or some such triviality. Covered with mahogany stains, the children were dusky urchins, unrecognizable in the evening light.

I listened to one of them stutter along, talking to Ben, and recognized Tom's timorous voice. I looked down and saw that the boy had accidentally splashed the toe of my shoe with a spot of paint from the brush he was holding. I moved back and waited impatiently for Ben to finish. Across campus, in the Library, I knew that all the people in their tuxedoes and gowns were waiting, many of them quite happy to give Ben Delacruz a standing ovation. I couldn't understand Ben's reaction to Rockhorn's acceptance. Did he take this acceptance to heart? Was he grateful for it? I suppose the answer should have been obvious: of course not. I suppose it didn't fit with being an outsider. In so many ways, this gathering at the Library would be Ben's coming of age at Rockhorn.

I interrupted his conversation with Tom and took the evening's gold-embossed invitation from my jacket pocket. I held it out to him. "Didn't you get one of these?"

"Of course I did," he replied mildly.

"Then why—" I asked "—are you going to miss this night?" Did he not know that people had spent valuable time putting this together? Perhaps he had forgotten it? Perhaps it had slipped his mind, or had failed to end up on his calendar?

Instead of immediately answering my questions, Ben looked at me for a long moment, until I looked away. Then he asked me a question in return.

"Do you know what it's like to be a rare coin collector?" he said.

"What?" I answered. "Rare coins?"

"I'm just asking if you know what it's like to collect anything small and valuable—stamps, watches, jewelry, rare coins? Are you familiar with what that experience is like?"

"Um, no," I said. "Not really."

"There's a story I want to tell you. You should know what that is like before I begin."

I checked my watch. "Well, I don't know, Ben. The festivities have just begun. I mean, I do have a small collection of antique fountain pens, but they're hardly as valuable as coins. I don't want to arrive too late, you know. How about if we just call it a night and—"

"The story is short. It won't keep you long," he said. He sat down on the end of the thick timber he was sawing. I stared resolutely at the ground, clenching my jaw.

"There was once a woman who had a coin collection. I knew her. She had a house full of them—all of them were equally valuable to her, and I guess they were all of about equal value, as they were from the same era. The coins were given to her by her father before he died, and they were valuable to her not only because they were worth a lot of money, but also because of his care in choosing the coins to give to her. Each had a value in her heart that was worth more than the value they would have fetched on the open market."

"That's great, Ben. I'm glad you knew her and all. I'm always happy to hear about other friends of yours, even if you're no longer in touch with all of them. That's great. But just right now, I can't—"

Then he said my name, and for some reason that brought me up short. Just the way he said it, as if he were comforting me again, in the midst of my financial crisis, or in some difficult time with Jake. He said it again, and this time I looked up at him.

"Oh, go on," I said. For some reason, I felt overcome with nascent emotion, as if nothing had happened to separate us in the last few months. "Go on with the story," I said resignedly.

"The story is short—just listen," he said. "This woman lost one of her coins. And she didn't just say to herself that she had enough already, and that one less wouldn't really matter. This was the truth, you know—losing one wouldn't have mattered greatly to her overall net worth. No, she didn't say that. Instead, she searched the entire house. She lived in an old mansion, and it took her months of searching. Day after day she searched for this one silly little coin."

"Why?"

"Because it was hers, and because she cared about it. She cared about it much more than it was worth, you see. It was given to her by her father, and she couldn't bear to lose a single one."

"That's very sentimental, Ben. Quite a commitment."

"Yes. She found it, you know. She found it under a basket in the backyard. Someone had used it as a weight, under a candle, at one of her parties. A party much like the one they're having tonight."

"I see. And this story has relevance here exactly how?" I gestured in the direction of the Library, where I could see other party-goers congregating near the door. "I do have someplace to be, after all—and so do you."

"I know, and I'll be there." One of his students approached him, and Ben took his hand, motioning him to wait a moment. "When the time is right, I'll be there. Watch for me."

"Right, sure, I'll keep an eye out for you," I said dryly.

"But you asked about the relevance—isn't it obvious?" He looked down at the child who was standing beside him—a teenager, someone nearly as tall as me. "Which group do you think will miss me more this evening? Which group will care if I'm there or not?"

"Well, I guess I thought some of us adults *would* care if you were at the Library or not. Apparently not though." The frustration rose inside me, smoldering like a fire. "Look, my patience is at an end. First you're not going to come to this event—something that's been in the planning for months, and now you waste my time with some stupid story about coins and old women."

"Sure, it's just a story—it may be stupid to you. But the coins are like children, like the students I have here. And you cannot lose a single one."

As he said this, I realized it was the same old story, the repetition of losing and finding. "You know, Ben," I said. "I know this story, I know it far too well, and I really have more important things to do."

"But, my friend—the story is about the real world. That party you're going to, it isn't real, it's not real at all. What I've talked about though—the coins and the children—they're real, and they are the same thing. Each of them has no time to waste, no second chances, and most of them are lost…" He was talking to me, but I wasn't listening.

Ben stood there, instructing me about the lifestyles of junior high children, and I suddenly realized how much I disliked him. I disliked him more now than before I knew him. I didn't need his help any longer. I had successfully retained Rockhorn Academy as my client, and I would soon be a member of the faculty myself (with one business class to my name). I found myself looking through the eyes of a faculty member at Ben, and not liking what I saw. He still hadn't given me a straight answer to why he was out here instead of inside with the rest of the adults.

As he talked, I looked at the lines on his face, the wrinkles caused by smiles and by tiredness, and I saw that he didn't know. He didn't realize that I had grown to despise his brand of help—he'd never understand how, in a short season, I'd gone from asking his assistance to distaining it.

I suppose it wouldn't occur to him to contemplate the fact that I had accomplished my goals and cleared my name, and thus might not need him or his group of misfits anymore. Didn't he see that I was on the verge of achieving some power at Rockhorn, and that I didn't need to accede to his whims anymore? Yet he was so trusting that he just kept telling me everything—everything he was thinking about. As his voice droned on, I stood there hating him for being what I could not be—hating him for being so trusting, for knowing every childish answer to life's mysteries, and most of all, for liking misfits, and for trying to make me into one.

Quickly, I brought the conversation to a halt, said my good-byes and departed for the open door that waited for me across campus.

The Library was a hubbub of activity. I was pleased to see that the event was being carried off with as much class as Rockhorn could muster, which was considerable. Just outside the door, an antique-looking gas lantern had been installed for the evening: its flame glimmered and wavered over a valet who inspected and collected each golden invitation. Inside the doors, uniformed valets waited, taking coats and directing traffic. I used my coat to wipe the sawdust off my hand before handing it, with my gold-edged ticket, to the waiting valet. Then I glanced around the hall, a place that had been transformed into a truly grand room. They'd cleared out the tables and moved many of the freestanding book stacks for this evening. Candlelight gleamed off of the immaculate parquet floor; the room was suffused in a soft glow. The large cathedral ceiling of the central library was festooned with ornate fabric, and the walls were replete with artist's renditions of what the new Library would look like, hanging right alongside some of the best selections from Rockhorn's permanent Art collection. Along the walls, on credenza after credenza were gorgeous flower arrangements beside ice sculptures, champagne fountains, and pyramids of candles.

A string quartet played at the far end of the astonishingly spacious hall, right under the dovetail joint that had first drawn Laszlo Lindbloom's interest in Ben. Nearer to me, on the left, were tables of especially alluring hors d'oeuvres—French pastries, lobster pâté and black caviar. The presentation dais, where the announcements and the Argurion family presentation would take place, was standing to my right, hung entirely in damask with a faint silver filigree pattern.

As I stepped inside, I was overwhelmed for a moment by the mass of people. The floor was already filled with people in formal dress. The resplendent gowns of the women almost made me ashamed I hadn't brought a date—any of my recent paramours would have jumped at the chance to be seen in their company. Velvet, satin, fine fur and silk predominated, with the occasional gold or silver gown glimmering as a subtle highlight in the sea of deep velvet. In the candlelight, the profiles of the men turned like silhouettes cut from black paper, sharp as glass against the bright colors their companions wore. How could Ben have said that this wasn't real? I could feel the reality of the millions in the room—it was there in all the details: every brocaded gown, every designer necklace, every Rolex watch, every custom-tailored tuxedo, and every perfect hairstyle.

Several people came out of the crowd immediately to welcome me, but there were less who greeted me than I had hoped. After all, besides the Argurion grant, the second important item to be announced this evening was the reorganization of the administration and their support staff, and as I saw it, Ben Delacruz and myself were the two new star players in the Administration. I felt that at least some of the attention that was being lavished on Catherine Foss should accrue to me, as hell would probably freeze over before Ben made an appearance this evening. But although there was a pause in the crowd as they evaluated the recent arrivals, there was no spontaneous applause or anything of the sort—not that I had really expected such a public display. But the few who did greet me were among those who mattered most this evening, and no doubt this was taken note of by the crowd: Bartimus Santos, Mack Demson, Catherine Foss' assistant Sandy Hedron, and Joe Matheson. And because their time was valuable, I did most appreciate their kind gesture in greeting me.

Joe, for example, was incredibly busy that night, but he still took a moment to see me. There were some words bandied back and forth about my new non-profit activities at Rockhorn, and some cheerful discussion of how the endowment money was being allocated. In the time we had, I congratulated him on the Library's conversion to a ballroom and he told me that it had taken weeks to move the book stacks, as the work required some very careful negotiating with Catherine Foss and her staff. But all of Joe's hard work was worth it, as far as I could see. The Library was truly transformed. It wasn't everyday that this kind of grant money came to a small private school.

"It's good to see you, sir," said Bartimus Santos in his formal tones. "Now I have to get back to my post, if you don't mind." He gestured at the tuxedo-clad crowd behind him, and I realized that Board members were scattered throughout the hall, talking solemnly about Rockhorn's future. (I had been exempted from this duty, as I was receiving special recognition this evening.) The Board members, at their regularly spaced "posts," were not exactly doing a sales pitch, but they were definitely telling Rockhorn's story, for those who wanted to hear it. I imagined Ben here in their stead, telling the story in any of his multiple languages, telling about how Rockhorn was open to people of any ethnic descent, about how Rockhorn provided opportunity, and proving by his very presence and evident erudition, that Rockhorn was a private school which any parent would consider in the same class as the Etons or Exeters of the world.

Part of me looked forward to the day when Ben would join such events with anticipation, and part of me didn't think that he'd ever want to wear those shoes—I suppose, to be truthful, part of me knew, even then, that it would never happen.

As my well-wishers faded back into the general crowd, I took notes on the crowd myself. The conversation was of a high caliber. I soon spotted both Martin Waite and Norman Alan Foss, looking regal in their custom-cut suits and shining silver hair. Apparently, they had brought a number of business associates with them, because the hall was packed with people I recognized as clients and former clients of mine.

Yet along with local philanthropists and school supporters, Joe and Mack had also had the foresight to invite a number of well-known personalities in the artistic community. I spotted the conductor of the symphony orchestra, resplendent in his white mane of hair and half-tailed coat. He was holding forth to a group of women with his European accent, a snifter of cognac in one hand. Joe had also let me know that somewhere here this evening were several well-known authors, among them Doctor Lucas Scribin, a neurosurgeon who had authored a best-seller which combined case histories of neurosurgery with his own observations about cultural psychology. He was said to be working on another book about—oddly enough—religious sensibility and neuroscience. I was also pleased to see his friend and constant companion Theo Philus, last year's national Poet Laureate, who had been the first to encourage Dr. Scribin to write. Philus himself was now rumored to be on the short list for this year's National Book Award in poetry. And there were gallery owners and artists scattered throughout the hall. In fact, every now and then one could hear one of the pieces of art on the walls being discussed in arch tones. Overall, I was very pleased with what Rockhorn had done. It was an ideal but real fête champêtre, taking place here at Rockhorn, within the walls of our own hallowed Library. I immersed myself in its reality by first obtaining a nice Cosmopolitan from one of the uniformed bartenders at the east end of the Library hall.

I continued to discover niceties in the hall that added to the festive atmosphere. For example, a complete model of the expanded Library facility had been constructed—it rested under spotlights on a low table near the entrance. To display all of its properties, oversize posters had been hung on every wall that magnified details of the imagined new facility, so that one looked up to see a sketch of book stacks or bathrooms five times bigger than you were, drawn in excruciatingly detailed precision. In the illustrations, I especially liked seeing the busts of famous intellectuals who graced the corners of each book stack. To further inspire our largesse, plaster mockups of these same busts had been placed throughout the hall this evening, with the names removed. Drawings for each bust would be held at the end of the evening—each lucky person who was the first to correctly guess their names and dates of birth and death would take home one of them as a memento of the Argurion Grant party at Rockhorn Academy. With the busts in place around the hall, the place had turned into a veritable monument to rational progress: I recognized Einstein, Isaac Newton and Galileo side by side, while Socrates and Nietzsche shared pedestals above the bar. The others I didn't recognize, except for Abraham Lincoln and Richard Wagner, who both looked rather unhappy in their perches above the string quartet.

However, there were other things happening this evening than the Argurion Endowment granting ceremony. One of the tables along the hall also solicited different contribution amounts for recognition. For the correct donation category, individuals, families, corporations, or philanthropic trusts could have their names embossed on large floor tiles which would cover the front entrance hall floor when the facility was completed. The names of contributors who dared to go up into the millions would end up listed in a special engraving on the wall near the front entrance of the Library. There was a mock-up of the engraving, with the Argurion name, and the name of several local firms who evidently had contributed prior to this evening's festivities.

There were also contributions solicited for Rockhorn's music department—the string quartet turned out to come from the school itself. The two violins were faculty, while the bass was an alumna and the viola was a current student. There were also other incentives to give. The largest contributor that evening at the music table would receive an in-home concert from the same string quartet playing this evening. No doubt, most of the crowd entertained on a scale similar to this, and could certainly use the addition of a discreet string quartet at one of their summer parties, to set the atmosphere just right, and to serve as a subtle reminder to their friends and business associates that they had been the ones to win the largesse prize at Rockhorn's winter fête.

Finally, against the north wall, there was a silent auction taking place, all of it to benefit the Library endowment. The items being auctioned off were choice pieces from Rockhorn's history and art collection, and most of the bids started in the six digits. There were two of the original eighteenth century chandeliers from the Library, several small works by well-known modern artists—I thought I saw a de Kooning and a late Warhol—and an extremely old copy of the history of Rockhorn (the placard said it was a duplicate of the one in a glass case near the school entrance).

I glanced around the selection, and was surprised to see a complete set of objects d'art from the Chapel, including the colored glass I'd seen in the far window that evening and the "Our Father in Heaven" inscription that had hung over the rough-hewn table at the front. I stepped nearer and examined all the pieces. On closer inspection, the ornate carvings of words and images from the religious past were exquisite works of art, each detail done with such care that each seemed to become a small artwork in itself. Then the entire object was covered in gold leaf, which was now beginning to divorce itself from the wood. Ultimately, I wondered who would care about purchasing them. It was a collection of relics from a bygone age.

However, seeing these things here did set my heart at ease. Apparently, a decision had been made already, and now I would merely be the accessory to the fact. From all evidence, the buildings in the Back Forty were being shut down—perhaps they were even condemned already—no matter what decision I made at this point regarding the food services, my business class, and a new building. My heart felt substantially lighter: I would not cause any disturbance by making public something that was already a *fate accompli.*

Then the music rose and halted suddenly with a crescendo. Mack was up on the dais, speaking into the microphone. "Welcome, welcome!" his voice boomed out. "My name is Nicholas Demson. I'm the Dean here, at Rockhorn Academy, and I'd like to welcome you to Rockhorn's Endowment Festivities! On behalf of the students, the faculty, and the Administration, I'd do hope you're enjoying the evening we've put together for you." There were positive murmurs about the hall, and Mack continued, buoyed up by the support. "Wonderful—fabulous! Please enjoy yourselves—and don't forget to visit the auction tables—" he pointed at the tables where I stood "—and to spend some time thinking about exactly how you'd like your name to appear on the wall or embossed in the tiles, in what is soon to be Rockhorn's newly endowed Argurion Library."

There were cheers around the hall, and I was swept away from the auction table, into the milling crowd. Mack continued talking, but most of the crowd had returned to their drinks and their conversations. At the conclusion of his little speech, a cheer went up, and there was a sedate push towards the food and drink.

I was happy to end up in the middle of the crowd. In every direction, as far as I could see, there were potential clients. Surrounded by velvet, rich satin, and matte black of tuxedoes, I felt suddenly important, as if this place mattered—as if I mattered. I nearly dropped my drink when I found myself elbow to elbow with Talitha Herodias, one of the wealthiest (and most reclusive) philanthropist in the Valley—after inheriting her father's oil fortune, Herodias had made additional billions as a high tech executive—yet here she was, chatting glibly to my right. Over on the other side of the room, I also saw the smooth profile of a well-known television actor. After my initial astonishment, I was gratified that so many eminent personages had managed to make their way to Rockhorn this evening.

The windfall of so many millions, given at one time, had impressed even these jaded patrons of the arts and sciences, and they had all come this evening, drawn like the proverbial bees to honey. The Argurion grant presentation looked to be the highlight of their season. Gossip regarding the Argurion family and how they'd arrived at the decision to endow Rockhorn could be over-heard throughout the length of the hall. As the evening progressed and more alcohol was imbibed, the gossip had a dirtier edge to it—snatches of whispered conversation regarding the various peccadilloes of the Argurion family could be overheard as well, if one listened in the right corners. The family itself, it seemed, had yet to appear. Currently, only the presenter, Mr. Jackson Malfais Argurion, had been glimpsed walking quickly with Joe Matheson, talking quickly and concernedly about something. Most probably, Joe and Jackson Argurion were preparing for the presentation and the speeches to follow. I could imagine that they were taking care of last minute details—checking the microphones and editing their speeches. They had no time to waste gossiping with us down on the floor.

Now Mack Demson was back up on the dais. "Thank you all for being here. However, there are some special guests that I'd like to welcome by name," he said. "And there are also some introductions. First, I'd like to thank Miss Catherine Elizabeth Foss for welcoming us into her beautiful library this evening. Thank you, Miss Foss, for your hospitality." Applause rose delicately from the crowd, like perfume. "Of course, I'd also like to thank Mr. Joseph A. Matheson, the Headmaster of Rockhorn Academy and coordinator of the Grant and Endowment program. Thank you, Joe, for your generosity, in putting this wonderful evening together for us!" Now the applause was more pronounced. Mack went on to recognize other Rockhorn faculty members, some of whom emerged from the crowd and made specific mention of benefactors of their departments. My attention wandered when Mack moved on to thank such people as Sandy Hedron, the assistant librarian, Sol Tharsen, who had donated many of the furnishings, and the school's own set-up and maintenance staff. The applause became sporadic, and I moved into the crowd.

As I traversed the floor, in every direction there were faces I recognized from the social columns and the television news. In fact, about the time I started wondering why there weren't any media here, I spotted a television reporter. She was wearing a brocade gown in dark blue with silver highlights, and she was making her way directly towards me, notebook in hand. I ducked away from her, and fled back towards the dais.

Mack seemed to be winding up his speech by noting the presence of various well-known personages he spotted in the crowd, along with their donations. Vaguely, I heard Mack mention Norman Foss and Martin Waite and their substantial contributions, the poet Theo Philus, and his contribution of a collection of first editions to the Library, the mayor Roderick Harper, and his continued support for Rockhorn, and a number of other philanthropists and personalities whom Mack pointed out, each of them glittering like jewels in the crowd. On these mentions, the applause was more pronounced—after all, the people were now all applauding for themselves.

I resolved to give the reporters something positive to report on about me. Instead of dredging up the past, they would be forced to look at my future, and at how I would be contributing to Rockhorn's growth. Since Ben hadn't bothered to come this evening, he would never hear me—he might not even know that I had made the final decision instead of Joe, and that my decision had gone against him. It was the only moment of glory I would be able to seize that evening. I managed to catch Mack's eye, and motion that I also had an announcement to make.

Mack seemed clearly pleased to see me, yet nonplussed that I was at the dais; he motioned that he'd be winding up soon. Mack made several last mentions of names in the crowd, and glanced around the room as he concluded. The rear door banged open, but Mack didn't take note of the latecomer just then. Instead, he wrapped up his remarks and pleasingly introduced me as a member of the Board of Directors and a major benefactor of Rockhorn Academy.

Ah, the gratification as I stepped onto the dais, the pride swelling in me as all the expectant faces turned toward me! The crowd waited, all of their faces upturned, leaving me alone, an island of attention in the midst of the suddenly silent mass of impressive faces, impressive resumes, impressive wealth—each moment to them worth more than many of the lower classes made in their entire lives.

Loudly, I told the crowd that I would be volunteering my time to reorganize and modernize Rockhorn's food services, including a new snack and drink service for athletic events. I also discussed the business class I'd be teaching as a further benefit to Rockhorn students. This didn't garner the applause I had hoped for, so I continued, making my decision on the spot regarding the money I was supposed to be receiving from the Argurion Grant fund. I opened my mouth for my last remarks, and just then I saw Ben Delacruz at the back of the room, taking off an old and threadbare coat to reveal a suit that barely concealed the various mahogany stains on his arms. A gust of cold air blew in the back door, and I saw that Ben was the one who had come in when Mack was speaking.

Everyone was waiting for my announcement. However, it wasn't quite the ringing pronouncement I had hoped for. Instead, it was somewhat stuttering and halting, perhaps because I had spotted Ben so belatedly. He began to turn towards the dais, to look at me, but I glanced towards Catherine Foss on the other side of the room, and bravely I continued speaking.

"As many of you know, I have requested the allocation of approximately one million dollars from the Endowment grant to improve Rockhorn's existing athletic facilities. With that money, I would have also been adding a new snack facility and announcer's booth for use at our students' events. But I am here this evening." I paused dramatically. "I am here to give this money back to Rockhorn Academy and the new Argurion Library! I'm giving this money back! Instead, for my business classes and for food during events, I have chosen to refurbish and renovate several existing buildings. Using only a small amount from the endowment, I'm going to turn these existing structures into a state-of-the-art lecture hall and snack facility!" No one said anything or began to clap, so I carried on. "I hope my contribution is valuable to the Library, and I hope to see all of you at the next Rockhorn home game!" At this point, some pockets of applause broke out, and I felt myself carried for a moment on that warm ocean of acceptance and affection.

21.

CATHERINE FOSS was quietly applauding for me, a broad smile on her face. I glanced over at Joe's face too, and shrugged in a self-deprecating manner. Although Joe looked disappointed, he wasn't grief-stricken. Joe would be fine with this change—the only things he'd really lost were the announcer's box and the new lights for the football field. No doubt he had a secondary plan in the works already for how to acquire them. He gave me a smile, as if to say 'Win some, lose some' and began to applaud with the rest of the crowd.

This gave me the courage to look back towards the door. Despite the weak delivery, I had received some scattered applause, and the applause kept building, even as I saw Ben turn in astonishment from the back of the room, and look at me. His gaze was penetrating. It went beyond injury, but I couldn't quite place the particular grief that afflicted him. It was something familiar, and it cut me to the core.

"Thank you, thank you!" said Mack Demson. He shook my hand before I stepped off the dais. And then Mack spotted someone else in the hall he wanted to introduce.

"Before I let you return to the excellent libations and the music, I'd like to introduce someone who has joined us—until this very evening, an important faculty member at Rockhorn. In fact, a very dedicated faculty member. So dedicated that until just moment ago, he was working to complete a last minute project for his class." Scattered applause broke out, and Mack held out his hand, calming the crowd. I looked at those happy faces applauding around me, and I thought how little they knew of him. "As we prepare to take down this building, and build a better one in its place—it's wonderful to have someone like him here to help us plan for the future. He's the capstone for our project, the top prize in our catch! He's our Teacher of the Year, and he's been extraordinarily important to the success of both Rockhorn Academy and the Ihme School this year. I'm happy to announce this evening that he will be taking on a larger and more public role in the newly expanded Rockhorn Public Relations department, working under Catherine Foss, and helping to promote our combined school to the larger Valley community. He hasn't formally accepted the offer yet, but I'm sure that he won't think long about moving from Wood Shop to the new post of School Ambassador!" There were chuckles around the hall. "A leader, a teacher, a mentor, a gadfly, an accomplished carpenter, a very good storyteller, a fisherman extraordinaire, and above everything else, an inspiration to us all here at Rockhorn, please give a hand for Mister Ben Cordero Delacruz !"

The applause that rose this time was hearty and sincere, full of hoots and hollers—even from so august a crowd as this one. Ben executed a graceful little bow at the back of the hall, and when that was seen, the applause grew even louder, to a deafening roar. The crowd parted in front of him as he moved towards the dais, and he progressed very slowly, for everyone seemed to want to shake his hand, even those who had never heard of him before this evening. He approached the microphone.

"Peace be with you," he said, and the crowd quieted. "There's not much I can really say to all this acclamation. I do appreciate it, and I know our kids—from Ihme and from Rockhorn—appreciate it too. Thank you, thank you all very much."

Applause broke out again, and Ben looked around. When it died down, he looked at Mack standing on the stage beside him and grinned. "Well, Mack," he said. "I'm a gadfly, huh? And I've got some authority now, don't I, as Teacher of the Year? I'd just like to say, as my first lesson, beware of those in new tuxedos bringing new positions because they also bring new responsibilities." There was laughter around the hall. Ben waved his finger at the crowd. "But don't worry—they'll suffer for it. I think they've punished themselves already—by hiring me!" There was more laughter, and then Ben concluded his remarks by looking at the stone walls on either side of him. "Well, it looks like they're going to take the whole place down, stone by stone. I guess they'll need my help to rebuild it." Everyone chuckled once more. "Thank you," said Ben. "Thank you, thank you, again."

As he left the dais, the applause was renewed, and it kept intensifying until Ben was lost from sight in the crowd.

Mack was making some last remarks about him. "— there will be a special presentation later this evening to Mr. Delacruz, for many of those here this evening—including myself—who wish to thank him properly for all of his efforts on behalf of our children and both of our schools."

I found myself with a sour taste in my mouth. I had supposed that both of us were guests of honor that evening, but at that moment, it felt as if he had been the only guest of honor, and I was merely an after-thought. The manner in which Ben had gracefully—yet with humor—accepted the honors bestowed on him also made me feel like a slovenly fool. Yet I was the one who had purchased the new tuxedo shirt, and had spent hundreds of dollars preparing myself for the evening, while all he had done was walk across campus, barely bothering to clean himself up for the occasion. All around me though, the conversations were full of anecdotes and accolades about Ben Delacruz, and I was roundly being ignored.

In the crowd of Rockhorn's well-wishers, several people tried to strike up conversations. My thoughts were whirling too fast to really pay attention to them, so I ignored them as best I could. Resentment at the way Ben had upstaged me was rising, but accompanying it was the fear that I'd gone too far. Ben might soon be much more powerful at Rockhorn that I'd suspected. Somehow I might be able to make up for the duplicity I'd shown. After all, I hadn't directed my announcement with the specific intent of offending him. Was it possible to make amends?

I looked around at the periphery of the crowd, and spotted Ben immediately. He was listening patiently to someone who seemed to be talking his ear off.

Soon I saw that Meredith was his talking companion. From my vantage point, I couldn't make out a word they were saying. It was strange watching from here: they were like tiny characters on a miniature stage, unreachable by anyone in the real world. She smiled and held out a small gift box. Then, as she passed it to him, the box slipped and I saw Meredith react with alarm. Moments later, Ben was picking up a small dripping box from the floor, and I could see chagrin all over her face. The tinkling crash the box had made as it fell to the floor was swallowed in the roar of the crowd.

People moved about. I saw Meredith mopping at Ben's hands, trying to wipe off whatever had spilled. And vaguely, I could hear Mack introducing the string quartet, and speaking about the donations they were soliciting for the music department. When the crowd parted again, I saw that a space had opened up where Meredith and Ben had been standing. A strong scent swept through the room.

Apparently, whatever she'd given him had been perfume, or cologne. Odd that something pleasant in tiny dabs can be so distasteful in a large quantity. As strong as formaldehyde, it cleared the crowd entirely in that corner, and I caught a glimpse of someone else dabbing at Ben's shoulder with a napkin. A collection of the valets frantically tried to clean up the glass and wipe up the pool of perfume. Ben, of course, didn't seem to care if his shoulder was wet and smelly.

Then an older man in an out of date tuxedo, someone I didn't recognize, came up to me. He bent his head in an inquiring tone. "Excuse me," he said. "But don't you know this Ben chap? I understand that you might be able to introduce me. I'm curious to know if he—"

"No, I'm sorry," I said automatically. "I can't say that I do. Does he work at Rockhorn?" I nodded a rapid good-bye and moved into the crowd. Maybe I could talk to Ben, and make him see that I hadn't intended what I'd done as a personal slight. Perhaps he'd understand if I talked to him directly.

But I was of two minds, and this confusion perhaps caused me to feel some paranoia. What if I changed my mind, and went the other way? Now that I had these thoughts, it seemed that everywhere I turned I saw people watching me. There was Catherine Foss, off to one side of the dais, glancing aside in what I thought was an attempt to hide the fact that she was keeping an eye out for me. Was my distress and indecision evident even across a crowded ballroom floor?

I turned the other direction, and saw Bartimus Santos standing close to the wall, holding a Scotch on the rocks, eyeing me again with what I thought was suspicion. He motioned me towards him. In frustration I turned back again, plowing the opposite direction through the crowd. I didn't want to talk to anyone. I needed to think.

Although I didn't necessarily want to rescind the announcement, if that was the only way to make sure that Ben understood, I was willing to contemplate it. I stared wildly around the room (no doubt making a fool of myself in the process), looking for Ben. But I could not spot him anywhere.

Soon, I found myself pushing through a group of several Rock-horn instructors, when one of them plucked at my elbow. "Hey," she said. "Didn't you know Ben's class from Ihme was using that building out there—the one you said you're going to take over and refurbish? Didn't you know that?" Her tone was shrill, as if she'd had one too many Martinis.

"No," I mumbled. "No, I didn't. Not at all." I craned my head and looked over my interlocutor. I was searching for Ben, trying to see if there was any way I could come close to him without being observed. Perhaps I could insinuate myself beside him and steal a moment alone to hear his thoughts. I just wanted to make sure that he understood that it wasn't entirely personal—but then again I didn't want to renounce it or anything like that. There were other considerations, not least among them the monetary ones.

I ended up at the hors d'oeuvres table. That was where I found him, finally. Our hands almost touched across a plate of kosher crackers. I jerked back in surprise, as if I'd had an electrical shock.

Everything seemed surreal to me in that moment. I noticed odd things about him. I was intensely aware of his fingernails, and I could see the wet spot on his shoulder. And the suit-jacket he was wearing didn't quite fit. Apparently, it had been borrowed from a valet at the door. The musky smell of spilled perfume surrounded us; he reeked of it. For a moment, I wondered if he'd been drinking—he was a mess. I realized that my hands were shaking. Ben seemed much calmer than me.

I laughed nervously. "I've been looking for you," I said.

Ben took note of my sweating brow and agitated hands. He reached out for some of the crackers, and then added a piece of sliced salmon.

"You're going to betray me, then?" he asked.

"Now, Ben, that's going a bit too far."

"Well, the first time might be an accident. The second time could be coincidence. But they say that if you don't recognize it by the third time, you're a fool. And come to think of it, I might be a fool here."

"But there are good reasons for all of this, Ben. There are grown-up reasons, real reasons. We should talk." I filled a plate with food from the table, not even noticing what I was taking.

He shook his head sadly. "Anyway, I'd best be going."

"But where? What do you mean?"

He nodded at me portentously. "You know where I'm going," he said. "The real world."

"I don't know what you're talking about, Ben."

He backed away from the table, walking towards the crowd and the auctions table. He turned his head and looked back at me. "You can't go where I'm going—but trust me, you will follow. You'll see!" Then he pushed himself into a gap in the crowd.

"What?" I spoke loudly, startling even myself. "Ben, don't do anything! Come back—all we need to do is talk about this!"

The Argurion presentation was in a few moments. I found myself standing up near the dais, holding a plate of things that didn't really go together—kalamata olives, crab legs, strips of veal, and the like. I caught a glimpse of Joe Matheson brushing off his tuxedo near the back of the room, no doubt preparing himself for the big moment. Mack Demson was up on stage, discussing something in hushed tones with one of the uniformed assistants.

The volume of conversation in the hall continued to rise, until it threatened to drown out the string quartet's gentle arrangements. The continued absence of the Argurion family led to more heated discussion. Rumor had it that they'd all appear together. They'd make a grand entrance. The crowd buzzed with the excitement of the coming presentation, humming like a high-tension wire.

Mack went to the microphone and began to make lesser presentations. First, they were announcing the people who had correctly guessed the names and dates for each of the busts placed around the hall, and would be taking them home this evening, each presented with a special plaque commemorating the evening at Rockhorn.

I looked at the crowd. Some of the faces were turned up so that they caught the light, and they seemed frozen, enraptured as they watched Mack. Many of the rest of them were still talking to each other, glancing up and down, evaluating and comparing their gowns against the one worn by the person they were conversing with. I saw Ben on the other side of the room, raising a glass as he conversed with someone I didn't know. I watched him in a daze, feeling the best possibility for a real friendship that I'd ever had slip away from me.

Then the crowd closed across my vision. For a moment my sight seemed to blur, and I rubbed my eyes, shaking off the moment.

Mack's sonorous voice boomed out again. Now he was speaking about the various pieces of art that were being auctioned that evening as a benefit to the Library endowment. He described the chandeliers and their entire history in excruciating detail, and finally called the winning bidder up to the dais for a presentation of each item. Then he moved on to the various pieces of art, starting with the least expensive—a recent watercolor landscape of Rockhorn's buildings done by Joe Matheson himself—and moving ever so slowly towards the more notable artworks.

In the back of the room, there was a second crash of glass that evening. For a moment, I thought I heard someone applauding, but it wasn't applause at all. It was a voice shouting. The disturbance continued, and the crowd moved uncertainly forward, towards the dais. I could hear the voice from the rear shouting, "This is shitty. It *stinks!* You all stink!" There was a second crash—by the sound of it, an entire table had been overturned. Some reveler who had imbibed too much, I imagined. But the crowd seemed truly disrupted. People even began moving towards the front exit, but the event couldn't be over already. The Argurion announcement and presentation hadn't even taken place yet, and Mack was caught in mid-speech. I looked up at him, and saw his face distraught. Obviously, he could see more than I could. What was going on?

I looked back, but all that could be seen was the milling of the crowd. People came to the front in an increasingly frantic manner. I saw a brace of valets congregate at the back of the room, and things seemed to quiet down. Despite the momentary confusion, Mack began again, concluding his monologue about the art pieces with only a slightly nervous shake in his voice. The main event was nearly upon us. At the east end of the hall, I could spy the Argurion family standing regally, preparing to make their entrance. Joe flitted onto the stage, to whisper something in Mack's ear before flitting back off again.

To recover from the disturbance, people mobbed the bar and the liquor tables, and soon the crowd was serene again, the conversation once more loud and boisterous. In the interlude, the string quartet struck up a Mozart waltz; the light and happy tempo lifted the mood.

The party looked to proceed well into the small hours of the morning. At the end of it all, we'd all drift home like so many floating champagne bubbles, dreams of Rockhorn's future filling the air.

22.

IT WAS not to be. Joe Matheson was soon at my side, whispering urgently to me, telling me that my presence was required in the anteroom off the main Library. Apparently, there was some sort of an emergency meeting that was being convened immediately, before the presentation. When I came into the room, I saw Bartimus Santos, looking grim, and other members of the Board. Soon, there were ten or twelve of us at the front of the large anteroom. Joe came in after me, pulling the door closed behind him. He was out of breath.

"This was all of the Board I could find, on a moment's notice," he gasped.

"It's a quorum—enough to take action," said Bartimus. "Where's Miss Foss though? I thought she was going to join us."

At that moment, Catherine Foss burst into the room. Her face was pale and drawn. "The authorities have been notified," she said. "I called the police and the fire department."

"I'm not sure that was really necessary," said Joe Matheson.

"It's my Library," said Catherine. "If he damages one of those pieces of art, or if he does something to any of the books—you'll all pay for it. This place tonight contains priceless treasures of our cultural history, and I will do what is necessary to preserve them."

"Not to mention the good will of the philanthropic community," said Mr. Tharsen. "They're here for the first time this evening—we don't want to lose that good will."

"Well, that's precisely why we shouldn't have called the police," said Joe. "He'll calm down soon enough—and we'll have a good laugh about it. I can't imagine most people are leaving. The Argurion announcement is yet to come. But if uniformed officers mob the place, our guests sure to depart quickly."

Then Sandy Hedron came rushing into the room. "Pardon me for interrupting," she said. "But I thought you all should know—apparently he's left the building. He's gone."

"Wait—what's going on?" I asked. "Who's gone? What are we meeting about?"

"There's been a disturbance on the floor," said Bartimus. "Someone throwing things. Breaking glasses."

"It was Ben," said Catherine Foss bitterly. "I knew he wouldn't go along. He just went berserk."

"Then why were you the one to offer him—" I began.

"He's dumped a table over too," said Sandy Hedron. "And before he left, he attacked several of the auction staffers."

"So it was Ben I heard shouting," I said.

"Truly outrageous behavior," said Bartimus. "Shouting obscenities."

"I only heard him say that people were full of shit."

"Well, yes," said Joe. "But that's enough to clear a room like this. A crowd of this caliber wants everything to be perfect. I talked with him, and I thought I'd calmed him down, but then he began throwing things. He was frightening people."

"That's why I called the police," said Catherine. "It's a legal matter now."

"You shouldn't have called them," said Joe. "You know, we have our own security staff."

"A fat lot of good they did us," said Catherine.

"Yes, but –" Joe snapped his fingers. "I just realized, we have Mr. Avecet already here this evening. He's out on the floor."

"Philip—?" said Tharsen.

"The Chief of Police, Philip Avecet. I'll ask him to join us." Joe disappeared from the room.

"We will wait for Mr. Avecet," said Bartimus. "He may be able to provide assistance in formulating a plan of action."

Individual conversations broke out around the room as we waited for Joe to return. I gulped my drink. "It was wrong what I did," I said to Mr. Tharsen. "I didn't know it was that important to him. Why does that old building matter so much? It was dishonest, what I did."

"You know, you might have a point. He was going on about the building out there."

"He was?" I asked.

Tharsen sneered at me. "Oh sure, you were the one to be friends with him and then give away the buildings he was using. You'd know all about honesty and dishonesty—why don't you tell us exactly what's wrong with what you did?"

Bartimus looked over his glasses and rescued me from Tharsen. "Well, sir," he said to me. "I do understand that you believe what you did caused Ben to become upset, and that you believe it was wrong. But there's no help for it now."

"I just had no idea that he'd commit himself to a fight for that building," I mused to myself. "I'll take it back—I'll go out on the floor, and take back my announcement, and then I'll find him and tell him. I'll change what I said."

Tharsen moved on to other prey, and Bartimus came nearer. He leaned close to me, so that he was almost whispering. "In fact, I share your sentiment, sir. It was a shameful thing for you to do. I believe in heritage and history, and perhaps Ben Delacruz was trying to remind us of where Rockhorn first came from, with this business about the Chapel. I believe that I've been blind all along about Mr. Delacruz, but there's no help for it now. We've got a group of people here who are more intent on making money from that crowd than they are on the question of honesty."

"But what if I took it back—what if I found him, and changed my position, couldn't we just go back to the way it was?"

"No, at this juncture, it wouldn't make any difference. We've gone too far now. And he's gone too far as well." Bartimus sucked on his pipe, and then he spoke again. "We really can't let this stand. It's reprehensible—both ways."

"C'mon, I should go talk to him. I can't make it worse, can I?"

"Well, unfortunately, you wouldn't be helping the case by reversing yourself—no one trusts you, everyone thinks you have something to gain in all this. You sir, in fact have established a habit of reversing yourself when a matter comes to a Board vote, and I for one, must beg you to keep your peace during this discussion. You will not improve things—you could, in fact, make it much worse."

Joe entered the room again, with Philip Avecet in a tuxedo and several uniformed policemen. Carefully, Joe closed the door behind them. "They're all happy on the floor now—except the Argurion family. The family can't understand why we're delaying the presentation, and they don't like it much." He wiped sweat off his forehead with a napkin.

"As soon as things are cleaned up, we'll move directly to the Argurion announcement and presentation," said Joe. "No further delays. Let's push through it quickly."

"Where's Dean Demson?" asked Bartimus.

"Mack's still out there—curtaining off the damaged tables," said Joe. "And keeping the Argurion family happy."

"What do you need us to do?" growled the deep voice of Philip Avecet. "Is the perpetrator still in the building?"

"No, he's not," said Joe. "I'm sorry about this. I think you yourself could have resolved this entire situation quietly, sir, without other ·uniformed assistance and without any fuss. But now that your men are here—"

"They should go and arrest him!" said Catherine. "He's probably still on campus."

"Well, there is some damage to school property," said Joe. "But he is still an instructor at Rockhorn, after all. Chief Avecet, I'd prefer that you simply have a psychological evaluation done, and see if there's something else causing this kind of behavior. He's usually so gentle and mild-mannered—it's not like him to do something like this. Not at all like him."

"Oh yes it is," said Catherine. "It's just like him—as you've seen this evening, at heart he's violent and destructive. He's threatened me before, and since he couldn't touch me this evening, he took his rage out on the event. He's out of control, and I don't want him treated with kid gloves. I want him prosecuted!"

"Well, whatever you do with him—there has to be a comprehensive psychological evaluation first," insisted Joe. "Check for mood-altering things: drugs, alcohol, allergic reactions that might have affected his behavior. Is that clear?"

"I think we can accommodate you," said Chief Avecet. He looked around the room, and chose his words carefully. "If we take him into custody, I can have him transferred to Moolston immediately, before we book him. But you have to understand, I will have to take him into custody if we find him."

"That's fine, sir," said Joe. "Just fine. You do your job, and we'll do ours." He turned to go back out onto the ballroom floor.

Philip Avecet cleared his throat. "Ah, hmm. Just one question, Mr. Matheson," he said. "Where do you think we would find this man? If he's still at Rockhorn, where would he go?"

Joe walked across the room. Now he was standing beside me. I stared straight ahead at Philip Avecet's pleated tuxedo shirt.

"This man can help you," said Joe. He put a hand on my shoulder. "He's been spending time with Ben for months now, and he knows all of the places Mr. Delacruz frequents around the campus, especially after hours."

"All right, officers," said Chief Avecet. "You heard the man. Follow his lead, but don't take any unnecessary risks." He held up a black police radio. "I'll be monitoring you from here, and I'll be on the police band as well. You'll have back-up if you need it. Let's go!"

I opened my mouth to protest, but found that the room was rapidly emptying out. I felt that Mack Demson would have been a more appropriate choice, as he'd been spending the most time with Ben in recent weeks. Perhaps Mack would be more effective as well—I wasn't sure how Ben would react to seeing me again. But soon there was no one to protest to.

Only Catherine Foss, Sandy Hedron, the police officers, and me were left behind in the room. Catherine smiled thinly at me. "Unfortunately, I have to stay behind for the presentation as well, but Sandy will go with you—she'll be happy to help."

I would now be missing the presentation. Joe had promised to introduce me to the Argurion family, and now I would be missing my chance to meet several of the wealthiest people in this hemisphere— one of whom was a Rockhorn alumni. I resented Ben for this, but apparently not as much as Sandy Hedron resented him. All the way out of the Library, and across campus, as the four of us walked towards the back forty, Ms. Hedron talked incessantly about the dangerous behavior that Ben had exhibited, and about how frightened many of the children and faculty at the school apparently felt about his influence there. She seemed to be making as much up on the spot as she could. In sordid detail, she described the worst particulars of each member of Ben's group, and she made it sound as if they were all presently engaged in the very activities that Ben had removed from them. It was almost as if she planned to incite the police officers to have quick trigger fingers and itchy reactions when they encountered Ben and his little group of juvenile delinquents. Perhaps she was simply upset by the previous events of the evening, but in any case, I do not think that her words were warranted. Her conversation definitely did not help to calm my already frayed nerves.

I led them directly to the site of the last campfire I'd attended—the one right after Mack had fallen in the water. It was as if my feet were impelled to travel in that direction themselves, as if they knew the way without my help. I knew—somehow, I knew—beyond a doubt, that Ben would be there that night.

When we arrived at the campsite, a low fire was already burning in the pit, and we could see many dark figures standing around the periphery, in the shadows. I could see Ben himself standing quietly by the fire, facing away from us, as if he'd just concluded telling a story. The place seemed packed with people—some of them Ben's juvenile students. I had become genuinely nervous about the armed policemen who were with me. After all of Ms. Hedron's rhetoric, I felt that they might shoot first, and ask questions later. So I brought my little group to a halt ten or fifteen yards away, well outside the circle of the fire.

"Look," I said. "He's just ahead. Let me go alone, and pull him out of the crowd, so that there isn't any unnecessary upheaval."

"I don't know, sir," said one of the policemen. "How about if we go in first instead?" He un-holstered his gun.

"No," I said. "This is what I'm doing. I don't want any violence tonight."

"Which one is he?"

"He'll be the first one I talk to. Arrest him—not anyone else."

I stepped forward, into the firelight. Standing quite near to me was Ben. I said his name, but he didn't seem to hear me, so I stepped closer, nearly close enough to touch him, but still he stood there, staring across the fire, seemingly mesmerized by the flames. I looked where he was looking, and saw Zeb, the father of Jimmy and Jon. His face wore an expression as angry as any I'd ever seen on the faces of his homicidal sons; the firelight flickered across his enraged face, and the light played off the gun barrel he was holding, pointed directly at me.

Sandy Hedron spotted the gun about the same time I did. I turned to look back, and I could see the glint from the guns held now by the two officers.

"Look out!" cried Sandy. "He's got a gun!" But she pointed at Ben. I glanced down at Ben's hands in sudden horror—had he been holding a weapon on me this entire time? With relief, I saw that his hands were empty, but the officers were raising their guns, pointing them at Ben and at me. They were coming from the side into the firelight. Soon, they'd be visible to everyone who was standing there. I was sure there was going to be gunplay.

I thought to say something, to step forward and clarify that Ben had no weapon on him, to try to save the situation. But Ben beat me to it. He raised his hands high in the air, showing them empty.

"What? Do you think I'm some sort of revolutionary? C'mon, you should have arrested me inside. Don't worry yourselves—I'm not holding a gun."

Immediately, despite his calm assurances, the officers wrestled him to the ground. I've never seen a person be immobilized so quickly and so forcefully. In a matter of seconds, he was face-down in the dirt and his arms were cuffed tightly behind his back with plastic zip-cuffs.

We were still surrounded. All around the circle of the fire people were standing –people of all types: women, men, young children, adults, old men. We couldn't see their faces, but they could see us silhouetted against the flames. The officers read Ben his rights in a rapid-fire monotone and pulled him upright again.

The officers prepared to push through the gathering crowd of onlookers and supporters. They wanted to take their prisoner back to the main campus. Then I heard a sudden yell—a loud sound like an animal bellowing. The large shape of a man lunged out of the crowd. Without warning, the man was in the circle of firelight, and then he was less than two feet from me, roaring like a wild animal. It was Zeb, and he looked angry enough to kill. Caught unaware, I jumped sideways, trying at least to put the flames between Zeb and me. I slipped to the ground and felt the shoulder of my tuxedo rip. Somehow, I ended up on my knees behind the fire, facing the officers instead of Zeb. Suddenly, there was a deafening roar. Zeb had fired a shot at nearly point-blank range, right behind my head.

For a long moment, I couldn't hear at all. I saw Ben urgently mouthing silent words, and I saw one officer put a hand to his ear, and grimace as if in pain. Then my hearing returned, and the sound of the gun echoed in the forest like some lost thing. Oddly, when my hearing came back, so did my sense of smell; the acrid stink of the powder immediately set me to coughing.

I watched them all from a strange vantage point, as if I were underwater. Everything seemed to have slowed down. I found I'd put the other sleeve of my tuxedo too near the flames. It was smoldering, but I couldn't feel any heat at all. I attempted to stand up, but stumbled. Somehow, I'd hurt my leg. Vaguely, I could hear Ben talking loudly, repeating over and over again: "Put it away, Zeb. Put it away." One officer was clenching his gun firmly, not taking his eyes off Zeb, while the other officer took his hand away from an ear that dripped blood and muttered in an absurdly absent-minded manner, as if he'd merely cut himself shaving, "Just a nick, a little nick." Then I saw both officers lunge towards Zeb. First, they collided with me as I attempted to stand again, knocking me to the ground and bowling me over. Something snapped in my knee. They ran right over me in their pursuit, but they missed him in the end. Zeb's huge shape twisted and slipped away in the dark, leaving his coat behind in the policeman's grasping hand.

Now the officers began to back up, out of the firelight and onto the path towards the main campus. They stared wildly into the surrounding wilderness and pointed their guns at the forest. Even hustling sideways like crabs, dragging the bound Ben with them, they moved quickly. Sandy Hedron was far ahead of them already, running as fast as she could to the safety of the buildings. I was nearly left behind, still kneeling on the ground beside the fire.

I forced myself up off the ground and ran to catch up. "What about the rest of them?" I shouted.

"We don't have the men to take them," said the first officer. "We can't keep our prisoner, and hold off these crazy guys at the same time. We've got to get back."

The one with the nicked ear spoke into his belt radio. "Back-up," he said. "Officer hit. We need back-up out here." But even before he was done speaking, the crowd had melted away into the darkness. All of Ben's friends and supporters were gone. We were alone.

23.

THE PRESENTATION was long since over when we returned to the Library. I could see a few guests emerging from the front door of the Library; the people were beginning to depart. Under the antique gas lantern, their jewelry flashed and sparkled and their sleek coats shimmered with the light. Across the road, we could see the bright headlights of Jaguars and Mercedes as the valets pulled them slowly to the front of the Library.

From across the square, I heard the faint sound of a woman's polite laughter, an artificial chuckle echoing out of the door. After the gunshot and the fire, and Zeb roaring at us in the darkness, all of it seemed unreal. It was as if these people were living in a dream. I could still hear the explosion ringing in my head, and now that the adrenaline was wearing off, it was very cold. I was shivering uncontrollably.

A tall man in a tuxedo came out of the Library door and flagged his car down. A pair of diamond cuff-links caught the headlights of an Audi TT and flared brightly for a moment, burning our eyes. Then the Audi pulled forward, cutting off the glare. For a moment, in my half-deaf and exhausted state, a strange delusion swept over me. It was as if all of the people emerging from the door were celebrities—actors on a false movie set—and we were the real characters, coming back to explain the story to them.

I shivered again and the hallucination faded away. We were scratched and muddy. My neck was blackened and throbbed from the powder burn and somehow we'd gotten water and soot stains on all the knees of our clothes. Both arms of my coat were now ripped; my tuxedo was utterly ruined.

"Hey, you," said one of the officers to me. "Does anyone recognize him inside the building? Do they know that he's a teacher here?"

"He was inside earlier—he gave an acceptance speech. They know him."

"Well, we don't want anyone worried about what's happening. Chief Avecet said to make sure not to upset anyone."

"Not to upset anyone?" I said. "What about this?" I pointed at the powder-burn on my neck.

"Yeah, there's that," said the officer. He held up Zeb's coat. "But we got what he was wearing."

"Here," said the other officer. "Use this." He pulled a piece of black cloth from a pouch on his belt. He yanked the cloth over Ben's head, and tightened a string around his throat. I saw that it was a bag designed to cover a prisoner's entire face. Ben could no longer see. Apparently, this was designed to keep a prisoner from running away. It would also serve to make him unrecognizable as we came into Rockhorn's Library.

The officer went one step further—he pushed the fabric of the mask into his mouth and yanked a strip of tape around Ben's head, rendering him mute for the moment. I suppose the officer thought that we had had enough shouting in the Library hall for the evening, and I quite agreed.

Thus, instead of disrupting the proceedings, we were the evening's capstone curiosity. With a bound and gagged prisoner in our possession, we received a small smattering of applause from those who were still present. The police and their guide were returning triumphant, with the perpetrator of the disruption in hand. As gracefully as we could in our mud-stained clothes, we accepted their accolades and tried to disappear rapidly into the anteroom.

This time, the Library anteroom was crowded with people. Every member of the Board seemed to be present and accounted for; they stood shoulder to shoulder. I saw Catherine at the other end of the room, next to Bartimus, who was engaged in a deep discussion with Wallace Steg. A hubbub of worried conversation filled the air.

"Ah—they're back!" Catherine Foss touched Bartimus on the shoulder. "They're back—they have him," she said.

Reluctantly, Bartimus looked away from his conversation. "Yes, I see…they've come back. Ah—Mr. Avecet, sir, if I could have your attention," he said. Chief Avecet then turned and saw us. He stared for a moment, taking in our muddy appearance, our bound prisoner, and my tattered tuxedo. Then he turned his back again. For nearly ten minutes, he stood and talked to Catherine and Bartimus about us, while I felt the weariness sweep over me. Catherine seemed to be trying to convince Chief Avecet of some important point. I couldn't hear what they were saying over the continuing conversation of the Board members, and I couldn't understand why they had to wait. Couldn't we be done with it all?

Although I couldn't hear them, I watched Catherine closely as she talked. Her eyes and cheeks gleamed, ruddy from the after-glow of the Argurion Presentation, and she seemed to have accorded herself additional powers and importance following the presentation. In her eyes, it seemed, the moment she was handed that check for $30 million dollars was worth every struggle, every weakness. I wish I'd been there to see her bow her head under the outpouring of applause from her assembled benefactors. Already, I could see her savoring the moment, recapturing the goodwill of the assembled eminences. She'd be savoring it for decades to come, cashing that check every time she asserted her right to power.

Evidently, she won this initial discussion. Chief Avecet and Bartimus Santos parted to stand on either side of her. Catherine clasped her hands together and looked at us with shining eyes. Apparently she was in charge now. Perhaps she already was, all along, only I was too dim to realize it.

Catherine picked up a wine goblet and a spoon. Quickly, she struck it, sending up a chiming cacophony of sound.

"Ladies!" she said loudly. "Ladies and gentlemen of the Board. May I have your attention, please!"

Gradually, the conversations died down. People turned, and when they caught sight of us, their attention was riveted. A slow silence came over the room.

"As you can see," said Catherine. "Our errant instructor has returned." There was a collective sigh of acknowledgement around the room. A few whispered conversations broke out anew. Catherine spoke up again, over the whispers and mutters.

"I have prevailed upon our gracious Chief of Police, Mr. Philip Avecet, to allow Rockhorn Board to clarify a few important matters with Mr. Delacruz before he is booked and charged for his acts of vandalism."

"—And psychologically evaluated," broke in Joe Matheson. "I really don't see how Ben could have committed such heinous acts of destruction, and I don't know if we should be holding him responsible for his actions before we understand whether or not there are extenuating circumstances. Perhaps a mental imbalance of some sort—"

"Yes," said Catherine firmly. "There is a mental imbalance. But there is no question that Mr. Delacruz is responsible for these actions. We have many witnesses. And there are many angry people here this evening, not least among them Mr. Jackson Argurion, whose presentation was sullied by these unfortunate events."

"Well, I would like to talk to Ben," said Joe.

"By all means!" agreed Catherine. "Let's find out just what manner of human trash would cause such a disturbance."

"Please—" she said to the officers. "Would you mind taking off the hood and tape? We'd like to hear Ben's response—if there is any response."

The officers removed the gag and the black bag they'd placed over Ben's head.

Catherine Foss began speaking as soon as the officers went to work. She had a lot of hateful things to say, and apparently she feared that she didn't have enough time to say them all. Every now and then she would throw in questions that seemed designed to trap Ben in contradictory statements. I didn't listen to her entire monologue. I gathered that she was angry, and vengeful, and wanted Ben to acknowledge his crime, and explain his actions. My attention wasn't really with Catherine though; I was tired, and I was watching Ben.

When the black bag was removed, he blinked and squinted in the sudden light. Underneath his nose, a sheen of blood caught the light. Ben's entire face looked swollen, his eyes bloodshot and unrecognizable. I looked closer, and realized that at the campfire struggle, he had split his lip open and possibly broken his nose. Between the campfire and the Library, the bruised flesh had become inflamed and swollen, filling out his usually narrow face. After he glanced around the room, catching many hateful glares in response, he turned his face towards the floor, apparently to allow the blood from his damaged nose to drip onto the floor.

Soon, Catherine paused. Evidently, Ben wasn't responding in the way that she had hoped. I presume she had hoped to snare him in one of her convoluted word traps. His lack of any response just seemed to make her angrier and more irrational. Soon she moved from rational questions to raging, groundless accusations, hoping to provoke some response—any response—from Ben. I found myself shrinking back a bit into the crowd, anxious about the consequences of such rage.

As he saw Catherine become more enraged, Philip Avecet seemed to share my apprehension. Midway through a ringing speech in which she accused Ben of intentionally doing shoddy workmanship on the Library, in order to make it fall down on this very evening, Philip Avecet cut her off.

"I'd like to hear from him," said Avecet. "Mr. Delacruz. Do you have any response to any of these things that have been said? Have you done all of these things?"

Surprisingly, Ben turned his face up from the floor and looked directly at Chief Avecet. He seemed to be attempting to smile.

"Why, yes sir. I actually plan to take the new Library down brick by brick and then to become the new Librarian myself. The Librarian next in line to be Headmaster of Rockhorn."

An uproar broke out about the room at these ludicrous words.

"Mr. Delacruz ," warned Avecet. "I'm in no mood for jokes."

"Oh, I'm not joking," said Ben. Ben had more to say, but my knee was hurting and unaccountably, I felt faint. So even as Ben continued speaking, I went out the side door of the anteroom in search of a glass of water.

The ballroom floor was empty, and the cleanup crew was taking down all of the wall hangings. After I collected my drink, I looked out at the large empty room and imagined all the people who had been here earlier in the evening. For the first time, I saw that suspended from the ceiling, covering the cedar rafters, was a huge artificial ceiling made of cloth, with faint clouds of white and blue with silver edging in them. I had not noticed it earlier, and the sense of unreality struck me anew. The expansive cloth hung over the entire ballroom floor. It was all like a vast movie set, with the actors all off-stage.

I thought back to earlier in the evening, when Ben had been up on the dais, thanking the crowd for their support, and I imagined him actually filling the role he'd joked about in the anteroom: Librarian, and then Headmaster of Rockhorn. If he'd been a different person—less confrontational, less obscure and enigmatic, less dogmatic and prickly—perhaps he could have gone there. He would have been a much less political, and a much more effective Headmaster of Rockhorn than Joe Matheson. But soon the police officers would take him away. I shook my head and glanced back at the false silver-edged clouds. All around me, the lights were dimming; the cleanup crews were shutting down the hall, and I was left in darkness.

When I came back into the anteroom, Ben had apparently finished speaking, or whatever Philip Avecet had said in reply had so abashed him that he had stopped. In any case, he was looking down at the floor once more. A tiny trickle of blood stained the tiles at his feet, but no one had thought to clean it up.

Now Philip Avecet was showing Catherine Foss the brunt of his frustration. "Miss Foss, I really believe that a psychological evaluation might not even be necessary. It seems clear that this is just a petty act of vandalism—a small internal political struggle that became a bit bigger than anyone at Rockhorn had expected."

"Yes," said Joe Matheson. "What if you both just take a few days to cool off?"

Philip Avecet stepped closer to her. "Do you have proof for these extraordinary accusations that you have made tonight?"

Along with the rest of the crowd, I was surprised to hear the response. Quickly, she spoke up. "Why yes, Chief Avecet, we do."

She gestured at the back of the anteroom, where the door to a storage closet was almost obscured by the standing Board members.

"Sandy," she called. "Please show our friends in."

The Board members parted, and the storage room door opened. At that moment, I realized that the entire sequence with Chief Avecet might have been a set-up; Catherine Foss may have been preparing for this moment for months now. It would be like her to prepare for such an event. This was her grand opportunity to exact retribution for real and imagined slights.

A hesitant trail of three or four students filed into the room, along with one parent. All the students were all upper-classmen. I recognized at least one of the children as a member of Ben's group, and I recognized another as one of the athletes Ben had confronted with a hammer outside his classroom. I watched them as they passed. I'd never seen any of them have a problem with Ben. Red-eyed and worried, each of these juveniles seemed to have been threatened with evisceration or at least expulsion unless they cooperated this evening.

"Chief Avecet," said Catherine Foss. "I'm sorry for only bringing forward these individuals now. However, each of them approached me separately as the only person they felt they could truly trust at Rockhorn Academy." Catherine sighed dramatically. "They approached me, and each of them had pitiful stories—simply horrifying stories—to tell of the negative influence Mr. Delacruz has brought to Rockhorn. As you've heard, we've had to deal with this problem—with Mr. Delacruz's many problems—for months now. Drugs, deception, intimidation, gang activity." One of the students nodded solemnly.

"So why didn't these people come to the police?" asked Joe.

"It seems that they were afraid of others in the faculty. Each of them were so afraid of the possible consequences, that they said that they would only come forward if and when Mr. Delacruz was in police custody." The same student nodded again. I felt he was overdoing it, but as I looked around, I saw that most people believed his reaction was genuine.

Now it was Avecet's turn to sigh. "All right—why don't you come back to the station house? I'll take some statements."

"Oh, but I told them all that I'd permit them to say their piece just as soon as he was apprehended. I told them they would be able to confront Mr. Delacruz with the evidence of exactly how he has ruined their lives. You wouldn't deprive them of that chance to speak the truth, would you?"

I rolled my eyes. I had had little idea that Catherine would take it this far. I wouldn't have led the police out there if I had known.

"I see," said Philip Avecet suspiciously. "However, I want to remind you that this is not a court of law. None of these 'witnesses' have been sworn—and all of it would have to be thoroughly vetted before being used in some prosecutor's case. Mr. Delacruz hasn't even been charged with anything."

"Oh yes, we know that." Catherine glared at the group until several of them nodded again. "However, this is their one chance to confront the man who is the cause of their difficulties here at Rockhorn."

I could see now that Catherine really didn't care about carrying any particular charges forward. What she cared about the most was the court of public opinion here at Rockhorn, and despite what happened once Ben left Rockhorn in police custody, she wanted to assure that any lingering respect the Board had for him was stripped away—she wanted to guarantee that he was never coming back here.

Chief Avecet sighed again. "Carry on."

Now that this was beginning to turn into a show trial, I could see him regretting his decision to allow Catherine Foss to ask some questions. He looked despairingly at Bartimus Santos, who simply shrugged.

Sandy Hedron spoke up first. She told a quite amazing story about what we'd found at the fire this evening, replete with men in gang costumes who assaulted the police officers, a cloud of marijuana smoke in the air, crack pipes around the campfire, and half-naked children who Ben might or might not have been sexually molesting. I looked around for the officers, astonished that they hadn't objected to these incredible details, but they were nowhere in evidence.

I thought about speaking up—I really did. But there was my past history against me, and the words that Bartimus had said earlier this evening had stayed with me. Who would believe me, a person known for duplicity? And by this point, I was too tired; my head was still throbbing and my knee ached. I found a comfortable chair on the other side of the room and sank into it in relief, waiting for the constant drone of Sandy's voice to pause for a moment. Then, I told myself, at the end of her statement, I'd speak up. Then I'd correct the particulars.

I must have dozed off in that chair, because soon someone else was speaking. Reluctantly, they were repeating the words that I'd heard shouted this evening—and adding to them everything Mack and I had once heard around the campfire. "You're like toilets, all shiny and white ceramic on the outside, and inside just full of shit, full of stinking shit. Toilets—all of you. Full of shit."

There were gasps of horror from several of the old biddies on the Board. And then, of course, the person telling the story went on to add all sorts of other obscenities that Ben had reputedly taught to even the youngest children in his Shop classes. I thought it was particularly shrewd of Catherine to have someone take note of this. No, in a criminal trial it wouldn't matter, but at Rockhorn it did. Despite the lack of religious ideas, the old guard at Rockhorn did pride themselves on bringing up children in an environment clean of the lower classes' predilection for crude language, slang, and obscenity. Ben's crude— and particularly apt—language would be the straw that pushed the Board's opinion of him over the edge.

I drifted away, hearing only the ringing of the gunshot still in my ears. Intermittently, I regained consciousness, hearing fragments of a purported drug deal orchestrated by Ben and finally, a distorted version of Ben's first fishing trip. This version contained boys who were encouraged by Ben to try to drown other boys in some sort of twisted gang ritual. (Of course, I wasn't there—so how was I to know that Jake's version wasn't distorted?) I faded out again.

Yet unaccountably, I woke up for the end of another tale of drug deals at Rockhorn. No doubt Catherine Foss was very pleased with the direction this evening was taking; by this point, her 'witnesses' had finally engaged Philip Avecet. He was furiously writing in his notebook: drugs at private schools were something he could sink his teeth into.

"And when did this deal go down?" said Chief Avecet eagerly.

"Um, on September fifteenth," said the boy. "Yes, I'm sure. On September fifteenth."

Avecet scribbled rapidly in his notebook. Then he looked up. "Wait a minute," he said. "You just said that the biggest drug deal on this side of town went down on September fifteenth, with Ben bringing the drugs themselves and doing the deal. Fifteen kilos of cocaine."

"Right," said the young man who had spoken.

I stood up to watch this exchange, and found Mack Demson by

my side. His tuxedo was muddy too, and he seemed out of breath. "Where have you been?" I mouthed silently? But Mack put a finger to his lips—apparently, he didn't want me to draw attention to his presence.

Avecet flipped a few pages back in his notebook. "But according to this other statement, Ben Delacruz was up in the mountains, on this fishing trip with about thirty children and their parents, on that night. Doing who knows what strange things."

"Oh," said the young man. He slid a glance in Catherine Foss' direction. "Um, I don't know. Maybe he came back down?"

"He doesn't have a car," said Joe Matheson.

"And he drove one hundred miles each way, and he made it here by six p.m. and back without anyone noticing?" Philip Avecet shook his head in disgust. "These stories don't match," he said. He closed his notebook.

Soon, other police officers arrived from the back forty, bringing other prisoners from out in the back forty. There was a motley collection of students, and of adults, all of whom had been seized as possible accessories to Ben's acts of vandalism this evening.

"Look at all of these kids," I whispered to Mack. "C'mon—the charges for them can't be very serious at all. Only Ben was actually in the hall this evening, throwing things around. No one else. What are they going to charge them with? Aiding and abetting their own teacher in the performance of his duties?"

"Silence," said Catherine Foss at the front of the room. Evidently, someone had asked a question of Ben, and Catherine wanted it to be obvious that he was refusing to answer.

"You forget," said Mack in my ear. "It's a Rockhorn party, and this was Catherine's big moment—sullied now forever by the memory of the vandalism. Sure, they'll let most of them go. They'll have to. But for now, they can make them sweat. I'm just glad I didn't get nabbed. I told Ben I'd join him out at the campfire after the party was over, like all the rest of these people here. I just managed to get back in time, before the police arrived."

"Aren't you going to answer at all?" said Catherine. "These are serious charges. Aren't you even going to try to help us sort out the truth? Tell us what really happened?"

But Ben said nothing. He simply looked straight ahead at her, as if his indomitable will had triumphed, even here this evening, under these ignoble circumstances.

Mack, on the other hand, seemed frightened of the police. They were scanning the group in the anteroom now, as if they expected to find someone. Mack soon slipped away to the ballroom, out of sight of the Board and the police officers. Now, it was as if Mack's fear was contagious—I found myself looking over my shoulder, wondering if I'd be seized next as a possible accessory. I sank back into the chair, trying to conceal myself from the officers, and from Catherine's probing eye.

Yet Joe Matheson hadn't caught Mack's fear. Apparently he felt that by this point, some sort of a victory had been won for Ben.

Joe walked over and put his hand on Ben's shoulder. "Now, of the actual charges the police are going to bring, I can't imagine any of them are really weighty," he said. "He's been through enough tonight—let's let the police book him and he'll spend a night or two in jail. That's about what the going rate is for vandalism, isn't it, Bartimus? One or two nights." He put an arm gently around Ben. "When you get out of jail, then why don't you come to my office, and we can talk it all over, and figure out what happened, and how we can work things out in the future." Then quietly, I heard him say to Ben, "I really want to keep you here, buddy."

"Two or three *Nights*?" Catherine exploded. "That may be the going rate for petty vandalism. But not if Chief Avecet goes through with the psychological evaluation at Moolston that you requested, Mr. Matheson. And although I questioned it previously, I now believe that the psychological evaluation is absolutely necessary. At the very least, Mr. Delacruz will be inside Moolston for a matter of weeks. Am I right, Wallace?"

Wallace Steg solemnly nodded at her. There was a muttering in the crowd, and someone pointed at Joe, as if to shame him. Gradually, the Board was turning against Joe. I could feel the tide changing in the room, even as Catherine continued.

"*After* he is discharged from Moolston—if that ever happens—then he will be booked and charged with the crime. And when that happens, I plan to prosecute to the fullest extent of the law. Willful destruction of property, mayhem, incitement to mayhem, child endangerment. You name it, I will ask for it. And although there are some small disparities, I believe the substance of these other very serious allegations against this Delacruz character will stand.

"Mr. Matheson, I am asking you to back me up on this. I am asking for you, as the Headmaster of Rockhorn, to pledge your complete support for the charges that I expect Rockhorn Academy to bring against Mr. Delacruz. If not, I believe the Board would be entirely justified in asking for your resignation this evening."

Bartimus Santos took his pipe out of his mouth, as if he were about to say something. But he did not. Like the rest of the Board, he simply stared at Joe, waiting for an answer.

Joe was caught entirely flat-footed. He stood in the center of the room, right beside Ben. For a long moment, he looked down at the floor, for all the world like Ben's fellow criminal-in-arms. The stares of the entire Board rested on him. No one seemed to breath. Then Joe looked up from the floor.

"Miss Foss," he said hoarsely. His eyes were wet and rheumy. "What has been done to Rockhorn tonight is, of course, inexcusable. Of course I will support all charges brought against this man. There is no need to further encourage me in the performance of my duty towards Rockhorn." He reached out his hand to Ben's shoulder and stepped away. The effect was as if he had pushed Ben—in fact, Ben took the touch like a punch to the shoulder and slumped to the side for a moment. Perhaps Joe really had pushed him, as he left his side.

"Now," said Catherine Foss. "I know that Mack Demson wanted to say a few words." She looked distastefully around the floor. "I believe he felt there were some words that might be said to defend Mr. Delacruz's indefensible actions." She sighed. "Of course, there are two sides to every story, and I suppose we'll have to hear his."

She glanced around again, pleased not to see Mack in evidence. "Mr. Demson? Nicholas Demson? Is there anyone else who wants to say a word on Ben's behalf? Oh, Mack? Mr. Demson?"

But Mack was gone. A dead silence filled the room for a moment. Then, oddly, I could hear laughter. Someone was chuckling quietly to themselves, in a high uneven tone. No one else seemed to care, but the sound to me was eerie and chilling. I glanced around the room, and found that the sound came from Sandy Hedron, who apparently couldn't contain her mirth at Ben's ill fortune.

Philip Avecet spoke up before anyone else really caught wind of Sandy's laughter. Clearly frustrated by the chaotic nature of the accusations and counter-accusations that had been heard this evening, Avecet was trying to bring it all to a close. He wanted a clean resolution.

"All right, I'd like to hear from you, Mr. Delacruz ," he said. "What's the truth of what happened here? Just the facts, as you see them."

"What is truth?" said Ben mildly, as if he'd just taken a stroll in the park. It was something a mental patient might have said; a statement that entirely did not fit the moment. And it was then that I knew he was out of our reach.

Heavily, I stood from my comfortable chair and moved toward the door. My knee had seized up and the going was slow and laborious. Every stumble cost me greatly in pain, but I was determined to clean myself up a little before I went home. Perhaps I could find a doctor somewhere, who even at this late hour would look at my neck and my leg. I was worried that by morning I wouldn't be able to walk at all. It was a shame that Dr. Lucas Scribin had already departed.

I got myself to the bathroom, and scrubbed the powder burns and the mud off of my face and neck. I managed to comb my hair and remove my tattered suit jacket. I would be cold when I walked out to the car, but at least when I arrived in my own kitchen to greet the child-sitter, I wouldn't look like someone coming back from the grave.

While I was out of the room, Philip Avecet removed Ben from the humiliating discussion in front of the Board, probably provoking Catherine's ire in the process. Avecet had him formally taken into custody. According to the record, he asked for Ben to be taken to the police station for administrative processing and transfer.

At Joe Matheson's request, the police were then supposed to transfer Ben immediately to Moolston. Joe still held out hope that the County's psychological evaluation and a complete physical examination might reveal the presence of some hitherto-unknown symptoms that afflicted Ben. I gathered that he thought discovery of extenuating circumstances—mental illness, hypoglycemia, reaction to medication or something else—might prevent them from booking him at all. Such a discovery would save him the ignominy of a court appearance, and a later indictment on his record. A psychological debriefing was much less damning to a teaching career than an arrest and an arraignment.

When I returned to bid all of them adieu, the room had emptied. Joe, Catherine, Bartimus and a few others were left behind, arguing over what had happened this evening. Joe apparently was still arguing that it had been irresponsible to call the police.

"We could have handled all of this on our own," he said. "There was no need to call in the authorities. I mean, this was just a minor political contremptus—no need to go all legal on him."

"But that's precisely why I called them," said Catherine. "We don't have the authority to arrest, or to prosecute. Only they do—they needed to be here."

Joe shook his head. "I'm not sure it was really necessary."

"Neither am I," said Bartimus.

"I thought it was," I said. After all, I said, they weren't out there in the cold, feeling the irrational anger of the crowd, hearing shots whistling by them. "They were out of control on the school grounds. It was absolutely necessary."

But no one responded to what I said. Their argument was with Catherine, and it seemed that now my part was done, they could simply ignore any opinions I had about the matter. It came to me, watching them continue to argue without me, that I had only been a disposable tool, one that wasn't worth taking into consideration any longer.

I turned to go, and Catherine pulled herself out of their discussion. She walked with me out of the room, and she opened the door of the Library for me. A gust of wind wafted the gas flame toward us, and I could see a light drizzle beginning to fall across the campus. As she opened the door, Catherine surreptitiously held out her hand.

"Thank you for your help this evening," she said. She pulled her hand away, leaving behind a slip of paper in my palm. It was a check.

Even as I realized it was there, the wind caught it, and blew it down to the ground.

I bent over and looked at it on the floor. The check held a large number, a sum far beyond that which Catherine had originally promised me. All those zeroes on the check stared up at me, all full of emptiness.

24.

SOMETHING WENT horribly wrong in the time between Ben being taken by the police and the time he was released from their custody. As far as I can make out, his papers were misfiled with another person's papers. The other man, a certain Sabbarab Munos, apparently had a vaguely similar name, was also of ethnic descent, and was charged with vandalism at about the same time. There were critical differences between the two men, however. This Sabbarab had a rather lengthy criminal history and had just been re-apprehended after breaking out of a low-security jail cell the previous week.

Thus, instead of being gently tested for mind-altering substances and receiving a proper evaluation by psychiatric professionals, Ben Delacruz was treated like a hardened criminal, and placed in a maximum security cell with the more extreme elements of the jail population. Like any major metropolitan area in these united states, our incarceration system is filled far beyond the legal maximum: instead of two men in one room, there are three, or four, or even six stuffed into a cell. Once they're transferred to federal custody, there are further legal constraints on treatment, of course, and the prisoners receive all the protections of federal law. But in our Valley, the voters haven't approved such luxuries as working toilets and new jail cells for all of the incarcerated. No one cares. And it's easy to lose a man in a system that is this overpopulated and broken-down.

Sabbarab Munos received the initial psychological evaluation at Moolston that Ben was supposed to receive, and passed it with flying colors. He was released to the general population soon thereafter. His whereabouts are currently unknown.

When Joe Matheson received no news about Ben from Moolston after a reasonable period of time, he made inquiries. By that time, perhaps, it was too late. Obviously, Philip Avecet, despite his evident interest in the situation at Rockhorn, didn't have the time or the in-clination to keep an eye on every petty vandalism or drug case that came through his offices. So he didn't catch the error for about three days, all during which Ben was rotting in a jail cell, suffering from a possible concussion and an untreated broken nose, and possibly other undiagnosed injuries. In the general prison population, I can't imag-ine what else might have happened. In any case, I do know that by the time Ben was transferred to Moolston, he was essentially beyond our assistance.

They told us that at Moolston he had to be forcibly sedated.

According to their records—presented to us later by Wallace Steg—Ben had become violent and irrational. He was raving in a paranoid fashion about being persecuted and about bets being placed on his death. Whether this was prescient or not I do not care to speculate, but the records show that rapidly, he was slipping downhill.

The actual case history notes are expunged at a certain point—os-tensibly to protect the privacy of the patient, but there are probably other reasons that have been concealed from me. I can speculate that there was some kind of altercation with the staff handlers at Moolston. A psychiatrist's name, a Dr. C. Turion, is listed as one of those receiv-ing injury, but his remarks are blacked out in the record of Ben's case. Again, they sedated him.

The second time the drugs went in though, it seems that there was some sort of negative reaction, or perhaps they accidentally gave Ben an over-dose in the midst of struggling with him. Perhaps the staff felt it was necessary to be a little firmer with a patient who was taken into their care directly from police custody, and they became a tad over-zealous. I wouldn't put it beyond them. In any case, their word in these circumstances was law, and Ben's side of the story was gone with him. I suppose we'll never know exactly what happened. I per-sonally believe that it was probably a combination of a choke-hold and sedation which caused it. There is also the possibility that Ben's various undiagnosed and untreated injuries had already retarded his metabolism or compromised his immune system to the point that a standard dosage of sedating drugs would be lethal.

I do not know. No one knows for sure. I do know that if Ben were still in touch with his family, there most probably would be adequate justification for filing a suit on the grounds of negligence leading to death, and possibly cause for a malpractice suit against Dr. Turion as well.

They attempted to revive him. A breathing apparatus was brought in. Chest thrusts were done. In the final extremity, electric paddles were applied to his chest and his heart was shocked with many volts of electricity. But there was no heartbeat at the conclusion—there were simply bright red marks left on his chest from their exertions. And in the end, he was just as dead.

Ben's family did not come forward. I doubt if they still, even now, know of his death. But as soon as the news of his death was made public, there was a surfeit of regret and self-flagellation from the community. Students began to cover the area near Ben's last campfire with a patchwork of photographs, drawings, letters, flowers, and candles, until half the back forty was filled with these remembrance items. The daily newspaper carried a very long story about Ben's influence and activities at Rockhorn Academy under the headline "Turning Point at Rockhorn: *A Champion of Special Needs Taken Away*." The story opened on page 1 with a cover photograph of Ben in profile, taken at the Library Endowment ceremony, and the rest of the story was filled out by other photographs of Ben in the classroom with Rockhorn and Ihme children, Ben at his lunchtime table, and Ben working in the Shop. Each of them were credited to Rockhorn's own student photographers, and each of them brought a pang to my heart.

Along with the factual news stories, there were tales and rumors that emerged, percolating into the atmosphere of controversy that now surrounded any discussion of Ben Delacruz. I gave no credence to most of these stories, as the majority were even stranger and more outlandish than Catherine Foss' concocted accusations against Ben. Soon, there were many other stories, most of them rapidly taking on the characteristics of urban legend. A few, of course, had a certain basis in fact, but the majority were the kind of myth and legend that children make up about their heroes.

Instead of merely rescuing a few boys on the fishing trip, Ben was now veritably walking on water. He didn't merely work with special needs children—he healed them. He found coins inside carp when he fished (a more believable tale than many of the rest), he brought speech to the autistic and sight to the astigmatic. Of course, most of these so-called events happened when Ben was alone with a group of his students on a fishing trip, or alone in the Shop room with the same close-knit group. It little mattered to me that I had once been considered part of that group, I wasn't about to get sucked into a morass of superstitious zealotry.

I believed none of the stories, and thus I've related none of them here. Why do I need to complicate the truth of his life? Shouldn't it be enough for them to realize that he was simply bigger and better than all of us? That he was cut from a different cloth, a material that most of us can only aspire to?

Given the public outcry of support, Joe Matheson proposed to hold a school-wide funeral at Rockhorn, which he would open to the civic community at large. I was still disgusted with myself for having been party to Catherine Foss's petty machinations, and although I had considered destroying the check Catherine had given me, I ended up giving it to Joe, who was soliciting donations to permanently enshrine some of the spontaneous memorial items in the back forty, near the sports fields and the campfire circles Ben frequented. With my additional funds, Joe was able to receive Board approval to actually inter Ben Delacruz on the school property and create a permanent memorial on the school grounds.

This proposal seemed straightforward—there had once been a graveyard on Rockhorn's back forty, after all. If one searched hard enough, one could supposedly find the grave marker for several Rockhorn family members, buried under mounds of brush and overgrowth. Joe was simply proposing to add the grave of a revered instructor to that unused graveyard. The Board and the Student Council had no objections, so Joe prevailed upon various friend sin high places to release the body to him immediately, so that we could proceed with a funeral and burial. None of us knew that there would be any further bureaucratic complications surrounding Ben Delacruz.

The very next day the funeral was held in Rockhorn's Auditorium.

Although I had felt an open coffin was distasteful, there was much demand to see him one last time. So after some consultation with a funeral director, Ben's nose was put straight and his features cleaned of the grime that had accumulated during his time in jail. During his time in the morgue, I was surprised to see that his expression had not hardened into an ossified leer. Instead, he seemed at peace. Against my will, I was indelibly reminded of the one other time I had seen sleeping all alone, the night-sounds of the forest rising quietly around him.

At the funeral, the outpouring of public acclamation for Ben and his good works was simply astonishing. Mayor Harper spoke and of course Catherine Foss was able to articulate her deep and heartfelt regret at being deprived of Ben's potential, just at the pinnacle of his career at Rockhorn.

The funeral was designed, I suppose, to lift Ben to a point of heroism that I doubt he ever really achieved in life. I mean, we had to turn people away from the Auditorium on the day of the funeral. Yet how many teachers could realistically touch the lives of the vast number of people now coming forward and claiming to have been directly affected by Ben's influence? Where were the naysayers now? They had to be out there somewhere, but instead of hearing their stories, we heard only the glowing reports of incredible insight, humility, and the recitation of lives changed for the better by Ben's influence.

By the end of the hour, I was growing tired of it all—little of it seemed to have anything to do with the Ben I had known. Then, as I leaned back in my seat beside Jake, I heard something that made me certain that Ben's iconoclastic and otherworldly spirit remained alive in his students. Near me, Jake was talking quietly with another young Rockhorn student. Jake's friend leaned over and whispered, "Ben's in the real world now. The real world."

"Yeah," said Jake. "The real world, man. Someday we're gonna follow him."

For some reason, this exchange sent a shiver up my spine. Both because I knew that Ben had concocted this fantasy world for the amusement of children just like these two, and also because these two children didn't know that it was a fantasy—they took the idea quite seriously.

The school groundskeepers had hired a local firm to dig a proper grave near the last campfire site, and the tombstone was already in place. For some reason, it was important to Joe for the grave to be a perfectly symmetrical rectangle. He supervised the digging of it himself. The grave was in a beautiful location, mid-way between the firepit and where the cattails grew at Albe Creek. It was near to the old Chapel.

In the afternoon after the funeral, Joe was instructing the groundskeepers as they prepared to transfer the coffin by hand from the Auditorium to the grave, when a representative from the State Coroner's office and a supervisor from Moolston arrived at the school. They were accompanied by a special State Police detail. The man had come from the Coroner's office specifically to take Ben's body back to the Moolston morgue, where a complete autopsy would be performed. Afterwards, the remains were required by law to be buried on state property.

Apparently, there had once again been a bureaucratic oversight. Technically, it seems that Ben was still "in custody" when he passed away. State law required an autopsy when a suspect dies in custody, but the good doctors at Moolston had once again failed to realize the exact legal status of their patient, even after his death. Furthermore, the bodies of indigents who were in the custody of the State when they passed away were not to be released to any person who was not a family member. It seems that the state had jurisdiction in any case where a deceased had no known domicile and no legally registered family. They were always, without exception, buried on State property. No matter how much Joe's powerful friends had been able to bend the laws in this regard, the bureaucrats had spotted the violation in time to retrieve the body from us.

Thus, with regret, Joe relinquished Rockhorn's claim on Ben's body. Under the circumstances, what else could he have done?

Several days later, there was one last twist to the strange story of Ben Delacruz. The State Coroner's office and the State Police detail returned. In hushed tones, they told Joe that evidently the body had been misplaced. The Moolston supervisor assured them that the body had been placed securely in their morgue, and prepped for autopsy. However, once the Coroner's office requested the autopsy results, no one could find them. Further inquiries were made, and it also appeared that no one could locate the remains. Finally, they had circled back to Joe Matheson, wondering if perhaps he had held onto Ben's body in order to bury it on the school grounds, despite State law.

Nothing of the sort had happened, of course. But the body did not appear, in anyone's custody. It was a very strange ending to a disturbing sequence of events.

Joe's perfectly symmetrical grave, with the ornately carved tombstone, sat empty on the school grounds, gradually filling in with winter leaves and underbrush, until it had moldered into an unrecognizable depression, a shallow pit that was soon falling away into the earth itself.

25.

JAKE'S LIFE with me returned to much the same pace as before. We had our little arguments and our little reconciliations: our faltering attempt at being a family. Jake was more independent now though—without fail he walked to and from school on his own. When I offered a ride so that I could find an excuse to drop by Rockhorn, Jake usually refused. I never met his friends anymore. Somehow, he seemed embarrassed or ashamed to have me seen at Rockhorn. And increasingly, I felt this way myself. I was vaguely uncomfortable and out of place there now, as if I was coming back to a place where I'd once been employed but was no longer. I resigned from the Board and from the various Committees on which I had served. Technically, my volunteer project with the snack items and food services wasn't paid employment, so although I was able to recoup the promised sums from Joe Matheson, I gradually begged off being on campus for more than the absolutely necessary time. My business was coming back as tax season loomed closer, and Joe volunteered to take over my business class.

Soon, there was little reason for me to have anything to do with Rockhorn Academy, and I preferred it that way. Jake and I had found that we had little to say anymore about his schooling—he was growing older, to the age where his classes and his activities didn't require my oversight or participation, and I was now busy enough that any extra activities outside of work were burdensome.

One day a week we managed to be home about the same time after school, and I tried to prepare him a snack, just as I had in the old days. Usually it was a pretty non-communicative affair. Jake would munch on his sandwich or his quesadilla, and I would read the paper or talk about my day at the firm.

So it was with surprise one day, after I had prepared his snack and was reading the Wall Street Journal, that I saw Jake running wildly towards our front door. He flew inside and threw his backpack on the floor, bursting with the need to tell me what had happened to him that day.

"I saw him!" said Jake. "He's here. I swear to God, I saw him!"

"What? Who?" I said with bemusement. After a long period of confusion, the story came out. Apparently, Jake had been walking on his usual route home from school, down Shekinah Road, left on Paton Lane and over Albe Creek, when he encountered a man who looked vaguely familiar. They fell into conversation, and the man turned to Jake and proceeded to tell him that he had once gotten entirely soaked in that creek by someone who was walking while reading a book and collided with him. Then he winked at Jake and asked "Did I ever tell you about that time?" At that moment, Jake claimed to have recognized Ben Delacruz's mannerisms and expression, and thought that this man was in fact Ben himself.

"All right," I said carefully. I set the sandwich down on the table. "Do you want your snack?" I wanted some time to think about how to deal with this hysterical interlude. Perhaps Jake had never properly processed his grief over losing Ben.

"No, no," Jake said. "I had something with him. He had some dried fish, and offered me some, and we had a snack together. It was great, Dad! Maybe I'll see him again tomorrow."

I did my best to calm Jake down, and as soon as he retired to his room, I called his therapist and scheduled an emergency session. I was concerned that he was polarizing his life-experience into two levels: those experiences that included Ben and those that did not include Ben. Sadly, it seemed that any experience without Ben was a negative one in his book. Furthermore, I told the therapist, he was attempting to make any single male adult he met into a Ben-like figure. But as the therapist pointed out to me over the phone, perhaps this had more to do with my lack of fathering skills and less to do with Ben.

I was concerned about Jake once more, but this time it wasn't as clear that his delusions were the result of a crowd of external negative acquaintances. With that problem, I could simply not allow him to be around certain people. This time, however, all of his problems seemed to exist inside his head, and I had no access to that world. We did a number of follow-up sessions with the therapist, some of which I attended. But Jake did not seem to improve.

Then, a week later, another child was rumored to have encountered Ben Delacruz. Moira, of course, was this other child. She claimed to have seen him after school as well, and also claimed to have had an elaborate fishing trip with Ben, in which they went swimming together and caught fish, and finally roasted fish up by the fire. If she would have left a few of the details out she might have been more readily believed. Perhaps the most telling detail that condemned her story to derision was her description of the red electric seared spots on Ben's chest from the paddles that they'd used—unsuccessfully—to revive him in the psychiatric ward after his death. There were ways by which she might have made a more convincing story out of it, but she took none of them. As it was, her story was so fantastic, so detailed and overboard that she was roundly disbelieved, even by her gullible peers.

Yet despite the fact that this was now a shared delusion, it was very sad to me that my boy, Jake, had been the one to succumb. Even though he lived under a dark cloud, he was always the most levelheaded child. It was pitiful to me that for a week or more he was lumped together with Moira in this self-deception. After therapy didn't seem to be working, I considered taking him to see a more rigorous psychiatrist, perhaps the same psychiatrist that treated Moira's multiple mental ills with a spectrum of mind-bending pills.

Then Tom asserted, in his stuttering way, to have seen Ben as well—this was the third child now, and soon there was a fourth and a fifth. I realized belatedly that we were dealing with some type of mass hysteria. By the time there were ten children or so who claimed to have seen him—not including my child and Moira—I was convinced that this was some version of that shared hallucination that caused unidentified flying object sightings and black dogs in the night. This was what convinced me, in the end, that we were dealing with a near-religious hysteria.

There was nothing to be done for it.

All of our children saw psychiatrists. Some families talked about it among themselves. Some didn't. Some children were medicated—one to the point of temporary institutionalization—and some went into the wide world with their hysteric hallucination intact. There was no sure and certain cure. There was only that great healer to rely on, time.

During this mass delusion, Ben's legend continued to increase, to a level far above that which I felt was appropriate. All of this posthumous excitement didn't seem right to me; in my estimation, Ben Delacruz was just a small everyday man who happened to land an instructor position without even a degree to his name. But with the children in an uproar about these "sightings," the ant's nest of rumor, speculation and hero-worship had been stirred up once more. Soon even people like Laszlo—who should have known better—and Bill Girus were telling stories about Ben. Apparently Bill's disabled daughter had been quite affected by Ben's work with her, and in order to keep Bill quiet on the topic, Joe Matheson finally had to call him into his office and ask him to stop telling all visitors to Rockhorn about Ben. However, I suppose it was part of Ben's legacy that many of the disabled students who had worked closely with him managed to stay at our school. No one had ever gotten around to telling their parents that they shouldn't be at Rockhorn any longer—and now no one would ever have the temerity to do so.

The only person who was unaccountably quiet on the topic of Ben was Mack Demson, and I couldn't get a word out of him. I tried one day. I came to Mack's office in the early morning, when I knew he was usually free, and I shared my concerns about Jake. Then I went further, and I asked what steps Mack was taking to shut down this mass hysteria.

"What do you think of all of it?" I asked. "Is it just the children missing their best friend, their confidante and playmate? Why are they imagining these bizarre encounters?"

"I don't know," he said. "Of course, it wouldn't help at all if I told anyone that I'd seen him too. I'd lose all credibility."

"Well, have you seen him?" I asked.

But Mack refused to say anything else on the topic. He went to his window and gazed out at the back forty, where the football field and the outbuildings stood. He said, "I've been visiting the Chapel that stands out there in the field, you know."

I looked out at the Chapel too—the place I was supposed to use for my business classes and snack endeavor. I wondered if it would ever really get off the ground now. "Oh," I said. "I've never been back." But there it stood, gray and silent. As far as I know it's still useless and empty. Thanks to Ben, no one is making any other use of it, but no one quite knows what to do with it either.

Finally, the day came when Jake saw him again. It was a Friday afternoon after school and Jake had a soccer game. We had left the LakeStrand district and were proceeding through some of the less prosperous districts. We were heading towards a soccer field on the edge of town.

A stoplight at a major intersection brought us to a halt. On the street corner was a mob of day laborers waiting, and as we pulled away from the light, Jake called out loudly, startling me. "Look—" he said. "There's Ben! I see him, right there, on the corner! He's telling a story!"

I slowed down to glance over the crowd, and indeed, there were a group of hard-worn men gathered in some sort of a makeshift circle around a man who seemed to be talking. The man in the middle was sitting on the ground, as Ben often used to do, and for the life of me, I couldn't be sure it wasn't Ben at that moment, his beard grown out again, his features strong but swarthy in the half-light. I sped up, moving on even against Jake's protests, and we never knew for sure.

Even now, despite my better instincts, and despite the calm demeanor I present to Jake, I can't seem to disabuse myself of the possibility that it might have been he. As the years go by, wherever there is a crowd of itinerant laborers, as we pass them on the street corner, I see them gathered around the fires in the barrels, huddled around a few equally destitute leaders, and I imagine for a moment that I see Ben.

Wherever there are the poor, the dispossessed, the outcasts, I imagine with my son Jake that I see Ben among them, his face looking silently out from the crowd, yearning for nothing but understanding, pleading nothing but peace.

finis

THOMAS SINGE is a community-builder, lecturer and writer. He is a lay member of the Episcopal Diaconate. Thomas Singe formerly studied to become a Catholic priest.